THUNDER WELLS

TERRY W. ERVIN II

Gryphonwood

Gryphonwood Press

THUNDER WELLS. Copyright 2016 by Terry W. Ervin II.

Published by Gryphonwood Press
www.gryphonwoodpress.com

ISBN-10: 1-940095-56-5
ISBN-13: 978-1-940095-56-1

Printed in the United States of America

THUNDER WELLS

Nobody ever said surviving an apocalyptic alien invasion would be easy, let alone possible. For Jack Fairbanks, there's no other option than to try.

Jack, a college sophomore, survived the plague, wasn't near a coast when the tsunamis crashed ashore, and dodged the kinetic bombardment. While destroying great swaths of humanity, the Mawks delivered a series of EMPs, wrecking the electrical grids, communication networks, and all but the most rudimentary elements of transportation.

To finish the job, the Mawks seeded Earth with dozers and crawlers, tracking beasts created to crave the taste of human flesh, and hunt what remained of mankind to extinction.

Despite Jack believing humanity's fate as a doomed species, he spends his waking hours scavenging, and patrolling the metro park claimed as his territory. Brutish dozers and relentless crawlers aren't Jack's only concern. Vile human gangs want Jack's buried stockpile of food and supplies. Twisted cannibals desire his flesh.

Lucia, a hardened urban survivor, is Jack's single connection outside his park. That is, until what remains of the Ohio National Guard comes calling. Rather than hold out in his park and wait for the end, Jack offers his food and supplies, and his rifle, in a bid to change the course of the invasion. To give humanity one final sliver of a chance.

Neither Jack nor Lucia know exactly what the soldiers are up to, and why their column is moving south. The Mawks might be in the dark as well. Nevertheless, even as Jack pieces together the Army's goal, part of a secret global effort, the Mawks finally descend from orbit and bring their technological might to bear.

Books by Terry W. Ervin II

Thunder Wells

Crax War Chronicles
Relic Tech
Relic Hunted

First Civilization's Legacy
Flank Hawk
Blood Sword
Soul Forge

Collections
Genre Shotgun

Dedication

This novel is dedicated to Peggy Jester and Laura Eckstein. Why? As both my career and that of my wife drew us away from family, Peggy and Laura opened their homes, offering daycare to our daughters, Genevieve and Mira. The love, support and care provided to Gen and Mira in those formative years has played a significant role in the caring and responsible young ladies they've become.

Acknowledgements

First, I would like to thank Kathy, my wife, and Genevieve and Mira, my daughters, for their patience and understanding in allowing me the countless hours to imagine, plot, research, write, revise and edit—all things necessary to complete a novel.

Second, I would like to thanks my co-workers, family, friends, and the members of Flankers, all of whom encouraged, questioned, and prodded me along to finish Thunder Wells.

The character Luther was named in honor of Jessica's recently deceased grandfather, intended as a tribute to his caring and wisdom. Jessica was selected from the hundreds who signed up for the chance to name a character in my next novel. It was a pleasure to work with her while watching as 'her character' brought added depth to the plot.

Finally, I'd like to thank the folks at Gryphonwood Press, especially Melissa Bowersock for editing Thunder Wells, and David Wood for not only believing enough in my first novel to publish it, but for his advice and insight, and continuing to provide an avenue for me to reach readers, offering them the tales I want to share.

That leaves you, the reader. You're the primary reason I wrote Thunder Wells. Thank you for choosing my SF novel from the hundreds of thousands available. I truly hope you enjoy the story. With that in mind, don't hesitate to send an email or post a review to let me know your thoughts. And, as a last note, if you opt to receive my newsletter, you'll automatically be in the next drawing to name a character—if you desire. Visit my website (www.ervin-author.com) for the newsletter link.

Chapter 1

The crawler moved slower than me, even though I was on foot. But like all its kind, it was relentless. Endurance and near flawless tracking, those were the crawlers' hallmarks. That, and when they brought you down, they ate you.

The first time I'd seen it happen was several months ago, not long after they became a lethal concern. Through my binoculars I'd spotted an old guy fleeing on a ten-speed bike. He should've discarded his overloaded backpack and retrieved it later, because his unstable bike's narrow front tire hit a rock and the guy went down. Back then the biggest crawlers were only ten feet long. Now they reach sixteen feet, with a fifty inch girth.

That's not the only death I'd witnessed—from a crawler. Even so, witnessing one such death is more than enough for a legion of nightmares. The arthropod alien didn't bother to squirt a jet of venom on the downed man. It wasn't necessary. The crawler ran down its hobbled victim within seconds. Its mandibles crushed the old man's body parts into a bloody, pasty mess as it feasted, starting with the screaming man's feet and legs.

Those cries of pain and terror are worse than the actual viewing. They echo in my nightmares louder and longer. And I've heard more than my fair share of crawler killings.

Even if I'd been nearby, there was nothing I could've done for the old man. All I had with me at the time was my slide-action .22 rifle, and a similar calibered single-action revolver. Crawlers are like a horror movie cross between a giant centipede and an armored millipede. Their layered carapace is resilient as steel backed by reinforced concrete. I'd heard that a .50 caliber round can get through, and some specially jacketed .44 and .357 magnums, and high powered hunting rifles might, if you're lucky. But standard lead bullets like I had? No chance.

Shooting the alien vermin back then wouldn't have

saved the old man. It would've put the crawler on my trail. Back then I didn't have my obstacle course. Fortunately, I had one now. And one of my shotguns, this one gripped tightly as I ran.

Glancing over my shoulder, boots thumping down through the tangled weeds and deep meadow grass, I caught glimpses of the crawler. It was a big one, maybe the biggest I'd ever seen. This one's carapace had more red in it than brown or orange, at least what I could see before it trailed me into the overgrown meadow. The waist-high weeds slowed me, but high-stepping and determination kept me moving. Skill, and a little luck, kept me from tripping. The tangle near the ground hampered the crawler as much as me.

None of the flesh-eating alien creatures tired as fast as humans. Steady and relentless would've been their motto, if they were intelligent enough to have one. They were smart enough to track and to keep on a human's trail. That was more than enough.

My angle of flight brought me to the old dirt road that led into the metro park's woods, mainly maples with a few oaks. Once on the road I picked up my pace, allowing me to increase the distance from my pursuer. They all had a steady five MPH rate, no matter their size. Sure, I could keep ahead of it, for a while. I was nowhere near a marathoner, and it'd take one to have a long term chance. Or a bike. Even a car, but those attracted dozers. And a dozer was far worse than a dozen crawlers.

Rather than rely solely on my feet, I used my brain. Formulated a plan to take advantage of the crawlers' predictability and their anatomical weakness.

I kept far enough ahead of the crawler that I didn't need the poncho folded and stuffed in my backpack. Actually, it was a brown canvas book bag with lots of pockets and heavy-duty zippers. I just called it a backpack, although I had an actual backpack too, stored away. I had a lot of stuff hidden, stored away.

The crawler was fifty yards behind me, and I was beginning to feel a little winded. The price I paid for carrying a bunch of gear, and scavenging more than a mile from my base of operation. Next time I'd think harder about bringing one of my mountain bikes. Having a bike stolen beat being run down and eaten every day the week.

There wouldn't be a next time if I didn't kill the alien menace chasing me.

I took the second trail, angling to the right. The crawler would follow, sensing my path. They picked targets by sight, then followed by scent, or something akin to scent tracking. It wouldn't cut the angle. Predictable. Even if it did attempt a short cut, I was on the trail and it'd face pressing through tangled undergrowth.

Then I spotted what I was looking for, ahead. I cut a sharp left, tearing through a stand of ferns before angling right again, making the forty yard run between fallen logs I'd placed, leading to the ladder ramp.

About eight feet tall and standing at a sixty degree angle, my ladder was nothing more than long limbs about three inches thick, lashed together by rungs eighteen inches apart. The ladder was braced at an angle, like a lean-to, except there wasn't anything to fill the gap between the rungs. Those opens spaces, I needed.

Slinging my single-barrel shotgun over my shoulder, I climbed up and over, hang dropped, then ran straight to the small tree I'd chopped down, leaving a V in the stump. That's where I'd rest my shotgun's barrel. Breathing hard, I needed the post to help steady my shot. If I missed I'd have to make it to my secondary ramp at the other end of the park. I wasn't sure I'd make it there ahead of the crawler.

Breathing deeply, I watched for the alien creature through the ramp's rungs. Head and mandibles slung low, it came on straight. Settling my breathing wasn't easy. Nothing like those snipers in the movies.

Something raised the hairs along the back of my neck—well, further than they already were. Someone, or something else, was nearby. These were my woods; I could tell. If it was a dozer, I was doomed. Another crawler? Maybe I should've put on my rain poncho.

No, I told myself. The poncho would've slowed me down. Made it harder to climb the ramp. Harder to aim and shoot.

If it was a person, a human or three, they wouldn't mess with me. At least not until I'd taken care of the crawler.

It came on, the swirling mess of reds and browns and orange, like a melted twist of crayons, and those hard, crystal eyes. Venom spewing eyes. And the mandibles hanging low, rhythmically flexing, opening and closing, edges glistening with toxic saliva.

Ten yards…five yards…up the ramp…climbing…the head passing the third rung. The vulnerable underbelly showing between the rungs.

Blam!

The 12 gauge deer slug flew true, slamming into the crawler, toppling it backwards off the ramp.

The predatory creature rolled and writhed. Its dozens of clawed, segmented feet spasmodically twitching as the alien beast screeched. Its agony sounded like amplified violin strings gone wretchedly evil.

I had to put the creature down fast. Silence it before the death cry drew unwanted attention. Breaking open my shotgun, I loaded a 00 buckshot shell. I kept four of those in my green plaid shirt's right pocket, and four slugs in my left. If I used those up and emptied the revolver on my hip, if my foes took *that* long to take me down? Nobody that dumb and incompetent was still alive. If the crawlers or dozers hadn't gotten them, predatory humans—gangsters— would've eliminated them by now. A lot of dying since the alien attack and subsequent seeding. And when the seeding bloomed, the crawlers and dozers emerged. They hunt canines and, I've heard it said, equines as relentlessly as they do humans.

I didn't want to get too close. Sometimes, in its death throes, a crawler spurted venom from ports beneath its eyes. Not always. The toxin caused a rash if it touched skin. Blinded any eyes it touched. And if it got in your mouth or in an open cut? Near instant paralysis. Locked up like being afflicted with advanced stages of tetanus. Immobile and in horrid pain, until the poison reached your diaphragm. Then you suffocated.

And if you didn't get it off your skin? Paralysis followed, but taking minutes instead of seconds. Hard to clean off the sticky toxin while running for your life. Times like that, a river might be the only answer. Hard to tell for sure, as I'd never had to remove the pea-green squirt of death.

Normally, a healthy crawler shoots venom to bring you down, and you're crushed by mandibles and eaten alive long before dying from suffocation. That's why I carried a poncho, and yellow-tinted shooting glasses—protection from venom spurts.

I slipped on my shooting glasses. Those and the brim of my dingy Toledo Mud Hens baseball cap should work, if I kept my mouth closed and ducked any random squirts.

I glanced over my shoulder, still wary of something unseen, before striding around the ramp with my shotgun shouldered. The crawler wasn't going to shut up and die anytime soon unless I helped it along.

I had cases of 12 gauge shells, but what I had needed to last…well, for as long as I could make them last. Maybe a lifetime.

I dropped to one knee fifteen feet away from the screeching alien, kept my shotgun shouldered, waiting for it to spin and writhe just right and expose its underside again. Its under skin, if you could call it that, was tough as boiled leather. Thick, but not tough enough to stop a bullet, or buckshot.

"Get out of the way, Jackass."

I got to my feet and stepped back, turning to face the only person who called me that.

She must've been behind me when I shot the crawler. The sturdy Hispanic woman, Lucia, trotted around the other side of my ramp, holding her compound bow. She'd nocked some sort of homemade arrow tipped with an oval stone. It was an opaque crystal lashed to the end of the arrow she'd made out of a branch. She'd done a better job than a cub scout whittling one from a lilac branch, but not by much.

With a menacing grin, Lucia aimed and shot the crawler in the head. The crappy arrow penetrated, sinking at least five inches deep. Immediately the creature fell silent. Its rows of two-clawed feet continued twitching, but it was dead.

Luther had told me a regular hunting arrow *might* pierce a crawler's carapace an inch or two. That meant the shaft would get snapped as the creature rolled around, dying. And good arrows were harder to find than shotgun shells.

The homemade arrowhead she used? What the female gangster just accomplished impressed me. That didn't mean I was going to ask her; it was exactly what she wanted.

"Lucia," I said, "I thought you were just screwing around with that primitive arrow. Thanks for the assist."

She scowled at me. I could count on one hand the times Lucia produced a genuine smile in my presence…discounting the instances Luther or I mentioned someone that had died suffering, especially if it was someone she hated. And she hated a lot of people.

Fewer to hate now. So many people had died, brought down by dozers or crawlers, or fellow humans. Or the aliens.

Lucia was maybe five-foot four, dark skinned like most Hispanics, with long black hair. She kept her straight locks in a single thick braid. She wore sturdy black boots, faded jeans, and a black T-shirt under a jean jacket. I imagined she'd been heavyset once. Not anymore. More toward lean now. Lean and angry, and mean. Mostly mean.

I had six inches on Lucia and probably forty pounds. Still, I wasn't sure I could take her in a fight. And if I did, probably not unscathed. The Bowie knife she carried on her left hip was faster than my hand axe. She knew I'd bury my axe in her without hesitation, if it came down to it. Plus, I might be able to draw my revolver before she could draw her Glock.

"*Eso es cinco para la valla?*" she asked.

"You know I don't speak Spanish," I replied. I did

understand it, a little. She said something about 'five' and the word 'for' was in there, but I didn't know what *valla* meant.

"That's because you're ignorant, Jackass."

"That's better," I said, grinning, "but I don't think that's what you said."

"Thought you only know English."

"I know *cinco* means five," I said. "You know, *Cinco de Mayo* and all?"

She shook her head. "You've got everybody fooled but me," Lucia said. She attached her bow to a sling across her back. "They think you're some jacked-up survivalist. Some sort of expert hunter and marksman."

"What about those six new bodies on my fence, feeding the crows? Cannibals."

Killing people wasn't tops on my list, but anyone trying to steal from me? Can't let that happen. The only warning shot they get is if my aim is off. And cannibals? Shooting them is a public service, for what remained of the public...remained of the human race.

"Yeah," Lucia said, "that pack skirted the city. Planned on fattening up on you, Jack. A loner they heard about."

I could guess how they heard about me. "Only thing getting fat around here are crows and vultures. And maggots." Flies weren't a terrible problem in the park, but with all the dead bodies to be had, the fly population erupted. Pesky and buzzing, but easy to learn to ignore. Mosquitoes bothered me more.

Lucia spat on the ground. "Scavengers," she said. "And the crawlers and dozers."

It was odd. Normally I spoke more like a college boy, and her, an inner city girl, but for some reason we sometimes met each other half way.

Risking a little by taking my eyes off Lucia, I scanned the area. "Let's not stand here. That screeching might've drawn unwanted attention."

She nodded. "Your little park, Jack. Where to?"

I pointed my shotgun's barrel down at the dead crawler. "You willing to help me drag this over to my fence?"

"*Sí,*" she said, surprising me. "Looks dead enough now."

"Okay," I said. "Give me a second." Along the base of the ramp I'd buried a short length of rope, wrapped in a plastic grocery bag. After retrieving it, I began looping it around the back end of the crawler.

"That's the third time I've seen you take five steps—"

"You mean *cinco*?"

"Shut up, Jackass. What are you? Some kind of psycho squirrel, burying your shit everywhere?"

"No," I said, offering her one end of the rope.

One thing this park did have in abundance was squirrels. Every now and then I took a slingshot to one of them. Easy prey, they having been conditioned to ignore the humans that once frequented the park's trails, usually jogging. The people ignored the nature around them in favor of music directed through earbuds.

It was over a quarter mile to the secondary entrance, where I displayed my warning carcasses, both human and alien. The crawler was heavy, and its carapace was dimpled, like an orange. We were quiet, both of us watching and listening as we approached the silent main thoroughfare that ran across the front of the metro park. My park, now.

We made it across the asphalt parking area and were within sight of the split rail fence standing twenty feet from the road. Most of the human bodies were picked clean. Bones and skulls of the older examples littered the ground around the fence. The crawlers, however, had only begun to rot. Crows, vultures, and any vermin around wouldn't eat them. Flies didn't lay eggs on them because their maggots couldn't feed on their bodies. Only bacteria was able to break the alien flesh down, and not very quickly. Maybe it was their own internal microbes that eventually began the process. What might happen once those microbes became established in the local ecosystem? That was going to happen, whatever I did or didn't do. Worrying about it would accomplish nothing.

Whatever the case, they smelled horrendous, like rotting

potatoes mixed with burnt rubber, accented by stale urine. Being close made my eyes water and my nose run, sometimes lasting for a couple hours, if I lingered too long. Why it didn't bother the crows or other scavengers? Another mystery I didn't have time to ponder.

Lucia slowed. "Got something to trade."

I stopped, lowered my end of the rope, leaving us between two big trees. The deep grass and a few smaller trees offered additional concealment. We'd be difficult to spot from most angles. What she wanted must've been important to her. Lucia visited only when she wanted something, or had something to trade. Helping me drag the crawler? Not her style.

"What do you have?" I asked. "And what're you asking?"

We both squatted down less than a stone toss from the alien carcasses draped over the split rail fence. It was nestled in high grass between the main road and an asphalt drive that swung around to one of the park's parking areas.

Lucia glared at me, her brown eyes cold as stone. They didn't move even though her lips did. "Information. Whatcha got for that?"

"Depends on the information," I replied. I started to cross my arms, but decided against it. Squatting, it'd be awkward to defend myself if Lucia tried something. But it'd be difficult for her to make a quick, decisive move. Better to stay low and out of sight. After checking the sky and looking for danger, I met her harsh gaze with one of my own.

Lucia was a sort of freelancer. She travelled among the gangs in the city and the few suburb groups that had formed for survival. More resources needed for groups, but sharing of skills and responsibility, and more defensive firepower often outweighed that drawback.

The female freelancer dealt with loners like me, too. She'd warned Luther and me of marauding groups, allowing us to make ourselves scarce when their numbers or expertise were too great, and once when a dozer was on the way. Now she was here, dealing with just me.

Dozers stuck mainly to the cities, hunting humans there. Crawlers were more widespread, crisscrossing fields, woods, suburbs and urban developments without apparent preference. I had most everything I needed. Gear for the upcoming winter, even stuff to survive outdoor subzero temperatures. Living in structures? Houses, apartments, garages, churches, factories, warehouses? Not a good idea. Dozers hunted those, mainly. They tore into them like half-starved bears clawing for honey in a rotting log. Wood, brick, steel? Doesn't matter. Nothing can withstand their claws. Maybe one of the Army's Abrams—like there was an Army left, let alone one with tanks. Images of a tank's scarred turret and chassis, gouged by a dozer's claws, flashed through my mind.

"I know you got antibiotics." Lucia flicked her head, indicating my park back over her shoulder. "Buried out there somewhere."

"*If* I do, not for information."

"Not even if the pills were for a young kid, sick and dying?"

It surprised me that she could say that with a straight face. Like she'd care about a young kid. I chuckled and shook my head. "Someone you know got VD more like. Wants to stop the burning."

That got her attention. Her hand moved to grip her Bowie knife's hilt. Mine went to my hand axe.

"You insinuating somethin', Jackass?"

"Yeah," I said, not flinching from her gaze. "That you're lying."

I did have antibiotics, mostly from when Luther and I raided two veterinarian offices, and pet stores. They were more valuable than guns or bullets. Even food.

We might've gotten more, but that would've meant entering nursing homes or hospitals. Neither of us had the stomach for that. First, because any medicines there were needed by the patients. Second, without power, they were certain to be hell holes. Anyone needing anything electronic to keep them alive, pumps, oxygen machines, monitors or anything, they were dead. Probably thousands, dead and dying in the first day. And third, those facilities would be filled with deadly microbes, eager to latch onto any host that came into contact, physical or airborne.

Lucia's hand hadn't left her knife's hilt. "You'd be the one to know about having STDs, Jackass, not me."

"Oh," I said. "You thought I was referring to you, giving it to someone?" I laughed, and that caught her off guard. "Lucia, you know the mating habits of praying mantises?"

"What?" she asked.

"You know what praying mantises are, right?"

Her hand slid from her knife to her hip. "I do. Who doesn't?"

"Actually, a lot of, let's say, urban dwellers don't."

"What's your point?"

"I imagine any dude having sex with you would end up like a male praying mantis." I paused for effect. "The female mantis kills the male during sex. Chews his head off."

She took a half step back, cocking her head with a raised eyebrow. "You shittin' me, Jackass?"

"Thus, Lucia, I would never imply some guy got an STD from you. He'd be dead before any infection could take hold."

She rolled her eyes and shook her head. "That's why I like you, Jackass. I put up with your crap because I have no idea what you're talking about half the time. But it's entertaining."

Lucia scanned the sky, watching for vultures or crows while I scanned the area. We both listened.

"Seriously, Jack, you got any antibiotics?"

That she used my real name indicated she *was* serious about trading. "I got guns," I said, pointing to the most recent human corpses, or what was left of them, along my trophy fence. "What they had. Decent shape. Not a lot of ammo though."

"Maybe some other time for those."

"If I had meds like antibiotics," I said, "I'd kinda be

more interested in saving them for me, if I got an infected bite or cut, or got sick."

"What I have to share with you is important. Antibiotic important."

Not every house in the city or suburb could've been scavenged. I'd found a few bottles of medicine here and there when I did. That was a while ago. Maybe pretty much everyplace had been cleaned out.

"Not here," I said, pointing at the thoroughfare and the suburban houses on the other side, set a short way back from the intervening road, all with their tree-filled lawns. Not too far down there were even some front yards that had sported brick walls along the street. Those had been largely broken up by a dozer a month back.

Lucia said, "I got something to show you after we toss this crawler next to the others."

"Sure," I said, listening for a second while scanning the remnants of a garage burned down to its foundation. It happened before I arrived. Probably a squatter who kicked over an oil lamp or something. Only thing moving near it was a squirrel, scampering along one of the boards on its way to another tree.

Lucia followed my lead, hefted the rope, and helped me drag the alien creature the last fifteen yards. While we did, she asked, "You ever look close at crawlers' eyes?"

"Sure," I said. "Hard as rock, like a crystal. There's a venom sack behind them, so pushing on one, even when it's dead, can get you with a squirt." I watched her for some reaction, trying to figure why she'd asked me that. "Even for a week or two afterwards, because it takes that long for their flesh to start decomposing."

"Decomposing," she said with a laugh. "Using big words on me ain't impressive. Why not just say rotting?"

I shrugged as we crossed the narrow asphalt road. When we reached the fence I dropped my end. She did the same.

Lucia yanked out the arrow she'd shot into the alien beast's head. She glanced at the wooden shaft denuded of its crystalline tip. She cussed under her breath, then pointed with the damaged arrow along the fence. "If you don't know already, Jack, I cut the eyes out of your trophies."

The emanating stench was pretty intense, especially as a breeze wafted it our direction. I looked away as my eyes began to tear up. Lucia backed away while I hefted the crawler's front end and tossed it over the top rail.

After we retreated back across the parking area, and a few paces under the nearby cottonwoods, I blinked to clear my eyes. "That's your information?" I asked. "Collecting their eyes? For What?"

"Whatcha think I used for my arrowhead? They're like diamonds, and if you split them right, they're harder and sharper than anything."

Maybe she thought I'd be upset she dug out the eyes of those crawlers I'd killed. I shrugged. "You want to cut out the eyes of the one we just killed?"

She tilted her head, keeping her eyes focused on me. "What's the catch, Jack?"

"No catch," I said. "Next one I get, we'll share the eyes. You get them split."

"Deal," she said. "What about the antibiotics?"

Moving my hands from belt to pockets, checking my weapons and gear, I said, "They're not part of the deal."

Lucia put her hands on her hips. "So you *do* have some."

"I've scavenged houses, just like you. I've stashed some meds, but don't know if they're antibiotics." It was a half-truth.

"You got'em buried," she said with humor. "I just might bring a metal detector out here and dig them up."

"If I buried my meds…and if I put them in a tin can first…and if you can find a metal detector that survived the EMPs…sure, go for it."

"How long you think you can last out here alone, Jack?"

It was a legitimate question. "How long do you think you'll survive in the city, Lucia?"

She ignored my question. "What ammo you got for trade?"

"You don't want the guns?"

She shook her head. "Bullets are in shorter supply than guns."

"Bullets for bullets," I said, thinking a replacement pump shotgun would be handy. But those were even more valuable than antibiotics. The one I had, Luther's, was broken.

Lucia asked, "You want 22s for your carnival gun?"

"Those, 45 longs, and 410 and 12 gauge."

"Those are all pretty uncommon. What do you have?"

"A few 30-30s and some 45 ACPs." I tipped my gaze down toward her holstered pistol. "You know anyone that reloads expended bullets and shells?" I saved the brass bullet casings and expended shells whenever I could.

"There's one reloader that's competent, but what she charges is ridiculous." Lucia scrunched up her nose in thought. "Maybe in a year, and things dry up even more. Got any scopes?"

"Junk." I preferred to be honest, especially since she'd figure it out anyway—if she traded for the two I had.

"You got something personal for long range, Jack?"

I did. An old bolt-action hunting rifle, .30-06, with a good optical scope, and something even better than that. But I wasn't going to tell her. "What do you think?"

Lucia grinned, and we finished our negotiations. We'd exchange ammunition. She got the better end, as usual, but she was making the delivery and the pickup.

She promised to be back sometime next week, ending with, "Don't make me sneak up on your ass again."

"Wouldn't have happened if I wasn't occupied with a crawler."

She nodded acknowledgement, and smiled. "Then don't go shooting me for trespassing, like that dumbass, homemade sign near the main entrance says."

All remained quiet as the sun was near to setting. I wasn't far from the small river that meandered through my park. In most places it was less than fifty feet across and often shallow enough to wade across, except for the silty bottom. Years of old tires, plastic jugs and other trash littered the waterway. Fallen limbs littered its muddy banks as well, often extending ten or twenty feet out into the river. That made for good fishing, except for the snags.

I stood next to the grave of the man I inherited the park from. The man who shared it with me, and gave me a leg up on surviving when society collapsed, and it was every man for himself—or woman for herself.

The alien invaders came. Nobody had an actual name for them, at least no one I came across. Maybe the government or the UN knew they were on their way or in orbit. If so, they didn't share it until the Electro Magnetic Pulse Attack. Those EMPs wiped out virtually everything with a microchip, which constituted virtually every modern electronic device. If you had a TV in your basement that ran on vacuum tubes, it still worked. But what would there be to watch? Same with radios. There were sporadic transmissions. Coded crap I couldn't figure out without a key. Maybe the military coordinating with militias? If so, I hadn't seen them do anything.

Then came the impacts, right on the EMP attack's heels. Kinetic energy weapons. Not much more than rocks raining down from low orbit, counting on velocity and mass to do the job. And do the job, they did. From what I pieced together, they targeted military bases and major cities.

Downtown Toledo, not too far east of my park, got one. Knocked down a lot of the skyscrapers and set fires that couldn't be put out. Then the aliens did something to create tsunamis. Those took out the cities along the east and west coasts. Some in the Gulf of Mexico too, I heard. No reason they didn't do the same across the globe.

Exterminated us humans through drowning. The tsunami attacks took almost a week. Without cars or trains, or even effective communications to warn people to run inland…the fate of millions in the US, probably billions across the globe, was sealed.

Then the seeding. The small round pods that developed,

or erupted, into crawlers and dozers. We humans were too busy fighting among ourselves for what was left. Raiding stores and warehouses and packaging plants for food. Then roving gangs, those with guns and no morals—some would call an advanced survival instinct—fell upon the old, weak and ignorant.

Initially, I had the survival instinct, just not the violent variety. Later, I maintained the survival instinct, just a lot more prone to violence to ensure my survival. The man in the grave in front of me, the one person I talked to on a regular basis, was the reason for the latter.

We met just before the serious looting started, the day after the EMP attack. There was nothing in my college dorm room, and I wasn't in denial. I knew what'd happened. Not the aliens, but the EMP. Initially, everyone thought the power was out. The grid was down and the government would get it back up—or send help if they couldn't get the electricity flowing right away.

Nobody around knew it was caused by aliens—at least no regular civilian did. News had to spread by word of mouth.

No cars ran, except for a few old ones. No cell phones operated, or battery-powered radios. Nothing was being transmitted. No electricity, or satellites or computers meant no signals. The jets that fell from the sky the moment the lights went out, their fires announcing the collapse of modern civilization.

I was over a thousand miles from home, and on my own.

We met, Luther and me, in a veterinarian's office. I was there to get food, enough for the long haul. To survive I could stomach cat and dog food. I figured it'd be months or more. The grocery stores were already a madhouse. My next plan was a store with camping gear, to get water purification tablets and what I'd need to survive outside the city, beyond the suburbs. He, Luther, was there for the medicines.

The thin old guy with a wiry beard and mustache must've seen something in me. His wife had died just two weeks before, and he was alone, like me. After a brief conversation, the Vietnam vet survivalist took me under his wing.

Exhaling, I stared down at Luther's grave. "Killed another crawler today," I told him. "That ramp idea we devised but never built together. It works." I squatted down and patted my hand on the rock mound. "Thanks again."

With that, I stood and listened to the woods. Birds make noise, chipmunks and squirrels move about, rustling leaves and limbs, until dozers or crawlers show up. The alien beasts don't hunt them. They just ignore everything but humans and dogs, and maybe horses. Eventually, Luther and I figured that the local wildlife would begin to ignore them, much like the squirrels ignored people, who'd become part of the landscape. I wasn't so sure. The alien smell would continue to unnerve them. At least for a while.

I moved a rock that had tumbled off the grave back to its place. Must be smell or alien nature that unnerves the local wildlife, I reassured myself, hoping it continued. If it didn't, my chances of survival would go down.

It was getting dark. With shotgun in hand I trotted down the trail, planning to use my secondary sleep station. Being close to Luther, watching over him that night, felt like the right thing to do.

Good thing I did. It could've been that he offered guidance from beyond the grave.

Chapter 2

A sound out of the ordinary stirred me awake. My hammock and mosquito netting were stretched between the branches of a large maple. Someone—no, more than one person—was walking up the hillside leading from the river, putting them less than thirty yards away.

They were good. Nearly silent passing through the ferns and brush while approaching from the river's edge.

Were they stalking deer or other wildlife for food, or were they stalking me, for what I might have? My gut said they were after me. Didn't matter. Either way, they were trespassing in *my* park.

Luther taught me what to do about that.

They were moving my direction, slowly, about twenty yards a minute. Stopping and listening frequently. They weren't using any artificial lights. It took me a long time to get used to night, with its near total darkness. Since childhood, I'd been around artificial ambient light, from streetlights and homes with lights on, to night lights and the light from a digital alarm clock's numbers. The moon and stars don't penetrate thick canopies very well.

The intruders must've come in from the east. Used the interstate highway bridge, climbed the rusty chain-link fence that ran along the park's northern perimeter, then moved down along the river, to avoid being spotted. A challenging route.

Had the men scouted this area? Was that their current purpose?

Without Luther, I was only one man. I hadn't seen any signs of trespassing, but I wasn't a tracker. An inexperienced outdoorsman and an inexperienced hunter better described me. If the approaching men were good, like I thought they were, they wouldn't have left obvious boot prints in the sandy dirt that made up many of the trails. Even if they did, my rounds don't take me everywhere in my park. Not on a regular basis, so rain could erase their boot prints, which would be different from mine. Trails in the leaves? Unless they left obvious prints, I'd be hard pressed to tell the difference between them and a deer or a raccoon, especially after a day or two.

Then there were the paved trails with blacktop, or the boardwalks. Nobody, not even Luther could've found traces of human passage on them…not anyone careful, like these men were.

I held my breath and listened. In a minute they'd reach the trail. Of course, like any paranoid individual, I slept with weapons. I pulled my favorite revolver from its holster, one that could shoot both .410 shotgun shells and .45 rounds. Plus, I had a double-barrel shotgun in a sheath lashed to a limb. Those were good. Still, my advantage lay in Luther's night vision monocular. But shooting from a hammock, and not falling the forty feet to the ground? Or ending up a sitting duck stuck in a tree?

The security setup and the tripwire warnings near the trunk of the tree where I chose to sleep were meant to warn me if a crawler was about. I worried more about crawlers tracking me to where I slept than men hunting and finding me. My best bet with these men was to lie still, and quiet, and hide, until I could descend unnoticed.

They passed within ten feet of the tree that held me. Their breathing and a faint crunching of what remained of last fall's leaves, and the quiet creaks and swishes of fabric allowed me to keep track of their progress. The faint odor of cigarettes and stale sweat was in the air. For some reason they hadn't triggered my wire and bell alarm. Maybe their high stepping had tipped Lady Luck in my favor?

At more than fifty yards, I wouldn't have heard them. It must've been the sudden silence in the woods created by the men passing that stirred me to wakefulness.

A breeze whispered through the trees, reaching the ferns along the floor. It offered me an opportunity to shift my position and look over the edge of the hammock. Switching on the night vision scope, I looked down through it, picking up the green images of four men outlined by the darker background.

All four were armed with rifles or shotguns. One had a scope that he seemed to be looking through, slowly sweeping side to side. Was it night vision like mine? It had to be. What if it was thermal?

Cold sweat dripped down my forehead. Luther had been the cold-hearted, relentless survivalist. He'd tried to make me into one, just as protective and ruthless. He might be disappointed as to the extent of his success.

Defend myself? Yes. Shoot cannibals? Yes. But these men? I wasn't so sure, even if it meant not defending my territory from all intruders, possibly encouraging more to follow in short order.

Scope Man was taller than the others. He stopped, slowly scanning from left to right in a 120 degree arc. Something caught his attention and he signaled the three stationary men behind him. Using my monocular night vision scope I found what caught Scope Man's attention. A four legged image, standing still, watching. A small doe.

After the brief pause, the four men moved forward, at a faster pace.

If they'd been hunting for food, the deer would be lying dead. In any case, the animal's presence led them to believe nothing dangerous, like me, was nearby.

Me. I was their quarry. That settled my resolve.

They reached the Upland Woods Trail and moved south.

After lowering my knotted rope, I gathered my gear and descended to the ground forty feet below.

I was at a distinct disadvantage. There were four of them, and one of me. My shotgun, a short-barreled coach gun, had buckshot shells in both barrels. Luther said not to load slugs in it. That meant I didn't have the range of a rifle. Selecting it as a handy weapon while I slept made sense at the time, figuring on a close fight if someone, or something, attempted an ambush at night. My five-shot revolver had a three-inch barrel. The mix of .410 shotgun shells and .45

long bullets didn't offer the distance or the accuracy that a rifle did. And the four intruders had rifles, or maybe shotguns. Plus, they might have handguns. And their night vision scope might be better than Luther's—mine. The Mylar lining Luther had sewn into our hammocks protected me from detection, if their night vision gear was the more expensive thermal, or Scope Man didn't think to look up. Out on the ground, I didn't have any ability to foil being thermally detected, other than hiding behind something substantial.

Of course, they were on my turf.

Guessing at their intended direction, I cut off the main trail, especially as a boardwalk section was coming up, and took a deer trail. Not only would clomping across the wooden surface announce my presence even more than on the sandy dirt, but the deer trail would allow me to circle around and get ahead of them. Prepare my own ambush.

CHAPTER 3

The buzzing around my face suggested bringing along some mosquito netting would've been a good idea. Lying tight against a log, part of a fallen tree that park rangers had taken a chainsaw to several years ago, I listened for the four men. A few smaller sections of the downed tree were scattered among scant bits of underbrush growing beneath the tall oaks. One log rested at a sixty degree angle to the established trail, which offered some protection from observation if I miscalculated the invaders' approach.

I knew this spot, near the deer trail, because two months before I'd buried a plastic tub filled with supplies: canned tomato juice, kidney beans and stew, and a box of fifty .22 longs and a box of twenty-five 12 gauge shells, #4 shot, a pair of socks, leather work gloves, a book of matches, a Swiss army knife, and a plastic magnifying glass. Maybe Lucia was right. Maybe I *was* a psycho squirrel—one with a sharp memory.

Why were mosquitoes attracted to someone shivering with a cold sweat? I sometimes got this way when I thought about killing people. Crawlers for defense, or deer or squirrels for food? No problem. Sure, I was afraid of dying. I'd never been shot. It had to hurt. My pain tolerance was decent, but who looks forward to the possibility of being shot? And on my own, without hospitals? Being shot was a death sentence. Even being grazed meant an iffy chance of survival.

This kind of stuff was always easier with Luther in the lead. *Was*, being the operative word. A heart attack took him less than an hour after we dealt with a group like the one hunting me now. They'd been looking to take us out of the picture, thereby inheriting what food, supplies and gear we had. The current group was planning the same. This time it was only me to face them. Maybe they didn't know that. Not unless someone had been watching, and hadn't seen Luther recently. Or someone like Lucia told them.

Whatever the case, the four intruders believed they had a powerful advantage, especially with Scope Man's night vision gear. Functioning delicate electronics were more than just rare. For a night vision scope to be working, it had to have been protected in something like a Faraday cage when the EMPs struck. There weren't any factories or facilities to build or repair them. Night vision gear was hard on batteries. That meant having a powered and functioning one was an even larger unlikelihood. But like me, anyone who had such rare equipment would have a way to keep it energized.

My night vision monocular offered more flexibility in general spotting and tracking than a rifle-mounted scope.

Didn't Lucia ask about me having a scope?

No time to ponder that question. Movement, quiet and muffled, came from the trail twenty-five feet to my left.

It wasn't a particularly dark night, with a three-quarters moon and not many clouds, so some scant bits of light reached the ground. Not enough to see much unaided without intense concentration, other than shadowy movements.

I banked on them passing me by, enabling me to sit up, take aim and eliminate them from behind. Shooting trespassers in the back? They were hoping to surprise me in my sleep. They apparently knew that I didn't sleep in buildings, otherwise they would've chosen a different approach and direction of search. If they didn't find me tonight, they'd be back. I could better prepare for their return trip. They might be emboldened and less cautious. Or, they might bring more men.

No, if I was going to do this, better to deal with them in their first incursion…*if* it was their first incursion…

I couldn't afford the distraction and pushed aside any indecisive thoughts.

They stopped and quietly conferred. Ahead of them the path made a T. Beyond that was another trail, The Grassland Trail. If they took the current trail northwest, it broke into a large meadow. If they went southeast, it kept to the woods, bordering small spots of open terrain on their west.

Whispers. Nothing I could make out. The faint smell of cigarettes was on the air again. Cigarettes? Tobacco products were getting pretty scarce. That at least one of them smoked cigarettes, an addictive and increasingly rare product, suggested their relative wealth, or ruthlessness. Or both. It also suggested inexperience, bringing such an exotic smell to a park area.

I washed regularly, not with soap every day, so I didn't think they could smell me. Smoking and hunting wasn't a smart move. Maybe they weren't all that bright?

They hadn't passed my position, which played on my nerves. Did they suspect something? Were they going to split up? Or spread out? If I attempted to peek over the log at the wrong time, Scope Man might catch me. In scope spotting, human eyes, just like animals', stuck out like pinpricks of light. I didn't know what might happen if I was looking through my monocular. I never asked Luther. And if they had one of the more expensive thermal sights...

The whispering stopped. Sounds of movement, continuing toward the trail's T intersection.

I had to act fast, make sure I got a clear shot at Scope Man leading them while he remained within effective range of my shotgun. He was the biggest, most immediate danger.

With my monocular, I peered over the log. Less than forty feet, with only wide-scattered saplings between us. Letting go of my monocular, allowing it to dangle by its leather cord around my neck, I thumbed off the double-barrel shotgun's safety and took aim at Scope Man.

Rear Man, a short and stocky fellow wearing a ball cap backwards, whispered, "You hear that?" and turned my direction, rifle or shotgun held hip level, ready to shoot.

I squeezed my shotgun's first trigger, keeping my aim on Scope Man who'd stopped in response to Rear Man's warning. The 00 buckshot knocked Scope Man off his feet. A pellet must've clipped Second Man in the leg because he toppled to the ground.

Not waiting to see more after recovering from my gun's recoil, I aimed for Rear Man and pulled the second trigger. I dropped behind the log and reloaded while rifle shots flew overhead, and a shotgun slug slammed into the rotten log sheltering me. Rear Man saw my muzzle flash, and somehow, I must've missed him.

I popped up, above the log again, a few feet to the right from where I'd been. Second Man was crawling toward the prone, unmoving Scope Man. He was going for the night vision scope, so I sent a 00 blast his way and ducked again. There was no immediate sign of Rear Man or Third Guy. They were either on the ground, or behind cover, or both.

Without ear plugs, needing all of my senses before the ambush, my shotgun's blasts momentarily deadened my hearing, but not so much that I couldn't hear at all.

"He's behind that log!" To emphasize the point, another slug slammed into my log, rocking it a few inches.

If only Rear Man hadn't heard me and turned, ruining my surprise. Luther's voice in my head cut through my thoughts. "Hitting a moving target's a lot harder, son, than nailing one that ain't."

After reloading my used barrel, I grabbed a branch and tossed it behind me. Hunching down, I sprinted toward a pair of stout oaks to my right. Two gunshots rang out, but nothing hit me. Crouching low with my back against the tree, I listened for movement. Not hearing any, I spun around the trunk and sent a blast of buckshot to the left of the fallen Scope Man, and then a second blast to the right of him. Without taking time to see if my shots hit anything, I moved to shelter behind the next, slightly larger, oak.

A cursing groan let me know I'd hit someone. Was it the already downed Second Man or Scope Man? Or Rear Man with his shotgun, or Third Guy? From his firearm's report, Third Guy had a rifle, definitely one that fired something larger than a .22.

After reloading, I slung my shotgun and pulled my revolver. Ready with alternating .410 shells, with #4 shot, and .45 longs, I sprinted right and across the path, drawing fire. One shot rang out. The report sounded like a deer rifle. Without aiming, I fired my revolver toward the muzzle flash. After pulling the trigger, I knew I'd missed high. Third Guy was on the ground, firing from the prone position, hidden among some brush and ferns.

Hoping there was only one of them left, I turned toward Third Guy and opened up with my revolver, firing several times into the patch of ferns, hoping that if I didn't hit him, I'd at least suppress his fire.

By the time I reached Third Guy, he was rolling in the ferns, groaning and holding his hands to his face. Staying crouched down I tossed the wounded man's rifle out of reach and kept moving, over toward Scope Guy. I had only one shot left in my revolver, a .45 round. After making it to a tree for cover, I lifted my night vision monocular to my eye and scanned the area.

Scope Man wasn't moving, and neither was Second Man. Third Guy hadn't gone anywhere, and continued to groan. After a second, I spotted Rear Man, or at least his legs partially hidden by a log. He had to be laying on his back, and there was some movement.

After reloading my revolver and holstering it, all the while listening, I unslung my shotgun, checked the load and that the safety was off, and made my way toward Rear Guy.

I found him, clutching his neck. Despite the darkness, I could tell from the slick stains on his hands and the ground around him, he'd taken at least one 00 pellet to the neck.

With the toe of my boot, I lifted and kicked his discarded shotgun out of reach. His eyes widened, despite his panicked suffering, before he closed them. He knew what was next.

Luther drilled into me that bullets weren't to be wasted. This was a moment I wished for a knife like Lucia's. Looking around and seeing there weren't any other threats, I rolled the stocky man over with my boot and hacked with my hand axe. The steel blade severed his spine just below the neck. Third Guy was harder. He must've taken a face full of #4 shot. Lucky pull of the trigger for me. Unlucky for him. I kicked him over and he began pleading for his life.

After finishing the job, I looked around and listened. After assuring myself nobody else was around, I doubled over behind a tree and got sick. I'd be lying if I denied shedding a fist full of tears over what I'd done.

Shed tears over what I had to do.

CHAPTER 4

Before dawn I'd searched the bodies, stripping them of any valuable clothing, firearms, ammunition and other equipment. Then I wheelbarrowed the corpses and put them on display to deter others. This time I decided upon the chain link fence bordering the highway that ran along the metro park's north perimeter. A fresh warning across the direction from which the dead intruders entered my park. Their bodies would rot and feed the vermin twenty feet from the undisturbed section of the chain-link fence where Luther and I had cut a passage, and then carefully wired it closed.

After watching with my night vision monocular for an hour, I figured everything was safe. The survivalist family that controlled the Boy Scout camp just to the north probably heard the gunfire, but they wouldn't investigate any further than the highway once they saw the fresh corpses.

I'd taken the guns and gear to a maintenance shed. A Remington hunting rifle, .270 Winchester, with only eighteen rounds. The best part would've been the night vision scope. It'd taken a shotgun pellet during the fight. I also appropriated a 20 gauge over/under shotgun, with thirteen slug and a handful of birdshot shells. A .22 caliber semi-automatic with 55 rounds, and a Winchester lever-action rifle that fired .357 magnum or .38 special rounds. It was loaded with five .38 rounds, and a snub-nose .38 revolver that held three.

The firearms were in decent condition. Maybe they'd left a stash of ammunition, or maybe they'd traded it all for cigarettes. I found three unopened packs and a half used pack on Scope Man's body. Their shirts and jackets needed washing, along with a bulletproof vest one had been wearing. Luckily I'd shot him in the face. Their boots were well worn, and not my size. Other things like pocket knives, pliers, a compass, things like that, sat in a pile for my future attention.

With the birds singing and the sun having risen an hour earlier, I was exhausted and needed to get some sleep. And that was a problem.

When Luther was around, it was easier to sleep. One of us could always be on watch. Now, it was just me. Walking out of the shelter after listening a moment, I moved to a main trail to make my rounds. I carried my .22 caliber rifle, the carnival gun, as Lucia called it, and the Taurus Judge revolver, with its .410 shell and .45 long mix. The .22 slide-action rifle with an octagon barrel was light and I felt comfortable with it. Hidden around the park, I had other firearms, should I need them.

What I needed to do was to walk my trails, leave a fresh trail of my scent, past the climbing ropes and ramps and other contingencies, should a crawler or a dozer pick up my scent. The plan with the ropes dangling from sturdy branches overhanging the trails, just around a turn, was to offer me a chance to get above and out of a tracking creature's path. That was the theory, especially with a dozer, because unless I managed to shoot it in the mouth, most likely as it was preparing to take a bite out of me, I had nothing else that could stop it. And even that desperate measure probably wouldn't work.

Listening while walking my rounds, my mind wandered back to the concern of me being the only one holding the park. I needed to get someone else. Maybe two people. But who? Lucia? I shook my head. Not her, and not anybody she might recommend. I couldn't trust her. Really, who could I trust? It was a dog-eat-dog world out there. That thought made me sigh. The dozers and crawlers had targeted canines as hard as they did humans. It'd been weeks since I'd heard a dog bark, or a coyote howl. Sounds I might never hear again.

The lean-to shelter in the ravine. I hadn't slept there in a while. Luther always preached: Keep every advantage within your power; don't be predictable.

I watched the road and highway off and on for several

days, not exactly sure as to the type of person, or persons, I was looking for.

Most of Toledo's population was gone. Dead, or departed, and then died. Few, very few, migrated toward the city. Most fled the menace posed by crawlers and dozers, and predatory humans. Disease and starvation, fresh water being in short supply. Even suicides whittled away at what remained of humanity, a sliver of its original number.

Before the invasion, there were articles online where people theorized surviving a zombie apocalypse, and how it wouldn't be that bad, if you were prepared, both mentally and physically, had necessary training in firearms and survival skills, and stockpiled the right equipment to see you through. See you through to what? How much different was an alien invasion apocalypse as compared to a zombie one, especially when the alien one included dozers and crawlers, going around and trying to eat you?

Idiots. How many of those idiots were still alive? The survivalist family in the Boy Scout Park across the highway north of my park was probably as prepared as anyone could manage. Judging by the few encounters Luther and I had with them, surviving wasn't an easy thing, even for them. Long term, they were worried.

I stood on a maple's limb, leaning against the trunk. Although I was only fifteen feet above the ground, the elevation gave me a better view of the road, with the leaf-filled branches offering cover from observation. Wearing greens and browns, unless I moved sharply, human eyes wouldn't pick me out of the background.

I wasn't moving much, just flossing my teeth. I brushed three times a day, and flossed once. "Don't wanna get a deep cavity with all the dentists gone," Luther had warned me more than once. "No fixing them, just pulling. Without Novocain or sleeping gas." Now that I was alone, I'd have to do it myself, maybe with fishing string? No way I could manage it with pliers. Better to brush and floss. Luther had, then we had, and now I alone had, boxes of toothbrushes, and 10,000 yards of dental floss. Actually, 317 toothbrushes and 296 spooled four-packs, each spool containing 25 feet of floss. Not a lifetime's worth the way I used it, but close enough.

Too bad Luther got to the dentist offices after someone ransacked them, taking all the drugs and medications. The looters didn't have too much foresight. They left the toothbrushes, toothpaste, and floss.

This morning, a couple, a man and a woman, trudged along the highway past me. It wasn't hard to hear the tall, gaunt man berating his rail-thin, female companion. He pushed a mountain bike loaded down with sacks and duffle bags. What the mainly green and navy blue bags held, I couldn't tell, but the bike's load appeared balanced, maybe several hundred pounds. He had what looked like a hunting rifle slung across his back. His heavy work boots matched the grimy coveralls, like what a mechanic would wear. The feminine cat's eye glasses didn't fit the ensemble.

His companion looked unkempt, with tangled hair sprouting from beneath her brown knit hat. She wore a tattered sweater and faded jeans, and scuffed hiking boots. The day was going to be too hot for all of that.

She stared at the road, pushing a heavily-laden, three-wheeled baby stroller. Even across the distance, her bony hands and pinched cheeks showed her thinness bordered on emaciation. The man's language was laced with more cuss words than regular nouns and verbs combined, most of them directed at his companion. They were a distance from me, downhill, but his voice carried, even above the birds behind me.

Maybe having to wear women's glasses made the man angry. If he'd lost his, or they'd somehow got broken, it wasn't like he could pop in and see an optometrist for a new pair with his prescription. No, you made do with whatever you could find that fit the need, even if it wasn't fashionable.

I didn't know bird calls by species; couldn't pick out particular species, for the most part. Back when Luther was around, I didn't pay attention when he told me, figuring it wasn't important. He could tell me again if I ever got curious. I only knew blue jays, cardinals and crows, all loud species. The birds behind me were chirping out warbling songs and calls, not very loud, so I could hear the man. He was blaming the woman for their predicament, from what I could tell, having to leave, but why they left was never expressed. Rather his foul-mouthed rant repeated the same statements over and over, and over again, as they passed the abandoned vehicles scattered along the interstate highway. Sometimes he peeked in a window or through a windshield before moving on.

I had no interest sharing the park with their type. I sort of felt bad for the woman, but she willingly travelled with him—although she didn't have a firearm that I could tell. Could be that she didn't have a choice?

Less than a half hour after the couple had passed, movement along the highway, again moving away from Toledo, caught my eye.

I froze. The boxy creature, built like a bear on steroids, but covered in a thick hide that reminded me of a rhinoceros, trotted along the road. Its large claws clicked against the pavement with each step. They were sharp, four inch weapons, a darker shade of gray than the dozer's hide. They could tear through cinderblocks and car doors like razor blades through cheap fabric. Dozers didn't have a head or neck like a bear. This one, like all the others, had a beak, three-sided instead of two like a bird's. Sharp and serrated, and set between its shoulders, the beak made the dozer look even more compact and deadly. If needed, the beak could telescope out several feet and flex up to eighty degrees on the sinuous, muscular conduit.

Conduit. That's what Luther called the striated green tube ending in a ring of knotted muscle fibers that powered the beak.

The dark spheres, four of them spaced across the dozer's shoulders, above the beak, were sensing organs. Maybe eyes. Maybe more along the lines of motion sensors, or olfactory-related? I'd never been this close to one, never spoke to anyone who'd survived being close to one. From what I could tell, it was on the trail of the foul-mouthed man and his companion.

I had my .22 caliber 'carnival gun' and my Judge revolver. Neither would stop the dozer. Their hide was more resilient, or maybe the better term would be resistant, than layers of plate steel, or so I'd been told. No gun in my arsenal would be useful against that.

It trotted past, a seeming spring in its step as it edged toward a gallop, curving around and through the scattered abandoned cars and trucks.

Better the couple it was tracking than me. Sure, I felt some guilt at that thought, but not enough to call the alien hunting beast down on me.

Unless something sidetracked the dozer, it'd catch up with the couple in twenty, no more than thirty, minutes.

Twenty-three minutes later, while I was digging up a few dandelions along the edge of an overgrown meadow, I heard it. Two gunshots. Distant. Too distant to hear the couple's screams as the dozer took them down.

The dandelions available for harvesting were getting older. The leaves and the roots would be bitter, but that fit my mood.

The couple's demise meant another victory for the invading alien menace.

CHAPTER 5

Instead of running the trails to freshen my scent upon them and check for intruders, I went to the south end of the park to watch the road, not really expecting any travelers. I ended by making my way to the split-rail fence bearing the corpse of the crawler Lucia helped me kill.

There weren't any crows around, which made sense. The most recent 'trophy' wasn't something they'd eat. As I approached, I caught sight of movement across the road, near one of the houses. I approached closer, keeping low, with trees and patches of tall weeds between me and the movement.

Making it to a decent-sized maple whose trunk was surrounded by tall grass and flowering weeds, I took up position with my .22 caliber rifle ready. One person I recognized. Lucia. The other five—four black men and one woman of lighter complexion—surrounded Lucia, standing near the overgrown shrubbery along the east side of the brick ranch house.

The woman shoved a compound bow into Lucia's hand. It looked like Lucia's bow. Lucia didn't raise her hand from her side, holding it along her hip as if it were bound there. The distance was too great to hear any words exchanged. Lucia appeared to have a sour look on her face, but that was normal. At least two of the men were grinning.

All of Lucia's associates sported green and brown camouflage and carried rifles, three with scopes. The three with scoped rifles also carried some additional gear: belts, leather straps and metal leg braces of some sort. At a signal from the tallest man, one that carried a pump shotgun, the woman scampered toward the road, keeping low and watching, mainly across the road, toward the park, toward me. She stopped near the mailbox, knelt behind it and the leafy weeds that had sprouted up around it.

It was difficult to see her but, after a moment, she

must've signaled the others forward.

They strode through the deep grass of what had once been a well-manicured lawn, Shotgun Man shoving Lucia ahead of him. One man angled toward an oak tree along the driveway near the road. Its trunk extended up at least forty feet before branching out. The lanky man slung his rifle and placed the braces under his boots before strapping the framing to his legs. Then he slung his leather strap around the trunk of the tree and began to climb, using the leather strap and what must've been spikes in the braces attached to his booths and legs.

Was he climbing to achieve an over watch position?

Not good. But, even as the man climbed, the others, except for the woman and Lucia, began spreading out right and left. A tactical error. They should've waited for Over Watch Man to get into position.

Resting the barrel of my .22 on one of the maple's low branches, I prioritized my targets. I had fifteen rounds in my rifle. Having a higher caliber gun would've been handy, but Luther always said comfort and accuracy in a confrontation was more important than the size of the bullet. If you missed, it didn't matter.

Like me, most people didn't carry hundreds of rounds with them, so when I captured higher caliber rifles, I usually only got one, maybe two dozen extra rounds, maximum. Not enough to become comfortable and competent with a new gun.

When people entered the park, it wasn't to move in—at least not right away. It was to take us, Luther and me, and now just me, out. Take by force what I had.

Over Watch Man was still climbing and not an immediate threat. I didn't think Lucia was on their side, so the woman near her would have her attention split. That left two riflemen with scopes and one with a shotgun. Shotgun Man concerned me the most, so I targeted him.

Leading him slightly, I aimed for his head. A body shot would've been easier, but a .22 didn't have a lot of takedown power. Unless I got lucky, even a hollow point might not do enough to completely incapacitate him. At least they didn't appear to have bulletproof vests like the one I'd recently acquired and, unfortunately, wasn't wearing.

Exhaling slowly, I squeezed off one round. The man's head jerked. My round struck him in the neck, below the ear. Before he staggered two steps and fell to the ground, I was lining up my second target, the nearest of the two riflemen near Shotgun Man. Luck was on my side. The rifleman I chose stopped and turned to see what had happened to Shotgun Man, giving me a clean shot. The other, smarter, if not more experienced rifleman, dropped to the ground.

Not having the luxury of time, I took hasty aim and fired. My round must've struck Inexperienced Rifleman in the chest, as he flinched and staggered back a half step. Having .30-06 rounds right then would've been preferable to a tiny .22. Nevertheless, I pumped and squeezed off a quick third shot, half aimed, hitting the stunned rifleman in the gut.

He sank to the ground. Not dead, but out of the action—hopefully.

Three rounds expended. I couldn't see the rifleman who'd immediately dropped to the ground. The woman had drawn a knife and moved behind Lucia, holding the blade to her neck. Over Watch Man was climbing down. He was my next target.

The woman using Lucia as a shield yelled, "Drop your gun and give up, or she dies!"

Both I and Experienced Rifleman ignored her and fired. The roaring *crack* of his gun rang out far louder than my .22's *pop*. Bark sprayed in the wake of my bullet. It must've ricocheted into the Over Watch Man's calf as he cried out and jerkily fell the last ten feet to the ground. The belt slung around and attaching him to the tree slowed his fall, but the process slammed his face against the tree a few times.

Knife Woman standing behind Lucia shouted louder. "Last chance. Back off now!" She was taller than Lucia, with her right hand holding the large knife and her left arm wrapped around Lucia, holding her close. Knife Woman's face was tucked against Lucia, partially obscured.

I shifted to the other side of the maple tree and took aim at the woman's left cheek. That placed the trunk more between me and Experienced Rifleman.

I took a relaxing breath. Almost 150 feet. If I missed and hit Lucia, it would only quicken her already certain demise. If I hit Knife Woman, it gave Lucia a chance. Still, the odds were against Lucia, as I intended to back off, rather than press the fight. The attackers wouldn't follow me into the park, not when I was aware of their presence. Plus, I might be able to track those still alive and mobile back toward Toledo, and maybe finish them off. If I made my shot, Experienced Rifleman would be the only one not wounded. Shotgun Man, I figured, was dead, and Inexperienced Rifleman, with two hollow-tipped rounds in his torso, might not be far from the Grim Reaper's visit.

Thunk-Crack!

Experienced Rifleman's bullet imbedded itself in the maple tree's trunk, opposite side from me.

It made me jump, but I pulled my rifle's barrel back on target and pulled the trigger.

My bullet missed Knife Woman's face. It bit into her left shoulder instead.

Lucia knocked Knife Woman backwards, even as the taller woman clumsily jerked the knife's blade across Lucia's throat. I dropped to the ground and lost sight of Lucia's struggle.

Crack! Another gunshot whipped past overhead, probably where I'd just been standing.

Experienced Rifleman had a scope. I didn't. He had a bead on me while I had only a vague idea where he was. Time to back off.

Keeping low and using the deep grass and clumps of flowery weeds for cover, I crawled back to my right, attempting to put distance between me and Experienced Rifleman, who fired another shot my way.

"Jamal, look out!" The deep voice of warning was swiftly followed by two quick gunshots. They sounded like a pistol. A rifle shot and two more gunshots.

I came up next to a tree, a smaller one than the maple that previously sheltered me. I stood to see what was happening.

Lucia was on her feet, holding a pistol, taking aim at the prone Knife Woman who was feebly trying to crawl away from her. One shot and it was over.

Lucia's left hand was clamped along her throat, tucked under her chin. Even from my distance, it was easy to spot blood seeping through her fingers. Lucia turned my way, dropped the pistol and slowly sank to her knees.

I broke from cover, sprinting toward her, banking that Lucia took out both Experienced Rifleman and Over Watch Man.

Chapter 6

After dabbing the iodine solution on Lucia's stitched-up wound, I needed to give it a minute to dry.

Owing to her struggle to survive, the slash Lucia suffered largely missed her neck. Instead the cut ran across the bottom of her chin, not across her throat as I'd thought.

The two Vicodin from my stash helped dull Lucia's pain, not only from her wound, but also from the beating she'd suffered as evidenced by forming bruises. The times Luther had me practice stitching wounds on the carcasses of a pig, a deer, and a plucked duck before we cooked and ate them provided me some experience. But those were dead, immobile subjects that weren't bleeding and didn't tense up. And I couldn't have Lucia look up to give me a better angle. That would've open the wound more.

The stitches didn't look too ragged. It was a lie. She'd have a noticeable scar, but she was alive. She'd live with it if infection didn't set in. I had some tubes of antibacterial gel, and could use those later. They weren't handy at the moment and it was important to get the wound covered.

All in all, Lucia proved once again she was one tough cookie. I would've yelled, maybe whimpered if someone was sticking a little hooked needle in my flesh and pulling the wound closed with the tightening thread. Some sights bothered me. Fortunately for Lucia, somebody else's blood wasn't one of them. If I ever had to stitch up my own leg or arm, or stomach? That'd be another story.

I performed the medical procedure in the park ranger's house, which was situated near the park's southwestern border. Carrying her the short distance proved easier than anticipated. Adrenaline coursing through my veins had something to do with that. The ranger's small residence had been ransacked long ago. Nevertheless, the torn-up couch would allow Lucia to rest. She was tough, and should be able to endure the atrocious geometric patterned wallpaper.

Lucia appeared quite at ease, the pain pills having taken hold. She glanced over at the row of storage tubs lined up along the wall. The rainwater downspout was redirected through one of the broken windows into the first of the green tubs. A PVC pipe placed into a cut hole extended from the first tub to the second, and another PVC pipe connected the second to the third. She smiled, recognizing their purpose was to collect rain water. When the first filled, the overflow filled the second in line and so on. That had been my idea and Luther approved. We'd set up something similar in a few of the nearby homes, as well as in the manor house and the old school house located in the park. Sure, I had specially manufactured 'straws' that could filter out bacteria and other microbes, but those were for emergency situations. Food, shelter and fresh water. Those were the top priorities for Luther and me. That, and securing our location from looters and human predators.

"You need to lay on your back," I said, "and try not to twist your neck or stretch your jaw."

She glared at me, then did as I said.

After glancing out several windows to see if anyone was watching—or any alien beasts were roaming about—I said, "Give me a second. There might be a hand mirror in the bathroom so you can get a look at my handiwork."

Lucia frowned and nodded slightly.

"I'd be curious if it was you who sewed me up." A moment later I returned with a circular makeup mirror and handed it to her. "It's not that bad, but there's gonna be a scar."

While she held the mirror and tipped her head up, wincing at the pain, I prepared the gauze bandage and tape to cover the wound. Lucia's eyebrows rose, then scrunched down.

After I affixed the bandage, she said, "Not bad as I thought." Her words were muffled as she tried not to move her jaw as she spoke. "Thanks, Jack."

I nodded. "You're welcome. The whole thing could've ended up worse. We can talk about it later."

"I remember you on that crazy-ass old lady tricycle, with those wagons full of plastic tubs and who knows what the hell else. Pegged you for a crazy one." She snorted a half laugh and winced. "Crazy like a damn hoarding fox."

"If you say so, Lucia." I shrugged. "Now stop talking so those stitches don't get torn out."

Her eyes looked heavy, like she was fighting sleep. Probably the pills. Suddenly I wondered if she'd been on any medication, and if there might be some sort of bad drug interaction. There wasn't much I could do about it. Make her vomit?

Shaking my head, realizing paranoia was creeping into my thoughts, I picked up the pistol and holster sitting on a nearby end table. Pain meds made people drowsy. Everybody knew that.

Holding up the .45 ACP, the pistol Lucia used to kill the woman and other two male captors, I said, "It's loaded, with a round in the chamber," and showed her the safety was on. After slipping it back into the holster, I set it near her right hand, between her leg and the back cushion. "I've got to make the rounds. Toss those bodies on my trophy fence and see what they have on them."

She nodded in understanding, her eyelids still heavy.

"Don't you shoot me when I come back," I warned. "I'll knock on the door five times after calling your name." I moved the end table up next to the couch, within reach. "You hit this twice so I can hear, and know you're not gonna shoot me, okay?"

She rapped her left hand's knuckles on it twice in acknowledgment, then closed her eyes.

She was out before the door clicked closed behind me.

Lucia didn't escape infection. She ran a slight fever and a red tenderness afflicted her chin's wound, but a few days of Amoxicillin caplets gave her immune system the upper hand. Some of the vitamins I shared probably helped just as much. During that time she stayed mainly in the ranger's house, but stood two stationary, five hour watches after the first few days. That offered me a chance to catch up on some much needed sleep.

One evening watch, near the highway, Lucia shot at what she described as a 'scraggly man,' to drive him off. My guess was Lucia's warning was actually a missed shot, but it didn't matter. She grumbled about the rifle, one taken from the men who'd captured her. She cursed how messed up its scope was.

With the intervening foliage and the abandoned cars scattered across the highway, unless someone stood still, nothing was a straight out easy shot.

During her recovery, I kept to my pattern of patrols, and my stash locations secret, even as my thoughts drifted toward asking Lucia if she'd be interested in teaming up with me. She was smart, ruthless, willing to work and, most importantly, a survivor. Really, except for the first two days, we hadn't spent more than a few hours in each other's company, and then we were eating or I was caring for her wound.

Still, I had some questions, and more than a few reservations.

Even though her jaw and neck were still sore, Lucia sat down on the fallen log next to me and swung her left leg over so that she straddled it. The log was half-rotted and not so big around that it was uncomfortable for her.

She asked, "Is this really what you eat all the time?" She was referring to the bowl of dandelion and plantain greens I handed to her. They still had some of the morning's dew on them. I'd also tossed in a handful of dog kibble.

We were near one of the meadows along the Orange Trail, not far from the ball diamonds and the elementary school just outside the park's border. Large swaths of the meadow had deep grass, with shrubs and brambles filling the rest. It normally had a fair number of butterflies flitting around, and that day was no exception.

I took a step back and sat on the other end of the log. Offering a sincere grin, I raised my matching plastic bowl.

"Yes. Eating greens and whatever else the land can offer while it's available. The preserved food, that's for winter and emergencies."

She glared at me.

"Maybe after I take a nap," I said, "we can catch some fish. But, until then, it's dog food for protein. Plus, additional nutrients and calories, to keep our strength up."

She tasted the plantain and stuck her tongue out. "This is nasty-bitter. Your cattail concoction tasted better."

"Actually, if I recall, plantain, you can make a tea with it, and maybe an ointment from it, too. Good for stomach ailments and to help fight skin infections. I'd have to check the book."

"Book?"

"Yeah, Luther had one, on local edible and medicinal plants." Actually, there was a stack of them that I'd hidden around the park. No reason to tell her, at least not yet.

"And you have it now, Jack?"

"Not on me," I said, smiling and patting my pockets.

"That's not what I meant, and you know it."

I gave her a sarcastic look. "No, I buried it with him."

She sneered at me. "Jackass. Just trying to make conversation."

I ate a few bites. She was right, the plantain was noticeably bitter, even more so than the dandelion greens. How many people were starving, with 'weeds' they could eat growing around them? How many plants around me were edible that I wasn't aware of? I drank a mouthful of water from my plastic bottle to wash the taste down and stared at Lucia out of the corner of my eye. She took a drink from her bottle and glared back at me.

"Okay," I said. "It was a long night. You watch the north end, near the highway while I catch a few hours of shuteye, and we'll go fishing."

Her facial expression was difficult to read. Anticipation mixed with disgust?

"So," I said to Lucia, tossing my fishing line out about ten feet into a bend in the river. The lead sinker reached the bottom of the slow-flowing area. Most of the river was slow, shallow, wide and muddy. Cleaner, I could tell it week by week, as mankind's industrial and other polluting activities had ceased.

The red and white bobber settled on the surface. "Those men and that woman that brought you here. They weren't your friends. That was clear."

I paused, watching the bobber for a moment, then continued. "You haven't made any noises about going back to the city, wherever you...dwell, when you're not lurking about here verbally harassing me."

Lucia, standing on some flat rocks along the bank next to me, scowled. She inexpertly tossed her line out, managing not to cross mine. I'd had to show her how to put a worm on the hook and explain the bobber. This was obviously her first time fishing.

Her bobber settled about seven feet from mine. "Haven't decided where to go, yet." She stared out at the pair of bobbers.

Our fishing poles were short sticks, thick as my thumb. We didn't need the rod and reel gear stuffed in the rafters of the park's old school house. I'd wrapped about twenty feet of fishing line on each stick. The setup was compact and easy to coil up, and I could press the hook's tip in the end of the stick.

"They got into my bunker," she continued. "I shot their leader in the throat, and stabbed another one. That's why their plan was so messed up."

She'd kept her language clear of cussing. That probably meant something. Squatting, I stared at the floating bobbers and listened to the woods around us. A few birds singing, and a breeze in the leaves above.

"They wanted me alive to get to you. Wanted your drugs. Medicines are in short supply. Worth more than bullets, for barter."

I shrugged, recalling her previous visit, and her questions about antibiotics.

"To be straight with you, Jack, the local citizens figure I'm dead. Someone had to see them leading me out this way. My bunker's cleaned out for sure. My bolt holes? I've got a bunch, but don't know about them. That's what I've been trying to figure."

I asked, "Many folks, citizens, left in Toledo?" My park was on the western edge, tucked into suburban type housing.

She thought for a moment. "Four, maybe five thousand. Less each day."

I shifted a little forward, still watching the bobbers. "Only the toughest, most ruthless ones left?"

She smirked at my statement and squatted down next to me. "You'd think, but it ain't worked out that way. Sure, there's some gangs and loners nobody'd dare cross. Not even think about it. But meanness, guns and muscle, ruthlessness, guile don't always protect you. From the humans, it mostly works, but someone might pop you from a distance. Payback for something, or figuring to take what you're carrying."

She shook her head. "There's some that are just wild-ass crazy.

"Nothing like that keeps you safe from the crawlers and dozers." She sighed. "Being smart and sneaky might, if you've got some luck. Keep them from spotting you. Getting on your trail. You know that, Jack. You lose that luck? If it ain't your day, don't matter how mean you are, how many in your gang, how well you're armed and bunkered in…"

Two long minutes passed before she continued. "Actually, with the eye-crystal arrows, the crawlers ain't so scary. You can kill them easy now, if you got arrows, or a spear to stick them. But with fewer people, they're hunting in packs now. Tough to get them all. And dozers? Don't anything stop them, except a meal."

Lucia jumped a little. Her bobber had jiggled, and dipped once.

"Careful," I warned. "Wait for a good hit."

She held her stick ready. "What's a good hit, Jack?"

"That was a nibble, a good hit—Now!" I shouted when her bobber went under.

It was funny. Lucia's look of disgust while sticking a worm on a hook, and struggling to remove the hook from the three bluegills she pulled in, compared to the ease she displayed gutting and preparing her fish for cooking. I only had to show her once how to prepare bluegill for cooking. I was expecting to catch bullhead, but you take what you can get.

Lucia's Bowie knife, the one the female intruder had confiscated and used to slice Lucia's throat…she insisted on using it, as opposed to my fillet knife. She handled the big blade like a natural extension of her hand. That almost balanced the need for the finesse of a smaller blade to efficiently fillet a fish. Fortunately, the bluegills were all about ten inches, and that helped.

The experience relayed volumes to me. Although Lucia was ruthless and a survivor, she wasn't an experienced outdoorsman, or outdoorswoman. The city was her familiar territory. Her insistence on using her Bowie knife, when a more suitable one was on hand…

"Using your knife," I said, "cuts weren't as clean. We lost some meat."

"That flexible little one might work better, Jack. But it's not the one I'll always have on my hip." She slapped the blade in its sheath hanging from her belt to emphasize the point. "Better to learn using the tools you always got, right?"

While I didn't agree, believing that if you have the proper tool on hand, use it, I saw where Lucia was coming from. "Do you know how to build a fire without matches?"

She pulled a lighter from her pocket and smirked.

In turn, I pulled a magnifying glass from my shirt pocket. "Better to use something renewable like sunlight, and save matches—or a lighter—for cloudy days."

"My little brother likes to kill ants with one of those," she said, then frowned, probably remembering her brother, more than likely lost, like so many.

I missed my family too, and tried to keep them from my thoughts, tucked away with the hope that they were still alive. But my dreams? Those I couldn't control. There they appeared regularly, and revived thoughts of their death. Those haunted me.

Florida, where they were, was too far from Ohio to consider a trek home, to find them, if they were still alive. Too many dozers and crawlers, too many gangs and predators, too many miles of danger, with uncertainty of food and shelter. Water, with my ceramic-filtering safety straws, wasn't a problem. Unless someone took them from me. Someone who got the drop on me in unfamiliar territory, or a group that simply had more muscle, more guns…

Once I'd shown Lucia how to build a proper teepee campfire, I left her to cook so I could patrol the southern portion of the park.

Later, over our meal of fish wrapped in dandelion greens, we came to an agreement, without any formality, or even a handshake. Lucia would remain with me, in my park.

Now *our* park.

"I'll tell you where all of my bolt holes are, and what I've got stored in them," Lucia said, while kicking dirt on the fire. "If you think you can remember."

I laughed at that. One thing I had was a good memory. "Take a bike tomorrow, and see if any of them have been found and looted." I helped her kicking dirt onto the fire's coals. "Might be best to keep any supplies there, in case we end up needing them."

"We can do that, Jack."

She looked down at her outfit, a mishmash of her clothes—boots, jeans and jean jacket—and what I'd stripped from intruders and collected from abandoned houses over the past months. She'd put on a brown T-shirt with cartoon drawings of two tusked monsters. They were ogres, based on the shirt's caption, Dueling Ogres. It just didn't seem to fit her personality. Or the facets of her personality I'd seen.

The shirt was a little tight across the chest. Maybe she picked it from the folded stack for that reason? Or maybe she just liked cartoons?

I put her attire selection aside. "Anyone left in the city that learns you're out here now," I said. "That should deter them."

"Maybe," she said, a lack of confidence in her voice. "Maybe not. For a long time, I sort of stretched the truth, about you and Luther, and then just you, making you sound more dangerous than you are."

She studied my face, expecting some sort of reaction. Offering no expression, one way or the other, I stirred the dirt and dying coals with my boot.

"You knew, Jack, that I was going to betray you? They were gonna force me to lure you out into the open. But how'd you know they—we was coming?"

"I didn't, Lucia. Pure luck I was there." I kicked more dirt on the few surviving red coals. "Saw a dozer trailing two people heading west along the highway. Came to the south end of my par—our park—to create distance should the dozer return, still hungry."

"Could be fate looking at you and me, Jack."

Something felt wrong about Lucia. It didn't sound like her. Not the hard-ass woman I'd known. Had the intruders that captured Lucia broken her? Was it the loss of her independence? Entering into a sort of codependence with me? Or had it all been an act, and she wasn't playing the part anymore?

When I didn't say anything, Lucia said, "I'll take first watch tonight while you sleep. Then, in the morning, after you get a few hours shuteye, I'll ride into the city. Check on things, be seen alive, and let folks know you kicked ass, Jack." She grinned wickedly. "Let'em know they'll have to deal with both you and me if they think about coming around."

Her words sounded a little more like the old Lucia. There was a hint of the ruthlessness in her eye. But the ferocity, the confidence wasn't there. Would the others notice?

"Sounds like a plan," I said. "Focus your watch over by the Manor House."

She nodded before slinging her rifle. I grabbed my slide-action .22 and nodded back.

CHAPTER 7

Lucia pedaled steadily, watching over her shoulder, and to the left and right, giving extra time to the houses on her left. She appeared to be looking up and around, especially above roofs and trees, which seemed odd.

Nevertheless, she moved with a purpose. Bicycles offered more rapid and efficient travel, while also creating vulnerabilities. Of course, boot-hoofing it had plenty of drawbacks. In general, moving slower wasn't the better option.

From my perch in the cottonwood, I watched to see if anyone, or any creature, appeared to be trailing her. The area trees and their leaf-filled branches made it challenging. If I remained relatively still, they made someone else spotting me more than challenging.

Nothing followed Lucia toward the park...at least not yet.

She turned and passed close by my tree without looking up, taking the mountain bike through deep grass and onto one of the roads leading to the main entrance's parking lot.

After lingering twenty minutes, I climbed down the oak, using the few strategically carved hand and footholds. Using ropes was easier, but looping for easy release took time. Leaving a rope behind, tied to the tree's upper limbs? That was an obvious clue to any observant passerby or scout considering intrusion. Better to keep them guessing.

We met at our rendezvous point, on the west side of the Ottawa River, at the entry to the concrete walkway leading to the covered bridge. Lucia had already stowed the bike in a stall in the women's side of the public restroom building.

Instead of waiting, Lucia trotted up to me. Her wide eyes and frown said something she'd seen, or learned from her contacts, that wasn't good. She stopped about five feet short and signaled me to stay away. "Some disease is going around, Jack. Maybe more than one—part of the reason they wanted your medicine stash. The smart ones had a feel an outbreak was coming."

That gave meaning to her keeping a distance. "And you're contagious?"

"I don't think so. Guessed you'd wanna know before you got any closer to me."

"What is it?"

"Dr. Gurrie, she's an animal doctor—"

I cut her off, clarifying, "A veterinarian?" I didn't recall Lucia mentioning this person as one of her contacts.

"That's what an animal doctor is, ain't it?" As Lucia's hands slipped to her hips, her hunting rifle's sling hung precariously from her shoulder.

"Go on," I said. Doctors were a scarce commodity. Many died early on while treating patients in the failing hospitals, succumbing to rampant disease brewing within what had recently been state-of-the-art medical facilities. Apparently the rest, including nurses and technicians, joined the exodus from the city. Where to? I could only guess.

"Well, she's smart," Lucia said. "What doctor ain't?"

When I didn't reply, Lucia continued. "She says measles. A bad variant that previous vaccinations don't help. Measles, and cholera."

"I might have medicine for cholera. Antibiotics, but nothing really for measles."

"*We* might have medicine?"

Over the past two weeks, Lucia had jumped right in, going above and beyond to patrol and learn anything she could about outdoor survival. I showed her places to ambush or to make a stand. Those with good cover from front and back, formations of trees and logs, plus escape routes. I showed her where she could cross ravines on logs, or where she could descend and climb safely and quickly, and where she could run along the bottoms and hide, and more. All she needed to know, that I could think to share with her.

Lucia was a quick learner, and she accepted her position as the junior partner, but she insisted on our partner relationship.

I refrained from rolling my eyes. "*We* might. Did you see anyone with it? Red bumps and rash, and fever. That'd be measles. Diarrhea, and fever, that'd be cholera." Then I thought a minute, and sidestepped so that I wasn't downwind from her. "You said 'had a feel an outbreak?'"

"That's just part of the shit news, Jack. Only one of the moves the aliens are making."

I held up a hand. Aliens making moves? "Tell me about the outbreak first. Then the other...bad news."

She said, "There's some good news, too."

"Save that for last then." I pointed to the bridge. "Want to sit down there, out of the sun?"

"Yeah." She reached for the canteen on her belt. "Keep your distance until I tell you the happenings."

We walked the short distance to the bridge. I leaned against one railing, and she on the opposite side of the bridge.

"What Dr. Gurrie said was a group of refugees in a yellow school bus drove into downtown, along near the crater, loud and slow. Crates of food lashed to a frame they'd welded on the roof. One person riding on top with a shotgun. The Bankstreeters shot the guy and the bus tires. The driver gave up without a fight, and the three women weren't even harmed.

"The wooden crates were labelled in red paint: cookies, dried fruit, beef jerky. All riding on top, showing like billboards. Who the hell does that? They asked to get jacked."

"Where was the bus from?" I asked.

"What?" asked Lucia. "What does that matter?"

"Did your doctor friend say?"

"She ain't my friend, Jack. She's a contact." Then Lucia's tone softened. "She's tough but smart. Got guts. Gangs and independents trust her. She's done surgery and stuff to save people."

Lucia's eyes widened as she recalled. "Sandusky Schools."

"The bus was from Sandusky?"

"That don't matter, Jack. The women sick with the measles. The Mean Measles is what they're calling them. Kills about half that catch it. Some that fight off the fever end up blind. Anyone cares for the sick, catch it.

"The food was contaminated. Anyone that ate it got cholera. Most that got the Mean Measles got cholera too, but the cholera didn't spread too far cuz the Bankstreeters hoarded the food. They're all dead now. People burned their hotel and bolt holes. Bus too, the one from Sandusky," she said with a smirk.

"Dr. Gurrie says nobody's caring for anyone that gets sick, now. They shoot them and burn the body."

"Is that working?"

"Nobody knows."

"Nobody?"

"Nobody's out traveling. Not only 'cause of the disease, but because there's the alien drone."

That caught my attention.

She nodded. "They're big, like giant metal Frisbees. Dr. Gurrie says they kill with a sonic beam weapon. Causes brain bleeding—she said hemorrhaging."

"Was that why you were watching above the houses before you entered our park?"

Lucia nodded. "Bill Fiver, he's with the Cops Coalition."

I nodded back, signaling I understood the connection. Lucia mentioned them a few times over the past two weeks when she tried to explain what was happening in the city. They were a group formed around the surviving police officers, firefighters, city workers and some ex-military. They and their families took over the mall.

"Some of them got sick, but they had a ham radio guy who discovered the same thing happened in Cleveland and Columbus. The aliens brainwashed some people, infected them, and sent them in to be…" She paused, in thought. "To be disease vectors."

"What about the drones?" I asked.

Lucia held up a hand, telling me to listen. "The cops left

the mall. Just left it and all their stuff there. Anyone with the Mean Measles, too. That same day the drone started showing up. Comes from the east. Doesn't go near downtown, even the cratered part, and stays above the buildings. Anyone out in the open? It gets them. Sometimes it gets them in buildings, too.

"Dr. Gurrie says it hunts about twenty hours a day."

I took a moment to look around and listen. Even glanced skyward. There were a few buildings in the park. Only one big one, but nothing like a high rise apartment or a skyscraper from downtown. My mind raced, trying to think where I'd hide.

I let out a long breath. "Does she think it'll come out here?"

Lucia nodded. "Pretty soon."

"Did anyone try to shoot it down?"

"It's got armor or something. People shot it with rifles. She said Razor Stick shot it with his .30-06. Shot it twice before it got him. He had a scope, too. Anyone that shoots at it, gets chased down and killed."

"Only people that shoot at it? Threaten it?"

"No." After shaking her head, Lucia's eyes followed then settled on a horsefly landing on the bridge's railing next to her. With a lightning-quick slap of her hand, she crushed the biting fly with her palm. "Anyone it finds, it kills."

"Only one drone?"

She used the edge of the railing to scrape the dead fly from her hand. "One's enough."

"Anybody know anything about the aliens?" I asked. "The ham radio operator. Did he know anything more about them? Anyone seen one?"

Lucia shook her head, then stared down at the bridge's planks.

I couldn't get a reading on her feelings. Blank expressions weren't her normal mode. "You worried about getting sick?"

"I didn't touch anybody," she replied. "Only got near Dr. Gurrie. Didn't eat or drink anything, or do more than ride past my bolt holes."

"So you should be safe?"

"If I get sick…"

"What's the incubation period?"

"What's that?"

"Incubation period. How long from contact to showing symptoms—getting sick."

"I don't know, Jack. Like three days. That's how long it took the Bankstreeters, before they started getting sick."

The Bankstreeters. Lucia talked about them before. They were well-armed and aggressive, but didn't have any interest in spreading out to the suburbs, or my park. Even if they had intentions to, it wasn't going to happen, since they were dead. Their greed and shortsightedness cost them. They should've recognized it as a ploy, a bus with crates out in the open, labeled food containers.

Of course, hindsight is 20/20. And food could be getting scarce.

I thought about Lucia. She was brazen in many ways, but cautious in others. "You'll be okay," I said.

"Jack, you don't come near me for three days," she said. "We'll just patrol different places and not share a campfire."

Her eyes grew wide with worry.

"I might have some anti-viral medications," I said, recalling Luther had some medications from a pharmacy, used if you came down with the flu. The flu was a virus, so it might help. "If you do get sick."

"If I get it, you don't come near."

Our gazes locked for a moment.

"We'll cross that bridge if it comes," I said, unsure what I'd do. If I'd risk my life for her. Trying to lighten the mood, I added, "I can toss you meds in a bottle from a distance, if it becomes necessary."

She caught my grin, and returned one of her own. It was forced, but then again, so was mine.

"So, Lucia, what's the good news?"

"Dr. Gurrie said you did a good job stitching my chin. Good for an amateur."

"That's the good news?"

She shot me a crooked grin. It appeared genuine. "No. Just wanted to tell you that."

"Okay," I said, after taking another moment to scan the area, the sky, too. Lucia did the same.

"Okay?" she repeated.

"The good news?"

"Oh," she said. "Nobody's seen a crawler in days. They hunted them down. And Dr. Gurrie said everyone learned something from Kenny, the ham radio guy."

She paused, watching and waiting for me to ask.

I was curious, but could wait. She wanted to tell me more than she wanted to force me to ask.

"Nobody can figure a way to consistently kill a dozer yet, unless you can drop something that weighs a ton on it from about ten stories up. But there's a way to irritate them enough that they'll leave you alone. At least for a while."

That got me to lean forward, all ears. "And what's that?"

"I don't know, yet," Lucia said, looking from me to the bridge's floor planks. "Dr. Gurrie said she'd tell me and get me what I needed if I brought her back some antibiotics, and something else, to make it worth her while."

Lucia knew where I kept two stashes of antibiotics, and even the anti-viral meds. Buried in plastic tubs, double bagged in sealed plastic lunch bags. Buried in three different locations. Those weren't the only three stashes. I had two smaller ones with antibiotics. Luther kept a lot of stuff from me, initially. It took him months to finally share. He was a good role model, a good example to follow.

It wasn't solely my call, but I was the senior partner, like Luther had been.

"I can see why she's a contact, and not a friend," I said, crossing my arms. "A friend wouldn't extort medicine from a friend for life-saving information, like how to keep a dozer from killing you." Then I thought a second. "She isn't sick—the veterinarian—is she?"

"It's not extorting," Lucia said with a huff. "That's the way things get done now. You gotta give something to get something."

I snorted a laugh.

"Hey, Jackass, she warned me about the Mean Measles and the crawlers for nothing."

"Nothing?" I interjected.

"I told her I was working with you, now that Luther was dead. Most people already figured it out, so it wasn't really anything. Told me about the drone, too."

"That's just so you could be on the lookout for it," I said. "Better chance of you returning with the antibiotics."

"Well, you wanna know how to drive off a dozer?"

I thought about it. "I'd rather know how to avoid getting killed by the drone."

"She don't know that," Lucia said, placing a hand on her hip. "I got most of that info from Little Marvie."

"What did that cost you?"

"He owed me." She said it with a tone that suggested she wasn't interested in explaining.

"Okay," I said. "You know where we have a lot of amoxicillin hidden. When I dig some of it up, I'll show you where some more is buried. And a bottle of actual aspirin, half full."

"You and Luther scavenged the houses around our park for medicines, right?"

I nodded. "Where do you think I got the Vicodin for you? Not the veterinary clinic." Luther and I hit two suburban clinics, not one in the city, where Lucia's contact's clinic was apparently located.

I turned and walked off the bridge, and down the cement path leading from it. Wooden railings lined with wire encased the dog-leg curving path. Lucia followed, keeping a distance. "If you did catch anything," I said, "with three days incubation, I suggest you go back to the doctor and trade the pills for the information right away. We might need it.

"While you're gone, I'll try to think of a way to conceal ourselves from the alien drone."

"There's a few more that owe me," Lucia said. "Everything's all messed up and moved around in the city, but if I can find them, I'll see if there's anything else they know about the drone."

Chapter 8

I was crouched along one of the small streams that flowed through the park and fed into the Ottawa River. I preferred this rocky section for washing clothes. The water was relatively clear, and the shore wasn't muddy. It was easy to dip clean water into my plastic wash tub and dump it without taking in a bunch of mud or silt.

Lucia never got sick, and the disease wave in the city ran its course. Lucia and her veterinarian contact figured it killed at least five hundred.

As always, I listened to the wildlife around me, mainly the birds. Their silence warned of any predators in the area, human or alien. It was a quiet morning, except for them. Scattered rays of sunlight reached through the branches and leaves above. Upstream, a few water striders danced along the surface where the sunlight struck, causing it to shimmer.

One thing I'd worried about early on was that humanity would strip the land of everything living…birds, rats, cats, once the food ran out, and eventually prey upon itself. Cannibalism. When people became desperate and starving, it's what I thought would happen.

I doubted I could bring myself to dine upon human flesh, but there had to be those out there that would. Sure, people banded together for safety and survival, like I latched onto Luther. But wouldn't like-minded predatory people, those without inhibitions against killing and eating their own kind, become a growing concern?

That never materialized, at least in the local region, probably for two reasons. One, the fact that an alien species was lurking out there, somewhere in Earth's orbit, waiting for us to be eradicated, kept humanity from falling into total anarchy, every man for himself. We humans had a common enemy to face. Add to that, the second reason: The dozers and crawlers. Humanity was a hunted species, out of its element. No power, no modern machinery, communications, or ease of travel. There wasn't time to fall upon each other. Sure, there wasn't an overabundance of food, but with the kinetic weapons impacting around cities and the tsunamis striking the densely populated coastal regions early on, we hadn't depleted food stores as rapidly as I anticipated. I could still venture to some of the suburban homes and find what I needed, including an occasional cupboard harboring a few canned goods. Part of that was a risk-payoff calculation. Moving about, especially in unfamiliar territory, made you an easier target for the dozers and crawlers.

Luther and I planted crops, anticipating food shortages. Those shortages would eventually come. But so would the aliens, I was sure of that. They weren't in a hurry, it seemed. Of course, maybe they were more interested in Europe or tropical regions? Maybe they were avoiding the USA because we were armed to the teeth. If they could travel between the stars, they had to have weapons that made our rifles seem like a caveman's spear. But even a flint-tipped spear could kill a modern soldier. Europe would have fewer guns, fewer flint daggers and spears for the aliens to face.

Lucia'd won at rock-paper-scissors, so I got to do the laundry while she sat watch near the highway. I'd finished rinsing and was wringing the water from one pair of Lucia's jeans, when the sound of distant gunshots reached my ears. First one or two, maybe a pistol and a shotgun, from the north. Then more guns joined the fray, like a desperate firefight had broken out.

Within thirty seconds each firearm's report ended, one by one, the shotgun being the last, followed by a truncated scream…maybe. Or maybe it was my imagination. Then silence, including the birds.

I stood, realizing gunfights didn't usually end that way. After unnecessarily checking to see if my Judge was in its hip holster, I picked up my .22 slide-action rifle. Deep down, something in my gut told me that neither would be enough.

Lucia's voice, racing beneath the breeze-driven leaves in the upper branches caught my ear.

"Drone, Jack! The drone…it's coming!"

CHAPTER 9

The culvert running under the railroad tracks was just outside the park's western border, and less than fifty yards from where I'd been washing clothes.

The culvert was four feet in diameter and ran for more than forty feet. A narrow stream ran through it and into the park. The culvert running beneath the tracks meant a lot of overburden. That enabled it to bear the weight of trains and their freight. Hanging from the culvert's curved ceiling was the plastic crate I'd secured there. I snapped it open and pulled out the blankets lined with Mylar sheets, plastic tubes and bowls. I kicked the five rocks placed next to the cages into the water. They'd cause additional turbulence in the flowing water after it moved past the floor of cinder blocks I'd built. Even without the rocks kicked in, there was already some rippling turbulence caused by the water flowing through the hollow portions of the cinder blocks. Then I uncovered the two cages, which were actually dog crates liberated from a nearby home. Their presence made for a crowded tunnel at its center, but the culvert's length made maneuvering manageable while keeping everything a good distance from the culvert's entrance and exit.

Each dog crate held a raccoon that I'd caught in a box trap, after hatching my plan to fool and evade the alien drone.

Lucia thought hiding in a crawlspace under a house would be better. I didn't, especially as it'd leave only one option for escape. Admittedly, my culvert idea only offered two, and they weren't too distant from each other.

The other hidden area, also sporting two boxed raccoons, was under the cement walkway leading to the covered bridge. That one, however, offered less concealment—protection—from discovery than the culvert idea. Lucia, of course, didn't like the cramped and trapped feeling the culvert afforded, and expressed her opinion on that more than once.

The two pet crates shook a bit as the two big raccoons jostled and threw their version of a hissy fit. If they were expecting a feeding, it wasn't happening today. That they were riled up some helped my plan. Instead, I unlocked the padlocks from each cage, and hoped the ingenious pair didn't figure out how to release themselves. That'd screw up my plan.

Lucia had been patrolling the northern edge of our park, so my reaching the intended sanctuary before her wasn't a surprise. But then I thought, maybe she'd decide her covered bridge retreat was better. Maybe she'd even stocked one of the nearby homes, or even the park ranger's crawlspace with her own gear and supplies, and would make a run for that. I trusted her and didn't keep an eye on her. Besides, I had to sleep sometime.

If the drone entered the park, seeking to exterminate us, she would either join me or she wouldn't. Carefully, I arranged everything so that it wouldn't get knocked into the water, and waited.

My plan was predicated on us reaching the culvert ahead of the drone. Thinking on this, my mind began racing through all of the things that could go wrong. The result was sweat forming on my brow. Facing alien creatures, dozers and crawlers, was bad enough. Facing alien technology, equipment, directly? It apparently defeated the survivalists in the Boy Scout Camp in short order.

The sound of tearing through the tall weeds reached my ears. I placed a hand on my revolver's grip, then relaxed a bit. Of course, it was Lucia. A flying drone wouldn't make that sound.

Gravel and dirt cascaded through the grass and foliage, and into the stream outside the culvert as Lucia slid down the bank. She must've run part of the way along the tracks.

With my hand I signaled for her to hurry, while also putting a finger to my lips, reminding her to keep silent.

We'd spent several hours, off and on, speculating how the alien drone might find humans. Observation and movement, and sound seemed the most likely candidates. Chemical signatures, like pheromones or scent trails like tracking hounds could follow? Infrared or other spectrums? They were aliens that travelled between the stars. Maybe they could pick up on the electro-chemical activity of our brains?

That last one was my idea, which Lucia scoffed at. Nevertheless, dropping her rifle and slung bow, she huddled down on the cinder block seats running along the culvert's curved side. She huddled close to me and put on her baseball hat wrapped in aluminum foil sitting next to her. We both wore one, making us both look pretty stupid. Whether it'd make a difference or not, better stupid looking and alive...

Besides, it was pretty dark in the culvert.

Lucia pointed toward our park and then motioned with her hand, like something flying toward us.

She checked the plastic tubes, one for me and one for her, and placed one end in the water and pinned them to the stream bed by moving one of the cinder blocks. In the meantime, I made sure my fishing lines running through the circular eye screws drilled and glued into the culvert's concrete ceiling weren't crossed or tangled. They led to the release pins securing the latches on the crate doors.

In an instant the agitated raccoons held behind those crate doors fell silent.

Without urging, Lucia handed me my tube while inserting hers into her mouth. I did the same. As practiced once, we shoved the blankets between the cinder blocks and down into the stream to soak up water. The blankets had two layers of Mylar stitched between them, because I thought it might block alien sensor devices as much as the cold water would block our body's warmth from being detected.

We then pulled the waterlogged blankets over us. I made sure to keep hold of the two fishing lines without tugging them hard enough to dislodge the release pins.

Less than a minute after huddling under the waterlogged

blankets, a whisking hum approached. We remained still as possible, breathing in through our noses and exhaling through the tubes, so the carbon dioxide-laden air went into the turbulent water. Insects like mosquitoes homed in on carbon dioxide. An advanced alien device might do the same thing.

The drone sounded like an electric lawnmower on whisper mode.

Lucia gripped my hand. I squeezed back, reassuring her as best I could, trying not to tremble. The drone had survived at least a dozen of the survivalist's gunshots, maybe more. The survivalists failed to stop it, and it killed them. Then it discovered and tracked Lucia. The guns we had wouldn't change a thing. Creatures that could traverse space, and built ships that could withstand cosmic radiation and impacts with objects while traveling at interstellar speeds? They could armor their drones to withstand gunfire. Maybe they generated an energy shield, making them proof against all human weaponry? Or at least small arms fire. Probably not nuclear weapons, which released radiation and heat blasts rivaling the sun's…

What was I thinking? Refraining from shaking my head while condemning my stupid line of thought, I forced myself to remain still. To breathe slowly…as quietly as possible.

The sound didn't move on. It remained steady for what seemed like an eternity. That 'eternity' was probably less than two minutes. Were they analyzing us? The situation? Was the drone's controller, or the drone's AI, using an array of sensors to determine if there were humans hiding nearby, if there were legitimate targets?

What else could we do? I could pull the pins. But the raccoons were silent, seemingly as unmoving as Lucia and me. I'd duct-taped the tops of the carriers with aluminum foil and Mylar to mimic our blankets, but to a lesser extent. Had that been a mistake?

Could the drone's sonic weapon reach through the gravel and dirt and concrete down to us? That's what Lucia said the drones used to kill. What her contacts told her.

Could the drone move to one end of the culvert and angle its weapon at us? Was it even directional like that?

Maybe if it lowered to the level of the culvert's opening, I could climb out the other side, get above and shoot down on it? Tanks were heavily armored on the front and sides, but weaker at the bottom. Would drones be the opposite?

How fast did the sonic weapon work? Lucia never said, and I never asked.

The short scream from the camp across the highway after the final gunshot told me the drone killed fast. Painfully, and fast. *If* I'd actually heard a scream.

Water from the blanket soaked into my shirt and pants, causing a chill to run through me. No doubt more than just water was causing the chill.

The whisper-mode mower sound faded as another, metallic sound rose. A warbling sound, like a copper trash can lid wobbling as its rim undulated atop an oak table. The thing was, the warbling didn't settle or stop, like a lid on a table would. Rather, its intensity increased.

Within seconds every inch of my skin pricked and tingled, like ten thousand ants raced across it. My muscles squirmed, like worms were boring in between the fibers, and my bones rattled as if they were a struck tuning fork.

Next to me, Lucia grunted once as her body tensed up. She, like me, fought to keep silent. One card left to play. The raccoons screeched and squealed. I managed to tug the fishing lines, opening the crates holding the panicking animals.

They leapt down and shot out from beneath the culvert. Concealed under the blanket, I couldn't see them, but their departing animal cries let me know they'd been flushed.

An earsplitting sound, like a giant hacksaw dragged across jagged sheet metal, preceded a brief pair of piercing death cries.

A second later, the hacksaw sound ceased, followed by the warbling. Immediately the intrusive sensation afflicting my skin, muscles and bones faded.

The first thing I noticed was that I'd bitten through the

plastic tube. I placed a hand on Lucia, still huddled next to me, signaling for her to remain still.

The whisper-mode mower whirr reversed course, back over the culvert, and continued east, into our park, opposite the direction the raccoons had fled. Or so it seemed…maybe it just went straight up.

Neither Lucia nor I dared speak or move for a quarter of an hour. We continued breathing in and blowing air into the submerged tube, getting colder and colder, soaked in water from the blanket, with our backs against cold concrete. Finally, I pulled my pen flashlight and met Lucia's gaze. Cold sweat covered her face, same as mine.

I pointed to me, pointed up, then made a walking motion with two fingers, and raised an eyebrow. She nodded.

Crawling out from beneath the heavy blanket, edges dangling in the stream, I made my way out the western end of the culvert, figuring to put the railroad embankment between me and the alien drone. That didn't mean I moved quickly, nor did I spare listening as I went.

The sky held no sign of the alien drone. On the ground, the two raccoons lay dead. One hadn't made it out of the stream, lying atop a flat stone, its hind legs gently bobbing with the stream's flow. The other made it only a few yards further, lying a body-length up the gully's edge, toward the trees. They didn't even make it to the bike path between the railroad tracks and small business plaza less than a stone throw beyond.

After listening and assuring myself that the alien drone was long gone, I moved toward the nearest raccoon. It was sprawled out with a spatter of blood on the rock around its head, spurted from its nose, mouth, eye sockets and ears, like someone had lit off a firecracker inside its skull.

I'd seen my share of dead animals, but this sight was disturbing. The short distance to the second dead raccoon told me the drone's sonic weapon didn't take long to kill. Lucia came up beside me, bow in hand. A mixed look of pity and disgust clung to her face as she viewed the same gory scene.

I felt a tinge of guilt for the animals. But I could live with it. If it hadn't been for them, Lucia and I would be lying dead, blood and gore having burst from our skulls.

How many humans had the drone already killed?

How long before it returned, and when it did, would we be as lucky?

"Go wring out the blanket," I said. After glancing skyward, I continued, something not settled with me. A gut feeling. "I'm going to check the plaza."

"Sure, Jack," Lucia said. She kept her voice low, but it carried that confident edge I was used to. "You're not getting out of finishing the laundry."

"Uh huh," I replied, stepping around the raccoons and walking along the stream's steeply angled bank. Climbing up out of the gully, I reached the bike path. Crabgrass and other weeds had overgrown the path's edges. I crept across the paved blacktop, hunched over and peered westward, trying to spy between the trees and undergrowth. Something large moved, big and gray, like a van.

It wasn't a van, but as big as one. Six foot at the shoulder and nearly as wide, with a spring in its legs as it trotted through the litter-strewn parking area, in my direction.

A dozer.

A big, damn dozer.

Chapter 10

I backed away, trying to avoid drawing the dozer's attention. The fact that the huge alien predator was approaching our park at this very moment, moments after the drone's failed attack, meant it'd been somehow sent to clean up what the drone had missed.

Maybe the drone hadn't seen me, but odds were it'd picked up on Lucia as she fled. When technology fails, send in something organic, something more up close and personal to pick up the trail. It's what *I* would do.

Did the aliens, or possibly their AIs, think like humans?

Human hunters strive to think like their prey. Deer hunters study the habits of deer. Were the aliens studying the habits of humans?

Those thoughts and questions raced through my mind while trotting along the stream bank. Thankfully my partner was in the culvert.

"Lucia," I said in a sharp whisper. "Stay hidden. Dozer on my tail."

The deep, snorting grunt behind me said my whisper had given me away, so I ran. Up and over the tracks and back down, into the park.

I needed to make it to the Upland Woods Trail, then about 200 yards along it. Keeping ahead of the dozer, out of sight long enough to make it up the rope hung just for this purpose, and pull the rope up…and then, hope. Hope it followed the scent trail left by doing my rounds day after day, week after week, hope it fooled the dozer.

I cut through the trees and brush, and onto the trail, my boots pounding along it. The mink oil kept them dry while under the wet blanket but my jeans and shirt were wet. Stray leafy strands of encroaching weeds reached out, but this trail was wide, I didn't brush against them, didn't leave that type of evidence of my passing. My boot prints? There were already several layers of them, going both directions. A few of Lucia's as well, so I didn't think my new ones would immediately give my trail away. If I could keep far enough ahead, the dozer would have to rely on smell to track me, maybe by sound, too. Keeping far enough ahead might give me enough time to survive.

If it found Lucia, I'd get more time to make it to the rope. It'd take a while to dig through the culvert to get at her. Maybe the top would collapse down upon it?

What was I thinking? If that was happening, she would've screamed, or at least shouted a curse or two. Arrows didn't make sounds, if she tried that from within the culvert. Gunshots seemed more likely. Curses or gunfire, either way, I would've heard it by now.

The rope was new, knotted and dangling down from a large maple's overhanging branch. I slowed and leapt, catching it, and immediately began climbing the forty feet.

I'd seen YouTube videos of old gym classes having to climb ropes, but my gym classes never had to. I had, however, practiced. Refusing to look over my shoulder, I climbed, hands gripping, feet in place, arms and legs lifting. Moving up, knot by knot.

Would it be fast enough?

I reached the branch and climbed atop it, using leverage offered by the additional rope lashed to the limb. Breathing hard, I began hauling up the knotted rope, now risking a glance down along the trail.

Hanging the coiled rope on a stainless steel hook, I straddled the limb and waited—for about three seconds.

Around the turn trotted the massive dozer. How could it bound forward like its legs were made of springs, instead of lumbering like an elephant, or galloping like a rhino? That indicated massive strength. Strength to power the deadly claws on the end of its feet. Claws that could dig through rebar-reinforced concrete and, given time, gouge and tear through steel. Hiding in a bank vault wouldn't mean safety. Not if the dozer was determined.

That reminded me of the tube of construction adhesive stuffed in my jean's front pocket.

And then I saw it. My clothes, still wet from hiding under the blanket, were dripping. Water drops striking the dry path below. I slowly stood, so my pants would drip on the limb. But the trail…my sopping-wet clothes left a sprinkled trail pointing right to me. The incriminating spatter of dampness highlighted where I'd climbed the rope.

It wasn't a lot, but for an alien creature that regularly tracked prey? Would my scent trail left after traveling the paths day after day be enough to fool the dozer?

My movement caused the dozer to slow its trot. Then it sat back on its haunches, allowing its fist-sized sensory buds an upward degree of…sensing. Hard and crystalline, or so it was said, were they visual, auditory, olfactory? All three, or something else? Bats used sonar. Maybe the dozers used that to sense and track movement.

I leaned against the trunk, absolutely still, to no avail. The dozer grunted, which seemed odd for a beaked creature. Then it began snapping its tri-beak as it trotted ahead to stand beneath the big limb that extended over the path.

It again sat on its haunches and arched its back. Before I knew what was happening, the beast leapt up toward me, front claws extended. I stood frozen, watching as it came within five feet of the limb before dropping back to the ground, sending an impact vibration up the tree.

That snapped me into action. I dropped down onto the branch, again straddling it. If the dozer leapt up and caught my leg, I was done for. If it extended its beak, it might have a chance. My money was on it trying to knock the tree down. A few shoulder charges, and the tree might be broken, if not toppled.

I was right, sort of. After gazing up at me—or whatever it took a few seconds doing—it stepped over and took a massive swipe at the maple's trunk with its claws, shearing away a four inch gouge. That would've taken me at least a minute with a sharp axe. The tree shuddered from the blow, making me glad I was straddling the branch.

I pulled my revolver, pressed the release and flicked open the cylinder. Then I ejected the .45 bullets and .410

shells into my hand. I holstered my revolver and shoved the three .410 shells into my shirt pocket. On reflex I closed my hand on the bullets just as the dozer swiped again at the base of the tree. I pulled the tube of construction adhesive from my jean's pocket and twisted the cap off with my teeth. Maybe its contents were toxic, but I'd have to live past the next thirty seconds to endure that possible agonizing death. Suddenly thoughts of being eaten alive, my leg snapped off by the dozer's beak, and getting to watch the dozer swallow it…

Trying to ignore the dozer below, I used my teeth again and tore away the plastic foil sealing the tube. Then I began filling the hollow point tips of the three .45 caliber bullets with the construction adhesive. Only a dab. But with the third bullet, the dozer's next swipe caused me to cover the entire bullet, along with part of my hand, in adhesive. I couldn't risk that one to clean fire—then changed my mind. I stuffed the adhesive, what was supposedly painful, maybe even toxic to dozers, into my shirt pocket. Then I wiped excessive glue off the third bullet. If the dozer knocked me to the ground, maybe I could shove the gun into the beast's beak and fire before it chomped my arm off.

Pulling my revolver, I realized what a fantasy that was. I looked down. After it swiped again at the tree, causing it to creak, I slid the three adhesive-tipped bullets into the revolver's cylinder and closed it.

I didn't think the bullets would pierce the dozer's thick hide, but it was all I had. Its eye or sensor buds were crystal hard, like a crawler's. Maybe if I could get a shot inside its beak? Reaching behind me, I grabbed and tossed the coiled rope down.

The braided rope struck and then draped across the dozer's shoulder, causing the beast to back away. It examined the rope as it swung side to side. Lightning fast it lunged forward and snapped its beak. The dangling end of the rope fell, severed like an errant strand of cobweb clipped by hedge shears.

Having seen that, and the damage done to the maple

tree keeping me out of reach, I knew that my time on Earth was about to end…except maybe as fertilizer, after the dozer below crapped out my remains. That notion galvanized me. I wasn't going out like a stricken dove fallen into a tiger's maw. More like a rabid-crazed squirrel. Maybe I wanted Lucia to know I'd gone down fighting. I screamed curses at the dozer as it maneuvered for another swipe at my tree. In any case, the sound of my gun, and the dozer silencing my shouts might warn her, give her a better chance.

I shifted my revolver to my left hand and pulled my hand axe. I was a better shot with my right, but my left wasn't worth a darn throwing. The fact that my hand axe's blade had zero chance of penetrating the dozer's armored hide didn't register. Get it to look up and open its beak. I wanted that, along with wanting it to remember me as more than a quick meal.

My hurled hand axe glanced off the alien beast's shoulder, like I'd thrown it at a Brinks armored car.

The dozer didn't even flinch, or stop to look up. It swiped again and moved to the left, likely so the tree didn't topple down on it after its next blow. The exertion of throwing my axe took my cursing and frantic anger with it. Higher functioning thought patterns re-emerged.

Rather than as a crazed squirrel, I'd go down as a defiant one.

I gripped my revolver with both hands and aimed at one of the dozer's sensor bulbs. Where it emerged from the thick hide might be vulnerable. If so, shooting it there would give it reason to remember me, if the creature worked on more than pure instinct, and could remember such things.

The same instant I fired, an arrow shaft appeared to sprout from the dozers flank. I had no idea if I'd hit or missed, but the arrow caused a reaction. The beast bellowed like a bull being branded, and spun about, searching for its new adversary. I laughed to myself, at my notion of equating myself as its adversary.

Telling Lucia to run wasn't an option, not now. And, deep down, I didn't want her to run. If I'd been on the ground when it bellowed, beak splayed wide open, I would've had a shot into its throat. Of course, if I were on the ground, I'd be snapped in two like a twig facing my hatchet.

I shouted and fired another round, striking the dozer in the beak. It emitted a gurgling snarl in response. That's when Lucia hit it again, another split crystal-eyed arrow, presumably freshly coated with construction adhesive. The second shaft protruded inches above the monster's beak, a little to the left. Maybe I'd messed up her shot? Maybe she aimed for its opened beak?

The angle of the arrow's flight said Lucia was elevated above the ground, in a tree. I fired my last round, missing the beak. My bullet struck and then rolled off the alien beast's back as it leapt forward, toward Lucia.

I hoped she was in a big tree.

From thirty feet up in a red pine, Lucia got another arrow off, piercing the charging dozer in the back, near its spine—assuming it had a spine.

The dozer veered off, bellowing like a dozen red-hot branding irons were at work on its flesh. We heard it depart the park, straight south, glancing off trees, its bellows fading.

I climbed down first, having to hang drop about four feet after reaching the end of my sheared rope. I ran over to Lucia's tree.

"You think it's gone?" she asked.

I started to say something smart-alecky like, 'Would I be down here and alive if it wasn't?' but decided upon, "You drove it off, Lucia. Your vet doctor's info about hurting dozers was right. Thanks."

Her wide-eyed look of concern shifted to a grin. She started to say something, then hesitated, probably reconsidering what to say, like I had, and climbed down instead.

When she was standing next to me, holding her compound bow, she said, "We're even, Jack."

"No," I said, and she cut me off.

"Yes, Jack, your plan fooled the drone."

"No," I said again, holding up a hand to forestall her objection. "We're not even, we're partners."

She brushed my hand aside and gripped me in a tight hug. "*Gracias*," she said, emotion filling her word.

More than a little surprised and confused, I hugged her back. "You're welcome, Lucia," I said, not exactly sure what she was thanking me for. "You're welcome."

Chapter 11

Lucia and I once again were under the blankets layered with Mylar. This time, not in the culvert. Rather we lay on our stomachs, shoulder to shoulder, on a 1950s vintage metal-framed set of bunk beds. Plastic covered the beaten-down mattress.

"Your binoculars are better than mine," Lucia complained.

We'd pushed the bed up to a basement window pried open a few inches, allowing us a view of our park across the street. I'd also duct taped a layer of aluminum foil and Mylar across the window. Lucia's 'survival paranoia,' as she called it, and my gut feeling, said the hunting drone would return.

Propped up on my elbows, I shrugged, holding my binoculars to my eyes. "You have a better knife than me."

The morning was still cool, aided by the previous night's thunderstorm. The basement, being underground, helped as well. If not, with the Mylar-lined blanket resting from our shoulders down to our feet, both Lucia and I would be sweating up our own storm.

She snorted a laugh. "Don't try feeding me that shit, Jack. You like your hand axe more than any knife."

We lay quiet for another few minutes, occasionally peering through our binoculars. We took advantage of the wrecked sections of the stone walls near the road. Shattering the walls provided the single instance of usefulness ever shown by a dozer. At least in my experience.

It took less than thirty minutes after Lucia drove off the dozer for us to gather food and gear, and depart the park for the basement. We selected the house, not only for its view and proximity to the park, but because its garage held one of my sets of water-collecting plastic tubs.

Lucia asked, "Is there time to replant the corn and beans?"

While digging up a cache of supplies near one of the

large gardens planted by Luther and me, I observed the wilted corn stalks, nearly flat, like they'd been pelted by a barrage of quarter-sized hail. It only took a few seconds to see that the drone had decimated every plant in the garden plot. Did the damage after it lost track of us. My guess was that the drone used its sonic weapon to destroy the plants' cell walls. Everything in the plot was dying, the leaves turned to a pasty sludge that was beginning to dry out.

"If we do," I said in answer to Lucia's replanting question, "it'll have to be on different ground. Whatever the aliens did might've killed all of the soil bacteria and other micro-organisms."

"If you say so, Jack." She thought a minute. "If the drone killed a lot of the people in Toledo, less people for us to worry about. Plant the garden in the backyards of these houses. They got flower beds nobody's gonna be using."

Her words made me think. If the aliens had killed off a lot of survivors, those that survived the tsunamis and initial bombardments, and the plague of crawlers and dozers, those that managed without medicines or treatments…weren't among those killed because other humans preyed upon them, or just didn't have the knowledge or skills to survive without electricity and other modern conveniences…how close were they to victory over humanity? To conquering us and wresting control of the Earth?

Lucia bumped her shoulder into mine. "Good idea, huh?"

"Yeah," I said, trying not to sound depressed. "Might work better. Soil'd be easy to dig."

"You and Luther had extra seeds, right? If not, we could try scavenging some." Then her eyes returned to the sky, what limited portion was visible from our angle, looking through the twelve inch tall and thirty inch wide window.

Her thoughts were the same as mine. Being out and about, scavenging, would leave us even more vulnerable to death by drone than we were by crawlers and dozers. And those two menaces were still roving about, albeit reduced in number.

"Maybe the drone will move on," I said. "It moved from the center of the city, outward."

"Maybe," Lucia replied. "And what'll they send next. Some incurable disease?"

"No," I said. "Probably not that."

"Why not? It's not like there's any hospitals or colleges to study and find a cure. No factories to make the pills or shots."

"That's true," I said, "but I think they would've done that earlier, while there were more to spread it, if it was contagious."

Lucia started to object, so I interjected with a thought that came to me out of the blue. "That measles epidemic, might've been created in conjunction with collaborators."

"What?" she asked. "That's crazy talking, Jack." Then she went back to her original line of thought. "How do you know how the aliens think?"

"I don't," I said, thinking there really wasn't a reason for the aliens to collaborate with any humans. They were winning handily enough as it was. "But they must be smart. Have to be to figure out how to travel across space." I paused, taking a deep breath and scanning above the trees of our park. "This probably isn't their first rodeo."

"Experienced conquistadors..." Lucia trailed off mid-sentence. After a few seconds, she whispered, "Listen."

Even before she said that, I caught the sound. The growl of an engine. Internal combustion, not the whirring of a drone.

Chapter 12

"Is that a tank?" Lucia asked.

Rolling down the street was what looked like a tank, tracks and all, but it wasn't. The main gun was too small, its muzzle's bore being about an inch in diameter. While the tracks weren't doing the street any good, the weight of a battle tank would've been tearing them up. I wasn't up that much on military vehicles and equipment, but I thought I knew what it was.

"That's an armored infantry carrying vehicle, not a tank. A Bradley, I think."

"Looks like a tank to me, Jack."

"I think the Army built them to survive on a battle field alongside tanks, Lucia. My question is, what's it doing?"

The window was too narrow to climb out. Still, I was tempted to run up stairs and flag the vehicle down, but it had already rolled past. Maybe there'd be another.

Then it slowed down, at least by the sound of the engine, and stayed in place, just out of sight, I guessed near where my trophy fence was.

I threw the blanket off and climbed down, just in time to hear an amplified loudspeaker.

"Yo, Jack, Park Guardian. The Army says they sendin' a squad in to talk to ya tomorrow. Don't shoot at them or they say they'll frag your spooky ass.

"Archer Woman, if'n he ain't shot you dead, and you hearing me, relay the Army's message. If you can't tell by my voice, this is Chisel Z, telling you straight. Out."

Muffled conversation continued over the speaker. "Sit down what? Where—"

Lucia was still on the bed. With a raised eyebrow, I said, "I'll ask you about him later, and your name, Archer Woman."

Before she could respond, the Bradley's engine revved and it returned, backing down the road past us. The main gun began booming, firing about a round a second at something in front of it, about 2 o'clock, coming out of the park. A dozer, galloping full speed right for the Bradley.

The coaxial mounted machine gun opened up as well. As the main gun's rounds began to hit, they staggered the big beast. The rate of fire increased; each hit of the main gun was like the beast taking a punch. It staggered but came on. The Bradley stopped and a rectangular magazine began to unfold from the left side of the turret.

Lucia got off the bed, and grabbed a tube of construction adhesive from her backpack leaning against the wall. Something in the adhesive's mixture caused dozers severe pain, like being stung by a hornet, if it pierced the alien beast's nearly impenetrable hide.

She picked up her quiver of arrows, four of which had the split crystal heads.

Over the sound of cannon and machine gun fire, I asked, "Seriously, you're going out there?"

"Archer *Woman* my ass," she said, fuming. "I'll show that bastard archery."

Out of the corner of my eye, I saw the dozer stumble to the ground about fifty feet from the stationary Bradley. Another dozen rounds hammered it. Each struck like a 90 mile per hour fastball hitting the side of a canvas tent. And after each round, the dozer's thick hide didn't bounce back, a four inch diameter divot, an inch deep remaining. Where another cannon round hit inside an existing divot, the depth increased an inch or so.

I pushed the bed away from the window, and Lucia stood next to me, watching the downed dozer, its legs kicking feebly. After another few rounds slammed into its back, and another peppering from machinegun fire, even the twitching stopped.

"That's a good sight to see," I said.

Lucia pointed, angling up above the trees. "That's not."

The same time I caught sight of the distant alien drone closing in, a rocket jetted out from the Bradley's deployed magazine. "That's a TOW missile, I think. Wire guided." If my videogame memory was accurate.

"TOW?" Lucia asked.

"I don't know what the acronym stands for," I said, "but they're designed to take out Russian main battle tanks."

"Think it can take out the drone?"

"We'll see," I said, watching the missile's tail exhaust, gyrating slightly in its ascending collision course. "If the gunner doesn't miss."

A pop of a fiery explosion caused the drone to tumble from the sky—for about thirty feet before righting itself.

It came on again, slower. The main gun elevated and opened up, sending a few rounds and hoping for a lucky shot. Then a second TOW missile launched from the magazine.

"I think they only have two before needing to reload," I said to Lucia, not sure why. Maybe it was more to myself.

"We better get hidden," she said, moving over toward a far corner of the basement, next to the washer. There wasn't any water pressure to wet down the blanket, but we'd brought a few gallon jugs of stream water.

"In a second," I said, wanting to see the results. "It'll be more interested in that Bradley than us."

"If whoever, or whatever's running it, picks up we're here, Jack, after it kills everyone in that infantry tank, it'll come over and kill us next."

The drone shot straight up, the missile trying to match the new course. The drone continued upward, easily passing two hundred miles per hour. The missile followed, then went wild before flaming out.

The Bradley's engine roared and it raced forward, turning and driving across a lawn two doors down. The crashing sound said it'd blown through the white picket fence. The engine sound faded as I scanned the sky for the drone, the best I could from our angle.

"Get your stupid ass over here now, Jack!" Menacing anger hung in her voice.

It didn't matter if the drone detected her and me, or just me. With nowhere else to run and hide, we'd both be dead.

Before I managed to empty the first gallon jug onto the blanket, an explosion sounded, like ten tons of dynamite went off beside the house. I lost my footing as the ground shook. Dust from the overhead floorboards cascaded down.

The aliens were sending kinetic energy strikes from orbit to take out the Bradley.

Ten seconds later, another sounded, shaking the house. This one a little less powerful, probably due to increasing distance.

Lucia and I huddled under our half-soaked blanket, hoping the Bradley and those soldiers inside it got away. Even more urgent was my hope the house above us didn't collapse, trapping us in the basement.

Chapter 13

Six hours later, we emerged from the basement, figuring the drone would've moved on. Besides, we were both cold and wet.

Standing next to the house, which had survived, and looking through my binoculars, my heart fell. "It's down, but the damn thing's still alive." I kept my voice low and steady.

The dozer hadn't moved. It was lying on its side, but I could see its chest, where its ribs would be, if it had ribs, slowly rise and fall.

Lucia unslung her bow.

I stepped to block her path. "No. Shooting it with the adhesive might cause pain, but won't kill it."

She sneered at me.

"Look, it survived like fifty rounds from that Bradley's cannon."

She signaled and I handed her my binoculars.

While she looked, I scanned the sky and listened. A few birds were flying about, making noise. The smell of burned wood, rubber and plastic was in the air, along with three columns of smoke a block behind our house and extending southward. The kinetic energy projectiles must've been small ones, maybe not launched from high orbit.

"Its mouth is open. Looks like it's gasping for air," she said. "You told me a bullet down its throat would kill one."

I remembered telling her that, once, when I showed her the hanging ropes around the park and explained the reason for walking the paths as often as possible. "It should. If its throat and insides aren't as tough as the outside, and you get a lucky shot."

"You never said a thing about luck, Jack."

"I also never said 'would.' I recall saying 'could.'"

She leaned back against the house's brick exterior, now cracked in several places. After scowling at me and biting her lip, she asked, "You think it'll heal?"

I took my binoculars back. "That might be the one you nailed with your arrows. There's some darker discolorations. Welts where you shot it. At least that I can see from this angle."

"You didn't answer my question, Jackass."

That seemed pretty uncalled for. "Are you asking me, as me, or as an expert in alien monster physiology, Lucia? Or should I say, Archer Woman?"

She pushed off the wall and stood up straight, tense, with anger in her eyes.

Lucia's true colors appeared to be returning, but now wasn't the time, and this wasn't the place. I raised one hand between us. "Sorry, about the Archer Woman thing." Handing her my binoculars, I unslung my single barrel shotgun. After breaking it open to check the slug round, I rested a hand on the grip of my holstered revolver.

The anger hadn't left Lucia's eyes.

"Two things," I said. "Have your bow ready if that dozer gets up off the ground." Taking a step toward the downed dozer, I stopped and shot her a grin, but couldn't wipe the worry from my face. "And watch for that drone. Walking toward a dozer means I'll be concentrating on not peeing my pants."

"Don't think for a moment." She grinned and pulled a tube of adhesive from her pocket. "That if you do, I'll be the one washing them."

The dozer lay sprawled on its side, half on the gravel, half on the road, its beak on the roadside, dipping down at a thirty degree angle. A good thing was, the Bradley's auto cannon had broken off one of the three beak tips. The one normally at the 2 o'clock to 6 facing, but now at the 10 to 2 o'clock because the dozer was on its side. A smidgen of luck. That gave me a little better opening to aim for.

Steady, deep breaths, but with a hint of wheezing, told me the dozer was hurt, but not ready to give up the ghost right away. Lucia might be right. With the alien's physiology, maybe it could heal faster.

I took a few steps closer, getting to within fifty feet, ready to turn and run at the first sign of determined movement by the dozer.

Then my mind began racing again. The way it jumped when I was up that tree. How could a creature so large do that? And not get injured after landing? Something like that would bust up nearly any animal, except maybe a big cat, like a tiger. But a dozer was built more like a cross between a rhino and a bear, except for its springy legs. Those were like an oversized gazelle's. The alien beast's species could be from a heavier gravity planet. That meant stronger muscles, maybe greater bone density. I hesitated in my measured stride, about forty feet away. The insides, the flesh and organs might be denser, able to resist a shotgun slug, if it was a creature with genetic selection based on a high gravity planet.

Did it even have genes? DNA?

I shook my head and dropped to one knee, raising my shotgun. I couldn't convince myself to get any closer.

The dozer hadn't taken notice of me, or at least hadn't reacted to my approach.

Aiming. Holding my shotgun steady wasn't easy. In the heat of battle, I'd managed it...to shoot straight, but now? Taking a deep breath and exhaling, I concentrated on the beak, the opening, leading into its throat.

I aimed, counted to three and pulled the trigger.

Like always, the shotgun kicked.

The slug must have found its mark somewhere inside the beast. It grunted and squealed, like a hog getting its testicles cut off—or what I imagined it sounded like, just maybe an octave lower, and three times as loud.

The dozer rocked and bucked. Me? I turned and ran, not even looking back. The sign I caught that suggested I might live was Lucia. She held her bow, with an arrow nocked, but not pulled back, ready to shoot. The other sign was that she was standing relaxed, not quite laughing.

"You didn't piss your pants, Jack, did you?"

"Hey," I said, coming to a stop next to her, knowing I

hadn't. After looking back and trying to catch my breath for a few seconds, I continued, saying, "If a man approaching a dozer ain't scared, he's got to be crazy or just plain dumber than rocks."

"Can one be two out of three?"

"Give me any more crap about this and I'll start calling you Archer Woman on a regular basis, Lucia." The words were out before I could check them.

"Sure, Jackass." She laughed and took a rag from her back pocket. Wiping the still wet adhesive from the arrow's crystal, she looked up at the wispy smoke columns. "We should see if they got that infantry tank."

We didn't find the remains of the Bradly in any of the three craters. Each was only thirty or so feet in diameter and about ten feet deep, being a little deeper where part of an inground pool formed the impact area. The pattern showed tracks of the armored infantry carrier weaving and tearing through yards and fences, avoiding the kinetic strikes. It appeared the aliens just gave up and let the Bradley go, it heading back toward the heart of the city.

From the gouges, ruts, and thrown topsoil, that Bradley driver was going like a bat out of hell. I couldn't blame him. It worked.

Heat generated by the impacts caused a few houses' siding to melt. Owing to the recent storms, they didn't catch fire.

Lucia and I decided to head back into our park. Since there wasn't much of the day remaining, we'd cut back on our routine of trail walking, maintenance, and patrolling. Rather we'd stagger getting a few hours of sleep. That'd give us time to think and sleep on what the Army might want before we discussed it over a post-sunset meal.

"If someone told me I'd be eating dried cat food, crayfish, and dandelion greens for dinner, and thankful for it, a year ago?"

Lucia and I both chuckled at my statement, huddled

near a small campfire built to discourage mosquitoes. I'd set a double row of trip strings with bells to warn us of any crawlers approaching. The sounds of the forest, crickets and the hooting owl, and more, let us know nothing worrisome, like a dozer or other humans, were nearby.

"So," Lucia said, after chewing and swallowing a few dandelion leaves. "You think the Army wants your supplies. Ammo, meds and food."

"What else is here?"

"You," she said. "Chisel Z, he'd heard me talk about you and Luther. Every one of my contacts did." The campfire caught her grinning white teeth. "You know I sort of built you up, made you sound like some sort of renegade Navy SEAL or something. Especially after Luther passed. No one to mess with, not if they wanted to live."

She picked a bit of the leafy green from her teeth that her tongue couldn't remove. "You killed enough to back up my story, cuz a lot of folks want what you got out here—or what they figure you got."

"You do know, Lucia, that the closest thing I have to military training is my years in the Boy Scouts. That doesn't count."

"Well, Luther trained you up. Except for running from that dying dozer, you don't get spooked easy. Your trophy fence? That's smart, like a gang marking its turf."

"I'm one man." I took a handful of cat food from the bowl. It did have a sort of gritty, fishy, tuna taste. "You, make it two."

"Men?" She dragged out the single syllable word.

"Survivors," I said. "But medicine and supplies are worth more. Look at the risk they took."

"Could be they want to use our park as a base?"

I shook my head while she took her turn eating a handful of cat food. "No. What's here that isn't available at the scout camp across the highway, or any other local metro park?"

Lucia shrugged.

"We'll find out tomorrow," I said.

"Where do you think?"

"The fence. You hang back and back me up?"

"Sure, Jack. I can think of a good spot." She grabbed her compound bow leaning against a tree, and pulled the bowstring back. "This should do wonders against that infantry tank."

"Bradley Infantry Fighting Vehicle," I said. "You have a rifle, you know."

"Right. That'll keep them scared."

"That's not the point," I said.

"I know, Jack. Just jerking your chain."

I pulled the plastic case holding the night vision monocular from my backpack and handed it to her. "You get first watch while I catch some shuteye. I'll use the hammock over by Luther's grave."

"What about ladies first. What if I'm tireder than you?"

"Surely not more than a Navy SEAL," I said, trying not to laugh. "I'm still recovering from all those years of training."

She laughed in return. "If they only knew you like I do, Jackass. If they only knew."

The name 'Jackass' should've bothered me. It didn't. The way she said it had a different tone than before. My guess? She was having trouble letting go of her old ways, while trying to fit into a new one.

She did seem happier than before, or as happy as one could expect in a post-apocalyptic alien invasion world.

Chapter 14

They didn't show up in a Bradley or a Humvee. Rather, six soldiers on bikes came pedaling down the road, turned into the main entrance and came to a stop. Kick stands down, they got off their bikes and spread out in a circular formation. Still vulnerable to sniper fire, but ready for something alien, like a crawler or maybe even a drone.

Each soldier wore a camouflage combat uniform, although they weren't the same. Some sported greens for forested regions and others had tan and brown for desert regions. One wore a mixed combination of pants and jacket. Each held an unslung assault rifle and carried a holstered sidearm in his belt. They had on some sort of brimmed cap instead of helmets, like I sort of expected.

No bike helmets. It made me laugh inside. Nobody wears bike helmets anymore.

I watched them for a moment from my concealment, where I normally watched this area, between three trees and among some deep weeds. I didn't want them to shout for me. Nothing good could come of that, so I backed out of my hide position and began striding down the road toward the parking lot.

Lucia was a little bit deeper in the park. She was in the next nearest tree line, with her scoped hunting rifle. We didn't think anything bad would happen, but better to be safe than sorry. The Army might demand something that I wasn't excited about giving.

I carried my .22 slide-action rifle. It would give me a lot of shots, without looking like I was aiming for a fight. Against what I guessed were M-16s? It'd be a pretty short gunfight. I had my revolver, loaded with three .45 rounds and two .410 shells with 000 buckshot. And my handy hand axe. My jeans, boots, and thin brown flannel shirt, a bit tattered, over a forest green T-shirt and dingy NY Yankees baseball cap didn't shout military. I'd even shaved for the occasion, instead of wearing three days of whiskers. A beard in the summer was sometimes too much.

One of the soldiers, a tall African American, spotted me. "Sergeant," he said, pointing my direction.

The sergeant, a medium height man, a bit thin—but who wasn't these days—with short dark hair, thin lips and what I thought were expressive eyebrows. He stepped from his position and out of the circle to meet me.

When I got close he extended his right hand to shake. "Staff Sergeant Eckstein, of the 37th IBCT."

As we shook, I asked, "IBCT?"

"Oh," he said with a smile, "Infantry Brigade Combat Team, of the Ohio National Guard." He looked over his shoulder. "Actually, like me, most of us aren't from the National Guard, some, not even from Ohio."

"Okay," I said. "I'm Jack, Jack Fairbanks. I'm not from Ohio either. Was studying Marine Biology at the university here when the attack came."

No sense wasting time, and I wasn't comfortable with a half dozen armed men standing around, staring at me. "The men in that Bradley took an awful risk to set up this meeting. What do you want from me?"

Sergeant Eckstein looked around, then up in the sky. "I recommend we move to someplace less exposed."

The sergeant had an honest look. His men, not so much. But they weren't some sort of riff raff. Their uniforms, although well worn, were clean, all things considered. Their guns appeared well maintained. They struck me as professional. Plus, they were connected to the Bradley that had taken down the dozer, still lying in the road, and mixed it up with the alien drone—and survived. That the U.S. military was still around and effective caused a bit of pride to well up in me, as well as a spark of hope.

"Sure," I said. "Will a shelter house do?"

The sergeant nodded. One of the men rolled the sergeant's bike up to him.

"I understand you have a partner, Mr. Fairbanks?"

"Jack," I said, signaling for them to follow. "Call me

Jack."

"You have any military experience, Jack?"

"Not a lick."

The sergeant walked next to me on the road, pushing his bike toward the shelter house. "Your partner?"

"Not that I know of."

"Not that you know of…" He glanced at my rifle. "You protect your park with that?"

"Sure," I said. "I have other firearms." I stared him in the eye and then back at his men with their bikes following us. "I didn't want to risk intimidating you soldiers."

That was good for a few snickers, but not from the sergeant. "Your partner?" he asked again, giving extra attention to the wooded area lining the road on our right.

"She'll join us, if she sees fit," I said, looking around for threats myself, out of habit, even though I had six soldiers with me. "What does the Army want with us, Sergeant, or our park?"

We walked along the paved path and then to a dirt one, going past some slides, swings and monkey bars.

"There's a plan to resist the Mawks. My superiors think you could provide assistance."

"Mawks?"

"That's what they're called, the alien invaders." He held his hand about four feet off the ground. "They stand about this high," he said. "Look like a cross between a praying mantis and a hawk. Like a photo-morphing program going from one to the other, froze in the middle."

"Have you seen one?" I asked.

"Me personally? No. Not many have come down from orbit. At least not yet."

"They captured some?" I asked, wondering how they managed that. Maybe shot down some sort of fighter or shuttle? Or maybe ambushed a landing party. Did they have landing parties? Or was that my mind being too hooked on antiquated episodes of *Star Trek*?

I'd wondered what the aliens looked like, and had settled on the gray, big headed and big eyed ones seen in movies and on those alien abduction shows.

We made it past the playground area and to the shelter. The sergeant followed me up the steps into the open air shelter. I gestured to one of the table's benches. He parked his bike outside. His men deployed themselves around the shelter house.

We sat down. The sergeant pulled his canteen off his belt and offered me a drink.

"No, thanks," I said, took off my hat and scratched my head, and put it back on. That was my signal to Lucia that all was okay.

He unscrewed the cap and took a short drink. "You not much of a Yankees fan?"

I glanced up at my cap's brim and smiled. "No. I tore off the white logo so it wouldn't stick out at night. Colored in another one I have with black ink."

"Makes sense," the sergeant said, returning his canteen to its place on his belt. "I can't tell you much of the plan. The colonel hasn't shared a lot with me, but he'd like your assistance."

"How is that?" I asked.

"Sarge," one of the soldiers said. A short one, with a healing scar across the bridge of his nose. "Must be his partner."

Lucia swaggered up to the shelter house. How she managed not to sweat to death in that black leather jacket, I'd never figure out. She thought it was important, however. She had her knife and bow, and a .45 Colt Automatic in a holster on her swaying hip. Her face? I hadn't seen that arrogant look of confidence since the first drone attack.

Both the sergeant and I stood.

"This is my partner," I said, "Lucia, the Archer."

Sergeant Eckstein extended his hand for Lucia to shake. "I've heard more about you than about your partner here."

She shook his hand. "And what did you hear?"

"That you're good with your bow, you know just about everyone in Toledo that's important, and that includes Jack Fairbanks, here." Sergeant Eckstein glanced from her to me and back. "Except what you've shared with others, he remains a mystery."

"Until today," she said.

He smiled. "Right. Let's get to my purpose for this meeting."

I was on my favorite hybrid bike, following Sergeant Eckstein and his squad from the suburbs into the city. The abandoned library where I was to meet with the colonel wasn't too far away, only five or six miles. Since it was mainly road travel, my bike, which was a combination road and mountain, was pretty efficient. Lucia came along, since it was such a short distance, and we were partners. She wanted a mountain bike and, thus, had to pedal harder to keep up, as the soldiers rode hybrids like me.

If we had to start cutting through yards and rough terrain, she'd have the advantage, but I was counting on the soldiers taking care of anyone or anything that might cause us trouble. If they couldn't, I'd get the jump on getting away. Cowardly? Maybe. But they were trained soldiers, and it was their idea for me to follow them to meet with the Colonel of the 37th.

The city looked deserted. Most of the houses and businesses had broken windows and doors left wide open. More than a few were burned, as were many of the abandoned cars, many in the middle of the streets. Cracked windshields and opened doors, gas caps tossed aside, or gone. Obvious signs their fuel had been siphoned out.

Every now and then I spotted a head in a second story window, tentatively watching us. There were even a few impact craters, small, like those made when the aliens tried to take out the Bradley.

Lucia, huffing next to me said, "Things look bad, Jack. Ghost town."

I'd only ventured more than a few blocks from my park once in the past few months. The smell of rotting flesh, death and decay hung in the air. It wasn't overpowering, but the rancid smell was there. So were the scads of flies. "Grave yard," I replied. The sky should've been filled with gray clouds to fit the mood descending on me. Not the fluffy white cumulus ones that occasionally hid the sun as they passed overhead.

We pedaled on for a few minutes in silence, until I broke it. "Maybe they're just hiding from the drone?"

"I don't think so, Jack."

"She's right," the tall African American soldier said. His stitched-on name patch read, Washington. "Some fled, but a bunch got killed. I heard the drone used dozers to flush them that tried hiding."

"Food's running out," the sergeant added. "There are still some locals in hiding, holed up deep. Same story in cities across the Midwest."

We were moving fast and maneuvering around vehicles left disabled by the alien EMP attacks. Anything that had a computer chip controlling them was dead, the delicate electronics scrambled. It was that way with everything. EMPs brought down jets in the air. They shut down the electric grid and water treatment plants, the hospital equipment and manufacturing plants. Virtually everything modern society once offered was the equivalent of a plastic door stop or scrap metal.

Food running out? I hadn't expected that. Not yet, especially with the reduced numbers. What was left in stores and homes shouldn't be gone, yet. Luther and I had done a lot of estimating, thinking on disease, infirmity, crawlers and dozers, and humans preying on themselves.

No fine dining, sure. Not starvation, yet.

"Are you, the 37th, based in or near Toledo?"

"No," said the sergeant. "We just arrived less than a week ago."

"We? How many of you are there, in the 37th?"

The sergeant looked back at me over his shoulder, giving me an apologetic expression, especially with his eyebrows. "Sorry, not something I'm at liberty to share."

"Why not?" asked Lucia. "You think one of them Mawks will capture and interrogate us?"

Private Washington chimed in, asking Lucia, "You ever been in the military?"

Her scowling look of disgust answered his question.

"Hard to explain, then. Sarge is right, though. He ain't supposed to talk about things like that, even with cooperating contractors, let alone regular civilians. Army's tightlipped that way."

Central and Sylvania Avenue were main thoroughfares, meaning there were a lot of abandoned vehicles, forcing us to sometimes travel single file on the sidewalks. Debris, including boards, garbage cans, even appliances like refrigerators, kept us paying attention to our path, making riding harder, at least for me. I wasn't able to observe the surroundings, not to my satisfaction.

Add nervous agitation to my growing depression. Definitely not a fun day out riding in the sun.

We reached the library where the 37th IBCT had established its command center. A semi-circle drive swung around in front of the Tudor-style building, with a mixture of stone and brick, reminding me of a cross between a house and a castle. I spotted two soldiers posted outside, but nothing really to suggest this place was any type of headquarters or command center. No military vehicles, groups of men, check points or anything. A bike rack that one of the sentries appeared to be keeping an eye on. That was all.

The library looked largely unscathed, with windows and doors intact. Probably why the colonel selected it. Also, two large churches, both nearby, seemed to be strong points, based on the number of soldiers moving in and around the stone and brick buildings.

As we pulled up to the bike rack outside the library's main entrance in the building's rear, Sergeant Eckstein ordered his men, "Disperse. Washington, report our return to Lieutenant Kuhn."

"Right, Sarge."

Each of the five privates pedaled their bikes a different

direction, while Lucia and I followed the sergeant's lead, parking our bikes in the rack, making a total of twelve bikes, most being mountain or hybrids. One was an old school, single speed bike with a banana seat and hi-rise handlebars.

I made eye contact with the nearest sentry. His darker complexion, straight dark hair and broad nose suggested Hispanic descent.

"This way," Sergeant Eckstein said, leading us into the main building. He made eye contact with the other sentry and nodded before holding the door for us. I signaled to Lucia to go in first. I kind of expected the sentry to attempt to disarm us. Maybe a compound bow and .22 caliber rifle didn't appear to be much of a threat.

With all of the windows and the high ceiling with ornate support beams arched to the apex, the library appeared a mixture of early 20th century and contemporary. That was in the main section. The books remained on their shelves. The large fireplace gave me the image of them being burned for warmth once winter arrived, if not here, then somewhere nearby.

In the main library area, beyond the checkout counter and behind a research librarian's desk, sat a man who I thought must be the unit's colonel. The metallic eagle with shield and clasping arrows with its talons on the mustached man's shoulders, some vague memory told me that was the insignia for a colonel.

The library's furniture, fixtures, and books appeared in decent shape. Apparently nobody thought holing up in a library or looting it was worthwhile. Maybe they had a vending machine in the basement, but if they had any books on edible plants or how to field dress a deer? On second thought, anyone thinking of a library would probably just know how to find such nonfiction books, even if computer searches were impossible. My mom had told me about card catalogues. Those, the Mawks wouldn't have destroyed with their EMP strikes.

Anyone searching by pulling book after book from the shelves? They'd give up before finding anything worthwhile.

The colonel looked up from the papers on his desk. He had broad shoulders and black-framed, bifocal glasses resting on a straight nose. He struck me as a man who spent a good part of his time with his eyebrows drawn together in frustration.

Sergeant Eckstein came to attention and saluted. When acknowledged by the officer, the sergeant said, "Colonel Davis, this is Jack Fairbanks, from the metro park west of the city. And his companion…Lucia the Archer."

"Thank you, Sergeant," the colonel said, and dismissed the NCO. Then he turned his attention to me. "So you're Jack Fairbanks, huh?" He pointed to a pair of chairs to the side of his commandeered desk. "Come on, you and your archer lady, pull yourselves up a chair."

I signaled for Lucia to go first.

By the time we'd unslung our rifle and bow, and rolled over office chairs, he'd moved his papers aside, putting a tattered file folder on top of them. Even in an apocalyptic end of the world scenario, like humanity was living through, the Army still had paperwork for its officers. Maybe he was writing orders, or doing calculations of his own? How much fuel did he have, how many vehicles, and how far could he and his men travel without scavenging? Counting on finding critical resources along the way could be iffy, depending on your destination, and the route taken.

Written orders seemed more likely, giving them to runners in lieu of radio communication. None of Sergeant Eckstein's squad had a radio. I didn't see one near the colonel.

I remained standing, but Lucia sat right away.

The colonel smiled at her, then said to me, "Make yourself comfortable."

He leaned back in his chair. "I appreciate you both making the trip. Short, but any journey out in the open is fraught with risk. Like wandering South Chicago after midnight—at least as it was a year ago." He folded his hands on his lap. "Same now, just extraterrestrial predators to worry about instead."

Lucia leaned forward. "You been to Chicago recently?"

"Can't say that I have," Colonel Davis said. "The Mawks are giving it more attention than Toledo. City of three hundred thousand, formerly, versus a city of two point five million."

Maybe Lucia was from Chicago. Had family there.

Before she could reply the colonel said, "Where are my manners?" He stood and offered his hand. "Colonel Thomas Joe Davis."

Lucia shook his hand first. "Lucia Rachella Hernandez, but I prefer Archer."

"If we were out drinking, I'd prefer Joe, but I don't know of any open bars, do you?" He grinned, and didn't wait for an answer. "Lucia the Archer, or Archer fits your measure better than Archer Woman."

"Chisel Z is an ignorant asshole." She glanced down at her bow resting on the floor next to her chair. "I should shoot his ignorant ass next time I see him."

The colonel raised an eyebrow, and said, "Hold that thought," before extending his hand to me.

"Jack Fairbanks," I said, and shot a sideways glance at Lucia. "I prefer Jack."

"Okay, Jack and Archer, now that we have the pleasant formalities out of the way, let me get down to why I invited you here."

We all three sat. If the colonel planned anything, me standing wouldn't change the results much.

Although we'd worked up a sweat, I noticed his formalities didn't include the hospitality of a drink. He could see the canteens on our belts, but still. Maybe that said something.

"The 37th IBCT is scheduled to travel south shortly, and our alien visitors have made the supply situation a concern."

Lucia looked over at me. "Guess you were right, Jack."

"What do you mean by supply situation, Colonel, and what do you have to trade?"

He leaned back in his chair again. "Not much that you'd probably want." He pulled the ballpoint pen out of his pocket and clicked it a few times. "I'm guessing you don't get a lot of news, so a little background on current events might be in order."

News, other than what Lucia brought back was about all I had. Most of my time and energy was spent patrolling the park and doing what I could to survive another day, with an eye toward surviving in the long haul. I figured the aliens—the Mawks—might eventually make humanity an extinct species. If that was the case, I intended to be one of the last Neanderthals standing.

If by some chance humanity drove them off, or got lucky like in *War of the Worlds*, I'd eventually learn of it. Not through cheering crowds, not with so many dead. But the return of military aircraft to the skies? Some ham radio operators would learn of it and spread the news. Lucia would find out that way, with her connections. And if the Mawks finished what they'd started, learning wouldn't matter the moment they laid me out for a dirt nap—or a meal for one of their aggressive exotic import species.

"Since cell phone communications are a thing of the past," Colonel Davis said, "PBS, Fox News, or CNN, if you prefer, are gone…hell even billboards, the postal system and smoke signals, for the most part. Try sending a radio message, broadcast anything for more than a split second, you're inviting a rock from orbit.

"The Army—all the services—learned that about the same time as the surviving amateur radio operators, or you might know them as ham radio operators. Those with old vacuum tube operating sets, or somehow had their equipment protected or hardened."

Colonel Davis gave us a grinning smirk. "There's a fella not too far from here that survived a near miss, and was one of the early ones to spread the word."

The colonel sat up straight. "He's a funny old guy, on the crotchety side. You ever met him?"

I shook my head.

Lucia said, "Yeah, he's a batty old bastard, but everyone puts up with his shit cuz he's about the only source of outside news."

The colonel seemed to be pretty friendly for an officer, or at least what I imagined one would be like. Could be that he figured being cordial would be more likely to get what he wanted from us.

"Okay, just nod your heads or interject as necessary as I go down the list."

We both nodded.

"You know about the failed plague, the EMPs—,"

I interrupted him. "Failed plague?"

"Okay." He shifted in his chair. "About nine months before the EMPs, remember news of that deadly flu strain? Well, it wasn't flu and they, they being the Mawks, didn't expect our immune system to be able to handle it as well as we did, or come up with a vaccine so fast. The CIA got that from one of the little suckers they've gotten ahold of."

He leaned back again. "EMPs?"

We nodded.

"Kinetic impact weapons…tsunamis on the coasts…the dozers and crawlers…crop and food stocks destruction—"

I sat up straight, as did Lucia. "Wait," I said. "That drone destroyed the crops we planted. Turned the leaves to wilted slime."

"Sounds about right. Some industrious farmers with really old tractors managed to put in some crops, with the Army or Marines keeping the dozers off of them. Recently, some sort of microwave directed down from orbit, and the hunter-killer drones on a smaller scale, wiped out what's been planted."

He clicked his pen and raised an eyebrow. "Food stocks?"

"What about that?" I asked, wondering if my buried and hidden food was gone, destroyed like my garden.

"The Army, surviving governments, gangs, citizen groups, churches, you name it, stockpiled food in one place. One building, warehouse, school gymnasium. What you'd expect. Large, dry, limited access. All in one place. Easier to guard, keep track of, dole out.

"As it turned out, also from space, a form of directed radiation degraded the foods, ruined everything. The targeted food stockpiles now are neither appetizing nor nutritious." He clenched his pen, clicking it a few times. "Except for whatever was stored in cans. Being in a metal building didn't help, but stored in cans did."

He tossed his pen back on the desk and shrugged.

"So, what you need from me and Lucia—the Archer— is food for your men?"

"I think going from house to house, business to business, now that the dozers and crawlers have largely been eliminated, and we have an apparent respite from the hunter-killer drone, might provide enough. Doing that now. But we might not have the time."

"Are there other kinds of drones?" Lucia asked. "Other than hunter-killer?"

"There are bigger ones, Miss Archer. They stay up about three to eight thousand feet. Intel drones. We believe they're the ones that located the larger food stockpiles. The ones that track large movements of men and materials, pick up and locate electronic communications. Maybe even direct the dozers toward a target. They're part of a network, reporting to a larger satellite, which reports to the Mawk ships in orbit.

"None of them are an immediate concern. Not at the moment."

"Then what do you want?"

"I hear you have medicines. Mainly looking for antibiotics."

"The Army doesn't have them?"

The colonel smiled a grim smile. "Maybe the Army does, but this little appendage of it, doesn't. It's my understanding that some gang gathered up most of what was to be found in the city, ransacked houses, intimidated and took, or killed and took, whatever else they could get. Tried to corner the market. And then burned them all to ashes trying to fend off a dozer. Destroyed all their ill-gotten gains."

Lucia snorted. "Yeah. The Gonzos, we call them that now. They're all dead. They was keeping everything in a bank vault. From what I heard, they threw Molotov cocktails on the dozer. On fire, it followed their gang leader, El Gonzalez Grande, The Big Gonzalez. He hid in the vault. Still on fire, it tore into the vault. All the crates and bags of drugs went up in smoke, and El Gonzalez Grande became the dozer's un-Happy Meal."

"Thank you for the details, Miss Archer."

"Archer," she said.

"Archer. I also heard you have water filtration gear. Ceramic lined straws. That would solve a lot of time and problems for my men on the road."

I glanced at Lucia. She gave me a questioning look.

Those were invaluable. Contaminated water could be drawn through them, like a straw, and it'd be filtered clean. No microorganisms, or impurities to speak of, and no toxic chemicals, unless you went drinking directly downstream from a chemical plant dumping into it. Worth more than their weight in antibiotics, since they could keep you from getting sick in the first place. All the time and effort gathering water was important. Having to boil water was a pain, labor intensive and time consuming, and drew the attention of dozers and crawlers, and maybe the intel drones."

"Colonel, all that you hear might not be all that accurate."

He laughed. "Oh, son, I'm sure it's not. You're supposed to be a former Navy SEAL. A dead-eyed killer. A survivalist on steroids."

He held up a hand, gesturing for me to let him continue. "I'll grant you, Jack, you've clearly got some critical skills, mixed in with some wit and guile. Navy SEAL?" He shook his head. "But the water filters? That information, I have a high degree of confidence in that."

No, I didn't look like a Navy SEAL. Not even close. And everyone I rode past today would eventually figure that out. And that meant trouble down the road. The awe and mystery that had apparently been built up, that bubble was burst, or soon would be. I didn't think about that before agreeing to follow Sergeant Eckstein in.

The colonel said, all expression gone from his face, "You look more than a bit perturbed, Jack. Nevertheless, you might consider moving your hand away from your revolver. See, while I don't have a Navy SEAL of my own, I do happen to have my own highly trained Special Forces member." His gaze focused past Lucia and I, over our shoulders. "Sergeant Yin, would you care to introduce yourself?"

I looked back over my left shoulder, while Lucia looked back over her right.

"No need, Sir. I believe you just did."

Behind us about fifteen feet, near the end of a row of young adult fantasy novels, stood a short, stocky soldier of Asian descent. His M-16 wasn't pointed at us. More sort of at the ground, but could be raised in a fraction of a second.

That wouldn't have happened, I told myself, if I were in my woods. Lucia's annoyed expression said he'd snuck behind us without her notice, too.

With a sneer, Lucia responded more directly. "You ain't gonna get shit from us."

I hadn't noticed my hand on the grip of my revolver until it'd been pointed out. Looking forward, back at the colonel, I removed it.

"Yeah," I said. "I see how it is."

"Really?" the colonel said, amusement in his voice. "Let me tell you how it is, and whether you give me any of your 'shit' or not, what's going to happen.

"I invited you both here to request your assistance—"

"Cuz you knew Jack has all his stuff hidden and buried where nobody can never find it."

"I'll finish, and then you can say your piece." His colonel, command voice now coming through. "Or not. Your option, Archer."

With unrelenting eyes, he waited for Lucia's agreement. After a few breaths she nodded agreement, gritting her teeth. She flicked a glance at me, and then focused back on the colonel. The scar on her chin and throat stuck out, like it wanted to burst and drown Colonel Davis in a shower of her blood.

"Believe it or not, as American citizens—hell, as one of the dwindling number of humans on Earth—I have your best interests at heart. I have been ordered to make a delivery. One that just might stem the tide of our extinction.

"Now, you can ride back to your little park and wait to see what happens. If my mission, and those of other units across the country, and if secure word has gotten out, some countries in Europe and Asia…" He shrugged. "If our global mission fails, you *might* live a little longer than I and my men do.

"But somebody's going to come for you, and what you have."

He smiled briefly. "Ever see any of those Mel Gibson *Mad Max* movies?"

Lucia was still fuming, and as the colonel had paused, waiting for a response, I said, "I saw one, but it didn't star Mel Gibson."

"Huh, too bad. Remakes are always inferior to the originals." He shifted in his seat. "Anyway, now there's roving gangs of marauders moving across the country, from city to city, devouring and destroying all in their path like human locusts. The aliens apparently approve, because they're not stopping them, not like other units of any size that form up and try to move with a purpose.

"Those barbarians are doing the alien invaders' work for them."

He let that sink in. "There's one in Cleveland now. It'll take them a while to clear out that city and its suburbs. Pockets of resistance, and a lot of territory. This one formed in Pittsburgh. Fifty-fifty if they take I-71 south and head toward Columbus, or follow U.S. 6, or maybe State Route 2 along the lake to Toledo, next."

He made eye contact with the Special Forces sergeant behind us. "Six or seven thousand strong. On bikes, old trucks and busses. It's reported that when they can't find enough food, human flesh is an appropriate substitute.

"Now, Jack, you and Archer might be able to hide from them. But the food's gonna run out here soon enough, and whoever is left is going to come for what you have, no matter your reputation, no matter the risk. Hunger and desperation does that."

If what he said about the food stocks was true, he was right. Coming here, being revealed as something less than a Navy SEAL wouldn't make a difference. Desperation? Folks would risk a dozen SEALs. Folks that are left, they're certain to have survival skills, combat skills, and luck.

The colonel must've seen a change in my expression, because he nodded. "That's right, lady and gent, we're facing the end. Given the enemy an assist from our own hand, our own kind.

"Now, the U.S. Army can't do a thing about the Mad Max Post-Apocalyptic Marauders until the extraterrestrial menace has been dealt with. We form up to meet them, rocks from orbit will rain down on us. Or worse.

"So, you can pony up and help me and my men, help your country, help your species. I've got some sick men that a little medicine will help. If I have to carry less water, that'd free up vehicles and bikes and even horses and wagons for food and other gear. And save time and energy. Make us stand out less by building fewer fires to boil and purify what we need to drink along the way."

He picked up his pen and clicked it a few times. "Or you can hoard your stash, pray I and my men succeed, the world succeeds, and that you're around to enjoy the fruits of that success."

With that he leaned back and swiveled in his chair.

He made a good argument, if all that he said was true. What did he have to deliver? Some sort of bomb and putting it where he thought the aliens might make a landing? Did they get that information from their captured Mawk? I didn't think Toledo, or anywhere in Ohio or the surrounding states had a nuke, certainly not anyplace that had survived. The only major base that might've had one in Ohio that I could think of would've been Wright Patterson Air Force Base, and my guess was that it was cratered worse than the moon.

Maybe they had some sort of biological weapon or plague to plant, or something chemically explosive? Colonel Davis might have a Mawk, newly captured, and needed to get it somewhere for interrogation.

I internally shrugged. Instead of guessing, why not ask? "What do you have to deliver, Colonel?"

"That, Jack, I cannot share with you."

"What?" Lucia asked, leaning forward, hands gripping the colonel's desk. "You think the...the Mawks will capture us and torture it out of me and Jack?"

"I have my orders."

An easy out, I thought. But it made sense. If there was a plan in the works...telling us that he had a delivery to make, that might've been stretching his orders. Or maybe not. Nevertheless, if he told us, who knows who we might tell? We weren't even soldiers under his command...but the country had been placed under Martial Law, so technically...maybe we could, or would, be? What was the term...conscripts?

I glanced at Lucia. Although her face no longer held a sneer and she wasn't glaring at the colonel, I could tell she was still mad as hell at him. She wasn't the type to cool off quickly.

"Colonel Davis," I said, "Archer and I would like to discuss your proposal."

"Of course," he said, his tone neutral as gray clouds floating across a late night black-and-white movie's sky.

Lucia's patriotic streak surprised me. She hated the colonel, but she liked the idea of doing *something* to F-over the aliens. After five minutes talking out by the bike rack, we walked back into the library.

The colonel was in his chair, talking to Sergeant Yin standing next to him. He swiveled his chair to face us as we strode up to the desk.

"Three things," I said, "and we'll share what we're able."

"Three things," the colonel repeated, again in a neutral tone.

Lucia said, "You send help to patrol our park and help us dig up the food and supplies."

"Sergeant Eckstein and his squad can be assigned to that."

"We get two days to replant my crops, again with assistance and men patrolling the park from intruders, both human and alien."

The colonel raised a questioning eyebrow. "You want my men to assist you in farming?"

"Affirmative," I said.

Lucia added, "Since you'll be cutting into our supply, we'll need something to harvest when we return."

"When you return?" Colonel Davis asked with a sparkle in his eye, confident he knew our next demand.

"Affirmative again," I said, "since we're going with you."

Chapter 15

We planted roughly three acres of crops. They included corn and beans, spread out to avoid a repeat of Mawk destruction, some carrots, radishes and onions, some under cover of a light canopy of trees. We planted in a few flower bed gardens as well.

Then 180 of 237 water purification straws packed in plastic tubs were dug up, along with 22 fifty-pound bags of dry dog food. The dog food wasn't buried in most cases, just hidden in scattered isolated areas around the park. The straws were hauled back by the soldiers on bikes, and the dog food by bike-pulled carts. That required several trips.

Lucia and I preferred cat food, which was also more nutritious in some respects. I also showed her some of the nearby houses that had coal bins, where Luther and I had hid some food outside of the park. I wrote out a rough map detailing all I could remember of buried supplies, which I was pretty sure was all of them.

We hid the list and map in a plastic bag, stuck under a rock, buried under a fallen log, fifty paces south of the rusted chain-link fence where we sometimes posted and watched the highway along our park's northern boundary.

I had to trust Lucia. She was my partner. If I didn't make it back, there was no reason she shouldn't be able to survive on what Luther and I had gathered and hidden. Someone should benefit from it.

That was, if either of us returned.

Lucia and I hadn't been able to get any information on our destination. Not from Sergeant Eckstein, nor from any of his men. They were tight-lipped, but pleasant, especially when we shared canned fruit with them after a long day of digging and planting. The sergeant insisted upon a prayer before eating. His men seemed to expect this. What I didn't expect was Lucia crossing herself like a practicing Catholic. Praying never hurt, so I went along without complaint. My private complaint was that God, if he existed, didn't appear to be on humanity's side.

I was pretty sure the privates under the sergeant didn't know much of anything about the colonel's plans, especially while listening to the soldiers pack up after the second day's hauling and planting was finished. The only thing of interest mentioned was one soldier asking the other what a 'thunder well' was. He'd asked the sergeant with no answer given. They concluded Sergeant Eckstein was doing exactly what was ordered. The Army way.

Sergeant Eckstein did tease me, and offer to provide me with a real firearm, as opposed to my .22 carnival gun. In response, I demonstrated my proficiency with it. As a result, a small amount of fresh meat was added to the menu when I nailed a squirrel walking along an oak's limb about sixty yards away. Shooting my small caliber rifle was second nature to me. Plus, I showed him some of the guns taken off the bodies of intruders, so he knew I wasn't using the only gun available to me.

Turned out there were a few other citizens invited to travel with us, and the soldiers took a few of the rifles and pistols and ammo back for their use. The rest, Lucia and I oiled, wrapped and sealed up in trash bags, and hid around the park. We wouldn't have been able to do it in such a short amount of time if two of the soldiers hadn't been on patrol. The morning of the last day they spotted a crawler prowling along the railroad tracks. At least in the Toledo area, their rarity indicated they'd become an endangered species, maybe because they didn't reproduce. Nowhere had Lucia or I spotted or heard about any pods. That suggested those killed wouldn't be replenished with a new generation.

Lucia nailed the lone crawler with her bow and harvested the eyes before Private Washington helped me drag it over to my trophy fence.

Three days after everything was done, Private Washington arrived an hour before sunset. "Tomorrow morning, sunrise, the Colonel says the 37th is moving out. If'n you want to join us, merge with the column taking the

475 highway."

That was the highway running along the north edge of our park. At least we wouldn't have to ride over and join up, only to backtrack.

That night, Lucia and I double-checked our bikes—this time she selected Luther's hybrid—and all of our gear. As per our routine, we split the night awake and on patrol. Funny thing was, neither of us managed to get much sleep. I spent a good two hours next to Luther's grave, feeling surges of regret over abandoning the park.

I closed my eyes a moment and listened, picking up movement in the brush and dried leaves. A big old raccoon, near twenty pounds, wandered up and sat on Luther's grave. Fearless, it stared at me.

"Okay," I whispered, knowing everything with Luther and the park would be okay in my absence. "You can watch over our park."

I climbed the nearby sleeping tree, rolled into my hammock, and caught two hours of sleep, feeling safe. My double line of bell tripwires, Lucia on patrol, and Luther, somehow keeping watch over both of us.

Chapter 16

The rumbling sound of an old diesel truck provided Lucia and I ample warning. We stood off in the weeds next to our bikes, shielded by a blue extended cab pickup truck. Both of its front tires were completely flat.

I checked the hitch and strap that connected the small luggage trailer to my bike. Lucia did the same with hers. Food, spare clothes and boots, cooking gear, extra firearms, ammo, and more, all in plastic storage bins. I'd lashed it all down with rope and a few bungee cords. Lucia had done the same, but added her bow and a quiver of arrows to the top of hers.

Then we shouldered our backpacks and watched a green International dump truck from the 1960s approach. Ahead of it were two soldiers with M-16s strapped across their backs. I could see them and the oncoming vehicles better than Lucia because of my binoculars. Any vehicle built decades ago, those without any computer components, hadn't been affected by the EMP attacks.

The dump truck had a sturdy iron-frame push bar welded to the front. Obviously, if an abandoned vehicle or two needed to be moved, there was the solution. Better than breaking windows, putting abandoned vehicles in neutral, and using muscle power. And if a vehicle had flat tires? That would wear a man—or woman—out in a short time, especially if the process had to be repeated often.

Fortunately the driver was able to weave around the scattered vehicles. I hoped the big old truck had power steering, or the guy was going to be tired, unless he had forearms like Popeye.

Behind the dump truck was a Humvee hauling a trailer, like our bikes', just a lot larger. Some of the desert camo paint was obscured by gear strapped to its sides. An alert soldier stood, his torso extended through the Humvee's roof, manning a machine gun mounted there. He wore a

Kevlar helmet and mirrored sunglasses.

Behind the Humvee was an actual four-horse team. It pulled a large wooden flatbed wagon with a railing erected along the sides that consisted mainly of stubby two-by-fours with two rows of boards nailed to them. The lashed-down crates and container boxes weren't as densely packed as in my cart, or that of the Humvee equipment. Easily accessible along the back edge of the wagon sat two disassembled military weapons. I knew they were mortars, I just didn't know what type. I'd seen them used in video games. Indirect fire, with smoke, white phosphorous and high explosive rounds.

They had an old maroon El Camino, also with a trailer that appeared to have originally been a boat trailer. They'd converted it with boards and plywood for its new purpose. It carried a load of twelve bikes, in two rows, braced upright in an old bike rack that had been cut in half, probably with a hacksaw.

A clickity-engined Dodge Dart, dark blue and definitely from the 70s, was weighted down with a driver and five passengers. Behind it was another Humvee, this one camo green, with a TOW missile system mounted on the roof. Like the first Humvee, it had several soldiers riding inside. Unlike the first Humvee, it had a large towed mortar with tires. They appeared to be designed for the gun, and not a later addition due to circumstances.

Scattered between and off to the sides of the vehicles were about a dozen soldiers and civilians, as identified by their dress, on bikes similar to mine and Lucia's. Only two, pedaled by a red-bearded man and an ample-chested woman, had carts like ours. Those had brown tarps covering what they carried.

"Aren't you glad you decided against your granny trike?" Lucia asked, a grin spreading across her face.

I shrugged, and handed her the binoculars so she could see. "Easier to pedal on auto pilot, with your eyes closed."

"Whatever, Jack." She handed me back my binoculars and I stuffed them in their case secured in the small basket attached to the front of my bike's handlebars.

I also had my solar-powered recharger in the basket, recharging the batteries used in my—Luther's—night vision monocular. Lucia carried the monocular in a case on her belt.

Seven or eight miles per hour, I estimated, probably slower in places.

"That dump truck has to get horrible gas mileage," I said.

"There should be enough trucks on the road to resupply," Lucia replied.

"If we stay on the highway."

Her eyes widened at the thought. "Right."

Neither of us knew where we were going.

"I thought there would be more," she said. "More soldiers. I didn't see Colonel Davis."

"This could be an advance group." I pushed my bike into view and gave a friendly wave. No sense getting shot by the two soldiers on bikes ahead of the group. "They probably don't want to bunch up."

As I thought about it, I'd want the bike scouts further than one hundred yards ahead. Of course, they didn't have radio communications. It was hard to be stealthy riding on a road. And they'd be vulnerable to just about anything they came across, like a dozer.

One of the scouts, a wiry, rail-thin woman, pulled up next to me. The name patch on her unbuttoned military fatigues read Barhorst. She had brown hair and a few freckles, and a big smile. Didn't strike me as military. The T-shirt showing under her fatigues was faded, with a stitched up hole. The U.S. Army logo was still on it, however.

"You must be Jack and Archer," she said, looking us over.

I nodded, and she signaled the other bike scout to continue on ahead.

Private Barhorst looked over our bikes and attached wagons. Seemingly satisfied, she said, "Lieutenant Kuhn is riding in the first Humvee. Check in with him, and he'll assign you a location within the column, and any specific duties."

"Will do," I said, and she raced off to catch up with her partner, swinging around the occasional vehicle stalled on the highway.

"Let's go, Lucia," I said and rolled away from the shoulder and slowly started pedaling, tracing the scouts' route.

"I thought that skinny soldier said to wait and speak with her lieutenant."

"We'll go slow. They'll catch up to us," I said to Lucia over my shoulder. "I am guessing we have a long trip. This'll make it easier."

She didn't argue. In a moment she was riding beside me.

I thought saying goodbye to Luther would make it easier. My gaze lingered up to the left, toward the park that had been my home, my sanctuary. I had some real mixed emotions. I didn't want to leave. I also wanted to be part of taking it to the aliens, the Mawks. It was better than sitting and waiting for trouble to find me, sitting and waiting for the end.

"So long, Luther. I'll tell you what happened when I get back." It came out a little shaky. I didn't add, 'If I get back.'

Lucia must've heard me. "You ain't gonna cry, Jack. Are you?" She probably meant to say it sarcastically, but there was an emotional longing in her voice, too.

I didn't turn my head to see if she had tears in her eyes. I had a few forming in mine, but they dried up quickly. A dozer bounded down an incline from an abandoned church parking lot. Picking up speed, it burst through an intervening chain link fence.

The two scouts spun their bikes around and shot back toward the main column, both blowing whistles held between their teeth. I reached back and detached the cart and pulled my bike around.

I'd attached and detached the cart hundreds of times. Lucia hadn't, so I knocked her hand aside as she struggled with the pin. I pinched it before yanking it out and freed her bike as well.

Then, without hesitation, I said, "Come on!"

Already the dozer was gaining on the scouts. I wanted to be ahead of them reaching the column. I had no intention of fighting, not with my little .22 rifle stuffed in its makeshift leather holster belted to my front basket. If it got to the point where the dozer was tearing into the soldiers defending with real guns and equipment, I'd be retreating back up into my park. The supplies in our carts could be retrieved later.

When going all out, dozers were faster than men on bikes. And they had more endurance too, for a long chase. Lucia and I just had to be faster than the scouts, who'd already built up speed and momentum.

The dump truck and other vehicles pulled off the road, all except for the rear Humvee. The soldiers within the vehicles were deploying, taking cover, with rifles aimed over the hoods of cars, or the cement barrier dividing the highway. The civilians on bikes kept retreating even after they passed the rearmost vehicle. Nobody shot at the dozer, which was good, because we were between it and them.

I hadn't decided what I'd do, if I reached the soldiers. Following the other civilians seemed like a reasonable strategy.

Lucia wasn't as strong of a cyclist as me. Private Barhorst was pulling ahead of me. She glanced back over her shoulder.

The clump and scrape of claws on concrete said the dozer was gaining. Probably less than thirty yards behind us.

Ahead the Humvee with the TOW missile launcher came to a stop.

Flames and smoke erupted from the launcher with the missile picking up speed as it rocketed right toward us— right at me.

"Scatter!" Barhorst shouted before cutting right, angling her bike toward the shoulder.

I did the same, and heard Lucia shout a curse as she clattered and skidded across the concrete.

There was a little red Mini Cooper between me and the dozer. Dropping my bike I pulled my revolver, knowing it wouldn't do any good. My construction adhesive was in my backpack—like I had the time to prep a bullet. Still, I berated myself.

Gunfire erupted from behind me, as did a three-round burst to my left, just before I fired off a round.

The other scout had made it to the concrete median, leapt off his bike and jumped over the barrier.

"Stay down!" I shouted at Lucia. She was flat on the road, staring back at the dozer, legs tangled in her bike. Knife in hand, she frantically kicked free.

The TOW missile impacted just to the right of the dozer's open tri-beak, then exploded, sending a concentrated searing jet of flame into the beast's shoulder. I wasn't sure the fiery heat was penetrating, but it did cause the beast to stop and turn to its left, like a giant grizzly bear chasing its tail. Tracers bounced off and .50 caliber bullets from the Humvee's machine gun bit into the dozer. Not penetrating, but indenting and tearing away small chunks of its hide. The hail of smaller caliber rounds, including mine, were probably more annoying than deadly, like a bride getting fistfuls of rice thrown at her.

Then two small arrows bit into the beast's right rear leg and side. Later I'd learn they were from hunting crossbows. They must've had wet construction adhesive spread over their split eye-crystal tips.

By the time I emptied my three .45 caliber rounds and two .410 buckshot shells into the dozer, Lucia had escaped the entanglement of her bike and scrambled off to the side of the road. Without looking back, she crawled on her stomach, making her way toward my Mini Cooper. To my left, Private Barhorst continued to fire off aimed, three-round bursts.

The dozer had had enough. Emitting a bellowing screech, it turned and limped away on three legs, the fourth held up, apparently unable to bear weight.

Nobody stopped firing, unless they were reloading like

me. Lucia stood up next to me, palms bloody. Her jean jacket was scraped at the elbows. She was probably bruised there, but not bloody.

Wild-eyed, she drew her .45 caliber pistol and took aim just in time to see a second TOW missile hit the beast on its left flank. Adding to it, another two crossbow quarrels found their mark in its flank.

The dozer went down on its left side, thrashing. Some of the gunfire abated as the roar of a massive diesel engine sounded. At twenty miles per hour the dump truck ran into and then over the downed beast. It was like the right side's wheels had run onto and then over a mound of bricks. And like a pile of bricks would, the beast's ribs and body gave way some, but didn't fully collapse.

That impressed more than me. Over the roar of the engine I heard Barhorst say, "Damn!"

Twitching and quivering, like a crushed insect whose limbs didn't yet know it was dead, the dozer took a few minutes to expire.

CHAPTER 17

While Lieutenant Kuhn got the column reorganized and prepared to move, I cared for Lucia's scraped-up palms. A little water, followed by peroxide and an anti-bacterial ointment, had her ready for sterile gauze to be taped in place.

Private Washington was the soldier who'd fired the TOW missiles, and received more than a few pats on the back. Despite this, Sergeant Eckstein had Washington and the others in his squad getting the Humvee ready to move.

He'd just returned from meeting with the lieutenant, after checking out the dead dozer.

He held up a knife. "You can't even stab this into its skin, except with a sledge hammer. Even then, it took a half dozen blows."

I believed him, looking at his combat knife's pommel. "My guess is it's from a high gravity planet. Dense skin and muscles and bones. Be like you and me being on the moon or something."

"What makes you say that?" he asked.

"Saw one jump over my height in a vertical leap. Imagine a rhino or grizzly bear doing that, and not getting hurt when it lands."

A couple of the nearby soldiers stopped what they were doing for a second and looked my way.

The sergeant tipped his head in thought. "Makes sense. Its blood, gray, was like liquid mercury, maybe even heavier."

Lucia asked, "You didn't touch it, did you?"

"Me? No," Sergeant Eckstein said. "I studied chemistry and biology. Without protective gloves and more, no way will I mess with alien fluids. Not willingly."

Lucia looked skeptical. "So, you're saying you're a scientist?"

"Me? No," he said again. "I'm a soldier now. Me and

my men, we man the TOW launcher." Then he flicked a thumb toward what his Humvee was towing. "And the one-hundred twenty millimeter mortar. I was a cannoneer, working with the M119, 105mm howitzer. Towed like our mortar, and since I'm one of the few under Colonel Davis that has training with artillery… I trained with the 81mm mortars, like we have on the wagon."

He paused and shouted, "Washington, where's Henderson and Rollins?"

"Taking a piss in the bushes—" he started, then remembered Lucia was right next to the sergeant. "Ummm, he's…they're…"

"Go get them."

"Yes, sergeant." The man trotted off.

Then Sergeant Eckstein focused back on Lucia and me. "The lieutenant wants you two near the back with us. Ride for a while, then switch off, putting your bikes in the rack."

"What about our carts?"

"Should be able to secure them to the back of the wagon." He pointed to one of his two men sitting in the Humvee. "Go check with the horse driver. About the possibility of attaching these carts."

The private trotted toward the wagon. That got me thinking about how the horses handled the dozer. They didn't bolt. Well trained. Good driver on that wagon.

Lucia asked, "Where's Colonel Davis?"

"He's with the main group. Once we get south of Toledo, we'll travel parallel. Provide supporting fire, if needed."

"Why'd he assign us here?" Lucia asked. "Cuz we knew you?"

"Maybe. He told me, since you were so generous with your supplies, and looking forward to returning to the park, he was going to assign you to the safer column."

I glanced up toward the dozer splayed out in the road. "Good thing there weren't two of them," I said. "Wasted a lot of ammo."

"Not wasted," Sergeant Eckstein said. "Hammering

them with a hail of bullets confuses them. Like being over stimulated. Keeps them occupied for a handful of seconds."

"Gave Private Washington enough time to take it under fire," I said.

"Right, Jack."

"Hey, what's our job gonna be?" Lucia asked, folding her arms across her chest, wincing when she accidentally put pressure on her palms. "I ain't cooking or anything like that."

"Far as I know, you'll be assigned to night watch, at least until the lieutenant gets your measure." The Sergeant grinned. "Except for wiping out on your bike, you both did well under pressure."

Lucia scowled.

"Naw, forget that. Neither of you panicked." He packed up the first aid kit, where I'd gotten the gauze.

I put the anti-bacterial ointment back in my backpack.

The sergeant winked at Lucia. "Heck, you've got to be a bit brave, or crazy, making a stand against a dozer from behind a Mini Cooper."

We all three got a good laugh at that.

"I'd heard that dozers and crawlers hunted humans, as well as canines and equines."

After four hours of slow travel, at an inconsistent pace, I parked my bike between several on the bike rack hauled by the El Camino. I then took a seat on the bench next to Elmore Foltz. He was driving the horse-drawn wagon. A thin but sturdy, sun-beaten man in his late fifties, he showed me a sincere grin.

We exchanged small talk for a while. He corrected me in that his four horses weren't Clydesdales, but Belgians. Brunhilda, Cadaver in the front, and Comanche and Bud in the back, Bud being the mischievous ornery one. He wondered at my vest, a bulletproof one taken from one of the park invaders. He started to say something about my baseball cap, before I'd interrupted him with my question about the crawlers targeting equines.

"Maybe so, maybe not," he replied. "The crawlers killed my dogs, but didn't bother my cats. Kept my team slathered in pig excrement best I could. Maybe I got lucky."

I thought about that concealment tactic a moment. "Where are you from?"

He lifted his tattered John Deere ball cap and wiped sweat from his brow with a blue bandana kept in his shirt pocket. "Farm in Ottawa County. Kids have gone west. Wife left me soon as they did, blamed it on my drinking." He frowned and looked ahead. "Haven't had a drink in months."

We both laughed at his small joke.

"You, where you from, Jack?"

"Florida," I said. "Came up here for college. Was going to study marine biology."

He politely didn't ask about my family. It wasn't something people asked, Lucia warned me. A sad and touchy subject. Surprising he mentioned his own, stopping short of speculating if they were alive or dead. Most of the time I didn't think about it. Out of sight, out of mind, sort of. Being so busy trying to stay alive helped with that.

"Know where we're going?" I asked, looking over the flat expanse of land around us. Fallow fields, a few farmhouses and barns here and there. Normally the fields would be green with corn or bean crops, not weeds.

"South," he said without expression, then leaned over and elbowed me in the ribs. "My guess, no further than Tennessee."

I didn't ask as to his source or reasoning. "Oh," I said. "Sounds okay."

"Yeah, Army don't like to share much, unless they have to."

It was a little before noon, and it was a warm but cloudy day. We were south of Bowling Green, still on I-75, slowly weaving our way through abandoned vehicles. After I'd finished my hour break, the lieutenant assigned Lucia and me to find diesel trucks and siphon fuel for the dump truck as we went along. We'd already emptied our carts and they were filled with empty gas cans, a few metal ones, but most were red and plastic.

The Army, at least the 37th's main column under Colonel Davis, had four Bradleys, an array of old cars and trucks, and dozens of bikes. One truck pulled a flatbed trailer carrying two refurbished museum pieces. Twin-barreled 37mm Anti-Aircraft guns from World War II. Or so Sergeant Eckstein had informed me. They even had two towed 105mm howitzers. Their effective range was at least as far as the mortars, but too far to be of much use without radios to control, if they couldn't stay close or within line of sight of the main column. Sergeant Eckstein said they had direct fire capability, which might be their best use, especially in dire circumstances.

Why the sergeant wasn't assigned to the howitzers, I wasn't sure and didn't ask. If I asked Elmore Foltz next to me, he would've said with a smile, "That's the Army, son."

During my second break, he'd used that exact phrase several times while making small talk as we ate our lunch. It consisted of dry dog food and a few swigs of water. Not balanced nutrition, and even worse tasting. Hints of broiled beef masked by chalky grit. But it was filling and had calories, and I had vitamins in my backpack to supplement the 'eat whatever is available' diet. Lucia did, too.

I was reflecting on how long it took to travel from one mile marker to the next. So slow and plodding, so unlike driving 70 miles per hour, sharing the interstate with countless other drivers, zooming along in their vehicles without realizing the technological wonder's inherent fragility. Less than one minute to drive from one mile marker to the next, now a fading memory.

That caused me to reflect further. Going from one rural crossroad to the next instead of going down I-75 like we were now, from one exit to the next, would be better in one important way. There wouldn't be any billboards with their faded pictures and tattered edges, with their marketing slogans peeling away. It all reminded me of what life had been like. Places and luxuries I'd never experience again.

"You know our mission?" I asked the driver, turning away from my depressing thoughts. "I've been told we're making a delivery."

"Right you are, there," he responded after talking to his team, encouraging them. I guessed the smoky diesel fumes from the dump truck annoyed them, like they did me.

To our right, on State Route 25 was the rest of the 37th. If I stood on the bench seat, I could spot them between stands of trees, on the road, a little ahead of our pace.

"Well, can tell you that I picked up the 'package' for the Colonel. Don't know what it is, exactly, but he didn't want to use a military vehicle to go up to the pier on Lake Erie."

"It came by boat?"

"Nope." The driver paused for effect. "Narco sub."

"Really?" I asked.

"Yep. It came up from the gulf, up the Mississippi to the Chicago River. Got past the locks or dams, somehow. Then Lake Michigan to some straits, Mackinac, to Huron to Lake St. Clair to the Detroit River to Lake Erie. All that way north, only to go south again…unless it picked up the package along the way."

"How'd you learn all that?"

"Spoke to one of the crew. A mixture of U.S. Navy sailors and some of the narco sub's original crew. One of them, not a Navy sailor, told me."

"He just told you?"

The driver feigned offense, then elbowed me again. "Shared two of my last cigarettes with him."

"How big is the package?"

"Well," he said, stretching out the word. "Probably shouldn't say." A smugness hung in his voice, which seemed uncharacteristic, at least based on our brief conversations.

"We weren't their first delivery, I can say."

The horse team's metal hoofs clomped and scraped against the hard cement of the interstate highway. Looking over my shoulder, I made brief eye contact with Lucia. She was riding in the bed of the El Camino, along with Private Barhorst.

"You ever hear of a thunder well?" I asked the driver.

"Thunder well?"

"Overheard the soldiers talking about it, when they were digging up the filtering straws hidden in my park."

The farmer reached into a wooden box affixed to the bench seat, and held up one of the thick straws that resembled a recorder, those plastic elementary school instruments every kid had to play at some time. "Have you to thank for this?"

I nodded. "Good for about four hundred gallons."

"So I was told." He paused a few minutes after putting the straw away. "You gave up a couple hundred of them?"

"Pretty close to that," I said.

After another few minutes, he said just above a whisper. "Flooding the zone."

Leaning close, I asked, "What?"

"We're just one of many groups heading south. Overheard the colonel on the radio."

"Radio?" I asked, incredulous.

"Right," he said. "Had some transmitter and receiver hardwired to his radio pretty far off. Short conversation. The aliens cratered the sending and receiving antenna, where the deception terminated." He paused. "Army seems to think the aliens have limited resources. Flood the zone."

Again, I remained quiet, letting him talk.

"Like in football, son. The damn aliens got the technology to wipe us out, easy as a hawk going down on a three-legged mouse. But if there's too many gimpy mice all at once, some might get through untouched."

"Hope we're one of the lucky ones," I said.

The driver nodded his head and laughed. "From your lips to the Almighty above."

I probably should've shouted it, because God apparently didn't hear.

Chapter 18

Lucia stood watch while I siphoned diesel fuel from a Ford F-350. It was an older model, early 1990s, but not old enough to resist the EMPs. She paced on the hood, making sure to watch all directions for any dangers—human or alien.

One thing there were fewer of was flies. No dead bodies to lay their eggs on. I didn't miss them. The other thing, being away from the city, was the stench of decay, of rotting bodies. Scavenging in homes, it was something you had to get used to. But my park was surrounded by suburbs really part of the city itself. And the breezes carried the stench with them. Like the flies, I learned to ignore it and didn't notice until we'd gotten south of the city. The air was fresher, without the stench. Whenever we came near anyplace of any size, the faint odor of death hung in the air. It was depressing, and affected everyone's mood, usually making them just a little bit more irritable.

The erratic pace and pattern the Army columns made…on the interstate, off the interstate, parallel state routes and county roads and back. Rest for five minutes, an hour and eighteen minutes. The disruptive pattern didn't make sense. That irritated me more than the sickly scent of death.

It was about an hour from sunset. Lucia and I would have to make our way off the interstate and back down the county road about a mile. An hour was more than enough time.

The highway seemed deserted. A red-tailed hawk perched on a long dead ash tree's branch. Nothing else alive, debris from wind and rain building up against the vehicles' tires.

"That Lieutenant Kuhn," Lucia said. "He's the reason for the piss poor progress. According to Barhorst, she says it's some sort of calculation to throw off the aliens." She made another three-sixty scan of the area. "Not like they couldn't find us if they wanted. Not as slow as we're going."

"I'll ask Sergeant Eckstein about that when I get the chance."

"Ask him why they got radios turned on in their Humvees, too."

"They do?" I asked.

"Yeah. They listen only. All they get is quiet static. If they speak into them, send a message, it'll be like a blip on an alien's radar screen." She scrunched up her face. "Not radar, but you know what I mean."

"I do," I said, pulling the hose and fitting the cap on the last of our gas cans. "We're done. This one had two tanks, both were nearly full."

"Let's go," she said. "Dark's coming soon."

We were just north of a town called North Baltimore. Nearly 40 miles south of Toledo, but much further based on the indirect route we'd taken. Another long day on my bike had left my legs tired. Not that I wasn't in shape, I just didn't use the same muscles bike riding as I did walking and jogging around the park. Getting up in the morning, stiff legged, or at night before my watch—it hadn't been specifically assigned yet—wasn't going to be fun.

Midway through the night, Lieutenant Kuhn had us up and moving, less than five-hundred yards, and re-establish camp, around another abandoned farmhouse. This one had the signs of a crawler attack, an eighteen inch hole chewed through the cinderblock foundation.

Years ago, that would've creeped me out. Now, it was just part of the scenery.

I was in my tent, had dozed off for ten minutes, when the kinetic strike hit. Left a forty-foot diameter crater right where we'd been camping not thirty minutes before. The main column avoided a similar fate by moving, too.

Lieutenant Kuhn went around to his men, spread out in barns, the house, and the garage, if they weren't on watch or trying to sack out in their vehicle. He told them not to worry. We'd dodged the bullet for tonight. Elmore had better luck calming his Belgians than the lieutenant did reassuring his men.

The rising smoke from the crater, and the fact that the farmhouse had been knocked off its foundation, played a main part of the insecurity. Pictures rattling off their hooks, and a tall china cabinet toppling over, nearly crushing Private Washington…it'd been like a five magnitude earthquake had struck, and shook more than the ground. It undermined our confidence.

Chapter 19

A chorus of distant whistles invaded my dream. In it I was watching Luther skin a possum. My father sat on the log near the campfire, just to my left, asking Luther why he made the initial cuts like he did. He was trying to learn the skill, just like I had.

All three of us stopped, taking note of the sound.

Sharper, louder whistles snapped me out of my nap. Brought me back to the present, where I was on the bed of the horse-drawn wagon, nestled between a pair of crates to keep out of the sun.

I sat up and looked around, my .22 rifle in hand.

Elmore pulled his horse team to a stop. He shouted over his shoulder, "Jack, the mortars, get them mortars off!"

In a second, I was scrambling to the rear of the wagon. Two soldiers had abandoned their bikes and were sprinting toward the wagon. The whistles stopped. Distant cracks, like firecrackers, sounded. Equally distant rifle fire answered them. So did thumps from the Bradleys' main guns.

While standing atop the wagon, a brief glance toward the sound of gunfire showed that the main column had been driving parallel to us, also on a narrow county road about a mile distant. They'd turned our direction, and were on course to cross ahead of us, back east, toward I-75. The plan had been to skirt wide around Lima, for some reason. I'd fallen asleep shortly before crossing U.S. 33, so I guessed we were past it.

Colonel Davis hadn't stopped to form a defensive perimeter. Rather, his men were in retreat. The four Bradleys and an equal number of Humvees had formed a rear guard, firing away with cannons and machine guns. Already two of the Bradleys were stopped and smoking.

They, like us, were on flat terrain, with mainly fallow fields and a few ditches available for cover.

The enemy, what I could see, had some form of domed

tanks, metallic and sort of oblong. There were four of them and they didn't look like they had wheels. But they were pretty far off. Flitting around them were what appeared to be smaller versions of the tanks, probably about the size of motorcycles.

I pulled the rope, quick-releasing the knot holding one of the 81mm mortars in place.

Two soldiers grabbed the gun tube and the plate while I untied the other mortar. Two more soldiers joined us, and hauled the parts of the second mortar off the wagon.

"Shells!" one of the soldiers yelled as he carried the tube across the shallow ditch and into the field to set it up.

"That crate to your left!" Elmore shouted. A crowbar tossed from his direction landed atop it. The wooden crate was too big to move, so I took the driver's meaning and wedged the crowbar in place to pry the lid off.

Lucia climbed up and helped me lift the lid.

A nearby *whump* sounded. Out of the corner of my eye, I spotted Sergeant Eckstein and two men next to the 120mm mortar. They were firing again, not even waiting for the first shot to burst. They'd need that to adjust targeting. One man already hefted another finned shell, ready to send it down field.

"Willie Pete, Jack!" Private Rollins shouted. "Get us some Willie Pete."

From videogames I knew that was white phosphorous, and hefted one out of the box labeled as such. I handed it down to Lucia. "Run this to them."

Lucia was stronger than she looked, so she managed the thirty pound, 120mm shell without too much trouble. Another two soldiers raced up to the wagon, and I slid the rest of the crate over to them. It only had five shells left in it.

The distant firing continued. The enemy killed another Bradley. I saw it rock from the hit and begin to smoke. A Humvee took a hit which sent it spinning. Another hit sent it tumbling, the driver and gunner tossed around inside like ragdolls. For better or worse, they'd been belted in. When the combat vehicle came to a stop on its side, even from a distance, a massive hole in its rear quarter panel clearly showed.

Bursts of smoke rained down between Colonel Davis's column and the domed enemy tanks and smaller personal combat craft.

I handed Lucia another box holding four 81mm mortar shells the same time two *thunk-woosh*es sounded, announcing the 81mm mortars' first volley. All of that continued to the backdrop of the enemy's fire punctuated by cracking *boom*s and the main column's diminished machine gun and Bradley cannon fire.

With the smoke in place, the colonel's surviving combat vehicles picked up their pace of retreat, beginning to cross in front of us over a half mile away.

"Scatter!" someone shouted. "Incoming!"

We all knew what that meant. I slung my rifle and moved to grab my bicycle, even as the wagon jolted forward, Elmore shouting, urging his horse team forward.

"Hang on, Jack!" he yelled over his shoulder as I stumbled and nearly tumbled off.

The wagon would clear the area as fast as I could on my bike.

Lucia was running the opposite direction, away from the crossroad, back the way we'd come. She didn't drop the mortar shell crate even though the forty pounds was slowing her down.

The situation was total chaos, for our side. Desperate retreat by the main column, now without any mortar support as we, the supporting column, had scattered without rhyme or reason to avoid what we had begun to fear.

Earlier in the morning, brief radio bursts in the Humvees reported kinetic impacts striking units forming to make a stand against the enemy, or just stopping. We'd avoided that fate, possibly following Lieutenant Kuhn's random movements and pacing. It didn't matter. Mawk tanks were on the scene, doing the job better than a kinetic strike launched from orbit could.

Several of the Mawks' smaller personal combat craft peeled off from the enemy formation closing on the main column. They, four of them, turned and headed our way.

Chapter 20

It took a few seconds to register what happened after I'd been knocked in the air and then slammed down, my shoulder hitting one of the equally jostled crates. The roiling explosion initially added to the confusion, but then clarified that I survived a near miss by one of the Mawk's kinetic impact weapons.

Elmore's horse team had shown remarkable calm and discipline, until that moment. They broke into a full gallop. The second, more distant kinetic impact targeted the main column. The result for me was tumbling from the shock-racked wagon and hitting the ground hard.

Trying to regain the wind knocked out of me, my mind shouted: Why did I ever abandon my park?

I rolled to my feet and staggered to where I heard gunfire. In the shallow ditch, Private Barhorst was lying prone with just her head and shoulder above the cover offered by the ditch. She was squeezing off aimed, short bursts, just like when we'd faced the dozer.

Behind me the horses and wagon were trying to catch up to the dump truck as it gouted smoke while rumbling through the fallow field. Our column's two Humvees were off to the left, firing their machine guns at two of the speeding personal combat vehicles. The alien machines wove back and forth, like sleek motorcycles navigating a slalom course. That meant the .50 caliber rounds concerned them.

Lucia would be over with Sergeant Eckstein and his men.

Still catching my breath, I unslung my .22 rifle and checked it while keeping below the ditch's brim. Private Barhorst calmly punched out her spent magazine and inserted a new one. She made brief eye contact with me before we both raised our torsos and rifles and opened fire.

The two small combat vehicles closed, but not at

lightning speed as I expected. More like thirty or forty miles per hour. What they didn't do was dodge or weave to avoid our rounds like those facing the .50 caliber bullets did.

Several *vvvvthddd* sounds whipped just over my head, followed by popping *crack*s reaching my ears. I'd played enough videogames to recognize they were firing railguns, with the slugs barely missing overhead. They tugged at air while speeding past. I belatedly heard the small sonic *pop*s from when the rounds left the muzzle, traveling well past the speed of sound. One thing a videogame didn't offer was the smell of seared metal mixed with burnt ozone.

All the while, I squeezed off two rounds, one of which probably hit the vehicle two hundred yards away and closing. My bullet, little more than a gnat annoying a charging, three hundred pound boar. No, I wasn't going to kill it, but my attempt might distract it enough that someone else might. Otherwise, we were dead. All dead.

While the railgun from the combat vehicle on the right missed me high, the one targeting Barhorst sent three rounds her way. The first impacted with a *thud*, kicking up several pail-sized clods of dirt, the second skimmed across the field's topsoil, creating a rooster tail of dirt.

Private Barhorst rolled left and came up again, ready to fire. The alien gunner anticipated her move. The third shot struck her in the shoulder, impacting like a sledge hammer traveling a thousand miles per hour. It obliterated her, slamming the pulverized mess of body and uniform against the far side of the ditch.

I ducked just in time as the *vvvvthddd*-ing slug's pressure wave snapped my head back, dragging my ball cap from my scalp as it passed.

Rather than fight the momentum, I went with it and lay back in the shallow ditch's bottom. The combat vehicle targeting me had been closing on a straight collision course.

That gave me a whacked-out idea.

After setting my rifle aside, I drew my revolver and thumbed back the hammer. Then I held the gun close to my chest and waited.

The mower on whisper mode sound approached, louder than the drone, and in dual mode.

Five feet to my right steamed the remains of Private Barhorst. I was too scared for my own life to get sick. Still, the coppery, charred flesh smell filling the ditch's local region turned my stomach.

I waited, not knowing what to expect. The approaching sensation made me feel like a hamburger pressed down by a spatula. I tightened my grip so the revolver's recoil wouldn't snap it back in my face and pulled the trigger.

Luck was with me, as both combat craft shot over the ditch, one right above me. The overpressure pinned me in place. It must've been due to some sort of anti-gravity mechanism, because I didn't feel the wind, like from a modern human hover craft. The effect wasn't enough to knock the air out of me, but it was close.

Blam!

Even if I'd had a plan other than to shoot and hope for the best, it wouldn't have mattered. It all happened too fast, except for instinct and luck to intervene. Picking out any detail of the small combat vehicle's underside was impossible, let alone target something. A blink and I'd have missed it.

My hearing, after the repeated gunfire and kinetic impacts, wasn't great. Even so, a few seconds after my shot, a *thump* followed a sharp *pop* and a radio static-tearing sound, like a live electrical wire was discharging.

Peering over the backside of the ditch, I saw one of the personal combat vehicles tumbling like a tin can, kicking up clods of dirt whenever the flat bottom's edges touched the ground. The other alien combat vehicle continued on for a moment, firing. One slug connected with the distant dump truck, blasting a hole in the back gate.

How far the railgun slug penetrated into the truck's cargo? No clue from my angle, but if the slug would've hit the wooden wagon, it would've been the end of Elmore. Probably the end of his horse team, too.

The alien tanks were pulverizing every vehicle in the

main column with repeated fire, despite the fact that each already appeared to be shattered hunks. The smaller combat vehicles were doing the same to the wrecked wagons and trailers. They ignored the few surviving soldiers on foot, making their escape. One soldier was trying to right one of the 37mm AA guns. He got a stream of railgun slugs for his effort.

Closer to me, both Humvees were wrecked, with the two small combat vehicles swinging around for another pass. Sergeant Eckstein and Lieutenant Kuhn, along with two other soldiers, were sheltering behind wrecked vehicles, throwing grenades.

Apparently they had the same idea as me, that the anti-gravity drive along the underside was vulnerable. The Mawks must have been unfamiliar with mine warfare, something the Army should take note of.

The four men threw grenades and then hit the dirt as the small attack vehicles sent two more slugs into the hunks of holed metal that had recently been a pair of working Humvees. Then they concentrated on a trailer that already looked like a sieve.

The grenades exploded. One went off directly underneath the nearest alien combat vehicles, sending it into a tumble. With that distraction, I left my ditch and ran toward the vehicle I'd taken down. If the Mawk inside was still alive, I intended to capture it—if I could figure out how to get at the alien inside.

I dropped to the ground when the large enemy tanks took the distant dump truck under fire. The surviving individual attack vehicle pulled away after the truck rolled to a stop. The second tank railgun slug set the truck's shattered contents afire. Amazingly, the driver emerged and sprinted away.

Two minutes later, the dump truck appeared to be a smoking wreck. All the while, I laid prone with my rifle trained on the wrecked alien vehicle, ready to shoot any alien that might emerge.

The surviving small combat vehicle sped to join the

tanks and other combat vehicles. They left the battlefield in the direction from which they'd appeared. At the same time, the three disabled combat vehicles nearby, and four others that had engaged the main column, exploded.

Spectacular flashes accompanied the earsplitting detonations. The blasts didn't fling shrapnel like an exploding artillery shell. The blast energy was directed straight up into the air, and down into the dirt, like a firecracker going off in a steel pipe. The concussive force knocked anyone within thirty yards to the ground, leaving them disoriented for a few minutes. All that remained were small craters and brittle hunks of metal that looked like they'd spent a month soaking in battery acid.

My guess was the energy needed to power the railguns had been used in the self-destruction. The Mawks wouldn't want humans tearing them open and figuring out their technology, or getting their hands on the railguns, and energy systems to power them. They would've done better to allow them to explode outward and kill anyone nearby.

There might've been room for alien drivers in the small combat vehicles, but none were found, although the destructive blast could've consumed the body. That meant the alien combat vehicles must've been controlled remotely, either by operators in the larger tanks, or relayed through the satellite system. Or they were driven by artificial intelligence, ones willing to self-destruct and eliminate themselves in the process.

Chapter 21

The lieutenant directed the reorganization of what was left.

Fifty-seven soldiers killed, two wounded. One lost his hand when a railgun slug connected with his thumb. The other, friendly fire in the calf.

That's what happens when you face alien tanks with railguns and the ability to call down kinetic energy weapons from the heavens above. Maybe an armored battalion could've done better, especially considering the enemy's tactics.

It surprised me that I wasn't more scared in a full-blown battle, that I faced the alien enemy and didn't just turn and run. Maybe I should've had a more powerful firearm. In truth, it wouldn't have made a difference. Unless my gun used .50 caliber bullets, anything I fired wouldn't have deterred the enemy.

Burying Private Barhorst fell to me. Her fellow scout and closest friend was dead, too. Private Washington carried the dead scout over, mainly his upper torso. Better to bury them together. He and two other soldiers were carrying what dead comrades they could to be buried next to those that couldn't be moved, those who'd taken a direct hit. You couldn't lift or drag pulverized remains without leaving half of them behind and a bloody mess on you.

I thought about trying to find my rain poncho, or tent, but Lucia and others were tasked with gathering the scattered food, gear and equipment, and we didn't have the time.

Soft earth beneath the grass made up the side of the ditch, maybe not as soft as the bottom, but I didn't think she'd want to be buried in the bottom of a ditch. Scattered along it were enough rocks to cover the ditch-side grave, deter erosion and keep Barhorst and the others covered.

I had to hurry. There were limited shovels, originally

intended for working with the mortars and such. Heck, I hadn't even thought about needing a shovel until that moment. We hadn't stayed anywhere long enough to make digging proper latrines necessary.

Storm clouds were rolling in from the west, wind gusts pushing them.

Private Washington laid down the torso of the other scout next to Private Barhorst. "This was Private Winst," he said. "James Winst. He was in the reserves. Worked for Wal-Mart."

"What did she do?" I asked, trying to keep a steady voice.

"Private Barhorst? Danielle Barhorst? I think she was a teacher."

The image of her, rifle shouldered, aiming, concentrating. Short, steady bursts. Maybe she believed she was indirectly defending her students? Doing that formed a better image than what was in front of me.

Digging graves, burying brave soldiers that died in a losing struggle, hadn't been on my agenda when I volunteered to join the column. This was war. What did I expect?

I needed to shake off those thoughts, and asked Private Washington, "What were you?"

"That don't matter now," he said, standing up straight. "We're all soldiers now. For however long *that* lasts." He climbed out of the ditch, mumbling, "Make it wider. You got another body coming."

Something was gone from Private Washington. So different from the day he'd fired those TOW missiles, stopping the dozer.

I dug faster, ignoring the worms and bugs. No coffin. Not even a blanket. Just the cooked shreds of their uniforms. I looked around. No marker.

She had a wedding ring, her left hand remaining intact. A husband. Did she have kids? Taboo to ask, or even talk about family, since the Mawks had invaded. So many dead or missing. Private Washington had edged close to that line mentioning her profession before the war.

Was her family the reason she was so steady in the face of danger? More likely than just the students I considered earlier. Was that her motivation—doing her part to save the world, to keep them, her family, safe…or avenged? Was that the root of her bravery?

Me? All I was trying to do was stay alive. Do the right thing, help humanity, sure. But staying alive counted for something. It had to.

I'd find this place again. Its location was burned in my memory. I'd return and place a marker, even though I'd never know the female private's whole story. I wouldn't know anyone's whole story.

And they wouldn't know mine. Not even Lucia.

Thunder rumbled across the sky. The rain was going to make digging a complete mess. Dealing with the ravaged bodies an even messier prospect. Everything would be harder. We'd all be that much more miserable.

Sergeant Eckstein stopped by the ditch where I dug. He was carrying his helmet and a small book. A Bible. I stopped and looked up.

"May I interrupt," he said. "This'll only take a moment."

"Okay," I said, and stood, looking at him from the bottom of the ditch.

He offered a prayer. I don't remember exactly what he said. And he turned to a page in his Bible, but he really didn't need it. He said the words without looking at them. His eyes were on the ravaged bodies I was preparing to bury. I don't remember those words either. Just something he mentioned was from Ecclesiastes.

After he moved on, I got back to digging. Nearby, some soldiers were singing. I recognized the song. A weird memory connected it to one of the *Star Trek* movies, where Mr. Scott played a set of bagpipes for Spock's funeral. I never went to church and didn't know the words, or I would've sung, too. Instead, I listened and shoveled, the bagpipe memory blending with their words.

The downpour did make burying our dead a muddy

mess. At least the storm drops hid my tears.

The cascading sheets hid more than just mine.

The aliens hadn't targeted our El Camino. The horse wagon escaped unscathed, and they also ignored the clickity-engined Dodge Dart that stalled out when the battle started, but was running again. Railgun slugs did strike the dump truck, destroying the tail gate and part of the dump bed. Most of the shattered cargo and equipment it carried had burned, but the storm's rains stopped the fire before it reached the fuel tanks or melted the tires. A few vehicles from the main column survived, including an old Ford LTD station wagon, with actual fake woodgrain panels, and a 1940s vintage Dodge pickup truck, refurbished, with a flame paint job and all.

They'd salvaged one .50 caliber machine gun, which was being bolted to the El Camino's bed. One of the 81mm mortars was intact, as was one of the 105mm howitzers.

Lieutenant Kuhn was bringing the latter along, which didn't make sense. We were already chaining our trailers together, to be hauled like a train with a short string of cars. That meant we'd have to stay more to roads and not cut across fields. My guess was that Lieutenant Kuhn figured the aliens wouldn't consider our column's remnants as much of a threat.

Deep down, devastating as the Mawk's attack proved to be, it could've—it should've—been worse. Their tactics and effective use of firepower, and the odd ventral susceptibility made me wonder. Had we faced the second or even third string forces? Were the controllers, if the units had been controlled remotely, inexperienced, or overwhelmed with the number of targets across the nation, across the globe, all moving at the same time?

Flood the zone, Elmore had said. The enemy was draining the flood, that was for sure.

And we all had bikes. A few had been damaged or destroyed. But with so few of us alive, fewer than forty, that wasn't going to be a concern.

Scuttlebutt was, Colonel Davis expected to die. Not a martyr type thing. He just knew that his main column was an obvious target. From what little I knew of him, mostly from our short meeting, and what others had said, he was just doing his part. Doing his job, his duty, no matter the cost. No matter the sacrifice.

I wondered if the men and women who died felt the same. I thought on that for about three seconds. Everyone around me was dedicated to the mission, even though we didn't know what it was. The Army wouldn't have asked its surviving elements to commit a suicide run, at least not unless there was a purpose. Colonel Davis believed it. His men believed it and, in the end, so did I.

I was one of his men. And that was just it. I was a man. A remnant of a hunted species on its way out. Maybe we all just didn't know we were already dead, even if not individually, then as a species.

We were still traveling south. I didn't quite know why. Maybe to maintain the illusion, doing our part to keep the zone flooded as best we could.

The enemy's tactics hadn't been exactly impressive, but they'd been effective. Their goal had been to destroy military vehicles, and shatter our largest wagons and trailers and trucks. They'd repeatedly shot them up, even when they were beyond repair.

Whatever we were going to deliver, that'd been their target. That they just destroyed everything military and mobile said they didn't know exactly what we were up to, what we intended to deliver. It also suggested they probably didn't know our destination.

We all were with Lieutenant Kuhn, determined to follow him, but broken. A mixture of going through the motions and stubbornness, a sort of fatalism kept us going. Sure, there was an underlying burning, loyalty to a cause. There just wasn't a lot left to fuel it.

That changed when the lieutenant shared something.

Something important.

Chapter 22

First Lieutenant Kuhn was a middle-aged man, tall with dark hair, a little gray starting to show. His hair was short, but not military short. Really, except for those that shaved their heads, people's hair tended to be a little on the longer side. Not shoulder length, for guys. More like mid-ear or a little below. It wasn't easy to find a barber. Beards, or at least a decent growth of whiskers, was common, too. And a little on the greasy side. We washed and cleaned up when we could, but physical labor and limited changes of clothes meant we weren't going to win any fashion awards. We would've offended our fellow citizens a year ago, if we were standing in line next to them at a fast food restaurant. But today? We were all used to it.

I methodically brushed my teeth, on a set routine. Lucia did too, as did most of the soldiers and folks traveling with us, even if it meant using a finger wrapped in cloth to rub their teeth clean. Everyone kept track of their water filtering straw, and they'd collected as many from the battlefield as possible.

Besides being a middle-aged officer, Lieutenant Kuhn struck me as smart. He thought before he spoke, and made quick, decisive decisions. Mischievous, too. Under other circumstances, I bet he was the type who loved playing practical jokes.

Times change, and his grim words brought me back to reality.

"Even though we got a few licks in, the Mawks thrashed us pretty good."

Six of us were gathered around the lieutenant and Sergeant Eckstein. In the meantime a few sentries stood watch a few hundred yards distant. The others were out of earshot, setting up camp, little that that entailed.

We'd travelled several miles from where we'd buried our dead. The storm had passed. This was the place where the lieutenant ordered a stop, near an entrance ramp onto I-75. Within sight was the burned remains of what must've been a massive warehouse complex.

My clothes were still damp, although I did get my backpack and poncho before we moved out. By then, the storm had soaked me. Soaked just about everyone, except Elmore, who'd had his rain gear stowed next to him on his wagon.

Our commanding officer stood next to the end of Elmore's flatbed wagon, with Sergeant Eckstein one step to his right. Elmore was there, on his bench seat, looking over his shoulder and listening while his horses snorted and occasionally stamped. We were the only two civilians at this meeting. The other four men were soldiers, a corporal and three privates.

The lieutenant continued in his baritone voice. "However, since they missed their target, our cargo for delivery, our trek will most assuredly continue.

"Our trek would have anyway. There are columns marching without a cargo such as ours. Decoys. But we are not one of those, gentlemen."

I wondered why he was talking to me about this, and to Elmore Foltz. Upon a quick second thought, Elmore's wagon must be carrying the cargo.

"Now, some of you may be wondering why I have decided to reveal this to you."

He made eye contact with each of us. "Because, besides myself, Sergeant Eckstein, Sergeant Yin, and Mr. Foltz, no one knows any details about the cargo. Other than me and them, everyone else is equally in the dark about our destination. Under normal circumstances, this information wouldn't be shared with privates and corporals, and two civilians, without such individuals undergoing detailed background and security checks.

"As you have probably surmised, normal circumstances evaporated the instant the first barrage of EMPs struck. Aliens invading Earth, as bad as any science fiction nightmare. Worse, because in those, humanity usually wins despite the odds. That, gentlemen, is fiction. What we're facing here is nonfiction, with the odds heavily against humanity."

The lieutenant lifted his shoulders before tilting his head to the left and right, like he was trying to get a crick out of his neck. "Corporal Jones, Privates Finch, Gorski and Vippin, I am ordering that the information I am about to divulge will not be spoken of without expressed permission, or if dire circumstances require. Mr. Fairbanks, I have decided to include you based upon Colonel Davis's assessment. He believed keeping secrets is part of your nature, as is an innate loyalty for humanity, which overrides your instinct for personal survival. Sergeants Yin and Eckstein concur."

Sergeant Eckstein made eye contact with me, a stern look, saying, 'Don't make me regret sticking my neck out for you.' Sergeant Yin had been the colonel's personal guard back in the library in Toledo and was currently organizing the establishment of our camp.

"While I am ordering the others, Mr. Fairbanks, do I have your word not to divulge what I am about to share, except in the case of dire need, which I don't believe is necessary to define?"

"I understand and swear," I said. "Dire need would be along the lines of you and all others are dead or incapacitated, and the success of the mission is in jeopardy." Really what else was there to say?

"Okay then," the lieutenant said. "Mr. Foltz, Sergeants Yin, Eckstein and, of course, myself, are the only ones remaining in the 37th IBCT that know what we're to deliver and exactly where.

"I shall share with you what we carry, with the intention to deliver. Exactly to where, I will share with other individuals. They, like you, will be ordered or sworn to secrecy. It won't be a mystery as to who knows what." He paused for a breath and gave an ironic smile. "I will be meeting with them as soon as I have finished with you."

The lieutenant flicked his head back, drawing our eyes

over his shoulder, toward the front part of the wagon. "If something should happen to Foltz, Yin, Eckstein and me, you should know that the crate nearest the bench seat contains a thermonuclear warhead. Four-hundred seventy-five kiloton yield."

Somehow, that didn't surprise me. My discussion with Elmore about the narco sub delivery hinted at something major. Nuclear warheads were probably the only weapon we humans had that could hurt the enemy in a meaningful way.

The soldiers that just learned of the cargo either nodded their heads or smiled. They didn't seem shocked or, even less likely, concerned.

And 475 kilotons of blast power. I did a high school history report and recalled that the atomic bomb dropped on Hiroshima was 15 kilotons. I was sure that the USA had more powerful hydrogen bombs, but the one resting less than twenty feet from me, the one I'd practically sat on while riding with Elmore, could do more than destroy a city.

Lieutenant Kuhn continued after his pause. "Colonel Davis determined that stowing it on what he called 'an archaic horse-drawn wagon,' as opposed to a modern combat vehicle, would increase the odds the enemy might overlook it, should they attack. It would appear he was correct. They didn't even press their attack on our old diesel dump truck, not like they did our Humvees and Bradleys."

The lieutenant was right. The colonel had been right. By the end of the fight, the Army's combat vehicles resembled coffee cans blasted by 00 buckshot, from three directions at once. Compare that to the fact that the aliens hadn't even taken a pot shot at the horse-drawn wagon.

"We were lucky," Lieutenant Kuhn continued. "They hit us with light forces, equivalent to what we humans might use in, say, heavily armed police in riot control. Not true military combat vehicles." The lieutenant shook his head while staring at the muddy ground. "From what's been reported, the Mawks' main battle tanks are festooned with weapons and can slough off armor-piercing discarding sabot rounds from our M1A2 Abrams. And their undercarriage is capable of withstanding anti-tank mines." He shook his head. "I feel for the poor bastards facing those."

No sense feeling for them, I thought. Anyone taking on one of those was probably dead.

Lieutenant Kuhn included Lucia in the second group, meaning she learned our destination, maybe more. I wondered what Colonel Davis had seen in her. I didn't ask Lucia what she learned, and she didn't ask me about the secret cargo we were delivering.

I think the battle changed me. It was different than fighting humans, or even dozers. Being part of an Army unit, even as an auxiliary or a conscript, that meant something, being part of a unit directly fighting for humanity.

We stood watch for four hours while most of the survivors slept, or worked to get the vehicles ready to continue our journey south. The battle had changed Lucia, too. A mixture of pride showed in the way she carried herself, probably like my realization of the greater purpose I was serving, looking beyond my personal survival. Still, there was also a hint of haunted look in her eyes. She'd seen death plenty, just like me, but the battle we'd survived was different. A harbinger of any upcoming battles.

I wondered if Lucia saw the same thing in me.

I didn't ask.

What would it be like to actually see a Mawk? Talk to one, if that was even possible? Fight and even kill one? I glanced down at my .22 rifle, wondering if my ability to kill one was even a possibility.

Chapter 23

"Get over here, quick," Lucia whispered. She sounded excited, but kept her voice low so that she didn't disturb anyone sleeping nearby. We were in an open field, along a rural county road, next to a stand of woods. About three hundred yards away was a farmhouse, a garage, and several barns. Abandoned and nothing really of value there, except for an unopened box of Cap'n Crunch with Crunch Berries cereal. Some kid had apparently stuffed it under his bed and forgot about it.

Lucia held the colorful '20% More' cereal box now.

She explained Private Washington found it while a squad scavenged the house. He shared a handful with everyone along the way and we were at the end of the line. That still left us luckier than most.

Lucia shared her handful and crumbs with me before we climbed into our bedrolls set up under our tent. It wasn't our original tent we'd brought. That was lost in the battle. What we had now was a canvas tarp set up into a small A-frame, with a few stakes, cord and poles. Not much, but better than nothing if it rained.

We were up and moving, a few hours before sunrise, getting ready for our turn at watch.

Still brushing my teeth, I walked over to Lucia, and looked up to where she pointed at the night sky, about thirty degrees above the horizon.

I took a swig of water from my canteen and swished it around in my mouth, trying to see what she was pointing at. Instead of spitting, I swallowed the water down. "That shooting star?"

There was a pin of light, like a small star traveling low across the night sky. Maybe it was a meteor, because it didn't burn out. It was bigger than Venus, with a blueish tint.

"It's one of their ships," Lucia explained, still

whispering. "That short private, Gorski, told me to watch. He said they're orbiting the world, up there. He don't know how many but sometimes you can see two or three. He said the sun's reflecting off them, and that you used to be able to see the International Space Station the same way, before the Mawks came and blew it up." Some of the excitement drained from her voice. "Before they came and blew everything up."

It was too dark to see her scowl, but I knew it was there, on her face.

I handed her my canteen and picked up my rifle. "You about ready?"

"Yeah," she said, after swallowing a drink. She screwed on the cap and handed my canteen back. While rolling up our blankets and folding the stakes and cord and poles in the canvas of our tent, Lucia continued in a low whisper. "He said the lieutenant saw a diagram with figures about the alien ships out there, their orbital patterns, and some of their satellites, and memorized it. That's how he knows when to switch directions to avoid getting hit by their space rocks."

Memorizing all that would be tough. I was good at placing things in my memory, like where I buried equipment, but nothing like what the lieutenant had apparently done. What I buried didn't move, and I guessed the orbiting ships and satellites weren't on a convenient twenty-four hour schedule.

"They must have some smaller maneuvering ships," I commented.

"Yeah, Jack. But there's a whole world of us running around and only so many of them. Gorski explained that the aliens got AIs programmed to watch the earth's surface. They got algorithms that they use to determine targets. Because of that, the lieutenant moves slowly, and he zig zags, like we're scavenging, making us look like we're not moving with a direct purpose. He said we have beasts of burden, too. All those lower us on the threat level. Means we're not good targets to them."

"There's a lot less of us targets running around than

there used to be."

Lucia bumped her shoulder into mine. "I've been learning you ain't a morning person, Jack. You never look for good things to happen until the sun's shining."

"Never liked outdoor camping much, even when I was a Boy Scout. Cabins okay. Tents with rain and bugs…"

"I wasn't ever a Brownie or Girl Scout."

Lucia picked up the blankets while I grabbed the tent.

"Well, we better pack this in the El Camino," I warned, still whispering, "and be on time for our watch, or the lieutenant'll double it tomorrow night."

Walking over to the El Camino, past sleeping soldiers, I smiled, thinking to myself: See, Lucia. The sun isn't even up and I'm anticipating that we'll survive through tomorrow night.

I got to drive the old Dodge Dart for a while. The engine sounded iffy at times, and driving meant little more than moving forward on idle. It was less work than bike riding. It was also boring, and gave me a claustrophobic feeling. Lucia, riding next to me, fell asleep.

The trunk and back seat were packed with sleeping gear and sacks of dog food, and the trunk also had some spare weapons and a crate with some water filtering straws. The trailer pulled behind carried bikes and backpacks and two sleeping soldiers.

If the aliens attacked while I was crawling along on this little narrow road, between fields, with ditches on both sides, behind the LTD station wagon and in front of the diesel-fuming dump truck, we were dead meat. But at least we weren't sucking the dump truck's diesel fumes, and would die with clean lungs.

Clean lungs were on the agenda as I sucked on the tube to get the siphoning going from the abandoned Silverado, a dually.

Since our force size was smaller and potentially less intimidating to any nearby residents, we avoided towns and cities along the interstate and focused on long rural stretches to scavenge for fuel. Bringing vehicles would invite desperate folks, so we used bikes and trailing carts as always. But, instead of just me and Lucia working as a team, Privates Gorski and Washington were with us.

Lucia stood in the truck's bed, while Gorski and Washington watched from different areas along the highway.

I got the siphoning job because I carried the wimpiest gun, according to Gorski, and I was the fastest at it. Plus, I suck at Rock-Paper-Scissors.

We'd had to cross a field and railroad tracks before using wire cutters to get through the fence. That allowed us access where the grass, while deep, wasn't filling a steep ditch. Anything having too steep of a drop, or climb, would make hauling the carts behind my and Lucia's bikes impossible. Gorski and Washington would help us across barriers, if needed. More importantly, they were our protection.

The column wasn't dry, or even short on fuel. We scavenged houses and farms, almost always abandoned. Once we even found a 500 gallon above ground tank, nearly full. That diesel dump truck, however, drank fuel like an elephant in the desert. They were also running short on lead additives for the older cars whose engines needed it. I didn't know what would happen once those ran out.

Still, even if we weren't anywhere near low on fuel, the lieutenant wanted to stay topped off.

"Woman," Lucia warned. "Old woman with a shotgun, coming out of that old house."

Since the truck had been southbound, and the old house about fifty yards from the northbound side, I was a decent distance from the woman. My back was also to her, so I began splitting my attention between the hose filling the first red gas container and the woman.

The old white house had a big dozer hole in the side nearest the highway, so it being empty and abandoned seemed like a good bet. She was wearing an oversized flannel shirt and bib overalls that were stained and patched along the legs. Glasses taped together and unkempt gray hair made her look a bit on the unpredictable side.

The fact that she waved and held her shotgun under the crook of her arm, pointed down, only made me feel marginally more comfortable. Lucia, above me, stood rigid, with her hunting rifle held so that she could raise and fire it with little delay.

"You there, boy," the old woman called. "I've been counting on that diesel fuel for my generator this winter."

I kept siphoning.

"Shoulda taken it then," Lucia shouted back.

The woman was near the wire fence that ran along the highway. "Stays fresh better in the tanks."

"Shoulda moved the truck then."

"What, and give someone a reason to explore my house?" The old woman looked to her left, toward where Private Washington was standing. "Army Man, you'd take what an old woman would need?"

"I'm betting she's not alone," I said up to Lucia.

"Can't see anyone in the windows, Jack. But that don't mean nothing."

Private Washington shouted, "How'd you survive that dozer that tore into your house?"

"That?" The woman gestured over her shoulder. "Me and Frank did that to make it look like a dozer tore into the house. You didn't answer my question, Army Man."

"Where's Frank?"

"You think I'm some sort of fool woman, Army Man?"

"No, ma'am."

"Frank's backing her up," I told Lucia while pinching off the flow as the first container was full.

"Uh huh," she replied, looking around, watching for a possible ambush.

"Jack, stop siphoning the truck," Washington ordered. He walked a little closer to the woman, not quite placing himself between the truck we were siphoning and her. He slung his rifle along the way.

"You want him to pour back what he's got?" Lucia

asked, sarcasm dripping from the question.

"Thank you, Army Man."

"Washington," he replied. "My name's Washington, and you're welcome."

"Well, Army Man Washington, you and your group better stay on the west side of I-75."

"Why is that, ma'am?"

"Unless you got a few hundred soldiers and tanks, which it doesn't look like you do," she said, pointing over her shoulder with her thumb, "there's a marauding gang moving down Route 235. I hear tell they're over by Indian Lake."

"How'd you hear that, ma'am?"

"You never heard of ham radio, Army Man Washington?"

We were on the road, moving south through the night. Lieutenant Kuhn didn't want to risk a confrontation. It could be the old woman made up the marauding gang to spook us into leaving the area. We had a lot more to lose by staying, if she was telling the truth.

Rumor had it, there was another military column moving south, down I-71 to Route 23, and another paralleling I-77. Someone even talked about a decoy group on Route 68 not too far to the east of us. This information came from Lucia, who'd shared it as I drove the Dart along the dark narrow road before she dozed off. It was hard for me to do much more than listen, as the cloudy night meant it was hard for me to see the vehicle in front of me. We never moved at a steady rate, and without lights, the chance of an accident, or missing a turn, forced me to concentrate 100% of the time.

Lucia was good at carousing. The male soldiers liked talking to her. Made sense, she was good looking. The scar on her chin made her appear even more dangerous, and attractive to the soldiers. And, since she'd joined with me, eating regularly, her figure had begun to fill out, maybe somewhat like it was before the Mawks arrived.

I smiled, knowing she wasn't one to ignore any advantage she had. A few of the soldiers had joked about us 'sleeping together.' That wasn't going to happen. Not the way they meant. We'd gone through a lot together, trusted each other. That kind of chemistry just wasn't there.

Sergeant Eckstein told me the colonel had forbidden any sexual contact during the move south. In addition to Lucia, there were two female soldiers still with us. Lieutenant Kuhn kept the colonel's no sexual contact policy. I knew better than to think it wouldn't happen, not if a man and a woman, or another combination, really wanted to do it.

In such a small unit, keeping that secret away from the lieutenant's ears would be tough, but not impossible.

Besides, as evidenced by Lucia beginning to snore next to me, the constant stress and long hours of movement and activity, simple bone weariness, made scheming to find even ten minutes to do the deed less appealing.

Thinking on that, I pulled my comb and ran it through my hair and smacked my face a few times, trying to keep alert and avoid drifting off the road, or into the station wagon hauling the 105mm howitzer ahead of me.

I missed Luther, and wondered what part he would be playing in the march south. He might've turned away Colonel Davis, but if he hadn't, he might've become the colonel's second man, after Sergeant Yin. Although Yin survived, when the colonel hadn't, it was more by luck than skill. Luther had average luck, so maybe he would've survived. Maybe not.

I wanted to look around at the countryside, using Luther's night vision monocular. Sergeant Eckstein had borrowed it. His assignment was to scout behind the column and watch for anyone picking up on our trail.

The sound of the clickety slant-6 engine—the column's mechanic told me that was what ran under the hood—droned on like a mechanical lullaby. After administering myself a few more sharp slaps, I figured I'd make it through the half hour. Then it'd be my turn to get some shuteye.

Chapter 24

Lucia was far more gregarious than me. My circle of friends among the column consisted of her, Elmore Foltz, Private Washington, and Sergeant Eckstein. The two soldiers were always busy, so I mostly chatted with Elmore.

It was a hot afternoon, the sun blazing down. The trek had worn heavily on his horse team. It was obvious, even to someone that knew so little about horses as me. After talking about that concern while I sat on the bench next to Elmore and finished a can of tuna for lunch, I broached the subject of the nuclear device we were carrying. Elmore already knew about it, and he talked to a lot more people than me, and I was getting curious. Nobody was within earshot.

I scanned the unplanted field to our right, covered in weeds, many of them topped with yellow flowers. Bees busy visiting them, collecting pollen for their hives. "You've seen those Mawk space ships crossing the night sky?"

Elmore squinted up at the one o'clock sun. "The white and blue dots, sort of like big stars looking to crash some time?"

"That would be a yes?"

He chuckled and spat over the side and onto the pavement of the narrow county road. "Once or twice, but mostly I sleep when you can see 'em."

"I've been thinking," I said, pausing to lick my spoon and sat the empty tuna fish can aside. "How we're going to use our cargo against them. If they came from subs, they would've had rockets attached. Intercontinental ballistic missiles. I think they were built to launch and reach space and then come back down over their target."

"Makes sense, Jack."

"So why separate them? They've got to be hard to put back together."

"Rattling around in a truck might scramble their

computer chip connections."

"I was thinking. They could shoot them down with their railguns. Their ships have to have railguns."

Elmore didn't say anything. He just nodded for me to continue.

"We had the tech to shoot ICBMs down, I think. Patriot missiles, probably something else. At least Israel had anti-ballistic missile rockets or whatever you'd call them. And we gave them money and technology. So why wouldn't the aliens have even better?"

"You got me with that one, Jack."

We rode in silence for a few minutes until I said, "Maybe we're going to sneak in and plant them in the cities they build or near their ships when they land."

I thought back to when I did my report on the atomic bomb dropped on Nagasaki. I recalled seeing a picture with a big artillery gun and a yellow mushroom cloud rising in the distance. "Maybe they're going to use them as artillery shells?"

"Like the artillery gun that sergeant is always watching over?"

"No," I said. "The one I saw in a picture once was a lot bigger. If they even rigged it so that it would work, I bet you'd be caught in some of the blast, or maybe radiation."

"If that's all it took to blow up one of their ships. Kill a few thousand of them, maybe more, I'd be first in line to pull the trigger." He grinned. "Well, I don't think Sergeant Eckstein's artillery gun has a trigger. Even bigger ones wouldn't either, I expect."

"I know what you mean," I said, thinking over what Elmore had said, coming to a conclusion. "You know, Elmore, I can't say I'd be first in line, but if I was asked, or had to do it, I would. Same as you."

"Ha," he laughed. "Thought you young folks're supposed to be more reckless than old guys like me."

"How do you think we know where they're going to land?"

Elmore gave me a sideways glance, like I was stupid.

"CIA or FBI interrogating them." He spat again. "Could be the KGB. They're ruthless bastards, you know. They'd share that kind of thing with us, if they found out."

I looked over my shoulder behind us, and then east, toward the interstate. "We have to make it there."

"You thinking on that gang of renegades the lieutenant is trying to outpace?"

"If they're following, trying to catch us." In truth, I was more concerned about another attack by the aliens. I glanced up at the sky, half expecting a kinetic weapon to impact along our line.

Elmore snapped the reins and urged his team on. "Brunhilda and Bud, they're doing okay. But in a few minutes I'm gonna send you to tell the lieutenant that Cadaver and Comanche need a rest. Must rest if'n he wants my team to keep pulling."

Elmore got six hours rest for his team. Everyone needed it, human and equine. We then pushed on past dark. Lucia rode her bike next to me as rear guard, watching behind. Periodically we stopped, listened and watched, using Luther's night vision monocular. Once we'd spotted a dozer coming in. Lucia with her compound bow, and six other men with crossbows, loosed a volley of arrows coated with construction adhesive. That drove it away.

Crawlers were even less of a concern, as long as we watched for them. Unless we were in camp, they usually came at us from the rear, picking up our scent and trailing us from behind.

"We're not making as many turns as we used to," Lucia said, left foot on the ground and right foot on its pedal, ready to start moving again.

"I think we're falling behind schedule," I replied, checking the road and countryside behind us. It was too dark to see much, and Lucia had the monocular. Mostly I listened.

We'd crossed over I-70 and word was the lieutenant expected to camp for the rest of the night after another hour.

Lucia held the monocular up to her eye one more time, and slowly scanned the area behind us. "Don't they say, 'Better late than never,' Jack?"

"Not if late means the end of the line for humans, Lucia. The end of the world."

She handed me the night vision monocular. "You really planning on saving the world with that carnival gun of yours?"

Despite the darkness, I knew Lucia had a smirk on her face. Slowly, from left to right, I scanned the terrain. "Why do you think I left the park, Lucia?"

She held the monocular's case open for me. After it was closed up and stuffed in my backpack, Lucia leaned into my shoulder. "You ain't no Captain America, Jack."

"No doubt about that, Lucia. I'm not planning on doing anything spectacular. Just throwing in, doing my part." I shrugged. "A worker ant marching out with the army ants to defend the nest."

A half minute passed in silence. I bumped my elbow into hers. "So, why'd you leave the park?"

She hesitated before answering. "I followed you, Jack."

Her statement was matter of fact. No sarcasm. No attitude.

Turning her bike around, she said, "Come on. We're getting too far behind."

CHAPTER 25

A dozen of us stood next to Elmore's wagon, listening to Sergeant Eckstein as he relayed Lieutenant Kuhn's orders. As usual, Elmore sat in his bench seat, listening. I'd scavenged a sturdy foam pillow for him, which he complained about, but put to use. The bench's original padding had been old and compressed even before the trek south began. The folded blanket supplementing the original padding made the ride only marginally better.

Lucia was on my right and Washington on my left.

Most of us were assigned to the LTD Station wagon, and the 105mm howitzer it towed. That included the sergeant, Lucia and Washington, and another private named Harpster. The station wagon was now towing a wooden farm wagon, probably one used to haul bales of hay. The howitzer was on the farm wagon, facing forward and chained down. Maybe spiked down to the wooden bottom, too. Lucia said that on concrete the howitzer couldn't be set up and stabilized. Firing it would probably wreck the gun, according to the sergeant. But, mounted on the large-wheeled farm wagon, it could fire over the top of the LTD station wagon, even in direct fire mode. Our own mobile cannon, so to speak.

My guess was that the setup made the artillery piece, indirect or direct fire, inaccurate as hell. But even if it missed, it'd make a big noise. I wouldn't want to be in the station wagon when it fired. Louder than anything, and there had to be a concussive force emitted when the shell was blasted out through the muzzle. The old LTD might somewhat shelter anyone inside from that, maybe.

Lucia was to be an ammunition handler—basically to relay shells from the back of the crates on the wagon, or from the station wagon. She said there were shells preset to detonate fast for direct fire, and even a few beehive rounds packed with fleshettes. Each shell was marked with grease pens so she, like everyone else not trained by the Army, could tell the difference.

Otherwise, Lucia was assigned to use her hunting rifle and scope.

Me and Private Garcia, a skinny Mexican-American who'd only had one week of boot camp when the Mawks arrived, were to provide cover for Elmore and his wagon. The thought was that the more people we put on it, the more attention it would draw.

It made sense. The horses were vulnerable, but so were all of our vehicles, especially their tires. Of course, we could find replacement tires on abandoned cars. Replacement horses was another question.

"Okay," the sergeant said. "Everyone's had at least eight hours rest. Mr. Foltz, you and your horses got twelve. Now, we have to push hard."

Rumors had already spread, even before reports got back to the lieutenant.

There was a well-armed and organized gang in Cincinnati. More members than in Toledo, all the gangs added together. Apparently the seeding south of I-70 had been lighter than north of it. At least in Ohio. I imagined, without Bradleys or Humvees, we'd look like a bunch of school busses, like the one the Bankstreeters in Toledo shot up to get its supplies.

We had some firepower, but didn't really know the lay of the land, and the lieutenant felt speed would be our best ally. Bypassing Cincinnati, which had been renamed Lucifer's Outpost by the gang who called themselves The Minions, wasn't really an option. There was an apparent deadline for us to make it to our destination.

Sergeant Eckstein summed it up. "We're moving fast, using the Cropper Bridge to cross."

That made sense to me. I'd driven across the main bridge on I-75. The highway leading to the bridge was surrounded by hillsides and overpasses. More places for an ambush. Once across the Ohio River, it was a little better, but pretty steep going up, if I recalled. The interstate loop to the west was less urbanized, with patches of trees and green areas, and some small lakes and ponds. At least according to the maps they showed everyone.

"Anyone gets shot," Sergeant Eckstein said, "anyone goes down, toss them in a trailer or vehicle. Any vehicle that gets disabled, set fire to it. Leave them nothing. Show them the futility of the exercise."

The soldier who'd lost his hand to a rail gun slug died a day afterwards. The guy shot in the calf wasn't doing well. Fever was getting him. Being on the move with no medical facilities or medicine to speak of made survival odds pretty long.

"Except for the horse-drawn wagon."

Everyone knew that, but only a handful, like me, knew why.

We were going for broke.

"If it comes to a fight, shoot back using cover, if and when you can, but keep moving. If we get pinned down, allow them to react and fully mobilize, we're screwed."

We were also signing up to be lunch, since The Minions, according to local reports, had resorted to cannibalism to help nourish its members.

Sergeant Yin had done recon. On his way back, he'd disabled two of their early warning vehicles, both old minibikes run on lawnmower motors. They had regular pedal bikes, mostly mountain bikes. Our target bridge was about eight miles from the main city, and we had to get across before word reached The Minions' leadership and they responded in force.

If they used radios, they risked bringing alien attention down on them. Oddly, for once, the Mawks' attack capabilities might benefit our side.

Sergeant Yin also made it to the bridge and back, removing several of a bulldozer's wires, disabling it. One of our mechanics had them, and could re-install them in a minute, as could Sergeant Yin. The lieutenant thought we might be able to take advantage of that, since they had the bridge blocked with debris and cars intervening in two places along the elevated approach. The bulldozer was preplaced near the bridge, ready to push an opening in the barrier, or add more wrecked cars to reinforce it. We could use it to unblock the way more effectively than with our dump truck.

We rebuilt the sides of the dump truck's bed, destroyed by railgun slugs, using scavenged plywood and boards. It wasn't as strong, but allowed it to carry more gear and equipment, and also shelter some soldiers. Their job was to provide defensive fire from within the truck.

The lieutenant had also spoken with a number of locals who lived in the shadow of the gang that controlled the city, and the bridge. They reported food was short, despite purges of those deemed disloyal to The Minions. They'd resorted to launching old boats with nets to fish the river. Two groups, not as well armed as ours, tried to cross. One got shot to pieces. The other tried to negotiate passage, giving up part of their supplies, and were promptly overrun and killed, or captured and feasted upon, to the last man, woman and child.

Now that we were near the city, we had to move fast, before word got back to the city's gang leadership. They didn't have a lot of scouting outside the city, as the locals—The Minions called them Ferals—killed them on sight.

Three locals even joined us. They were former military. That didn't mean I trusted them.

The sergeant made eye contact with each of us. "Everyone knows your primary and secondary responsibilities. Any questions?"

We all shook our heads. No questions.

I was to ride next to the wagon. Keep watch, and shoot anybody that shoots at us. If Elmore got shot, I was to drive the horses. Elmore had shown me the basics while riding with him. He even let me drive them a few times.

Controlling the horse team was harder than it looked. Bud was a real screwball of a horse, if that could be said of a horse. He liked to try to do the opposite of what I wanted him to do.

Elmore spoke up. "Sergeant, maybe it won't come to a fight."

Sergeant Eckstein raised an expressive eyebrow. "Let's just say, Mr. Foltz, it's better to prepare for the worst."

The horse driver spat on the pavement. "Just checking, Sergeant. If you agreed with that statement, I was gonna ask Private Washington to find you a straitjacket."

Chapter 26

We'd crossed over into Indiana during the night and waited until just before sunrise. A nerve-wracking night, on a road with tall trees on either side, hiding us.

Now we raced down toward the end of that road, a sign telling me it was Mt. Pleasant. Woods remained close in on both sides. They were supposed to keep us concealed until the road dumped onto a highway.

When I said 'raced' I meant a sustained five to eight miles per hour. The horses were slowing us down. Actually, they might've been a weak link, because they weren't fast over a really long haul pulling a wagon, and The Minions might see them as food and shoot them. But the Mawks had already proven they'd overlook them, and anything they pulled. Part of their computer targeting decision algorithm? For some reason, the lieutenant considered a Mawk attack a distinct possibility.

Elmore's horse team had only one vehicle behind it, our dump truck. It would be our last ditch effort to blow through the blockaded bridge, if all else failed.

Elmore had metal sheets, like a sandwich board, protecting him, and a helmet.

I'd given my bulletproof vest to Lucia. I wouldn't take 'no' for an answer, no matter how ill-fitting she claimed it was. She was up near the front of the column, with Eckstein, Harpster and Washington, and the howitzer. Lieutenant Kuhn intended to use it in direct fire mode. I did have a helmet, which didn't make me feel totally naked. I had my .22 rifle slung and my revolver on my hip, and my double-barrel shotgun lying in the wagon.

Elmore had an AR-15, which looked like a military rifle, but wasn't capable of automatic fire. He said he was a horrible shot, and offered it to me. I was a horrible shot with anything but my little .22. Maybe the inaccuracy was psychological on my part.

We merged onto State Highway 1. Scattered trees and open fields were on the hillside to our left. We passed a few abandoned buildings on our right. Teams on bikes ahead of the column were to check that out. It'd get harder as we closed in toward The Minions' territory.

So far there hadn't been any gunfire.

Soon there were scattered houses on both sides. I eyed the windows of each. A few had the commonly seen holes torn into them by dozers, and smaller ones chewed through by crawlers. I wasn't interested in those, unless they contained someone holding a rifle.

Supposedly our three former military friends had gone ahead with Sergeant Yin and Private Gorski. In theory, the Ferals would leave us alone, and not betray us. We were going to hit The Minions. The more cannibal gangsters we took out, weakening them, the better for the Ferals.

Then came metal guard rails, with a wooded hillside to my left and a drop off to my right. The drop offered glimpses of a railroad track and a narrow road, like the type we normally travelled along.

Lucia thought we'd get hit in the front first. My thought was that, if The Minions got word in time, they'd ambush us, hitting us everywhere at once, and folding us in from the front and back. It's what I would do.

We broke into the open, our column spread out for two hundred yards.

The column stopped just past a pond. Two bearded men in camouflage outfits, reminiscent of turkey hunters, stood next to four bodies draped over a fence.

They'd taken out The Minion outpost, maybe using the big knives on their hips and compound bows leaning against the fence, since I hadn't heard any gunfire. Blood still dripped from the bodies.

I hurried and filled buckets for Elmore's horse team. The fact that the Ferals acted on our behalf, and the chance for a breather, gave me hope. Maybe the lieutenant had shared something of our mission, and the need to reach our destination.

Fifteen minutes later, we pressed on. Although there'd been a Minion outpost, we were in no man's land, about two miles until we reached Minion territory. Then, about another two miles to the bridge. Every minute without warning meant less time for the cannibalistic gang's response.

Sergeant Yin estimated they had at least thirty armed men and women stationed at the bridge blockade, most posted on the north side of the river. A few more men appeared to be unarmed workers of some sort. The Ferals said those 'unwilling' workers were serving some form of punishment.

Better than being eaten.

The roads were largely cleared, with abandoned cars pushed off to the side or into ditches, allowing for easy advancement. That suggested the city's gang leaders wanted easy access and driving for what vehicles they had, and the Ferals didn't feel it was worth their effort to block the roads. Or they wanted easy travelling through no man's land as well.

Our cars ahead started up, the Dart's *clickity* sound standing out to me for some reason. Elmore did his own clicking, with his tongue and teeth, as he snapped his team's reins, getting them moving.

Pedaling my bike, I watched the terrain pass, knowing the chances of me spotting a gang member among the buildings and trees would be pure, fantastic luck. Like Sergeant Eckstein suggested, I kept my movement pattern random, slowing and speeding, weaving a little left and right. It was tiring, but better than getting shot…or at least making it harder for a sniper. Most everyone did the same, even in the vehicles. Elmore had difficulty trying to do that, so he just pressed on, more and more uncomfortable as the sun rose. It was probably a combination of nerves and the sun's rays striking his sandwich board armor.

The metal sheets were speed limit signs, and I'd seen plenty of bullets holes in similar gauge signs. But from an angle, or with a slower or smaller caliber round, what he wore could save his life.

Crack! An orange flare rising above the trees followed the sound of a single gunshot. An auditory and visual warning of our approach. The flare hung in the air, like the type fired by a boat in distress.

The race was on. Our front line slowed as the station wagon swayed left. From my vantage, I spotted a soldier abandon his bike and jump onto the vehicle's side. Feet braced, he reached through the window and began steering while someone else jumped in the passenger side. The gunshot wasn't an alarm. It killed the driver.

I took in a sharp breath, reminding myself that Lucia hardly ever drove.

She was hunkered down next to a crate holding artillery shells. Maybe not the best place to hide, but where else was there for her?

A second gunshot took out the soldier steering the station wagon, his body jolting forward before falling to the road. Our column's return fire tore into the trees. We in the rear were too far back to have a clue where to fire, so I just kept moving and watching, ready to unsling my rifle.

Elmore got his team moving at what I guessed was a canter, because it wasn't an all-out gallop or run. We were too far from the bridge for that. And once we made it there, we couldn't just stop and rest.

The sun was advancing its climb into the sky ahead of us, and the morning was already warm. Like seventy degrees. Maybe we should've tried to get closer, or made a run for the bridge at night. We could've seen the enemy's muzzle flashes then. On the other hand, the Ferals might've used the night to help clear our way through no man's land, and they just missed one.

We only made it a half mile before the road T-intersected from the north. Our advance scouts opened fire with their automatic rifles from behind the metal guard rail, announcing some sort of meeting engagement. Our vehicles raced past the intersection and Elmore brought his team up to a gallop. I was ahead of him, pedaling hard.

The ground shook, and a rumbling blast echoed from

behind, followed by a small shockwave. The hillside where we'd had our first shooting encounter had taken a kinetic weapon strike. That meant our column's composition and direction had been radioed in. That was bad. The likelihood of The Minions using continued radio communications was unlikely. That was good…depending on how badly they wanted to intercept us.

They had eight miles to reach the bridge, and we had a little over three. They could race through their territory, once organized. We had to fight our way through.

I slid my bike down next to the two soldiers maintaining fire on an old pickup truck, a little newer than our 40s vintage Dodge. The contents of my basket, water, ammunition and food, bungee-corded under a tarp, didn't spill out. The soldiers had shot the old pickup truck's tires out and shattered the windshield, stopping it about 100 yards away. Two bodies lay sprawled next to the disabled truck, steam rising from its radiator. Rifles lay on the ground next to the dead men on the uphill road. They didn't look like soldiers, both wearing blue jeans and dark green t-shirts. One appeared to be black, and the other one appeared white.

"Go," I said, resting my rifle on the metal rail. Gunfire rose from the truck, kicking up dirt to my right. Two men made a thirty-yard dash for the trees. My first shot hit one in the right leg just above the knee. The other required two shots, the first missing and the second hitting him, probably in the shoulder, just before he made it to cover behind a tree.

While I did my part, the scout next to me kept the enemy pickup truck under fire, while the other got up on his bike. Elmore's team galloped by with the dump truck kicking up smoke twenty yards behind him.

I shifted my attention to the disabled truck and fired off an aimed round. My shot turned out to be lucky and clipped a Minion in the face when he stood to fire on the horses. Another one of our soldiers who'd left his bike to crawl along a rock-filled ditch killed the other. It was a good thing because neither I nor the scout soldier next to me had an angle to get him.

"Good shooting, Jack."

"You, too, Ramirez." I didn't take note until that moment of who he was, my mind being in an 'us vs. them' mode.

We three got on our bikes ahead of the crawling soldier who'd taken out the last Minion. That had been skinny Private Garcia.

Already more gunfire erupted ahead. This time coming from a pale yellow house on the south side of the road, opposite another T-intersection. They'd managed to shoot out one of the Dart's rear tires. From behind the Dart, the driver hurled a white phosphorus grenade. It went off with a flash, releasing burning sparks and white smoke onto the wide porch.

The house was riddled with holes. There weren't enough shooters in there to pin us down. That didn't stop them from taking pot shots.

We closed about the time Sergeant Eckstein had prepared the howitzer and fired an explosive shell directly into the side of the two-story house. The station wagon had turned and maneuvered so that the wagon, and thus the artillery piece, faced the house. The recoil rocked the wagon back a good yard or two. Someone must've stayed in the LTD, kept it in neutral and had their foot on the brake, but not all the way down. Otherwise, the welded hitch would've snapped.

The artillery shell's explosion blew out the remaining windows, and probably brought down parts of the second floor onto the first. Plus, the fire caused by the grenade was spreading across the front porch.

The Dart's driver had already hauled the spare tire out of the trunk, while another soldier began setting the jack.

I pulled up next to them, the horses and dump truck already having gone around.

"You want someone to stand watch while you do that?" I asked.

The two scouts and Garcia didn't even slow down, trying to get back to their assigned places in the column. That should've been a clue to me.

"No!" shouted Private Gorski. "Get back to your position with the wagon. Everyone in the house is dead."

The station wagon was back on the road, towing the howitzer-bearing wagon again. The wagon was big and ungainly. It'd take time for Sergeant Eckstein and his crew to catch up and regain their assigned position. I didn't see Lucia, but felt confident she was still with them.

"Okay," I said to Gorski, and began pedaling, giving it all I had.

I caught up with the column after about a half mile. Each time I passed a house or building or road intersecting our two lane highway, I began weaving a little, remembering I didn't want to be an easy target. It was a stupid waste of energy. Why would anyone wait for a lone rider and ignore the previous, better targets?

Tension built in my shoulders as we continued south and approached a row of brick houses on the left, overlooking the road. There was an intersection not far past them on the right.

Nothing happened. Elmore, riding on his bench, met my gaze and grinned. Then he removed his helmet to wipe sweat from his forehead. It wasn't an easy thing to do, not with his metal-sign armor. Sure, they'd trimmed and bent the edges enough for him to work the reins and sit in his seat, but just barely enough.

We continued on, through a few curves and a turn, into a neighborhood like route, with small houses, many burnt and a few showing signs of dozer and crawler invasion. My guess was they tried to catch the alien creatures inside and burn them to death. I hope whoever attempted it was successful.

The horses were tiring, and Elmore eased up a bit. The truck behind us slowed down, too. I swerved wide and looked back. The Dart wasn't in sight behind us.

Not yet.

Then we reached a six lane, divided highway and I knew we were close. The overhead green signs still standing pointed to I-275 north to Ohio and south to Kentucky. Nobody would miss that turn. It also reminded me that The Minions were racing on good roads. The map showed one that hugged the river leading to the bridge.

It was only then that I considered why there hadn't been any abandoned cars on the road, like Sergeant Yin had reported. Now that was changing. Not blocking, but abandoned cars that would make portions of our run like a slalom race. It also offered advance firing positions for the gang members.

The column came to a stop just before taking the onramp. Several soldiers hurriedly clamped three hooks to the dump truck's push bar frame, adjusting them so they extended down to touch the road.

While they did that, the lieutenant had the Dodge truck move forward before he emerged and climbed up on the truck's bed, using his binoculars to observe the layout ahead. After only a few seconds, he gave some orders. One private ran toward the station wagon, the other back to the dump truck.

A familiar sound, the Dodge Dart's *clickity* engine let me know they'd survived and caught up. I didn't want to jinx it, thinking we'd done pretty well so far.

The *crack* of a rifle announced a change in our luck. The lieutenant was stepping down when the bullet struck his helmet. His head snapped to the side and he fell from the bed onto the pavement like a sack of corn.

Corporal Jones, the lieutenant's aide, picked him up and shouted. "He's still alive! You all know the plan. Let's move." Even as he shouted, another soldier helped Jones lay the lieutenant atop some of the gear in the truck's bed.

The dump truck drove along the shoulder to take lead position. The driver slid two metal sheets with slits cut in them behind the windshield for some protection. They slid a pair of highway signs sandwiched together behind the welded frame in front of the radiator. Those efforts offered some protection to the driver and vitals of the engine.

More gunfire sounded from down the highway. Some of our men shot back, missing the man retreating on a small minibike. He wove around abandoned cars, hunched low.

Our column moved forward, dump truck in the lead, followed by soldiers on bikes, then the El Camino, LTD station wagon and more bikes. Lucia, riding in the back of the station wagon, gave me a thumbs up. I waved, letting her know I saw her signal despite the wagon carrying the 105mm howitzer.

At the direction of Corporal Jones in the Dodge truck, the Dart maintained position behind Elmore's horse team. The horses were snorting and breathing heavily.

My legs were tired, too.

The horse team responded to Elmore's call to move forward.

So did my legs, responding to my conscious effort, working the pedals to drive me forward. Some of the resistance to advance was weariness, but there was also wariness. Who rides a bike into a gunfight?

Chapter 27

The dump truck picked up speed as it traversed down the elevated highway made up of two northbound and two southbound lanes. Maybe out of habit the driver stuck to the southbound side, going the 'legal' direction down the highway.

The truck received rifle and small arms fire from several men defending the first barrier, a row of cars blocking the road, but only two vehicles deep. The dump truck's hooks scraping the road caught a spike strip extended across the highway so that the spikes didn't pierce its tires, and wouldn't damage any of the vehicles following it. Perched in the front of the dump bucket, with only their shoulders and helmeted heads exposed, two soldiers returned fire with their M-16s. From my vantage it was difficult to tell if they hit anyone or anything. The way the truck was moving, it'd be tough to aim. Even if they only peppered the near and far barricades sheltering The Minions firing at them, it'd cause some of them to duck. Automatic gunfire coming my direction would make me flinch, or duck.

The dump truck slowed and pushed through the first barricade. Two Minions on mini-bikes attempted to retreat. Too late. Bullets from our side brought them down.

Then, from the southbound side, sheltered within that half of the car barrier, two men and one woman hurled Molotov cocktails at our dump truck. One flaming bottle struck and shattered just above the left front tire well. One hit the plywood-repaired side of the dump bucket. That bottle didn't shatter until it rebounded off and hit the cement road, doing no harm. The third one, however, arced inside the dump bed and hit something that shattered the bottle, causing flames to erupt.

The dump truck didn't stop. Instead its engine roared as it accelerated.

Soldiers on bikes right behind our dump truck took

cover behind cars in the first wrecked barrier and exchanged fire with the Molotov cocktail throwers. The gangsters didn't have much interest in fighting and tried to rappel with ropes over the side of the raised highway. The problem was, all three had the same idea at the same time and didn't offer any covering fire, spelling their doom.

Our column followed the path through the first barrier. The dying flames from the second firebomb bottle were only a nuisance for our vehicles and bikes.

The horse team, however, shied away. The gunfire and everything else was proving too much. The horses balked. I grabbed the fire extinguisher from the wagon and attacked the flames. Boy Scout training, how to activate and aim the extinguisher, emerged in the crisis. The step-by-step instructions provided to our troop by the lady fire chief almost five years ago took over. Before I knew it, the flames were out and the horse team moved ahead.

The dump truck crashed into the second barrier. This one was denser, with a four vehicle depth and more shooters defending it. The soldiers in the dump truck's bed climbed out the back. The front of the truck had to be riddled with bullets. I didn't think the driver could be alive. Still, he'd managed to dredge up the second row of stop sticks and plowed deep into the second barrier despite his vehicle becoming an inferno.

Our truck's front left wheel was flat and on fire, slowing it down.

A second wave of Molotov cocktails rained down on the truck as it struggled forward, shoving cars out of the way, clearing the far right-hand lane before stalling out.

Gunfire and hand-to-hand broke out at the second barrier, with sniping fire coming from the final barrier blocking this side of the bridge. Elmore held his team back, not wanting to risk them getting in the middle of a gun battle.

"You good?" I shouted over the din.

He nodded, struggling with the reins.

I tossed my bike on the horse-drawn wagon and ran

forward, hunched down and clutching my .22 rifle that now seemed totally inadequate. At least twenty Minion gangsters raced on foot from the far side of the bridge to reinforce the final barrier on the north side. From behind them, Yin, Gorski and three Ferals, former soldiers, climbed up from the side of the bridge and opened up on them. All twenty went down without returning fire.

Yin and his team were largely in the open when they began exchanging fire with The Minions sniping at us from behind and within their barricade.

Yin led his men to the bulldozer sitting on the southbound side. Gorski and one of the Ferals went down in the process. Although the defenders of the final barrier were now caught in a crossfire, between Yin's team and us, Yin still had some long range rifle fire to contend with from a few defenders still holding the south end of the bridge.

The dump truck became column of flame. There was no putting it out. The cement barrier between the north and southbound lanes made it impossible for our vehicles to switch sides. We'd either have to wait for the truck to burn out to get the horses past, or back track, and move cars blocking the northbound lane by hand, or by tow chain.

I climbed over the first barrier and made it to the second, sliding between cars, stepping over two dead Minions, bullet holes and stab wounds showing through their jeans and T-Shirts. I thought about grabbing one of their bolt-action rifles, but decided against that.

The big yellow bulldozer's engine roared to life.

Already the station wagon and Dodge truck had skirted around the blazing dump truck before one of its diesel tanks exploded. It wasn't a massive ball of flame, like in the movies, but the heat was too much. It caused the El Camino driver to stop and try to reverse, which wasn't easy with a trailer. Everyone else who wasn't in the line firing was lifting their bikes over the cement barrier.

The distance between the second and the third barrier was about seventy yards. Soldiers were lifting their bikes, squeezing through the cars. My bike was back with the horses and nuclear bomb. The Dodge Dart was behind the horse wagon, waiting for the fire to die down or someone to make a decision. There wasn't much I could do there.

Corporal Jones with the Dodge Truck, helping its driver to gather our wounded.

Lucia remained with Sergeant Eckstein and the howitzer, hunkered low in the back of the station wagon as it crept forward.

I decided to take aim with my little .22 and provide cover fire for the soldiers on my side of the barrier, the northbound, preparing to advance. It would also help Yin, who was driving the bulldozer toward the barrier from the other direction.

About eight surrounded Minions remained among the cars in the barrier, firing wildly. It took me three shots, but I hit one in the shoulder, causing him to drop his shotgun.

It became a slaughter. The Minions, as cannibals and criminals against humanity, couldn't surrender. So they went down, taking another one of our men with them. The final two gangsters were crushed between the cars when the bulldozer rammed into the barricade, pushing through the barrier.

I wove my way back between the sedans before Yin made it to the second blockade. He pushed through and then, after several efforts, knocked through the cement barrier separating the north and southbound lanes. That opened up a path for the Dodge Dart and pickup, El Camino and horse wagon to proceed forward.

Down the highway behind us, gunfire broke out. Mostly scattered rifle fire, with a few bursts of automatic. The Ferals were trying to slow The Minions' reinforcements from the city. We were running out of time.

Another one of our soldiers went down, hit in the neck by fire from the nearest of three barricades along the southern approach to the bridge.

Three seconds later, artillery thunder boomed as our 105mm howitzer, lined up on its wagon for direct fire concealed behind a pair of subcompact Hondas, sent a shell into the cars blocking our southbound path.

The first car in the barrier, a fancy purple Dodge Charger, was driven back and erupted, like a coffee can eating an M-80 firecracker. A few Minions defending the blockade, furthest away from the wrecked Charger, staggered away and fled on foot. Those stunned by the concussive blast died when the second round exploded a pair of small SUVs, sending them spinning and tumbling. The howitzer wasn't a tank, but it looked to have the same firepower as one. At least against unarmored targets.

Each time if fired, the farm wagon and station wagon rolled back. Their combined weight absorbing the artillery piece's recoil.

I rode next to Elmore as his team galloped forward. Once we and the Dodge Dart were through the bridge's northern barricade, Sergeant Yin, still driving the bulldozer, started pushing cars, reforming the barricade. I hopped down and helped pour diesel fuel inside and atop some of the cars. Two other soldiers were doing the same. Once all five fuel containers were empty, I grabbed two of them and another soldier grabbed three before we ran.

The remaining soldier shouted to us, "Go!" He held an unlit roadside emergency flare, with a backup in his hip pocket,

Who was I to argue? I chased after Elmore and his team across the bridge, ahead of Yin on the bulldozer.

Already the second barricade we'd blasted through was on fire, aided by our dump truck, and its driver. Amazingly the driver had somehow escaped before his vehicle was fully engulfed, and he hadn't been gunned down. His uniform was singed and he had an apparent shoulder wound, but he rode on the trailer behind the Dart with an M-16 in his good hand.

He'd dumped some diesel fuel among the scattered cars and eventually they caught. The barricade wasn't fully intact and the flames licking through it weren't intense, but they would prove a hassle for The Minions trying to close in behind us.

The gunfire from that direction ended. I doubted that the Ferals had actually stopped them. But even the five or ten minutes' delay might make the difference between our success and failure. Between our surviving, or our deaths.

Chapter 28

The carnage surrounding me. The assaulting smells of blood and bowels, of burning tires and burning flesh. Cries of pain and agony, dying gasps punctuated by gunfire.

Back in my woods, after killing intruders, I'd often vomit.

Private Barhorst dying next to me. Burying her had torn at my guts.

But now? I pressed on, numb to it all. We pressed on for survival, not only our own, but for humanity's future.

Would there even be a future, even if we won? If we destroyed the Mawks, or drove them off, or they just left? Or would we become mired in what once was, band together in savage groups, fighting over the scraps of what's left? How could we rebuild? So many of us dead or gone, society fractured, our infrastructure shattered, what encompassed humanity, broken.

After fighting through the remnants of The Minions on the south side of the bridge, we trudged upward. Elmore's team was spent, and they hitched the wagon to the bulldozer. It moved at a good jogging pace. The Caterpillar brand of equipment's horsepower ignored the uphill grade.

The rocky hillsides rose forty or fifty feet above the highway. It gave me a feeling of vulnerability, like we were being funneled into a trap. We raced forward, on bikes and in what remained of our vehicles. The barricade fires blazing behind us kept the pursuing Minions at bay, at least for a short time. Sergeant Eckstein pressed us to reach the first exit ramp and go west, away from Cincinnati, and Covington situated across the river from The Minion-held city.

The further we got from the cities, the further The Minions would be from their base. The more vulnerable they'd be. Maybe there were some sort of Ferals on this side that would aid us? Or would they attack us in our weakened, disorganized state? If we didn't make it to the off ramp ahead of any Minions that crossed the main bridge through Cincinnati and reached the intersection, we'd be caught in a vise. Them in front, and those behind us, still waiting for the heat and flames to die down enough to push through in pursuit.

We'd lost more than ten men, and at least three, counting Lieutenant Kuhn, were in the bed of a truck or trailer, being tended to, as much as possible under the forced movement conditions. I wasn't sure what they could do for a head wound, one caused by a bullet hitting the lieutenant's helmet, other than wrap his skull and keep him immobile. No x-rays or CAT scans. If there was a skull fracture, concussion or internal bleeding, there just wasn't much that could be done—even if we weren't essentially running for our lives.

I pedaled next to Elmore, who was leading his team, riding bareback on one of the team's lead horses, Brunhilda. He'd discarded his metal sandwich board armor and struggled to keep his team under control despite them approaching exhaustion. The removal of the wagon burden, especially on the long uphill run we were making, was a necessity. The fact that none of the horses had been shot seemed like a miracle.

Ahead of us, Sergeant Yin drove the bulldozer in reverse, pulling the wagon holding the crate bearing the nuclear warhead. It was tricky, because he had to veer around the occasional abandoned vehicle. He didn't seem to care, having shouted when we first started that the bulldozer moved faster in reverse.

Whether that was true or not, I didn't know. Fast as we were going, maybe eight or nine miles per hour, it didn't seem fast enough.

Maybe it was. Sergeant Eckstein, who appeared to have taken control, hadn't ordered us to toss our bikes in the trailers and hop in along with them. Two miles to the exit. We were nearly there, and burning of exhaustion began seizing my calves and thighs.

The land to either side of the highway became grassy,

backed by trees thirty or so yards off. We were no longer in the bottom of a gully. Only a fence and median separated the north and southbound lanes.

Sergeant Eckstein directed the station wagon's maneuver over to the southbound lane, dodging abandoned cars. The 70s vintage family vehicle hauled the wooden farm wagon to the top of the overpass and stopped. The sergeant and several men began unhitching the wagon, working to get the gun pointed east over the cement barrier. That wasn't good. Several other men were deploying in the ditch along the southbound entrance ramp. Seconds later gunfire erupted, coming from the east, threatening anyone in the northbound lane.

When the guard rail ended to our right, Elmore drove his team onto the grass, putting a little more distance between them and the erupting gunfire.

Along a road from the east rolled two early 70s Broncos pulling U-Haul utility trailers, the kind used for loading small vehicles and equipment. Each had at least a dozen Minions in their jeans and t-shirts, bandanas tied around their heads, and armed with an assortment of rifles and shotguns. Behind them was some sort of spoke-wheeled, whitewall-tired museum car, a black 1930s coupe with men packed inside and two riding in a back rumble seat. The passenger side even had a man out the outside, standing on the running board. His shotgun in one hand, gripping doorframe with the other. If they'd had fedoras and Tommy guns, it'd be a scene right out of the Bonnie and Clyde days.

One Bronco, the rusted out yellow one, continued on, toward the underpass. The other, a red one, rolled onto the grassy area between the entrance ramp and the highway. It came to a stop. That allowed its men to hop off the trailer. The coupe kept on coming forward, smoke spitting as it raced down the entrance ramp going north.

That split the fire of our three men along the ditch.

Whether the yellow Bronco was his intended target or not, Sergeant Eckstein shouted, "Fire."

The 105 millimeter explosive shell caught the top of the

Bronco but didn't detonate until it was over the rear of the trailer. The explosion tore into the dozen Minions. They'd already hopped off the trailer and were scattering. None made it far enough. Hot metal shredded them, along with tearing into the trailer and the Bronco's tailgate, rear window and tires.

I didn't have time to watch further. Instead, I raced up onto the southbound side of the overpass. My objective was to target the men in the red Bronco's trailer.

Yin had pulled over the dozer on the crabgrass along the southbound exit ramp. Elmore halted his horses to shelter behind it. Our Dodge truck and El Camino were ahead of them, pulled off as well, with most of our bicycling soldiers forming up in a firing line.

The two soldiers in the Dodge Dart were hunched low, making it up my way. That was good, since the red Bronco had stopped under the overpass. It was hard to tell, but it sounded like The Minions were dismounting and preparing to race around and up the steep, grassy sides leading to the overpass's northbound side. While that was good for Elmore and Yin and the soldiers deployed along the southbound exit ramp, it put me and the Dodge Dart soldiers, and Sergeant Eckstein and his three men, Washington, Harpster and Lucia, in real trouble.

"They're coming up the sides!" I shouted, in case the Dart soldiers and Eckstein and his team on their half of the highway overpass didn't know. With an open air gap of at least ten feet between the north and southbound lanes, there was no way we could consolidate.

Lucia had her pistol drawn and ready. Washington had his M-16 ready. Both of them kept their backs pressed against the station wagon, one watching north and the other south. Eckstein and the other soldier were trying to maneuver the wagon to aim the howitzer at a new target. Sporadically intense gunfire continued rising from the direction they were aiming. Although the wagon's front axle rotated, allowing the wagon to turn, the big wooden platform was heavy and ungainly.

Behind me the two soldiers had taken up positions on opposite sides of the Dart. The jittery soldier on my side of the car glanced at me before nodding. The other moved toward the Dart's trailer. I ran to the overpass's south end, toward the center gap. The western slope, Yin and others might have a shot at anyone trying to climb. With the inside slopes, they wouldn't.

Fourteen men in the U-Haul trailer, and five in the SUV. That meant we faced nineteen Minions.

Rather than wait, I pulled my revolver, popped up over the side and pulled the trigger at the first T-shirted target I saw. I pulled back and dropped without waiting to see if I hit the man. Lucky I did. A storm of bullets ricocheted off the edge of the cement and tore through the space I occupied a fraction of a second earlier.

Getting off the pavement, I crouched with my back against the cement guard lining the overpass. Four shots left in my revolver. While they were unhitching the horses near the bridge, I'd reloaded my rifle, so I had fifteen rounds there. Nineteen Minions, maybe eighteen if I just got lucky. Against seven of us on the overpass, with some fire support coming from Yin's way.

The howitzer fired again. No immediate idea if it hit Eckstein's intended target when the shell detonated a fraction of a second later. Repeated howitzer blasts and gunfire had to be damaging my ears, both of which were ringing. There wasn't an opportunity to find out what success Sergeant Eckstein and his crew might've had because gunfire erupted atop the overpass, bullets crisscrossing, tearing into flesh.

I added my own voice to the din, a .410 buckshot shell catching a Minion in the face as he leapt over the barrier, aiming his shotgun at the Dart and its defenders. He spun and fell, his bandana shredded by a pair of my pellets penetrating it and biting into his scalp. He wasn't dead, but was out of the fight.

The next Minion wasn't so reckless. He popped up, extended his arm and fired my direction, guessing based on the sound of my revolver. His Glock missed me, but clipped his fellow Minion lying in front of me in the shoulder. The unconscious man bounced with the bullet's impact, but nothing else.

I scuttled back, catching sight of a Minion over my shoulder, leveling a shotgun at one of the Dart's soldiers. I spun and dropped prone, firing wildly. My round missed but caused him to switch his target—to me. Luckily, he was too anxious and pulled the trigger before his shotgun's barrel lined up on me. The slug bit into the concrete a foot away, ricocheted off, sending blasted bits of stone in all directions. My next revolver shot, a .410 shell, took the shotgun-toting Minion in the leg, dropping him.

After a three round burst, a man behind me cried out in pain as he tumbled to the road below. One of the Dart soldiers must've got the Minion who'd popped up and missed me with his Glock.

I concentrated on my aim, last bullet in my revolver, and pulled the trigger an instant before the shotgun Minion got his gun leveled at me. I was aiming for his chest, but the bullet rode high, and took him in the chin, shattering it. The man fell back bleeding, his jaw shattered, his face wrecked.

I rolled to my left, turning over only once, again placing me next to the overpass's cement guard. Kneeling, I kept my head low. Rounds were still being fired, but fewer, becoming more sporadic. One of the Dart's soldiers was down, half of his thigh and neck missing. The other was still crouched at the rear of the Dart, inching between its bumper and the trailer, seeking a target for his M-16.

Lucia and Sergeant Eckstein were on the other half of the overpass. Safety off, I popped up, .22 rifle aimed their general direction. Lucia was down, tucked into a ball, half under the station wagon, Colt pistol lying next to her. Washington was near her, using the vehicle for cover, watching to his left. No time to worry about her now, I tried to tell myself. The adrenaline of battle helped me ignore what 'might be' and focus on my survival.

A Minion to my right, on the grass near the barrier

facing east, away from me. He was ready to pop up and fire on Washington, or maybe Eckstein, both huddled down near the howitzer's wagon. They were both alert with their M-16s. I snapped my rifle's barrel right, pulled the trigger, and nailed the man in the back.

Gunfire and shouts escalated below us, below the overpass.

The stocky man I shot in the back didn't go down. After flinching, he turned my way. Under his green hoodie with sleeves torn off, he must've had a bulletproof vest, because I saw the green garment pinch where my bullet struck.

Pumping, I fired off another aimed shot before the Sleeveless Hoodie Minion could get his bolt-action rifle pointed my direction. My aim was at his head, but I hit his right hand, near the trigger.

His rifle went off, hitting the cement barrier further below me. I fired again as he dove for cover under my half of the overpass. I might've hit him in the leg, but it didn't matter. A single burst from an assault rifle, the sound of an M-16 which I'd become used to hearing, ended his life. His last words were little more than a muffled scream.

We'd won the battle for the overpass.

There wasn't time to celebrate.

The surviving Dart soldier threw his dead partner and gear into the back seat of the car.

"Lucia!" I shouted, looking across to the other half of the overpass.

Washington was leaning over Lucia, helping her to her feet. "She took a round to the gut," he said. "But her vest stopped it. Knocked the wind out of her."

Still hunched over, Lucia forced a smile across her face.

Washington stuffed her pistol in its holster. "She'll have a bruise but be okay."

Seeing that Eckstein and Washington were struggling to maneuver the wagon so it could be hitched to the station wagon, I gave Lucia a thumb's up.

She frowned. I didn't see Private Harpster. He would've been helping with the wagon…if he were able. His body wasn't within sight, but that didn't mean anything.

I grabbed the dead Minion's shotgun lying next to me. A 12-gauge pump. It didn't have a sling. He did have a bandoleer that still held ten or twelve shells. I tossed it all through the Dart's open window, next to the dead soldier.

I didn't know the dead soldier's name, and the name of so many others, men that I'd shared a camp with, marched south with. How did that happen? Not knowing who was fighting alongside me.

There wasn't time to ponder. I pedaled my bike back down the overpass, working to catch up with Yin, again on the dozer, pulling the wagon. My assignment was to stick near Elmore and his team. Stick near the cargo we were planning to deliver.

Overall we'd lost four men defending the overpass, defeating the Minions sent to cut off our route of escape. Men whose names I didn't know, would never know who they were.

It came to me in an instant. When Private Barhorst had died next to me, it was then that I stopped trying to get to know the soldiers, avoided even knowing their names.

We lost four men, and gained a red Bronco with a trailer. The vehicle we needed, but it wasn't a good trade. Four lives and the lives of dozens of Minions, gone. Ended. And our side is happy to get a trailer and a decades-old SUV.

Red was the right color for it. We'd bought it with four of our men's blood.

North, behind us, the smoke was dissipating. The main blocking fire on the bridge was dying out.

"Keep moving!" Yin shouted, again driving the bulldozer in reverse.

Humans killing humans. It disgusted me. We were doing the Mawks' job for them. Of course, that was probably part of the plan. I hoped our plan, Colonel Davis's plan, the U.S. Military's plan, worked. Because, if it didn't, we'd all be dead within a year.

Deep down I knew, no matter what, I'd be dead, too. Even if I made it back to my park.

Lucia rode in the back of the station wagon. She flashed me a smile, half reassuring, half grimacing.

Even if she and I made it back to our park, the Mawks, using technologically advanced weapons, or creatures designed for killing humans, would bring me and Lucia down.

With The Minions still after us for crossing their territory, or for crossing them, or because they needed a good meal—fresh meat—and equipment, what remained of our column might not make six months. We had to deliver our nuclear package.

The race was still on.

Chapter 29

How far would The Minions chase us? We had a two mile lead, but we weren't exactly fast. Bikes, horses and a bulldozer, in reverse gear. If we'd had the Humvees with TOW missiles and .50 caliber machine guns, and armored Bradleys with 25mm auto cannons and their own TOW missiles, the vehicles we'd started out with, our survival wouldn't be in question.

Maybe an emissary of some sort sent ahead to The Minions, to negotiate passage, or even grant passage, based upon our mission to fight back on behalf of humanity as a whole? But I wasn't privy to that decision. According to the Ferals, from what I'd heard, it wasn't a viable option. The Minions weren't to be trusted, and hadn't honored any agreement since taking control of Cincinnati. I wondered if the Ferals were a reliable source of information on The Minions, being their enemies.

On the other hand, they'd guided us, provided intelligence info, and fought for us, and delayed The Minions in their pursuit.

We raced westward, on a somewhat rural highway, with light woods and hilly fields on both sides. Only a few random abandoned vehicles, and most of those were off to the side of the road, fuel doors open with gas caps hanging by their plastic tether. My guess was all were siphoned dry. That meant that survivors from somewhere, maybe from Cincinnati, had drained the vehicles of their fuel.

The old Dodge pickup was in the lead. Then came the red Bronco carrying our wounded in its towed U-haul trailer. A corpsman and an EMT were tending to them. It brought to mind Dr. Gurrie, the veterinarian Lucia worked with in Toledo. Could the vet handle bullet wounds, tourniquets, and more? Had she been looking for antibiotics to help those with chest and gut wounds? Wounds today that were a near certain death sentence. I'd shared some of my stockpile of medicines with Colonel Davis's column, but I didn't have the strong antibiotics, and not in the amounts needed. Six men were wounded and still alive, including Lieutenant Kuhn. Chances were, raging infections would end their lives.

After the bulldozer came the horse team, unhitched from the wagon. The bulldozer pulled it with ease. The El Camino, the station wagon and its wagon carrying the howitzer followed. The Dart brought up the rear.

There were only seven of us on bikes, including me. I rode next to the bulldozer, wondering how long the old piece of equipment would hold out. It was beginning to spew even more smoke and its engine, or something, began to rumble and clatter in an unhealthy way.

Yin, driving and watching constantly over his shoulder, didn't seem concerned.

The LTD station wagon was holding out better than I thought it would. Its old V8 engine did okay, especially as it was rarely called upon to top thirty miles per hour.

We came to a stop near an intersection where a road cut off south, just past a brick home.

Someone from a powder blue house up on the left, past the intersection, walked with careful steps down the gravel driveway. He carried what looked like a hunting rifle with mounted scope, and was covered in camouflage hunting gear. He had to be hot, especially with his big dark beard.

He was dark skinned and burly, which stood out as most people had lost weight and muscle mass since the alien EMP attacks. Corporal Jones directed him to the truck carrying the lieutenant.

A smile came to my face when Lieutenant Kuhn sat up and began conversing with the man. He looked unsteady, leaning heavily on the side of the truck. But he was up and coherent.

A second man emerged from the powder blue house, also carrying a hunting rifle, this one without a scope. He was dressed the same as his partner, but sported a full, red beard streaked with gray. He was on the lean side, with long, loping strides, as opposed to his partner's swagger. The long strides didn't show themselves until after he also gingerly made his way down the gravel driveway.

After a quick discussion between the new men and the lieutenant, Corporal Jones shouted, "Garcia, extra ammo, then front and center. Fairbanks, extra ammo, stow your bike, then front and center."

I grabbed a box of fifty .22 rounds and a box of fifty .45 rounds for my revolver, and stuffed them in my pockets, supplementing what I already carried. Then I tossed my bike in the El Camino's trailer.

Trotting up, Corporal Jones began giving orders before I even made it to him. "Garcia, with this man," he said, pointing at the red-bearded man. "Fairbanks, with this man." He pointed to the burly black man. "Add your firepower to the ambush. They'll be joining us, so catch up to the column with them."

With uncertainty, Garcia saluted. "Yes, Corporal."

I just said with a nod, "Will do, Corporal."

The burly man turned to me. "Let's go, Fairbanks. We're to hide in that stand of trees." He started trotting. I followed. "Once we're out of sight," he continued, "I'll explain."

"Okay," I said before he picked up speed to a near sprint. For a big man, he moved fast.

Our column was already moving west again.

As we ran past the station wagon, through its open rear window, Lucia said, "Nail all them muthers, Jack."

CHAPTER 30

The man led me across the road, along the north side, just past the T, toward a thick stand of trees and brush. "Follow me," he said. "We don't want to make a path in the grass visible from the road."

That meant we slowed and high-stepped until we reached the backside of a small ridge. Unless someone was in a big rig, looking to their right out the passenger side, they shouldn't see where we'd gone.

Most of the tree trunks were less than four inches in diameter. We wove our way through them up to the broad-leaved shrubs and smaller trees along the edge. The man already had a spot picked out, behind a hidden stack of broken concrete, probably thrown there by lazy road workers.

"Fairbanks, huh?" the man asked.

"I go by Jack." I extended my hand and we shook.

"Call me George, then, seein' we're on a first name basis." He grinned after saying it. "That's a little shit of a gun. You any good with it?"

George had a lever-action rifle, probably a .30-30, with what looked like a decent scope.

"Probably not as good as you with your scope."

"Well, either your lieutenant thinks you're expendable, or you'll make a difference."

"I've sprung more than my fair share of ambushes, George. Who's with us besides Garcia and the red-bearded man?"

"They're in the trees next to the blue house, near the fence. Across from us is another pair of us Ferals. And then six more in the house."

The powder blue house was a small one, with a porch sheltering the front door and two windows, and a small addition to its left with a front-facing window. It wasn't very far from the road, and didn't seem like a very good building from which to launch an ambush. A brick home we recently passed seemed like a better candidate.

"Twelve of us against all The Minions?" I licked my lips. "Should be interesting."

"Three to one, is my guess," George said.

"You're part of the Ferals from across the river, or a different group?"

"We Ferals are independent, just support each other. Me and Mannock canoed across the river. Set this up with some of our own over here, thinking you all might make it this far."

"Thanks," I said.

"You just don't shoot until I tell ya to shoot. And don't send any of your bitty bullets into the house."

I gave him a scowling glance, and smacked a mosquito on my neck. "I hear a motorcycle."

"That'll be one of their scouts," he said, checking his rifle and scope. "They travel in pairs, one ahead of the other. They have rocket fireworks for signals. Let 'em both pass. We want the main group."

"Not a problem. I won't shoot until after you do." I moved a few of the rocks to give me a better position to lean forward, still behind cover of the rock pile. That way I didn't have much foliage blocking my view. "What kind of firepower is in the house?"

"We got a .50 caliber machine gun and dynamite."

"Okay, George." I thought about asking where they'd got the machine gun, but that didn't matter. What did matter was that our side had it. "That might do noticeably more damage than me and my carnival gun."

"Let's hope so." George leaned forward, resting his forearms on the rocks. He held a finger to his lips. "Shhhh."

The motorcycle sound came closer, then slowed. It stopped quite a way before the T intersection, out of our direct view. Then the engine revved and the vehicle sped forward. Both George and I ducked a little further behind the rocks. Vines in the front, and the shadows, and low hanging branches provided our cover. Based upon my experience in my park, we'd be invisible, if we didn't move or make any noise.

It wasn't a motorcycle, but a three-wheeled ATV. The Minion wore a black windbreaker with a pistol holstered on his right side, and a rifle of some sort, its butt and stock sticking up, in a carrying sheath set along the seat just behind him.

He slowed to a stop at the T-intersection and switched off his ATV's engine. That left the sound of our column, mainly the bulldozer in the distance, and another vehicle, a motorcycle or another ATV a short distance back from where the Minion scout had come. My guess was that he'd been cruising about twenty-five miles per hour. More than enough to catch up with our slow-moving column.

He observed the area, his gaze passing over us. Then he looked down the southern fork before signaling with two fist pumps. Then he started up his ATV. After another look around he clicked it in gear and continued on the trail of our column, slowing to observe the powder blue house on his left. Satisfied, he increased speed in pursuit of our fleeing vehicles and horse team.

Thirty seconds later a pair of Minions on a beat-up Harley cruised past, going about twenty miles per hour. They'd slowed before reaching the intersection, probably checking out the brick house.

The woman driving the motorcycle wore a black helmet without a visor, probably to keep her frizzy, long black hair out of the face of the man riding behind her. Other than that, they were attired and equipped much like the first scout. The man kept his eyes trained on the north side of the road, and the woman on the left, looking for some clue or sign of where some of us might have turned off or prepared an ambush.

As with the first scout, he overlooked me and George completely. They took extra time observing the blue house, even pulling up along the edge of the gravel drive. It looked unused, along with the gravel lane less than twenty yards to the west of the driveway, running parallel to it, and past the house and its yard, possibly leading to some farms or fields down the way. I hadn't bothered to look, and couldn't see, even if I wanted to, from my current hide position.

The scouts were being observant, but not careful enough, not for the pace necessary to catch our column before we made it too far from Cincinnati, their center of power. Why George and his partner had so carefully walked down the driveway to meet us now made sense.

After the scouts moved on, I pulled my canteen from my belt and offered George a drink.

"Thanks, man." He took a swig and handed it back. "First time we've got a shot at them, when we know their path and they're not full prepared."

Taking a drink, I wondered if George and his Feral team member, Mannock, had brought bikes across the river with them, or had bikes or a vehicle already positioned across the river. No way could they have made it this fast on foot, so I asked.

"There's an old luxury van behind the house." He pointed to the road going south. "We went down that road and came up behind to hide our tracks."

He didn't exactly answer my question, on purpose I figured. There wasn't time to inquire further. The rumble of a big diesel truck sounded from the east, growing closer quickly. In less than a minute a black Bronco packed with armed Minions rode past, going maybe twenty-five or thirty miles per hour. On either side, just trailing, were two three-wheeled ATVs, like the previous scout had. By the time they reached the blue house, a big diesel truck, one of the old cabover models, reached us. The sides of the metal semi box trailer it pulled had rectangles about three feet tall and two feet wide cut into them. Firing slits, spread about four feet apart, if I had to make a guess, especially since a Minion armed with a rifle was visible through each opening. They were leaning on some sort of framing, and watched the countryside. Either they were very disciplined, or very nervous, or both.

Following to the right of the semi truck came a man on

a red scooter. It looked more like a minibike, probably going all out to keep pace. Last was an old turquoise blue Impala with a torn up white vinyl top. The cloud of smoke billowing from its tailpipe was a good reason for it to be bringing up the rear.

George and I leaned on the rocks, taking aim.

"I got Scooter Boy," I said.

"Uh huh," was his only reply, his right eye lining up his selected target through his rifle's optical scope.

Even as I said it, movement from the blue house's roof caught my attention. Three sticks, like spinning batons, arced toward the road. One landed just behind the black Bronco, ahead of the semi truck. Its end hit the pavement, causing it to skid to the road's far shoulder. The next hit the edge of the road and tumbled under the truck's trailer, and the final one disappeared from my sight, probably bouncing off the semi trailer's side.

Couldn't worry about what they were throwing. George said they had dynamite. I focused on keeping my aim just ahead of my distancing target.

"Now," George said, an instant before the blast of his rifle sounded.

I was used to rifle fire, so it only caused me to flinch a little. Within a half second, I had my aim readjusted and pulled the trigger. At the same time, the sticks of dynamite detonated. The first one blew a small crater in the road's shoulder. The second detonated under the semi trailer's rear wheels, and the third went off within the trailer itself. The thrower got lucky, or was skilled enough to make it into one of the slit sections.

More shots rang out, including a steady beat of heavy machine gun fire tearing into the Impala, piercing metal and shattering glass, destroying the vehicle's occupants.

My target, Scooter Boy, fell from his bike, clutching at his back. The Impala stalled and rolled off the south side of the road, toward the house. Gunfire continued to erupt from the wooded ambush sites and from the house. The Bronco sped away, someone leaning out one of the windows, wildly sending back a few shots. That was all.

George fired again. I think he hit one of the ATV drivers. I nailed my man in the leg as he crawled off the road, toward the ditch area.

Two men bailed out of the semi truck's passenger side.

"I got the first one," I said to George. It was almost like plinking tin cans on a fence when I was a kid. But these were living targets. Men. Humans…enemies hunting me and Lucia, and my fellow soldiers.

We both fired about the same time. The head of George's man snapped sideways, showering blood and skull fragments across the grass. Mine dropped while running across the ditch as his right leg collapsed. I was aiming for his chest, but got his knee. Close enough.

George finished him with an aimed shot as he crawled for deeper grass.

The machine gun sent a few bursts into the trailer, supplementing the gunfire from the house.

The gunfire died down even as someone shouted, "Stop firing, cease fire!"

As far as ambushes go, except for the Bronco getting away, turning off the road and tearing across a fallow field to escape, it couldn't have gone much better.

"Not bad plinking there, Jack." George patted me on the shoulder before getting to his feet. "You'd be a real helluva bastard with a scope and a real rifle."

"Why?" I asked, grinning and getting to my feet, ready to follow him out of the stand of trees. "You already got that covered."

It didn't take long for me, Garcia and the twelve Ferals, including George, to catch up with our column.

In addition to the Feral's 1960s Ford van, that had equal amounts of olive green paint as it did rust, we managed to pull the cabover semi truck away from its burning trailer. The truck only suffered a shattered window and a bullet hole in the driver-side door. We also gathered a few firearms and bullets and other gear stripped from the bodies and vehicles.

One of the three-wheeled ATVs survived the brief ambush as did the red scooter, which I got to drive. It ran pretty well, but thirty miles per hour was its top speed. In any case, the antique European scooter was better than crowding into the van with Garcia and ten of the other Ferals.

The luggage rack installed on top of the van held all of the Ferals' extra gear, tied down under a gray canvas tarp. The Ferals were a balanced combination of red-necks, former suburbanites and urban dwellers. Ten men and two women, and they had one thing in common: hatred for The Minions.

While I was glad to have them joining our column, they seemed a bit unruly, and I wasn't sure how well they'd fit in.

The drive through Kentucky proved uneventful. No major battles. A few sniping efforts from folks angry at us crossing their territory, and scavenging fuel was harder. A few times we had to siphon from one of our vehicles to keep another going.

We lost the dozer before twenty miles had passed, and the *clickty* Dart three days later. The hills were too much for it, and the water pump finally gave out.

The growing hills and small mountains were tough for anyone trying to bike. They wore even more heavily on Elmore's horse team. Most of the time his wagon was hitched to the cabover semi.

I'm not sure if any of the Ferals knew what our cargo was, but Lieutenant Kuhn continued to recover and kept them in line and busy. Lucia didn't trust them, and said so in whispers. The two women, Ruth and Ruby, red-neck sisters, were friendly enough to Lucia, but the tall brunette sisters had nothing in common with the Hispanic city girl.

George was assigned to Sergeant Eckstein's artillery squad, and he seemed to get along with Lucia. Some of his stories working for the sewer department made her laugh. A lot of people frowned upon talking about life and careers before the Mawks attacked, but George was such a storyteller that he made people forget about their troubles, at least for a few minutes.

We continued to stop randomly and make turns on back roads, sometimes leading us up and down narrow mountainside routes. Roads would be an overly kind word for some that we travelled.

One thing that I noticed was the near absence of flies. They were all over the cities, their maggots feeding on dead bodies. They weren't quite as bad in the park. If someone couldn't learn to ignore their buzzing around, it'd drive them batty.

I wondered if going back into a city would drive me batty. Already, I was getting used to the fresh air. Air without the faint stench of rot and decay. Whenever we neared a settlement along the way, the tainted air irritated my senses. My sense of wellbeing.

Twice we were attacked by crawlers, once by a pack of three. We lost one of the Ferals to that. Dozers weren't common in the mountainous rural region, which was a blessing. With the trees close in most of the time and the narrow roads cutting between the hills, one getting into the column or in our camp could've been a disaster, even if the guards spotted it early.

Lucia sometimes took my scooter to scout ahead. She weighed less than me, and weight was a factor in the scooter's ability to go up hill.

I wasn't sure why we didn't just dump the horses and the scooter and bikes, pile in and race toward our destination. Nobody really talked about the mission, sort of a taboo, like asking about family.

Sergeant Yin and I were scouting ahead of the column, along a narrow road in a relatively flat area of Kentucky, nearing Tennessee. Mountains were ahead, in the distance. That was when I finally decided to ask Sergeant Yin why we weren't moving faster, after he pulled his ATV over to the side of the road. My guess was going fast could put us more at risk of an ambush.

He said, "The lieutenant believes moving too fast will

draw Mawk attention. They track movements from their ships, or so the lieutenant believes. Plus, we don't want to arrive at our destination too early. We have an appointed day to shoot for. Too many simultaneous arrivals might draw attention."

Who was I to argue? Then I asked, "Why was I assigned to scout duty?"

"Because you're good in the outdoors."

I laughed. "What makes you think that?"

"Where did you live when Colonel Davis recruited you?"

"A metro park, tucked in along the suburbs of a city. I knew my park, nothing more really. I'm no outdoor expert, or tracking expert, or marksman."

"If I didn't think you were up for the job, I would've recommended someone else," Yin said. "No, you're not an expert outdoorsman, but you're observant and understand nature better than most. You're a survivor. And you're fairly intelligent and steady, able to think things through under pressure."

"At this stage," I said, "we're all survivors. And thanks for the 'fairly intelligent' complement."

Yin looked over his shoulder, seeing that the column was rolling into sight. He grinned before starting up his ATV. "I like you, Jack. You're unique."

"Why is that?" I asked, starting up my scooter.

"You ain't afraid to carry a small caliber rifle, but you carry a hand axe instead of a knife to make up for it."

With that he revved his ATV's engine and said, just above the small engine's growl, "And you're reliable." Then he pulled out ahead of me, to continue our scouting assignment.

Chapter 31

I had no idea where we were. Not exactly. That was a major point of the exercise.

We were in Tennessee, somewhere, amongst the mountains. Well, some in the column called them hills, but they were tall and generally steep, covered in pines and oaks, hickories and maples. Lying under the canvas tarp acting as a tent, I thought on Luther, and his grave, and the times he told me the types of trees so that I could identify them. And how I hadn't paid attention.

All of that, and my—our—park, seemed so long ago, when in actuality, it'd been just shy of a month. Lucia was tucked in next to me, under a thin blanket, her face protected from mosquitoes by mesh fabric. I had the same, held in place by my NY Yankees cap. The sun was close to setting. Lucia and I'd just finished a large cut of flame-cooked venison from a deer that Sergeant Yin had brought down, and we were turning in early since we were assigned the 2:00 am until sunrise watch.

I'd tied the rope supporting our tent between two saplings, on a relatively level area just above the small coal mining road where the column stopped to camp. Extra pine needles provided a measure of comfort on the hard ground. We were on the western side, so some fading sunlight still reached us. Morning's sunrise would come late with the sun emerging beyond the eastern hilltops.

Lucia rolled onto her elbow to face me in our cramped tent. "What's got you, Jack?"

I opened my eyes and turned my head to face her shadowy outline. Her long black hair was braided, as usual. Most women had cut theirs short, just like most men had grown beards. I, on the other hand, shaved every few days, using Elmore's straight razor. It was a tricky process to learn, and I nicked myself the first few times.

"Got me?" I asked, trying to gauge her facial expression

in the growing darkness. The mosquito netting made that even more difficult. Her voice didn't carry her usual sarcastic tone.

Over the past few weeks, sharing danger, guard duties and working as a fuel siphoning team, and sharing a tent, we'd become even closer friends than we were after sharing our park. There, we lived in the same area, but had different wake, work, and patrol schedules that didn't intersect much. Traveling with the column we often ate lunch in company with one another, in conjunction with Elmore and Washington, sometimes Garcia and Sergeant Eckstein, and lately George. The last man, George, could've had a career as a standup comedian, or even a humorist, if he'd had a notion to put his stories to paper.

"Yeah, Jack. Usually you're asleep two minutes after putting your head down. It's been almost ten."

The bustle of camp included a small fire, Elmore tending to his horse team, some of the soldiers checking belts and working on the vehicles in the fading light.

"Just thinking," I said. "About our park, and if I—we'll ever see it again. And Luther."

"You ever think about your family?" she asked, hesitantly. "I think about mine. Mostly my momma and little sister."

Luther, we knew and had in common. Despite the time together, neither of us brought up family. "Sometimes," I said. "But I wasn't tonight."

"Sorry," Lucia said, and rolled onto her back in a flop.

"No, it's okay." I reached over and gripped her hand, both of us facing the canvas tent above us. She squeezed back. Her hand was calloused and strong, and warm.

"My dad went to prison not long after I was born," Lucia said. "Died there when I was in second grade. My sister, really my half-sister, was four years younger than me. Smart, a book worm. She died in a fire with my mom. One of the rocks launched down from space hit near our apartment. Before then, ran the streets. Selling heroin." She quickly added, "We needed the money, my mom, Rita and me. Momma had a factory job. A good one. They closed down, and she couldn't get another good job."

Lucia sniffled a bit.

Factories, unemployment, college and working toward a degree. All of that seemed like a lifetime ago. Like it was part of a movie I'd spent most of my life watching. Then it ended, and the theater lights never came on.

"My family is, or was, in Florida. I was going to school—attending college."

"You don't know if they're alive or not, do you." It wasn't really a question. She knew the answer.

She squeezed my hand again. "You going to go look for them, when this is over, Jack?"

"Depends on what you mean by over, Lucia. Look how dangerous it's been to travel with a military column, ignoring the Mawks. If we win, and humanity gets its act together, if it ever gets its act together."

"If not, what are you going to do, then, Jack?"

"Try to make it back to our park."

"Won't that be just as dangerous?"

"You and me can make it. I think Elmore wants to go back, too. We know some of the route, and dangers heading back. Maybe George and his pals will be going that way, at least to the river."

"Okay," she said, sounding relieved. "These mountains, being in them feels weird. I've seen them on TV, but being in them is different."

She took a few breaths while I swatted a mosquito that landed on my hand holding hers. "You think it's like that for the Mawks, Jack? Coming here is like leaving the city for the mountains?"

"I think it's more like them trying to move into an apartment, and trying to fumigate it first, to get rid of the roaches."

She countered, "I think it's more like one gang expanding its territory into a rival's. Thinking they're bigger, meaner, stronger, with more men and better guns."

"Maybe," I said. "Except a losing gang can retreat. Split

up and get out of town. We can't do that. We don't have anywhere, any way, to run."

Boots clomping on the dirt approached our tent.

"You still up, Jack?" It was Sergeant Eckstein's voice.

"Yes, Sergeant."

"I was pretty sure I heard you. Anyway, after your watch tonight, before you get breakfast, report to the lieutenant."

Chapter 32

My meeting with Lieutenant Kuhn lasted less than two minutes.

After refilling my canteen from the boil pot, checking my rifle and revolver and that I had extra ammo, and putting some food and other equipment in my bike's basket, folding the canvas bag closed and strapping it in, Lucia came over to give me a quick hug.

"Delivery time?" she asked in a whisper.

I shrugged. "We'll see," I said. But she was right, and knew the answer. I figured that just about everyone did, except maybe the dozen Ferals that joined us after the ambush south of Cincinnati.

Lieutenant Kuhn was riding with Elmore on his wagon, pulled by his team. The horses looked thin and worn, but had recovered some of their strength after being freed from hauling the wagon up and down the mountains of Tennessee. Bud was rebelling a bit at having to pull the load, but Brunhilda set an example that got him going.

Garcia rode on the back of the wagon, watching, with his M-16 held ready. Sergeant Yin rode his bike, keeping in the lead by about seventy yards. Between him and the horse team rode Private Smoater. There couldn't be anyone who was more fidgety than Smoater. But that was a good thing. He was always watching and paying attention, and was an expert with a crossbow, in case we came across a crawler or a dozer. The lieutenant and Elmore each had one too, in addition to their regular firearms. I didn't know if either of them was a good shot.

That left me, about fifty yards behind, providing rear guard.

Such a small group, to guard the nuclear warhead. We'd left the other vehicles, the cabover semi, the station wagon and Bronco, the Feral's old Ford van, and the even older Dodge truck, behind, along with the rest of the column, including the Ferals. The lieutenant believed, and explained to me that the smaller the team, and the fewer the vehicles, the less notice we might draw from the Mawks. No vehicles was far better. Having something radioactive, even though shielded within a lead-lined box, was signature enough, if the Mawks were looking for it. But they had to be looking, he believed. And if they didn't take notice of us, they'd be unlikely to take note of the device.

How did the lieutenant know how the Mawk ships' intelligence-gathering array of sensors worked? He could've received intelligence information from our side, and extrapolated. Humanity once had satellites. The Mawks were supposed to be using something like satellites to control their killing drones, of which we hadn't seen any on our journey. Fortunate for us.

The Mawks had a whole planet to keep track of. Just like in a classroom, if the teacher was looking the other way, or distracted, or not paying attention, a student could escape notice and get away with just about anything.

The road we travelled was narrow and cracked. Getting too close to the edge invited the blacktop to crumble and give way, offering a steep drop down the hillside, into the tall trees below.

Twice, we passed some sort of sentries along the road. Soldiers clad in helmets, and green and brown camouflaged fatigues, and dark patterned paint on their hands and faces. They stayed in the trees, among the rising trunks, and rocks, and fallen logs, but showed themselves with movement and a wave. That gave me a small measure of comfort. The lieutenant signaled the sentries with a weird hand gesture, probably a prearranged code, or something in sign language.

Maybe Sergeant Yin spotted the soldier sentries. I was too busy watching the road behind us to know if he had. But if Yin hadn't, and if the camouflaged sentries harbored ill intent, I wouldn't have known of their existence. Not until they'd opened up on us with their automatic rifles. And then it would've been too late.

We pressed on after nightfall, only stopping to water the horses from a spring dripping from the rocks or a stream fed from something similar. My legs were getting like rubber and protested almost as much as Bud and Comanche. Even Sergeant Yin showed signs of fatigue. Traveling by starlight, in the silent night, except for the crickets and occasional owl hooting, or possum and raccoon scurrying along, was in a way relaxing, but also more stressful. Sure, I wouldn't have spotted any ambushes by the sentries along the way, but the illusion that I was able to effectively watch for trouble made me feel better.

We approached another crossroad. There had only been a few. This one, like the previous, was set in a valley between hills. Someone with a red-filtered flashlight stepped into the road and signaled Yin. He stopped while the rest of us continued forward.

I kept my distance from the individual holding the flashlight—it was impossible to tell if it was a man or woman. Whoever it was stood alongside the wagon and conversed with Lieutenant Kuhn in muffled tones.

I was then signaled forward, directed by the Flashlight Man, based upon his deeper voice, to take my bike and equipment, along with Garcia, who took Yin's bike, into a small clearing about thirty yards east of the crossroads. There we were met by a female, also armed with a red-filtered flashlight. Closer inspection showed it to be a crank powered one. She appeared to be wearing a combat uniform and I spotted a helmet near a folding stool with a canvas seat.

Private Garcia and I leaned our bicycles behind a tree along the back of the clearing. I kept my rifle and he kept his M-16. It would've been impossible to move around without stumbling or feeling our way along, if not for the flashlight's dim red glow.

A confident female voice said, "There are a couple old cushions there." A flick of the flashlight revealed them. "May as well sit on down. Your officer won't be back until after midnight."

After we placed the mats seven or eight feet from the stool, the woman said, "Scoot them a little closer, so we can talk. We're informal out here, but don't want to be too loud. I'm Staff Sergeant Gibbons." She paused for a breath. "You can't see him, and probably didn't notice him, but across the road is Private First Class Johnson."

Garcia didn't say anything about noticing Private Johnson standing watch, and neither did I. Garcia stepped closer and saluted, "Private Second Class Garcia."

Using specific ranks sounded sort of formal to me. Our column followed some military rules and discipline but, as it was half civilian, Lieutenant Kuhn let some things slide. They still saluted, and addressed the officers with respect, but with him being the only officer, some informality crept in, especially around the civilians.

I kicked our sack cloth cushions, probably stuffed with rags, closer to the stool. "I'm Jack Fairbanks. Call me Jack."

"That's fine, Jack, and Garcia. Out here, just call me Gibbons. Please, be seated." She lowered her voice to the point that it was just loud enough for us, sitting fewer than three feet away, to hear.

"If you've got canteens, I have some dried and salted venison, if you're interested."

"That would be great. Thank you, ma'am," Garcia said.

"And you, Jack?"

I decided to test the sergeant's notion of informality.

"I won't say no to that offer, Gibbons."

She reached over into a backpack and pulled out a couple strips, about six inches long, half as wide and a quarter of an inch thick. Both Garcia and I thanked her.

Gibbons clicked off the light. "I have a few things, other than food, to share. Information that you can take back to the rest of your men, and I presume, women."

"We have both," I assured her before biting off a piece of the jerky. Salty to the point of needing water on hand was an understatement. Still, it was tasty, and knocked back my growing hunger. I'd picked up some cattail roots just before sunset while we were watering the horses, and ourselves, each using our own filtering straw. It would've been those and some dried dog food, otherwise. After pocketing a few vitamins, I'd left the rest in my small bottle with Lucia.

"That's good," Gibbons said. "Like I said, I have a few things to share, and then, if you like, you can get a couple hours of shuteye. I won't be insulted if you don't, or do so one at a time. I understand, times have changed, and trust often has to be earned." She laughed. "Every group that passes through has had a different comfort level. Dark as it is, you probably don't know where you are, except in general terms. You don't even know what I look like, and vice versa."

"We've been traveling hard," Garcia said, acknowledging her statement.

"I believe you," Sergeant Gibbons said. "And just to let you know, in case you're wondering, I'm no Playboy pinup."

That was worth a quiet laugh.

Garcia replied, "Neither me or Jack have had time to work out at the gym these past few months, just to let you know."

Gibbons snorted, stifling a laugh. Then her next words came out in a serious tone. "Okay, here's what you need to know."

For some reason, I suddenly expected ominous news, like the Midwest was the last place humans were holding out against the Mawks, and that this last bastion was about to succumb.

"First," Gibbons continued, "the President thanks you for your service and sacrifice, and those men and women that started the mission, but fell along the way. And the risk posed by your continued service to this country, and humanity across the world."

"You met the President?" Garcia asked.

"No, Private Garcia. I am relaying a message. Please, allow me to go through this in order, so that I don't forget anything."

As if on cue, less than two minutes after Sergeant Gibbons finished her rendition of status and highlights of the invasion, another group of soldiers arrived, escorted by a soldier carrying a red-filtered flashlight.

It was hard to tell, but the group appeared to have arrived all on foot, a few more than half a dozen. Three of them continued on with their cart, in the same direction Elmore Foltz, Lieutenant Kuhn, Private Smoater, and Sergeant Yin had gone. Their two-wheeled cart, presumably carrying a nuclear warhead, was pulled by a pair of llamas, or alpacas. I didn't know the difference between them, but in the dim red glow, that's what they looked like. They definitely weren't horses, mules, ponies or donkeys.

We moved off to a small clearing just within earshot of Sergeant Gibbons, if we were silent and listened with great care. She shared jerky and spoke to five men, relaying the same tale of invasion and information, also to share with the rest of their unit upon their return.

Having learned what I had, there was no way I would be able to sleep.

The same was apparently true with Garcia as he asked in a whisper, "How do you think they learned all that? And how accurate is it?"

I shrugged in the darkness. "They probably kept the captured Mawks separate. After interrogation, cross referenced their stories, what they said."

"You think they got the truth? I mean, can they speak Mawk?" Garcia's voice began to rise. "What do they even sound like?"

I leaned close and put a hand on the private's shoulder. Me, an expert in alien psychology? If anyone was, it sure wasn't me. And what I knew of interrogations was limited to what I learned watching television and movies.

I removed my hand from Garcia's shoulder and swatted a mosquito that had landed on my neck.

Television and movies...something I didn't think about much. The trek south had been so busy and tiring, every time my head hit the ground, I was asleep within minutes. No late nights with popcorn, Dr Pepper, and friends. TV and movies weren't taboo like discussing family and lost loved ones, but there just didn't seem to be any interest. They weren't important.

Nobody in the column, except Elmore, even seemed to read. He managed only a page here and there. Some Louis L'Amour book, a western.

There wasn't time, and apparently little interest. We came across books in abandoned houses, so availability wasn't a problem. Lucia and I had brought one book with us, a small field guide to edible plants. That was the extent of our reading.

"The FBI, or the CIA or NSA," I whispered to Garcia. "They know what they're doing. Maybe some professors from colleges like MIT."

Sergeant Gibbons told us that the deadly, virulent flu that went around about nine months before the invasion was alien derived. Colonel Davis had already told me about that, information from the CIA.

Gibbons also said that the government at first suspected, and then knew, that the Mawks were out there in space, not quite in orbit around Earth. They'd been able to keep it quiet while they tried to communicate and discover their purpose. The government also worked quietly to prepare for the worst, trying to do so without the Mawks knowing. The aliens were probably watching and listening, and trying to learn more about us before they made their move.

Garcia then asked, "So, Jack, do you believe the story about the Mawks being on the losing end of a war? Their invasion, this colonization a rushed one? That they didn't have years to perfect their virus attack, but did better manipulating the crawlers and dozers so they'd hunt and feed exclusively on humans and canines, man's best friend, and to a lesser extent, horses?"

"I don't see why a Mawk would make up that story, but I'm not an alien psychologist."

"Who is?" Garcia asked, his volume again beginning to increase.

"The CIA," I said. "The—"

He cut me off, finishing in once again in a whisper. "I know, CIA, NSA, FBI."

A few minutes of silence settled between us. Where would they take the captured aliens? Cheyenne Mountain? Area 51? Someplace totally off the grid? How did they keep all of the other nations quiet too? How many even knew?

"How do you think we're going to attack them, Jack? With those nukes?"

"In orbit," I said. "If the government and military was preparing, while trying to communicate with the aliens, then they must have a plan."

Nukes wouldn't be nearly as effective in space. Heat and radiation, maybe, but hardly any shockwave. That required an atmosphere. I'd learned that in high school physics.

"With the nukes," I said, "with the radiation already in space, that probably won't affect them. Maybe the heat might. Their big ships might not be built to enter the atmosphere. Maybe they intend to wrap the nuke in some sort of cover, so it explodes like a grenade, with shrapnel that'll tear into the ships?"

"I watched *Star Trek*," Garcia said. "Their ships had deflectors to keep space debris and junk from hitting their ships."

This wasn't *Star Trek*, but Garcia had a point. "Maybe not from behind," I said. "Ships going forward would have to protect against space debris. Anything going fast enough to get here from another planet, it'd need protection. A deflector shield of some sort, or an armored nose."

"Huh. That makes sense, Jack."

I don't know why Garcia expected me to know so much. Maybe because he knew I'd been in college?

"My guess is, Garcia, that we'll use some sort of hyper velocity missile. Something fast that they'll have trouble responding to."

"Stealth technology," Garcia added. "The missile will have that, too, I betcha."

"Maybe," I said, thinking that trying to hide a rocket's

heat plume would be nearly impossible. Our satellites, when we had them, watched for ICBM launches from other countries. The Mawks could at least equal that.

"Regular ICBMs launched at them would be too slow," I said. "Easy to target, so they have to be fast, and stealthy."

Didn't Lieutenant Kuhn say we were on a time table for arrival? With other groups arriving here? "I bet we're going to saturate the air with too many targets to deal with. And decoys."

Garcia said, "Like *Missile Command*, but in reverse."

"What?" I asked, quietly.

"An old video game I used to play with my uncle." His voice trailed off. "A video game I played." Then he stopped.

"It's okay, Garcia. I understand."

He sighed. "Thanks, man. You were saying?"

"We took out their personal combat vehicles, and their light tanks. They're vulnerable from beneath. Maybe the Mawk ships are vulnerable from behind?"

"How many ships you think they got, Jack?"

I shrugged, even though Garcia couldn't see the gesture.

Our pause let us know Sergeant Gibbons was still talking to the other soldiers.

"The total number doesn't matter," I said. "If we hit the right ones."

"Sure," Garcia agreed. "Like in the Navy, you go for the carriers and amphibious ships."

I nodded. "Right. If they have colony transport ships, take them out. That would cripple them. Give us a chance long term."

"Yeah, Jack. That's right. If they're losing a war, and this is a desperate move, they won't be getting reinforcements."

We were quiet again, listening to Gibbons whisper her memorized information to the other soldiers. She was up to the virus.

"What worries me," I said, once again leaning close to Garcia. I could almost see his outline with the faint moonlight filtering down through the trees. "That we're going to have to draw off their forces, engage them in a meaningful way for our real attack to be successful."

Garcia grunted in agreement.

Details of that, Sergeant Gibbons didn't share, or didn't know. We'd have to wait for Lieutenant Kuhn to brief us with the next step in the plan, and our part in it.

"What happened, Jack?" Lucia asked.

We'd just made it back to our column's camp. It was a few hours after noon and I was sitting down, with my back against a large hickory tree.

Lucia handed me her canteen. She could see I was dead tired, but curiosity had her. Washington, George and one of the other Ferals with us, Marty, had gathered around, too.

There wasn't any TV or radio, texting or Twitter or Facebook or any other social media. The only way the true story, or at least true as Gibbons had shared it, spread was by word of mouth.

Garcia was more excited than me, had more energy as he rode on the wagon most of the time. He was telling a larger group while the NCOs met with Lieutenant Kuhn. Elmore was with his horses, uncharacteristically quiet most of the trip back. Morose would be the word. He'd probably seen or heard something more than I had, something he couldn't share.

Lieutenant Kuhn would share anything beyond what I knew when he deemed the time was right. The Army way.

I sat back and told Lucia and the others what Gibbons had told Garcia and me. Then I told them what Garcia and I talked about.

After that, I didn't hear what they had to say about it. Exhausted, I was asleep less than a minute after closing my eyes.

After the evening meal of half-burnt opossum, some dry dog food and collected greens, Lieutenant Kuhn spoke to everyone except Sergeants Yin and Eckstein, who stood watch.

Some sat and others stood in a large semicircle around

him. All that were left of us. It felt like sitting in a doctor's office, waiting to hear a diagnosis after an intrusive battery of tests. Deep down everyone knew the Grim Reaper was preparing to make some calls. You, the person to your right or left, or all three wouldn't be alive at the end of the week. Maybe the lieutenant's prognosis was so bad that none of us would survive.

"The Mawks know something's brewing," Lieutenant Kuhn said, and shrugged. "We humans are up to something. Everyone here knows that."

He didn't say how humanity knew that the Mawks knew, or suspected we were up to something. They might have captured equipment. Maybe they were listening in, had broken codes or encryption. The aliens could have taken prisoners and interrogated them, or worse.

"So, we're assigned to be part of a distraction. Everyone here is now, by order of the President, under Army Command committed to the mission. Call it drafted, call it conscription, call it volunteering."

Several of the Ferals sat up straight, jaw muscles flexing, looking at one another.

"I'm not much for speeches. Those of us still alive are the smartest, or the quickest, or the most skilled at survival. Or lucky beyond measure."

He placed his hands on his hips. "Conscription. Desperate times call for undemocratic measures, ladies and gentlemen. That won't change how we've done things up until now, but it might in the future. I don't believe it will. Then again, I won't offer up any promises."

He paused to let that sink in, and allow a kernel of contemplation to germinate. Lucia's hand found mine. She squeezed it, and I squeezed back, before she withdrew her hand.

"We're ordered to be part of a distraction," the lieutenant started again. "Force the enemy to take their eyes off the ball.

"Check your gear and pack up. Catch some sleep. At sunrise, we'll be moving to form up with some other units."

Lieutenant Kuhn took a deep breath and gazed around at the group. "By now you know part of the story, the plan, but not enough to spill the beans, if you were captured." His eyebrows rose. "Personally, *I* don't know enough to spill more than a handful of beans."

He rubbed his chin. "In any case, it'll all be over in a few days, one way or the other. I'm not telling you something you don't already know when I say, even if we win, a lot of us are going to pay the price for that victory."

Lucia came running, almost skipping down the hill toward me. I was sitting next to my scooter. I'd just finished cleaning my rifle, and was looking over my double-barrel shotgun that Elmore normally kept on his wagon for me. He sort of fancied it.

"Jack," she said. "Sergeant Eckstein said he recommended to Lieutenant Kuhn that I be teamed with you instead of staying with him and the artillery."

Before I could say anything she continued, saying, "Marty is going to take my job moving and preparing shells. Sergeant Eckstein said they'd probably be assigned to a larger unit of artillery pieces, and Marty is stronger and he has more endurance."

I raised an eyebrow, wondering why Lucia wasn't insulted and didn't argue that, even if it was accurate. "He said we worked well as a siphoning team, so we'll be assigned to rear guard, under Sergeant Yin. He checked with Yin. I'll ride with Elmore when you're on your bike or scooter, and then we'll trade off."

That made me happy. I liked working with Lucia. Having her nearby. But artillery wouldn't be on the front line. Sure, Sergeant Eckstein had used his howitzer for direct fire. But, if they were forming a larger battery of pieces, it wouldn't be near the front, engaging in direct fire against the enemy.

Something told me that Sergeant Eckstein didn't expect us to survive, and thought it would be better if Lucia and me died alongside each other, or at least in close proximity.

I just smiled and accepted her hug, and didn't share my morbid thoughts.

Chapter 33

We travelled no more than thirty miles, as the crow flies. Old sayings like that are probably destined to return to common usage. Eventually the vehicles will break down, and the fuel available for scavenging will be used up. Then it'll be bikes and boots. Those will wear out, too.

I had some spare boots and bikes back at the park, but those were hundreds of miles away.

What would happen when we humans ran out of bullets? Would we be able to fight the aliens then? Did the Mawks bring ships with manufacturing facilities, to build railguns and tanks to fight us? Or were they on a limited supply until they established themselves?

Lieutenant Kuhn said it'd be over one way or the other in a few days. Even if we won, my guess was that it'd be decades until society recovered. How many people with the know how to rebuild were dead? Electricians, bio researchers, computer techs, nuclear engineers...how many were still alive? How many of them had the same survival luck as me? Maybe the government rounded up a core of those with the skills, if they knew of the possible invasion. Or did the politicians only look after themselves? If they did, their supplies would run out, too. Maybe sooner than mine, and maybe not. Either way, they'd run out in the end.

My thoughts shifted to broader areas, and it was proving depressing. So much of my time had been spent in our park, trying to learn and survive. Then, doing whatever it took to deliver the nuclear device. Now that the delivery was done, and the park seemed like a world away, a focused urgency wasn't on hand to distract me. Sure, a day or two from now, I might be dead. I should be preparing for that struggle, but I didn't know my part in it. Not yet.

At least there was Lucia. She was an anchor to our park, and a reason to look forward. She was reliable and attractive. She put up with me, and was a little less volatile than before.

Okay, a lot less volatile, probably because she was even further out of her element than me. Or she'd started thinking about—come to realize before me—the future that faced not only her and me, and everyone in our column, but all of mankind. Even if we won.

And then, what if the Mawk's enemies managed to track them here? If they were even more powerful than the Mawks, what chance would we, a wrecked world, have against them?

Then again, maybe the other aliens weren't looking for trouble. Could be the Mawks attacked them and bit off more than they could chew.

Lucia stood next to me, at the base of a mountain along with the rest of our column, waiting for the lieutenant to return with our orders. We weren't the only group. A few Humvees and Bradleys sat silent, but it was obvious that they were in working order. Soldiers moved around them, checking engines, wheels and tracks.

We looked worn out and ragged. There wasn't a uniform that hadn't been torn and mended, and stained. Boots scuffed, faces unshaven. We smelled. Sure, we washed, when we could, body and clothes. Socks every day and hands and face every day. But with no deodorant and limited soap…must've been like this in the middle ages. In third world countries. The whole world was a third world country. We all smelled of body odor, but at least we weren't suffering from halitosis. Everyone in our column brushed their teeth regularly. Nobody had tooth paste, but ashes and just plain brushes with water worked well enough.

Lucia stared up at me, eyes wide, with one eyebrow raised.

"What?" I asked.

She leaned back against Elmore's trailer. He was with his horses, watering them at a stream guarded by several soldiers, so that nobody contaminated it. Not far away, a pair of llamas were being led by their owner. They were probably the ones spotted the previous night. I knew they were llamas because Elmore told me alpacas had shorter ears and were too small to pull carts. The llamas were off white in color and looked ornery and difficult to handle. Stubborn like mules are said to be.

"You haven't talked much today," Lucia said. "Not when we've been together, like lunch, or now." At first her hand rested on her hip. Then it slipped to her side and she looked away. "You mad that I talked the sergeant into me sticking with you?"

That caught me by surprise. "No, Lucia. What would make you think that?"

"You not talking. I know you ain't a big conversationalist, Jack." She frowned. "It's like you're mad, or pouting."

I leaned back against the wagon next to her. George and Washington must've overheard Lucia's tone and gave us some distance.

"I *am* mad," I said. "Mad at the Mawks. Since we made the delivery, my mind's been clear to think." I took a deep breath and exhaled. "Even if we win, Lucia, it's not going to change much. The world's wrecked."

"If we win, Jack, we'll still be alive and breathing." She folded her arms across her chest. "What else? There's more than that. It's about me?"

I weighed saying nothing, then shrugged. "You'd be safer with the artillery. They won't be on the front lines."

"You think with space aliens, there's gonna be a front line?"

"Initially, when they first attack there will be."

"So, it's fine for you to die fighting, but not me? When we go back to our park, Jack, you think I should hide out in that old school house, to be safe and all?"

I didn't want this to become a fight. Her voice and expression showed that was the direction we were heading.

"We're a good team, Lucia. But this isn't siphoning fuel, and watching for crawlers or dozers, or hostile scavengers trying to get the drop on us."

"I've been in as many army battles as you, Jack."

We were drawing attention. Most glanced our way and

then looked the other direction, taking a few steps further away.

"You have," I said, turning to face her. "My fault for not wanting to see you killed like Private Barhorst was. Blasted into a bloody pulp right next to me. Breathing and living and fighting one moment. Dead the next instant."

Lucia's hands went to her hips. "You had feelings for her, Jack?"

That was it. I was done explaining myself. "Screw you. If you think that's it, then you don't know me as much as you seem to think you do." I pushed up from leaning on the wagon. "Think I'll go back with the not talking route."

And walked away.

"We are now attached to the 194th Engineer Brigade," Lieutenant Kuhn said. "Our artillery piece, along with Sergeant Eckstein, Private Washington and Martin Tallman, are reassigned to the artillery company. Except for vehicle drivers, the rest will form Company C under Major Elbadin of the First Battalion. Organization and ranking officers are by necessity, nonstandard. My direct superior is to be Captain Nejem.

"My orders are to accompany our vehicles and drivers, which are to become part of the motor pool, which I will command. Any personal equipment such as bicycles will be marked and inventoried, and returned upon completion of the mission. More on that in a moment."

That didn't make sense, but it was the Army, an army whose organizational structure had gone to hell. Maybe they really needed the lieutenant at the motor pool to get things organized. Maybe Captain Nejem was a superior tactician? It didn't matter. Sergeant Yin and Corporal Jones would be with us on the firing line, giving orders when it counted.

"Mr. Elmore Foltz will be part of the mobile reserve," Lieutenant Kuhn continued. "Attached to the motor pool, but his first assigned duty is to transport all of our personal effects, those that you will not need in the next three days, to a holding area. He will issue you a written receipt, describing your equipment. He will keep a copy, and will submit a copy to the supply officer. Keep only what you are able to carry, including your filtering straw." The lieutenant's eyes locked on me for a brief second. "Rations will be provided. Carry as much ammunition as you deem necessary. If you are short, the Engineering Brigade to which we've been attached has a surplus of most military and common nonmilitary ammunition. If you need a KA-BAR fighting knife or if you are trained in the use of grenades, see Sergeant Yin or Corporal Jones, whichever happens to be your squad leader. Sergeant Yin will lead First Squad. Corporal Jones, Second Squad. Having only two NCOs, they will be in charge of two oversized squads. As I said, nonstandard structure."

Lieutenant Kuhn stood straight, with his hands behind his back. "First order of business, the sergeant and corporal will call off names of their squad members. So that there isn't a log jam at Mr. Foltz's wagon, the squad leaders will direct you to report to him and turn in your equipment. In the meantime you will inventory and prepare requests for ammunition or gear. Thus, taking care of your equipment needs and storage is your second order of business.

"Once that is accomplished, you will form up and move to your assigned sector, dig in and prepare to defend, under the direction of your squad leaders. Sergeant Yin will be in charge until Captain Nejem arrives.

"Sergeant Yin and Corporal Jones, establish and organize your squads while I do the same with the drivers and their vehicles."

Lucia moved up next to me and whispered, "You could replace that hand axe with a good knife, Jack."

While Yin called off names, I glanced down at her grinning face. "Why would I want to do that?" I said, then returned my focus to listening for my name—and Lucia's.

She took hold of my elbow. "Sergeant Yin already told me that we're both assigned to his, First Squad.

"Let's hurry," she said, pointing toward our column's surviving artillery piece being hitched to a Humvee. "I wanna say goodbye to Washington and Sergeant Eckstein."

"See how handy having a hand axe is?"

The local forces had provided saws and axes, shovels and pickaxes. The llamas were hauling cut trees from uphill for our two squads.

Lucia wiped sweat from her brow and cursed under her breath. Wearily digging through rocky dirt and cutting through roots put her in a foul mood. I was tired too, but building a bunker, instead of a shallow foxhole, was important. We might not need it. However, if we did, we were going to need it badly. Mawk railguns could chew through logs faster than any steroid-enhanced beaver on amphetamines. Better the destruction starts out on the logs than on my flesh. Rocks might offer more protection, sure. But dealing with flying rock shards, hot enough to blister any exposed skin they touched, wouldn't be fun.

Really, nothing about fighting the Mawks would be fun.

While we dug and built, a team of men were surveying the road leading past our position. They marked a broad line and numbers across the road every two-hundred yards. They also dug and hammered poles in the ground, next to the lines. Each pole had painted striping on it, corresponding with the road paint.

Yin said the marks were to guide artillery fire. If the Mawks came our way, someone in the hills would signal back to the artillery park. The plan was to relay, starting with someone on one of the hillsides. It was in place of radio, which made sense. How effective it would be was another question. Having premeasured distance established certainly wouldn't hurt. And it's especially helpful to make sure artillery didn't rain down on us.

A few engineers were also digging and placing some land mines along the road. Their uniforms looked a lot cleaner and less worn than anyone's digging in on the hill.

Again, some paint on the grass and road, this time red arrows, indicated the spots where we probably wouldn't want to go stomping around.

Lucia dropped her shovel and plopped down on the ground. I finished hacking a few stray branches from a pine log and dropped my hand axe next to her shovel. Then I squatted next to Lucia and offered her a drink from my canteen.

She took it and unscrewed the cap. "Why'd you take those grenades? You ain't trained."

"No, but when Sergeant Yin has a few moments, I asked him to show me the basics."

"He agreed?"

I pointed to the small crate sitting next to my backpack, rifle and shotgun leaning against a nearby tree. "He's the one that secured them for me."

We were digging in at the base of a hill, set about twenty yards from the road leading up to several mountains whose ridgeline ran pretty close north to south. They weren't the tallest set of hills, or mountains, in the region. Up the road about a quarter mile stood an abandoned town, most of which was burned out. 'Town' was a generous term. Maybe a gas station with a small diner and convenience store attached, fifteen or twenty homes, mostly small one-story deals, and what must've been a bar. A dozer had broken into most of the buildings, from the holes torn into their walls, those buildings that hadn't burned down. The residents probably set fire to one of the houses, hoping to kill the dozer while the beast was inside.

From the look of things, everyone died, or abandoned what was left, months ago.

Lucia and I were digging on the far end of First Squad's line with Second Squad beginning just to our left. To our right, two Ferals, Vinny and Roamer, were digging an emplacement for the .50 caliber machine gun used in the ambush south of Cincinnati.

Both men were lean and constantly scowling and cursing. Vinny was shorter and wore a green and black checkered flannel shirt that he'd torn the sleeves off of. He had a matching one with sleeves that he wore at night. Roamer wore a red Ohio State football jersey that was so tattered and stained the numbers were obscured. The white color was a mash of browns and grays. Both men kept their beards short, looking like a blind barber had trimmed them. The men probably kept their beards short using a knife, without the aid of a mirror. Or, using dull scissors, they trimmed each other's that way as a joke.

Across the road from us, also along the anticipated direction of an enemy assault, was a company from Alabama's 167th Sustainment Brigade.

Other units were further along the road and in place up the mountain sides, and some at the other end of the road, where it narrowed before entering this short range of hills— or mountains, depending on who was asked. There were also supposed to be some mobile units scattered in between.

A few hills over, south of our position, was our artillery, with more soldiers, both professional and conscript, digging in. Sergeant Eckstein was there, George and Private Washington were there.

What was to say the Mawks wouldn't just bombard us from space, or land on us with their tanks and combat vehicles?

Of course, all told, we probably had more than a regiment of soldiers. All of us in one area. A pretty tempting target to swoop in and eliminate. We were supposed to be a distraction, and if we managed to serve that purpose, we'd get hammered.

Vinny and Roamer were already finished and came over to help me and Lucia place the overhead logs behind the two we'd dug in behind a ramp of dirt. The best protection we could manage from the front.

"Building yourself a real fort there," Vinny assessed while helping me lift one of the trimmed logs into place.

"A lot of work," I said. "But me and Lucia might need it." She'd given up the name, Archer, since she rarely carried her bow anymore.

Lucia added, "He already scouted out a spot for a fallback foxhole for us." She pointed over her shoulder with her thumb. "Fifty yards up hill."

"You're hard core, Jack," Roamer said. "Hard core serious."

"About surviving, I *am* hard core," I said, kicking the newly placed log into position. "If we need to fall back, we'll need a good foxhole really bad."

"Tell ya what," Vinny said. "We'll finish helping you here and you help us up there."

Lucia grinned. "May as well. When Sergeant Yin gets back from talking to..." She eyed me, then continued. "...coordinating with them across the road, he'll order us to prepare a backup—a secondary position—anyway."

Lucia got up and began tying the ends of her shirt into a knot, revealing her tight, sweat-streaked stomach. "Get me your canteens, gentlemen. While you're doing the cutting and digging, I'll cross the road to the stream." She unbuttoned a couple buttons on her shirt and adjusted her chest with a playful smile. "Along the way I'll stop and talk to those professional soldiers burying land mines along the road. See why they gave us iodine pills, and whatever else they might know."

She turned and started to leave, then stopped and grinned back at us. "Jack's better at digging holes than anyone you'll ever meet. It's all he did back at our park."

Vinny and Roamer watched Lucia make her way across the ditch and toward the soldiers down the road. Once past the ditch, her stride changed to one that added emphasis to her hips.

Her jeans were a bit tighter since she'd joined me in the park. Despite the hard travel, we'd eaten well enough. Plus, she was getting chesty enough to offer an eyeful of cleavage when she wanted, and it was apparent that she wanted to.

"Fine looking woman," Roamer said.

Vinny shook his head and met my and Roamer's gaze. "Hides her womanly charms well."

I laughed. "Meaner than a rabid weasel, you get on her wrong side."

Vinny helped lift and set the next log. "You and her go way back?"

I nodded, kicking dirt around the log and stomped it into place. "She killed more crawlers than men before we started south from Toledo. At least those men that I'm aware of."

Vinny finished packing dirt around the log with his boot. "I believe ya, Jack. She's got that crazy pissed look in her, just waitin' to jump out."

After we emplaced the third overhead log, I said, "Let's get a few trees cut down before that llama team up there calls it quits."

"Jack, let's do halfsies again," Lucia said, holding up her can of pork and beans.

I was using my Boy Scout pocket knife's can opener on my can. I'd already opened hers. "Peaches. Sounds like a plan."

Thing was, the local garrisoning forces provided food, canned food, but some joker had torn off all of the labels. So, everyone got a can. Food roulette. Sitting in the fading light across from us, Vinny and Roamer were already digging into their canned dinner. Roamer had concentrated soup, split peas and bacon. Vinny had pinto beans.

Lucia and I had collected some dandelion leaves and Vinny had gotten some purple-flowered fireweed and clover near the road in front of our position. The gathered supplement for our meal proved to be a bitter mixture overall, but it added various vitamins and roughage to our diets.

Sitting next to the emplaced .50 caliber machine gun and the two huge boxes of ammunition, I nodded to it after switching cans with Lucia. "Where'd you guys get that?"

"Stole it from The Minions," Vinny said. "Knocked off one of their patrols. Didn't ask where they'd got it, seeing as how they were dead." Both Vinny and Roamer laughed.

I smiled and Lucia shook her head.

Roamer asked Lucia, "What'd you learn while plying your femininely charms?"

Lucia half closed her right eye and glared at him, trying

to gauge if there was any derogatory meaning in his question, then said, "Whatever," and titled her head before tipping the can over her open mouth to get out any final drips of peach juice.

Once finished, Lucia smiled. It was getting difficult to see as the evening darkness began to close in. "Tomorrow, the shit's going to hit the fan," she said, leaning close and signaling for us to gather around. There were other soldiers and conscripts, up and down the line, eating, cleaning their weapons or sleeping. "We're gonna be told tomorrow morning. The colonel in charge didn't want any of the new recruits to worry unnecessarily and lose sleep, or desert."

She pointed up our hill. "They got a radar up there somewhere. They also got a silo with a fake ICBM. Fake nuclear bomb attached. They wanna draw alien fighters and attack craft down. Other places across the country and world are doing the same thing tomorrow."

Skepticism reared its ugly head in my thoughts. "Those men know that? And told you?"

"Well," she said, a smirk in her voice. "They've been here since the beginning. Moved here in secret, when underground construction for the silos began. Before the Mawks attacked.

"No women around, until now, Jack, so I think they're telling me something truthful. Plus, they're telling everyone tomorrow morning anyway. Except about the fake bomb attached."

Vinny and Roamer grunted agreement. I wasn't so sure.

"Once they send their fighters and attack craft down and get distracted, that's when we hit them."

"How?" I asked.

"They wouldn't say." It was getting too dark to see, but she had a frown in her voice. "They probably don't even know."

"So," Vinny said, "we're here, digging in to make the fake attack more realistic, to fool the Mawks?"

"Decoys attached to the decoy," I said. "Drain their resources, maybe draw off their reinforcements.

"Iodine tablets?" I asked, thinking about the ICBM's warhead being a fake. We'd brought a real one all the way down from Toledo, or at least I hoped we had. All those people who died along the way, to be carrying yet another decoy?

Luther and I had a stash of iodine tablets, in case of radiation, like from nuclear fallout. We buried them beneath the slide in the playground area. Three feet from the ladder.

"Why the iodine tablets?" Lucia said. "They didn't know why, or weren't willing to tell me. I think they just didn't say, Jack."

Cleavage, even good cleavage after a long drought, is only so effective. But I wasn't going to comment on that. Agitating a potentially rabid weasel is never a good idea.

Chapter 34

"The captain didn't say nothing about decoying in this. We ain't plastic ducks." Roamer's loud complaint to Vinny carried to our bunker. The heavy downpour ended and the late afternoon skies were clearing. "Where was the bugle call to halt the rain two hours ago?"

In the absence of radio communication, they'd given us a bugler and a handful of bugle calls. Advance, fall back, open fire, cease fire, shift left, shift right, hunker down in the bottom of your foxhole.

"He's right," Lucia said, squatting down and balancing on the makeshift latticework of branches I'd stuffed in the bottom of our foxhole. Although the overhead logs, and the brim I'd built around the hole when I'd seen the rains coming, kept much of the water out, the two hour downpour wasn't to be denied its chance to make the bottom of our shelter a murky, muddy mess.

"We're in better shape than most," I said to Lucia. My voice lacked much conviction, although I suspected it was true.

"What's Roamer got that welding helmet for?" Lucia asked. "Where'd he get it? Hope he's not thinking it'll protect him from those Mawk railguns."

"Don't know where he got it," I said. Lucia and I both had Army helmets strapped on, as did just about everyone in our two squads. "He said if there was a nuclear blast, he wanted to see what was going to kill him."

"Stupid moron," she mumbled, presumably so that her comment wouldn't be overheard. Earlier, the cascading rain would've made sure of that. The scattered bird calls present now, wouldn't.

"Well," I said, "the visor plates protect a welder's eyes. He says the one he's got has the most protection available, whatever that is. And the metal protects his face and head, probably not as well as a helmet, especially not from the back. He plans putting it on at the last second."

"Will it work, Jack?"

"If he sees anything that's close, he won't have time to tell us about it. We'll be busy cooking from the blast heat, or being battered to death by the pressure wave. My guess is both."

"Thanks for the positive thinking."

"Better than dying of radiation poisoning," I said. "It's supposed to be a horrible way to go." I reached into my pocket for a small plastic bottle, remembering to take my next iodine pill. "If it's close, these won't help much."

"What do ya mean?"

"Like a Band-Aid for a bullet hole."

Lucia cursed, then asked, "Why take them?"

I grinned, after taking a swig of water—like I needed it, soaked as I was. "Maybe the bullet hole will be like one from my carnival gun?"

She slugged me in the shoulder, and took her pill, washing it down with her own canteen. She'd filled ours using one of the dripping rivulets of water that had fallen between the overhead logs. The muddy water filling the foxhole's bottom was retreating from the soles of our boots. At least our boots were waterproof, even though we both were drenched. Dry feet counted for something.

"If you had another bandoleer for your shotgun shells," Lucia said, "and drew a black mustache above your lip, I could call you 'el Bandido.'"

There wasn't time to reply. The bugle call for 'hunker down' came. Both Lucia and I looked up for a fraction of a second before ducking low in our bunker and covering our helmeted heads.

Intense humming, like an electric lawnmower, reverberating like giant Mawk hunting drones, was closing in on us. Then a sound like a giant weed whacker chewing the trees above us, passed overhead.

A handful of splinters rained down on Lucia and I, along with a gush of water. Some screams followed.

Lucia grunted. "Something's stuck in my back."

Above, one of our logs had been shattered, looking like it'd suffered a close encounter with a mega buzz saw. Two of the resulting shards were sticking out of Lucia's back.

She refused to wear the bullet-proof vest. Said it wouldn't close over her chest right, so what was the point? I wasn't sure it was true. Nevertheless, that left it for me.

"Hold still," I said, while examining her back, trying to ignore the nearby screams. Most, but not all, of the men in our squad, and the one next to us, had opted for the logs overhead. Those that hadn't were paying the price for their laziness.

I studied the two pieces of wood. They looked like a pair of four inch splinters, each dug into her back near the shoulder blade, about two inches apart. Both of the pieces had penetrated a quarter inch deep into the muscle.

She handed me a clear plastic box, our first aid kit. "Hold still," I said again, before pulling the wood splinters out.

She flinched and grunted.

"Just a little blood, Lucia. Shouldn't leave a scar. Help me lift the back of your shirt."

She untucked it while I tore the bandage wrapping open. I used my sleeve to wipe blood away. There wasn't anything dry to do better, so I squirted some antibacterial gel on the wound and slapped the patch on, hoping the adhesive stuck.

I carefully pulled her shirt down and pressed my palm over the wound, giving the bandage a little better chance to take hold.

Lucia winced.

I said, "Should've worn my bulletproof vest."

She looked over her shoulder and sneered at me. "Don't fit no more, remember?" Then she grinned. "When that bugle calls us to start shooting, you get to stick your head up first."

I was going to say, 'It doesn't protect my face,' but, again, the bugle interrupted me. This one ordered us to open fire. Grabbing my .22 caliber rifle, I peered through the slit, past the shattered trees and branches arrayed around us.

Across the road, the opposite hillside looked like a giant weed whacker had torn through the pine trees. From what could be seen, our side probably looked the same.

Off to the right, down the road near the town, there was movement. Smooth, metallic shapes. Mawk tanks and personal combat vehicles. At least twenty of the former and three times as many of the latter. Hopefully they weren't top-of-the-line Mawk battle tanks. Several even larger, bus-like, bulbous vehicles followed. They were either armored supply vehicles or troop transports.

Out of the corner of my eye, swooping down from above, opposite the ground assault's approach, two trios of Mawk attack craft appeared. They were oblong, disk-shaped, like the Cylon raiders from the old 1970s *Battlestar Galactica* series, but perfectly smooth with a raised central cockpit and large guns aligned along the end of the 'wings.' The weapons were sleek, built into the flying craft's design, but with bulbous ends along the back. One group of three was turning away. The other remained on approach.

Despite leaning back and looking out the side of our shelter, it was difficult to tell which side of the road the remaining V formation intended to strafe, if that was their intention. The mower sound indicated they were responsible for the attack moments before.

Instead of attacking us, they veered off and angled up the mountainside.

Looking behind us, Lucia said, "Look, Jack!"

With the trees ravaged by intense railgun fire, we were able to witness what could only be an ICBM rocketing upward from our mountain. Easy to say why the trio of attack craft pulled up, pursuing something they believed more deadly. Armed with railguns, it wouldn't be hard for the aliens to take out the ICBM.

Then, smaller rockets trailing smoke darted up to intercept the attack craft. One smoke shaft after another appeared until four were in the air. "SAMs!"

"What's sams?" Lucia asked.

"Surface to air missiles. They take out airplanes. Maybe

they can take out the attack craft."

Even as I explained, the booms of firing artillery rumbled, echoing along the mountainside.

The attack craft began radical spins and maneuvers, all the while continuing to climb. Before the SAMs reached them, the attack craft opened up with their railguns.

The ICBM disintegrated in a fiery explosion after emerging above one of the trailing storm clouds.

Seconds later two of the SAMs detonated less than twenty feet from their target. The damaged attack craft ended its failed evasion maneuver with a wobble. The Mawk aerial attack craft weren't nearly as durable as their ground counterparts.

One of the final two SAMs detonated near the stricken craft. The fourth and final missed, and continued upward without a target. The wounded alien craft tumbled out of control, falling behind an intervening mountain ridge.

Even as it did, several kinetic energy weapons struck the mountain top where the ICBM had emerged. The ground rumbled and the trees shook, emphasizing the results of the orbital space to earth strikes.

"Jack," Lucia said. "We got bad company coming."

Several artillery and mortar shells detonated harmlessly a full hundred yards behind the advancing enemy ground units.

Leading the phalanx of shiny Mawk tanks was one bearing a large T-shaped attachment that protruded from its front. The wings of the T extended five feet beyond the tank's forward edge.

Although we'd been given orders to fire, no one had opened up yet. It seemed senseless for me to use my little .22 rifle against armored tanks. A few seconds later, the .50 caliber machine gun began chattering as it opened up, along with some of the larger caliber hunting rifles. Experience told me they couldn't penetrate the alien armor. Especially not at the current distance.

The booms of our artillery firing recommenced. At the same time, explosions erupted from the ground in front of the accessorized tank. The attachment was some sort of minesweeping device. It allowed the enemy armor units to creep forward without taking any mine damage.

Then artillery rounds began falling among the tanks and smaller combat vehicles, some of them scattering small round bomblets. Those detonated beneath a few of the tanks, disabling them. The other rounds, high explosive ones, from the howitzers and mortars, knocked the smaller vehicles around, but didn't stop any of them.

The two surviving attack craft ignored us, and raced toward the artillery park. I hoped some spotters saw them coming because there was no way we could send a warning. The artillery continued firing and several thin columns of smoke showed smaller SAMs were rocketing to intercept the closing attack craft.

We couldn't see what happened as the first row of tanks opened up on us.

Lucia and I huddled in the bottom of our foxhole while the heavy railguns tore into First and Second Squad's defenses, keeping us pinned down as they hovered forward.

The artillery continued, in lesser volume, and the engineers dug in across the road detonated their command-controlled mines. I ventured a peek through our shattered front logs. Luckily our hole was deep enough that we avoided injury from any penetrating rounds. There wasn't any worry about splinters as most of the wood had been pulverized. On the other hand, the temperature in our foxhole had risen at least forty degrees within seconds. Smoldering bits of logs threatened to burst into flame at any moment. The soaking rain that drenched everything was the only thing that kept full on combustion from happening.

Three successive explosions, followed by the earth trembling beneath us, signaled kinetic energy weapons had impacted nearby.

A few seconds after my ears cleared, I realized the rumbling boom of artillery fire was gone, telling me the kinetic strike's target. Three impacts? Odds were Sergeant Eckstein, Private Washington and George were dead. What about Elmore and his team? Was he still in the area when…?

How was it we in this area were getting all this Mawk attention? Armor advancing, aerial attacks, and kinetic impacts. Wasn't humanity supposed to be flooding the zone with attacks across the globe?

I didn't bother to scan the distant hillside location where the artillery was supposed to be. Didn't want their deaths confirmed by the telltale signs: rising smoke and falling debris. Lucia could've been among those killed by the kinetic impacts, but she wasn't. She was with me. As if to emphasize the point, she yanked me down just before the sixteen mobile Mawk tanks raked our side of the line again.

Our bunker was worthless now, the logs gone and the dirt in front of us gouged away. The bugle call to fall back sounded. Vinny and Roamer were out of their hole faster than Lucia and me. One lugged an ammo box and the other, the .50 caliber machinegun and tripod. Roamer had the welding helmet strapped to his hip. What could I say? I carried an antiquated double-barrel shotgun in a makeshift canvas sheath strapped across my back. For some reason Roamer, with his welding helmet, had laughed at my gun and sheath, called me Ash, with my Boomstick…whatever that meant, some sort of movie from what I'd been able to gather. Vinny got the joke, but Lucia and I didn't.

Roamer reminded me of Darth Vader, with his black welding helmet. That should've been my retort at the time, but it wouldn't have made any difference. They were laughing too hard.

I fired my rifle twice in the direction of the tanks while Lucia scrambled up the mud-slick hillside. The two little *pops* from my gun seemed so out of place compared to cracking railgun slugs, SAMs, ICBMs, detonating mines and kinetic weapon impacts. Shooting back at the enemy made me feel better, even if it might make me a target. It'd give Lucia and the machine gun duo a better chance.

A few other rifles firing sounded along with mine.

After Lucia and the other two had a five second head start, I clambered out of our shattered bunker and chased after them. The railgun gouges and furrows, and shattered remnants of the trees, actually made our retreat easier.

From what I could see through the steaming ground and smoldering fires, less than half of First and Second Squad was up and retreating.

Chapter 35

Sniping fire took down a few of us, but the artillery-deployed mines delayed the enemy advance long enough for us to reach our fallback position. The tanks and individual attack vehicles turned to concentrate on the 167th Alabama's position opposite ours. They'd had five days to dig in, as opposed to our one. Hopefully that gave them more advantage than our initial line of foxholes and mini-bunkers had afforded us.

I climbed over the logs and plunked down into our foxhole, next to Lucia. My boots were in a half foot of muddy water. Before the attack, I might've complained about being wet and cold, the water seeping into my boots. But I was alive, with the ability to complain—if I wanted to—for the moment.

With a pair of roof-mounted dual gun turrets, the larger, bus-like alien vehicles laid down a string of lashing fire. The slugs didn't bite as deep into the trees, ground and logs as the tanks' did, but they came in greater speed and volume.

Peering through a crack in our logs, I spotted the vehicles disgorging ground troops.

The disabled tanks turned our direction, enabling them to better provide the alien foot soldiers covering fire. Fortunately for us, the mobile tanks and individual attack vehicles advanced on the defenders from Alabama across the road.

"They're coming!" I yelled. "Ground troops."

My warning mingled with the shouts from others, and the bugle call to open fire.

As described to me previously, the aliens were a wicked cross between a praying mantis and a hawk, about three-quarters mantis.

My first personal observation revealed they were about four feet long and stood a little over three feet high. They appeared to have vestigial wings and advanced on us using their four hind legs. They had the body and legs of a mantis, but were covered in feathers, blue, white and black—the splattered colors of a blue jay. A broad torso and short neck supported each Mawk's feathered head, which closely resembled a hawk, eyes and all, except for the beak. That could be described as a gray, double beak, with two hooked portions curving downward, and one curving up, in between, like an inverted V jutting up, into a cruel W.

Their two arms ended in talon-like hands, carrying weapons that looked like a shiny, sci-fi version of an AK-47, banana magazine and all. A notable exception was the line of mini matchbox-sized protrusions spread along each side of the barrel.

They didn't wear any clothing, gloves or footwear. Instead they sported black harnesses strapped along and across their bodies, coupled with some netting pouches. The purpose was obvious, as the outfit securely held gear, possibly spare ammunition and weapons, along their bodies.

At least they didn't have body armor, not that I could see. If they were partially insectoid, maybe their exoskeleton covered that. Would my .22 caliber rifle penetrate? What I recalled from my biology studies was that exoskeletons were much more efficient in offering strength and leverage. It's why ants and other insects could carry so much compared to their size.

Heaven help us if it was the same for the Mawks.

About sixty of them advanced on us, broken up into groups of seven or eight. One half of each group scrambling forward while the other half provided covering fire from behind shattered stumps and ditches gouged into the earth. The tank railgun slugs kept us down, taking out a bunker position every few shots. Despite this, the bullets fired by the alien infantry proved to be equally feared.

Their rifles fired three inch, needle-like bullets, with tiny stabilization fins along the back and a small bulge nearer the point. Each made a crackling *snap* sound as it left the assault rifle muzzles. They also *popped*, after hitting a target.

The explosions weren't massive, equal to a small

firecracker, which they sounded like. My first experience with the Mawk bullets was seeing one drive an inch into the log protecting the front of my secondary foxhole. The explosion that followed a fraction of a second later blew out a chunk of wood, three-quarters of an inch in diameter and a half inch deep. Luckily, it happened far enough away that nothing flew into my eyes before I closed them, and not with enough force to penetrate my eyelids.

The second experience was seeing the result of a bullet striking Vinny in the cheek. He was feeding the belt of bullets into the machine gun when his face snapped back and he reached for the needle bullet. Before his hand got half way to his face, the needle bullet's bulbous section detonated, shattering Vinny's cheek bone and tearing off half his face. Heat from the small explosion cauterized some of the gaping wound.

Vinny stood up, and staggered back. In the process, another round hit him in the chest, penetrating deep enough that, when it detonated, he dropped, dead before hitting the ground. Either his lungs, or heart, or both had been obliterated within his chest.

"Jack!" Roamer shouted.

Cursing myself for not doing it before, I slid on my yellow-tinted shooting glasses and responded to Roamer's call. My little .22 caliber rifle was useless. I had my shotgun, but it wouldn't be useful until they were nearly upon us. Without hesitation, I climbed out of my bunker and dove into the adjoining foxhole. In the process I was hit by one of the needle bullets, too. It tore across the skin of my right bicep and passed on, leaving a trail of blood on my torn shirt sleeve. Ten feet behind me it detonated.

The Mawk infantry continued their leapfrog advance, closing to within fifty feet. Being so close, their supporting tank fire abated.

Roamer had dropped his welding helmet over his face. How well he could see through the coated lenses seemed less important than getting hit in the face like Vinnie had. Twice, one of the rounds was deflected by the steel helmet, only to detonate behind us.

The alien bullets made sense, especially if they targeted a foe with an exoskeleton. The needle would penetrate, and then the detonation would rupture the protective outer shell. For us, if it struck dense muscle tissue, an internal bone or a mass of tendons, that was enough to trigger detonation.

Despite the confusion, I stood hunched down, with Vinny's dead body between my legs, feeding the ammo belt into Roamer's .50 caliber machine gun. Vinny, wherever his soul was, would appreciate me taking up the job in his absence. There'd be plenty of folks besides him to mourn later, if any of us survived.

There aren't any atheists in a foxhole. That saying came to mind. I was agnostic, and thinking about souls. Hopefully I had one, because ending up like Vinny was a distinct possibility.

Roamer mowed down at least a dozen Mawks as they closed. Everyone still alive was up and firing lead at the aliens. They came on despite our withering fire. When they closed to less than twenty feet they poured forward as one.

I pulled the pin and tossed a fragmentation grenade, and ducked. Lucia saw me throwing it and beat me and Roamer to cover.

Blam!

Pushing myself up off of Vinny's corpse, I peered over the top log, seeing that the grenade knocked down two that were coming right for me and Roamer. It also knocked our machine gun askew.

The Mawks that ate my grenade were on the ground, twitching and convulsing like dying cockroaches. They sounded like a pair of steam kettles going off. All of the dying aliens did.

The Mawk battle cry was a stuttering whistle, sometimes high and piercing, other times low and husky. Their war cry melded with our human shouts and curses as they overran our foxholes and bunkers.

I reached over my shoulder for my shotgun. Lucia must've been lying down in the bottom of her bunker, firing her Colt pistol, as a Mawk soldier staggered and fell back in conjunction with the sound of pistol shots. Its feathered body jerked from several on-target bullets hitting before collapsing. One Mawk earned a load of my buckshot in the side as it angled away from Roamer's machine gun and toward Lucia's bunker. The blast knocked it off its feet, spasmodically kicking as it strove to reach the foxhole. It died less than three feet from Lucia, failing to avenge the death of its fellow soldier.

Before I knew it, one of the Mawks yanked aside our foxhole's pockmarked top log guarding the front. The alien swung the muzzle of his assault weapon my direction. The way he tossed that log aside? Mawks were strong—stronger than me. Fortunately, I was faster, and he got my second barrel full of buckshot. It obliterated his face.

From somewhere behind the lines, near the captain's headquarters bunker, our bugler called. The trumpeted order for us to hunker down penetrated the gunshots and whistles and explosive rounds. Where he was, I didn't know. Not too far up hill, based on the echoing sound. The corporal with the antique bugle was the only man in our company with a receiving radio. If he issued that call while we were being overrun, the reason had to be dire.

The Mawks must've received an order from their own commanders, as they immediately broke off and fled down the hill, carrying their wounded and giving us their backs, heedless of the consequences.

My only thought was, Nukes!

Roamer's foxhole was a wreck, so I scrambled out and down into my and Lucia's foxhole, landing next to her. It still had one overhead log sheltering it. The bugle call stopped. All was silent, except for the moans of dying men and Roamer, wearing his welder's helmet and shooting his rifle at the retreating Mawks.

"Get down!" I shouted at him. "Nukes!"

"If I'm gonna die, Jack, I aim to see it coming."

See it coming, he did.

Chapter 36

The earth shook, rattling Lucia and I around the bottom of our foxhole like a pair of dice in a Yahtzee cup. The deafening boom rumbled like ten thousand bass drums pounding around my head. An instant before that, the world lit up like a lightning bolt flashing ten yards above us.

"Holy shit!" Roamer shouted. "Lucia, Jack, you gotta see this."

His words reached me like a man shouting across the car of a runaway freight train.

The earth's rumbling stopped, and the ringing in my ears faded. Reaching for the lip of our muddy foxhole, I leveraged myself up and gazed at Roamer. He'd tipped his welding helmet back to see unimpeded.

Tops of a nearby ridge had erupted, with three oddly shaped mushroom clouds billowing up from them. They didn't have the exact form seen in documentaries and movies depicting thermonuclear detonations.

A pair of metallic rocks, kinetic energy weapons, disappeared down into the clouds, striking the wrecked mountain tops. In comparison, an anti-climactic event.

Too late, I thought, feeling the tiny rumble brought on by the Mawk's retaliatory effort.

"You shoulda seen it," Roamer shouted. "Three blasts, pret near blinded me, like strobe lights firing together. Black rocks, or something black, shooting up into the sky faster'n crazy hornets outta hell."

Still staring upward, he wiped a hand over his eyes and down his face, ending in a tug of his beard. "Errrumm, ahhh, that's what I think I saw…"

"Thunder wells," I mumbled, recalling a name hinted at. It fell together, made sense.

"What's that, Jack?"

"Thunder wells," I repeated.

Roamer shrugged in reply, and looked down into his

foxhole, recalling his fallen partner. "Sounds about right."

Then he knelt, his head lowering out of sight.

Lucia tapped my shoulder and pointed down toward the road. The Mawk tanks and armored vehicles were racing off. The four disabled ones were being towed, two by the armored personnel carriers and two by fellow tanks.

"Too late," I said, knowing that the nuclear warhead we'd transported served its purpose. All those carried to this area, brought from north and south had been used. Further east, just barely in sight, a pair of mushroom clouds, similar to the three near us, rose into the sky.

How many thunder wells remained silent, built for a warhead that didn't get delivered?

How many men and women died while playing their part in flooding the zone?

The wind continued blowing eastward, away from us. That meant any fallout would miss us. Bad news for anyone down wind.

"What's that?" Roamer asked, standing again and pointing skyward. Something streaked high in the sky, burning across it like a cluster of meteors, falling stars.

"For my money," I said, "one of the Mawk ships, busted up and falling out of orbit."

"Could be, Jack."

"Those rocks, or slugs you saw shooting skyward. They were fired by those nuclear blasts, like a gigantic pop-gun, I bet. Blown out into orbit by super-heated air or steam or something. Mineshafts or something like them acted like gun barrels. Thunder wells."

Didn't someone tell us that our attack was coordinated? Everyone at once, any surviving human forces with nukes, shooting at once, flooding the zone on a global scale?

Lieutenant Kuhn knew the ships' orbits, knew when they crossed overhead. I'd watched some of them passing in the night sky, when the timing was just right and they reflected the sun's light. How they lined up those shafts in the mountains—maybe dug them before the Mawks detonated their first EMP...

That the shape or surface of the slugs might've directed them came to mind.

Lucia interrupted my line of thought with a question. "Where are those alien tanks going?"

Both Lucia and Roamer were looking at me, expecting an answer. There hadn't been any tank blasts or gunfire around the 167th Alabama's position, not since the nukes went off.

Sergeant Yin, along with several other men from First Squad, walked toward us. "To those mountains, Lucia," he said, tipping his helmeted head toward the mushroom clouds. "Too little, too late."

"What were we shooting at?" Roamer asked. "Some space carrier or frigate or freighter?"

"Did we hit it—them?" Lucia added.

Sergeant Yin smiled while shaking his head. "I'm too far down the food chain to know that."

We may never know, I thought, my eye catching something distant in the sky. One, then two dark specks. Watching them for a moment, they appeared to be getting a little larger…coming closer?

Private Parcell noticed me looking at something and held a pair of binoculars to his eyes. After five long seconds of observation he said, "There's three of them. Metal disks, like capsules from…the Apollo Program? They must be big, shiny with black undersides. Parachutes, three of them attached to each, slowing their drop."

Black. That meant they'd survived the scorching heat suffered while entering Earth's atmosphere at high speeds. Years ago one of NASA's space shuttles burned up because its thermal heat shields failed.

Lack of something in the sky to compare them to made size and distance hard to gauge.

"Escape pods," Yin said. "Can't be anything else." He tapped Parcell on the shoulder, signaling for the private to hand over the binoculars. "Go up there, Parcell, and find our bugler and Captain Nejem. They should be in the signals and observation post. Inform the captain and ask him to report what we're seeing." He pointed to me. "Jack, you go across the road, gather up what's left of the 167th Alabama and get them back over here."

I grabbed my rifle and started pounding down the hill. Behind me, Yin shouted, calling the survivors to gather weapons and ammo, and form up.

Why did he order me across the road, instead of Roamer or Lucia, or one of the regular soldiers?

Getting there was tricky, stepping over the broken trees and shattered limbs, and not slipping on the muddy hillside. The dozens of dead Mawks? I felt no remorse or pity for them. They were alien invaders, the ones responsible for siccing the dozers and the crawlers on humanity. The EMPs, and bombardment from space, the disease and tsunamis…all the suffering, all the death. They were the reason.

Upon reaching the road I glanced upward, trying to estimate where the escape capsules might land. Sergeant Yin was right. Escape capsules, that's what they had to be. They'd land in the flat areas as opposed to the mountainsides, if they could help it. With our luck, probably nearby, maybe on the far side of the abandoned town. My gut said they would. How far or close to it, I had no idea.

Chapter 37

Captain Nejem kept us on our bellies or standing behind the burned-out town's few surviving buildings. He was an older man, maybe from the Middle East, Arabic or Indian. I wasn't sure, and didn't see a reason to ask anyone.

The escape capsules were taking forever to fall. The nearest, and closest to the ground, had three large parachutes slowing its descent. The others appeared to have the same. Something other than the parachutes had to be retarding their descent.

The captain had organized the remnants of the 37th and 167th into squads. There were only seventeen of us left from the 37th Infantry Brigade Combat Team, so we comprised what he named Fourth Squad. The other three squads, conscripts and volunteers and regulars of the 167th Sustainment Brigade, made up the rest. I estimated no more than ninety of us total, armed with M-16s, shotguns, hunting rifles, a couple machine guns, and my .22 carnival gun. More units were supposed to be forming up two or three miles behind us. We were closest to the alien escape capsules, especially with them coming down nearly upon us. So, apparently, we were to be the point of the spear.

That didn't sound good. Us, taking them on, having to advance out in the open.

Even worse, if the wind shifted we'd be vulnerable to radioactive fallout. If the Mawk armored units returned, we'd stand up to them no better than a pee wee football team defending against the Pittsburgh Steelers' offense. Sure, we might disable a tank or two, same as a Steeler might twist a knee tripping over an eleven year-old while blasting through a line completely ill-suited for the task.

But there we were, preparing to get at them, or at least contain them, once they landed. It looked like that might take place within a quarter mile of the town.

"First Squad," the captain said, from his position behind

a rusted steel shed about forty feet to our left, "when they get within range, open fire with your M2s. Attempt to shred their parachutes and give them a hard landing. That will also alert us to any self-defense capability. Fourth Squad, hold your machine gun fire in reserve."

Roamer and another soldier named Young, who ironically looked a decade too old to be a private, were manning our M2 .50 caliber machine gun. They had it set on its tripod, muzzle extending from the tailgate of a battered Ford Ranger. The truck cap and tailgate wouldn't provide much protection from railgun slugs. The setup offered some concealment. Of course the tracers would point right back to them.

They were no better off than Lucia and I hunkered down behind an old blue U.S. Postal Service mailbox that someone had knocked over. We dragged it a half a block to be in line with our squad along the edge of town. I'd pried it open and dropped in several cinder blocks. My hope was that the steel side and the intervening cinder blocks would degrade the first on-target slug's ability to penetrate our barrier, and us. We anchored it by bracing the mailbox's stubby legs on either side of a fire hydrant, and wedging a two-by-four between the mailbox and the trunk of an ornamental dogwood tree. The theory was that a slug wouldn't knock the mailbox back into Lucia and me. If it failed, death from blunt force trauma might be slower than a railgun round traveling a small fraction of the speed of light. There just wasn't time to dig a proper foxhole and let compacted earth do the job.

Other soldiers were stripping oak doors from houses and hauling out old refrigerators to improve their defensive positions. Some followed suit and filled the refrigerators and washing machines with cinder blocks and other debris. That's how bad our position was. If the escape capsules had self-defense weapons, or any aliens inside had any heavy-duty firepower, we were in trouble. Against the explosive needle bullets, I had more hope. Unless we were ordered to advance out into the open.

I didn't tell Lucia that shredding the parachutes might not do much good.

The amount of time it'd taken the escape capsules to descend suggested they had to be generating some sort of anti-gravity thrust. Or, maybe not.

If the Mawks had communications going, landing in an area where twenty minutes before, a firefight had been underway? Sure, they were kicking our tails from Maine to Montana, but they hadn't wiped us out, and we'd done our fair share of damage, especially when they fell back after the nukes.

Lucia and I had trouble hearing Captain Nejem's orders. He wasn't directing them at Fourth Squad. As a contingency, he was telling his engineers, the guys who'd emplaced the roadside mines, their job was to affix what they had, including some C4, to the nearest escape capsule. Target seams or doors or vents—anywhere where they thought the hull could be breached.

The 167th had already expended their few TOWs and RPGs defending their hillside position. C4 and some dynamite sticks comprised our only hope. If we couldn't get at them, the Mawks could just hunker down and wait for help to arrive. Their tanks weren't too far away, and I didn't think there was much in the surrounding hills that could stop them.

"Sarge," Private Parcell asked Yin, "what if those escape capsules hold noncombatants?"

Parcell had set up with his M-16 between the Ford Ranger and our mail box, behind a pink and green plastic slide he'd dragged from a nearby back yard. That didn't impress me.

Yin was on our left, less than a dozen feet away, behind a picnic table he'd stood on its end and braced against a split-rail fence. He peered intently at the drifting escape capsules.

The nearest one was a quarter mile up and twice that far away. It looked big. Fifty yards in diameter and three stories high, although it tapered, so that the top was about thirty yards in diameter. The three huge round, jellyfish-shaped parachutes were attached. The escape pods were smooth, but faint seams could be seen in the nearest, making me think they wouldn't be as nearly impenetrable as one of their battle tanks.

Parcell's question about noncombatants was directed at Sergeant Yin, but I couldn't help myself. "What of it?" I asked.

I turned to face him. "What about all of the human noncombatants wiped out by the tidal waves sent against the east and west coasts?" It was hard to keep sarcasm out of my voice. The anger probably masked it. "How many human *noncombatants* did the plague of dozers and crawlers eat?"

Except for the captain and his engineers, everyone within earshot was listening. Taboo or not, I continued, bringing lost family into the conversation. "Who here doesn't have a dead husband or wife, dead children or parents, or grandparents, thanks to the Mawks attacking Earth?"

Nobody said anything. They glanced my direction, and then returned their gaze to the escape capsules.

"It's us against them, Private. Species versus species. It'll only end when we're all dead, or they are."

After a few seconds of silence, Sergeant Yin said, "Couldn't've said it better myself, Jack. I've heard they're here on a rush invasion job because some other alien race defeated them, and they fled." He kept his eyes trained on the escape capsule, not sparing Parcell a glance. "Don't know how well it'll work out for us survivors if the aliens that defeated the Mawks track them here to Earth. It will end badly for us if they find us cooperating with the Mawks. Living in harmony. That's for sure."

"All I've got to say," Lucia said. Her knuckles went white gripping her rifle. "Eye for an eye and tooth for a tooth." She spat on the ground behind our mailbox barrier. "They've killed billions of us, so I say we got lots of catching up to do."

"Aww shit," Roamer said.

The sun glinting off several distant objects moving on the road explained the Feral's comment.

Mawk tanks. They were returning.

CHAPTER 38

"Holy shit," Roamer said, this time shouting instead of issuing a grumbling curse. "Y'all hear that?"

Lucia nudged me, her eyes searching the sky, and not the direction of the escape capsules.

The distant roar of jet engines. It was so foreign for a sound once so common. These, however, had a deeper, more menacingly metallic growl than passenger jets.

"Where the hell're those coming from?" someone from Second Squad's assigned area shouted.

"Who cares!" someone further away replied.

Captain Nejem, not distracted by the hopeful roar of approaching jets echoing off the mountainsides, ordered, "First Squad machine guns, open fire!"

That chattering gunfire drowned out what I hoped was real help—something that stood a chance against the alien tanks. I hunkered down with my back against the mailbox. Lucia looked down from peering over the top and joined me.

Roamer mouthed the words, "Screw it." Or maybe he actually said them. He angled his gun's barrel up and pulled the trigger, taking his shot at shredding the escape capsule's parachutes.

Precise, devastating fire answered our machine guns. In under five seconds, tank-fired railgun slugs obliterated all of First Squad's machine gun positions. Roamer and his new assistant gunner fared no better. The hyper-velocity slug tore into their small pickup truck like a .44 magnum round through an aluminum beer can. The first one hit, tore into the truck, knocking it back. The second struck a fraction of a second later, sending the shattered mess tumbling.

I curled into a ball as the heat and concussive force knocked the wind out of me. My ears rang while I struggled to keep from vomiting. Lucia wasn't as successful as me. We huddled together, but I managed to see two jets, less than two hundred feet overhead, roar over our position.

Memories from movies and airshows identified them. A-10 Warthogs. Tank busters.

I rolled onto my side for a view down the road. What would happen when the American Air Force brought its firepower to bear?

The tank-mounted railguns were effective anti-aircraft weapons. One of the two Warthogs disintegrated in a fiery ball, showering shards of smoking metal over the advancing enemy's armored column. Fortunately, the doomed pilot managed to release his bomb load a second before his demise. The surviving A-10 pilot pulled up upon releasing his bomb load.

The bombs broke open, releasing clusters of smaller bomblets that rained down among the tanks. Rattling explosions erupted beneath the leading echelon. The Warthog continued upward, placing itself between the tanks and the escape capsules. The pilot was betting the Mawks wouldn't risk striking the escape capsules.

Out of the corner of my eye, I spied a second prong in the aerial attack. Like dragonflies, four attack helicopters appeared above the crest of the hill, ahead to our right, and released a volley of anti-tank missiles at the stalled tank column. Three out of four launched missiles impacted against a target. The smoke and debris made it impossible to tell if they penetrated the alien-crafted armor.

Before the Mawks could retaliate, the Apaches dropped back behind the mountain ridge. At the same time the surviving Warthog tore into the most distant capsule with its chin-mounted rotary cannon. It sounded like a giant zipper ripping open. Sparks showered the side and bottom of the disk-shaped pod. First Squad's and Roamer's machine gun fire had holed but failed to shred the nearest escape pod's parachutes. The Warthog's final burst before passing overhead left its target with little more than tattered remnants.

The stricken pod wobbled while descending at an accelerated rate before toppling end over end. A flipping coin in freefall. It crumpled against the ground like a cheap subcompact veering off the highway and slamming into a mighty oak.

A cheer rose up among our squads. We'd witnessed so few victories over the Mawks, it couldn't be helped.

The Apache attack helicopters popped up again, this time splitting their missile fire between the tanks and the nearest escape pod, now only a hundred yards above the ground. There weren't any rockets firing to slow its descent, but something was happening as its parachutes fluttered to the side. Some sort of antigravity engines like the tanks used were kicking in.

This time the Apaches didn't escape Mawk retaliation. One exploded like a beer can full of kerosene. Instead of ducking back behind the mountains while their fiery missiles impacted against the side of the escape pod, now slowing to land, the attack helicopters tipped forward and flew down the hillside mere feet above the treetops. They were like angry black dragonflies spitting hot metal from their 30mm chain guns.

The Apaches stood toe to toe, streams of bullets and their few remaining missiles slamming into the tanks and smaller attack vehicles. All the while the Mawks fired back, sharp thunderclaps as the slugs burst from their railgun muzzles. The Army pilots could've fled, but stayed, and were picked off one by one. Their fiery deaths were spectacular compared to the Mawk tanks, which simply dropped eight inches to the ground. Smoke seeped into the air from where they'd been holed, adding a toxic mix to the ozone-scorched air.

The smaller Mawk attack craft scattered, those few that remained. They must've sensed the lone A-10's return.

It swept in, rotary cannon spitting smoke and lethal rounds. Its fire was so intense that the plane appeared to stall, knocked back by the recoil of its spewing cannon. It shredded the middle escape pod's parachutes while biting into the escape capsule's top. This one didn't topple, but came down faster than it should have, sounding like a bass drum doing a belly flop onto a shallow pond. Its bottom crumpled and several oval escape hatches blew off.

The Warthog continued firing as it passed, adding its cannon rounds to the mayhem within the smoking tank column. The determined pilot, however, didn't escape. A tank slug clipped the combat plane's wing and sent it cartwheeling out of control into the mountainside.

"We ain't exactly winning," Lucia, said. "But they ain't neither. Not this time."

I crouched back behind the mailbox, leaning in next to her and checking my rifle one last time. "It ain't over yet. The tanker Mawks are abandoning their crippled tanks, and I saw some Mawk colonists climbing out of the nearest escape pod."

As if reading my mind, our bugler sounded the command to open fire.

Chapter 39

The air attack stopped the Mawk tank advance about seventy-five yards short of the town. The smoking wrecks extended back about another seventy yards along the road. The valley area was flat, reaching almost a half mile across before reaching sloping mountainsides. Humans could climb them, but Mawks might be better at it.

Beyond the tanks were the three escape capsules. The nearest was damaged, but had civilians pouring out and milling about. At least a couple hundred, with a dozen more emerging from the few blown escape hatches every few seconds.

We exchanged fire with a handful of surviving Mawk tankers. Their snub-nosed carbine guns couldn't hit us, except through luck, and our marksmen, including Lucia with her scope, were steadily picking them off each time one or two peered around a disabled tank or attempted to crawl toward a ditch running parallel to the road.

Rather than take pot shots, I observed what was going on with the civilians.

"Sergeant Yin," I called.

He was busy doing what he could with his M-16. "I know, Jack. If those civilian Mawks make a break for the hills, we'll lose a lot of them."

The alien escape capsules had to carry at least four or five thousand colonists. One damaged and one destroyed, that still left more than our eighty or so soldiers could handle, even if they were unarmed. Artillery would've been nice to call on, but that wasn't an option. A few more cluster bombs would've been handy, but no more air support seemed likely.

Down the line, from his position behind the rusted shed, Captain Nejem spoke into a radio. That was a definite risk, but the escape capsules meant the global thunder well attack had met with at least some success.

If a human naval task force suffered a similar surprise attack? There'd be too much confusion to respond to one small radio communication signal, right? That sounded convincing to me. Hopefully whoever the captain was speaking to would send us help, soon. Weren't there supposed to be forces organizing down the road behind us? They might've been hit, or were dealing with their own tanks or escape pods. My attention had been too focused on the three capsules and the air to ground battle to have any inkling of their situation.

Two runners left the captain, one sprinting toward Sergeant Yin. The other toward Third Squad holding the far side of our line.

After a brief exchange, Sergeant Yin ordered, "Fourth Squad, prepare to advance. Hold your fire. Do NOT shoot the Mawks unless I give the order!"

He paused. "We're to keep them from abandoning escape capsules. Keep them contained as best we can until reinforcements arrive."

After the gunfight between us and the Mawk tankers, they were either dead or retreated back to the nearest capsule. None of the tanks appeared operative and none of the smaller individual combat vehicles still around were moving.

I took a drink from my canteen after rechecking my rifle. I placed a hand on the grip of my revolver in its holster, and then touched the butt of the shotgun above my shoulder. I had two grenades and ammo in my pockets. Would it be enough?

Lucia glanced at me, her eyes wide. They didn't hold fear. The way she bit her lip said she just didn't know what to expect.

I directed her gaze to the wrecked pickup truck, Roamer's grave, still smoking. "Time for some real payback."

A few men around me nodded agreement.

Lucia's eyebrows pinched down and a sneer crossed her face. It reminded me of the days before we'd joined forces in the park.

"Eye for an eye," she said.

"Fourth Squad, we're to fan out to the right," Yin said. "Don't bunch up. Keep your gun barrels pointed down. *Don't* open fire unless I order. If I go down, Corporal Jones is in charge."

That last statement wasn't necessary, not for me, but maybe for the few remaining Ferals.

The bugle sounded, ordering our advance.

Sergeant Yin stood, and swung his arm. "Up, Fourth Squad, follow me!"

There were only fifteen of us left. Lucia leapt on top of and then off of our mailbox, sprinting out ahead of everyone else. Looking back, she stopped for a few seconds. Then trotting, she fell in line ten feet behind the sergeant. I caught up and followed her at a quick trot, with Private Johnson behind me. Somewhere he'd gotten his hands on a SAW, a light machine gun. Blood seeped from beneath a bandage taped over his brown cheek. His penetrating eyes reminded me of a boxer going into the final round, looking to deliver a crushing knockout.

His visage made Clint Eastwood look like a piker.

Mawks could probably interpret our facial expressions as well as I could their body language, which was nil. But, if they could, the look on Johnson's face would give them second thoughts about Earth's subjugation. Maybe thirds, because they were probably already having second thoughts.

Sergeant Yin led us wide around the defeated tank column. Like everyone else, I couldn't help but point my rifle toward it, expecting the smoking domes of metal to rise to life and bring their railguns to bear. They looked like the tanks we'd faced before. None were the main battle tanks. Lucky for us.

First Squad trailed behind. Their numbers more than doubled the size of our assault team. Approaching left of the road, on the other side of the tank column, visible only in glimpses between the wrecked tanks, advanced Second and Third Squads.

The smoke looked gray with wisps of yellow. It had to be toxic, so I looked away and took shallow breaths. The best I could do.

Around the nearest escape pod, Mawk colonists were gathering into groups of twenty to thirty, tending to their injured and largely oblivious to our approach. Several Mawks standing sentry issued stuttering whistles before retreating into the masses.

Unlike the ones we'd fought before, Mawks with more gray than blue plumage were represented in roughly equal numbers.

"The jig's up," Lucia said.

Sergeant Yin picked up the pace, angling us about thirty degrees away from the nearest crowd and its capsule. "Rifles pointed down," he ordered. "Don't spook them. Remember, reinforcements."

Agitation spread among the aliens as they turned to face us, their wings up and fluttering and their hand claws up and extended. They began whistling and clicking like a horde of swarming cicadas mixed with agitated songbirds. The larger ones placed themselves between us and the smaller and the wounded.

It's what we humans would do, and that said something positive about them as a species. That's where my admiration and empathy ended. The strongest would be the first to die.

Aliens continued to pour out of the escape capsule, expanding their numbers, especially those of the large, healthy variety.

Sergeant Yin came to a halt. We turned to face the alien horde growing outside the first capsule. We had the steep hillside twenty yards to our back, with the aliens less than fifty yards away. "Firing line," Yin ordered. "Form a line. Standing, kneeling, or prone position. Rifles pointed down or away. Wait for all squads to get into position. Don't shoot unless ordered by me."

Most, like me and Lucia, took a kneeling position. A few, like Johnson, took a prone position, despite the weedy grass being calf-high. That made sense for him, since it allowed the use of his SAW's bipod.

It looked like the other two squads led by Captain Nejem were lining up opposite us, but further down, targeting on the second capsule's aliens.

Yin moved back down the line. "Jack, Lucia, Johnson, you're our anchor. If the northern capsule makes a break for the hills on our side, Jack, Lucia and Johnson, do what you can to stop them."

Hurry up, I thought, watching the Mawks shift the wounded and smaller ones to the back, their whistles and clicks getting louder. Reinforcements weren't going to make it.

I clicked off my rifle's safety.

Lucia whispered, "There's an awful lot of them, Jack."

"Uh huh," I replied, thinking more men armed like Private Johnson would be handy.

One large Mawk stepped out of the alien crowd, holding up a white strip of cloth. Like all the aliens, it had harnesses strapped along its torso and abdomen, but nothing that looked like a weapon.

"Hold your fire," Sergeant Yin ordered.

"He's got a white flag," someone down the line said.

Johnson replied, "You think we didn't raise a white flag when they were bombarding us from space?"

I agreed.

"If I can talk to him," Yin said, "might give us more time. But if things go to hell, mow them down and keep mowing, until there aren't any more."

There were at least two thousand packed around the capsule, with more inside. We had enough individual bullets. Would we have enough time to use them?

A single gunshot rang out from somewhere. On Captain Nejem's side. The captain shouted. It was impossible to tell what he said because a second shot, and a third went off.

Things were headed to hell.

Yin raised his M-16 and fired. The white flag-bearing Mawk's head snapped back with a spray of greenish fluid—

blood erupting from the back.

Before Yin's target collapsed, and he finished yelling, "Open fire," every human opened up.

Rather than fire into the central mass, I picked targets along the northern edge. I had fifteen rounds before needing to reload. I couldn't do that as fast as those with M-16s with their magazines. Back in my park, the calculation that my .22 rifle would serve me best might've been wrong. Dealing with dangers in my park was different than the front lines of combat. I should've picked up an assault rifle along the way, whether I was proficient or not.

My anger shifted thoughts to an even colder calculation. Forty-two of us. We'd each have to kill a hundred Mawks to have a chance.

Lucia fired, aimed and fired. The rip of Johnson's light machine gun, the controlled three round bursts of the M-16s gave me hope. We knocked them back. Their whistling faltered. If the Mawks were a timid species, one that hides behind technology, uses kinetic strike weapons and beasts like crawlers and dozers to do the dirty work, a hundred kills for each member of our two squads wouldn't be a problem.

Of course, the Mawks weren't timid. Like most animals, when cornered, or their young were threatened, they responded violently. Like a wave of claws and snapping beaks, they surged toward us.

To Second and Fourth Squad's credit, no one broke and ran.

Six rounds left, I counted with each pump and trigger pull. Five, four.

The Mawks came on, shrill whistles drowning out the report of our rifles. They climbed over their fallen. The yards between us melted away.

Fifteen bullets expended. I dropped my rifle and pulled a grenade from my belt and hurled it. Not at the front line but into the middle, hoping to break their momentum. As the first arced above the enemy mass, I pulled the pin on my second—and last grenade—and hurled it.

Twenty yards. My grenades detonated, hopefully tearing

holes in their ranks. A few other soldiers lobbed their own grenades. With shotgun in hand I emptied both barrels. The blasts of buckshot dropped three Mawks and caused two more to stumble. Those following climbed over or knocked them aside.

Johnson finished slapping a new magazine into has SAW. His fire pushed them back long enough for me and Lucia to reload.

Two more buckshot blasts and a reload. Ten yards.

How many had we killed? Three hundred, five hundred, nine hundred, a thousand? How many had I taken down? Ten, twelve, twenty?

The Mawks were unarmed and smaller than us, but far stronger. When they reached our line, it'd be hand-to-hand. I drew my revolver, took aim and pulled the trigger. My .410 rounds slowing, but not killing. The three .45s did better.

Five yards.

Lucia dropped her rifle before pulling her knife and pistol.

No time to re-load, I grabbed ahold of my hand axe.

Payback. One or two more were going to receive payback before I became 'dust in the wind.' Payback for all the death and suffering their species caused.

Chapter 40

The clash reminded me of an old movie depicting a battle in the Anglo-Zulu War, where red-coated British soldiers, armed with firearms, fought against overwhelming numbers of inferiorly armed Zulu warriors. We were the British, about to be dragged down and torn apart. Except we were the side suffering invasion, fighting to defend our land, our homes, fighting for not only our lives, but the survival of the human race.

Swinging with all my might, my hand axe bit into the neck of the first Mawk to reach our line. To my right, Lucia was firing away with her .45 Colt Automatic. Private Johnson hurled his SAW at the charging Mawks. Either it had jammed or he was out of bullets. The machine gun caught one alien in the chest, knocking it back into two following close behind. That gave Johnson time to pull a grenade, yank the pin and lob it fifteen yards into the alien mass. So practiced was the maneuver, that he had time to draw his own pistol from its holster.

I sidestepped one Mawk grasping at me. I knocked aside the talon-like hand of another with my pistol in my off hand, and stepped forward, putting me between the Mawk I'd just killed and one of its fellows reaching for me. My hand axe connected with another one right in front of me, biting into its head. It was like chopping into a coconut.

There were at least two behind me and hundreds in front of me. The shrapnel of Johnson's grenade sliced into five or six. That might relieve the pressure for a few seconds, if he and Lucia could dispatch the seven or eight immediately in front of us, no longer being pressed forward by their alien kin.

Their pistols rang out and my hand axe hacked, and everyone in our fragile line fought like rabid wolverines, shooting, stabbing, kicking, and clubbing. But they were thousands. We were like a sand castle facing the waves of a surging tide.

Shouts, curses, and gunfire melded with aliens' screeches and staccato whistles, and…air horns?

Was it the cavalry arriving?

Arriving a little too late.

CHAPTER 41

The cabover truck plowed into the alien horde, crushing and scattering them. A waving American Flag flew, affixed above it, with a UPS trailer hauled behind it. The trailer's wheels finished off those stunned or crippled. The maroon El Camino travelled in its wake, carrying helmeted soldiers in its bed, hunched down with automatic rifles held ready. Two Bradley fighting vehicles fanned out to either side of the semi truck. Their 25mm auto cannons hammered out rounds that slammed into the alien horde.

The new attack surprised the Mawk mass more than it surprised me. Captain Nejem promised reinforcements. Most Mawks broke and ran like a school of fish evading hungry sharks. Most, however, didn't mean all. The ones overwhelming our squad didn't notice, or didn't care, or were interested in a little final payback of their own.

Near me, Johnson went down first. He'd picked up my double-barrel shotgun and used it as a club. He nearly beheaded one Mawk with a Hank Aaron swing, when three took him down from behind. Two leaping on his back and one sinking its beak into his calf just below the knee. At the same time, Lucia fell back, holding her assailant off with one hand while madly stabbing and slashing with her knife. Two more were closing in to pounce.

I turned and caught one in the back with my hand axe before it reached her. That left *my* back exposed. Really, it didn't matter which way I turned. With Lucia and Johnson down, my back couldn't be otherwise but exposed. One Mawk took advantage of that and clamped onto my axe-wielding arm. Another leapt on my back and drove its beak into my right shoulder. Like two hawks taking down a raccoon, with a dozen more circling in for the kill.

I smashed my revolver into the face of the Mawk holding my arm with its claws. It staggered under the blow but didn't let go. Instead, it tore into flesh. Another came at me, so I spun, dragging the stunned Mawk on my arm to interpose it between me and the new assailant.

That didn't matter. The piercing pain in my shoulder caused me to scream. I slammed my revolver down over my wounded shoulder. I couldn't get much force behind it, so I jabbed with the barrel, guessing where the Mawk's eye would be.

It let go, releasing torn cloth and flesh, and blood.

The shouts and cries of First Squad were dying with its members. Johnson was silent. Lucia's scream held pain and desperation. We were being taken down by a pack of ravenous wolves—wolves with hawk beaks and eagle talons.

I managed to bring the grip of my revolver down on the head of the stunned Mawk, causing it to release my right forearm. Before I could do anything else—help Lucia—another alien came in low and took out my legs, like a punt receiver clipped from behind.

The takedown saved my life. A split second later a hail of gunfire ripped into the Mawks doing their best to finish off Fourth Squad.

The shattering gunfire broke the aliens' morale. They scattered and fled, most scrambling for the safety promised by the wooded mountainside.

The direction I faced lying on the ground allowed me to see most of them mowed down. They weren't fast as humans, even with their vestigial wings fluttering.

Letting go of my pistol, I clamped my hand over my wounded shoulder and tried to put pressure on it to stop the bleeding. It hurt like a red-hot poker had been jabbed into it several times.

Five feet away, Lucia was on her hands and knees, struggling to get to her feet. She was alive. The left side of her face looked shredded, and she held her left hand over the right side of her ribcage, blood seeping through her fingers. She still gripped her Bowie knife, stained with green Mawk blood.

The pain in my shoulder increased. Was their bite toxic?

The Bradley cannons continued firing. The crack of M-

16s and large caliber hunting rifles still filled my ears. There was almost no sound of Mawk clicks and whistling opposing them.

Lucia staggered over to me. I tried to get up, but fell back.

Gray started to fill my vision, closing like an iris or camera lens.

"Jack," she said, leaning close, blood from her torn face dripping onto mine. "Don't die on me."

The gray retreated for a second, but clouds obscured my thoughts. All that came out was to repeat back, hesitant and unsure, "Don't die on me."

"I won't, Jack, if you won't."

My hand's grip on my tattered shoulder weakened. My eyes were open but I couldn't see anything. With her free hand she pressed down on my wound. The fiery poker gone, a dull ache filled my shoulder.

"Doctor!" she shouted. "Medic, anyone!"

CHAPTER 42

The sound of a bird, a cardinal, I recognized that. One Luther hadn't needed to teach me because even a city slicker knew that. Voices, too. Muffled.

Someone next to me was snoring.

I opened my eyes. They were dry, and it was dark. Not really dark but twilight. I was in a large tent, situated along the edge, in a cot. Snoring came from someone a few feet to my right.

My right forearm hurt, but not as bad as my shoulder, so I couldn't roll onto my side to see whose snoring woke me up. Well, I could've, but logic suggested the resulting pain would knocked me out. Plus, I would've screamed along the way, waking up the snorer. And everyone else.

It was male snoring, deep and nasal. There were others breathing, at least one not too far away moaning. Not loud, maybe dreaming, maybe doing his best to contain the noise, suggesting pain?

My left hand, attached to my good arm, rested atop my chest, on a thin blanket. Then I reached down and felt the rough fabric covering a pole, confirming I was in a cot.

Thirst. My throat was dry. But I was alive. The pieces began falling back into place. The battle, Roamer dying. The Mawk colonists and their escape capsules. The battle, the truck, and Lucia. I felt my face. Clean and dry. No blood.

Lucia's bleeding face. It was the last thing I remembered.

There was no presence of her breathing. We'd spent countless nights in our small canvas tent, sleeping next to each other. There were seven of us in the tent, a big one. Not one of them was her.

My shoulder, where I'd been bitten, hurt. Not piercing, not dull, but like hundreds of pinching ants were randomly biting and releasing, biting and releasing.

Despite that, and my thirst, and all my questions, I

managed to doze off, listening to the cardinal and other birds sing.

They had me sitting halfway up. A stack of folded blankets supported my back.

The sun was out and the smell of pine trees filled my nostrils. That, and the smoke of fires and the smell of gun oil.

I hadn't left my cot. Soldiers had carried it out of the tent so a doctor—actually a nurse practitioner—could examine me. We were still in the mountains. A camp, from what I could see of it—several large tents—along the edge of a woods filled with tall pines. I was between tents so I couldn't see more than that. I guessed we were still in Tennessee. I wanted to be back in my park. Actually, I wanted to be back in college, or home with my family. Neither of those were possible. Maybe my park wasn't possible, either.

A wavy-haired man, dark with streaks of gray in it, while balding on top, walked up to me. He had a stethoscope draped around his neck and a friendly smile. His rumpled uniform's patch identified him as Tuck.

He gestured to someone out of my line of vision, a gripping and tipping motion, before squatting down next to my cot, on my right-hand side.

My right forearm, resting along my side atop the pale green blanket, was wrapped in cloth strips. They weren't exactly white, but clean as could be expected. Sterile gauze fresh out of sealed plastic was a luxury of the past. The blanket covered my shoulders, which was good, since I had on nothing underneath except a pair of socks. My shoulder was bandaged, and still stung with the ant-like bites.

"You're Jack, or so I'm told. Touring from Toledo." Tuck grinned.

"I am," I said, my voice raspy.

A soldier carrying a canteen appeared from between the tents. He wasn't wearing a helmet, but had a slung M-16.

Tuck, who appeared to be a 2nd lieutenant, based on his

gold bar, unscrewed the canteen's cap and held it to my lips. After a couple sips, I nodded.

"We won?" I asked. My voice was still a little raspy, but the drink made my throat feel much better.

"That depends upon the scope to which you're referring." Again he offered a toothy grin. "Locally, we did pretty well. Some of the non-combatants fled into the hills, but they're being hunted down. Even if we don't get all of them, most don't appear to have the skills or knowledge to survive for long outdoors. Especially not in an alien environment." Lieutenant Tuck uttered that last statement with a hint of irony.

I nodded. Before the Mawk invasion, not many of us humans could survive alone, out in the woods. Those that were left? A different story.

"Let me fill you in on your current medical status and prognosis."

His words sounded ominous. "Okay."

"You may have surmised, you're going to live. You've been out for almost three days. I stitched up the talon wounds on your forearm. You'll have scars."

The scar comment made me think of Lucia. I recalled her face again, torn open by Mawk talons.

"Your shoulder, you can probably tell, is taking more time to heal." He pursed his lips. "Unfortunately, you're one of the few people allergic to Mawk saliva. Sort of how a small percentage of the population is allergic to bee stings, except the reaction is for the affected tissue to swell and become inflamed. Fortunately, they have very little saliva.

"We were able to flush the bite wound on your shoulder within an hour after the battle, which was good. That allowed the potential inflammation and complications to remain minimal. Yesterday I repaired the damage to the tendons and torn muscle tissue. You're bullet-resistant vest made the difference between what you received, and a crippling wound. With work, you should regain ninety percent of the original strength and mobility in that shoulder. Potentially, ninety-five."

Rehabilitation? Not like there'd be any weight machines or any sort of resistance equipment.

Lieutenant Tuck must've seen my frown. "Jack, healing will occur faster than you might expect. Blood loss is contributing to your weakness." He moved his hand and placed his fingers on my throat, checking my pulse.

Weakness? He was right. If pressed, I could probably stand, maybe walk, slowly, if I had assistance. My thoughts were still mired in cobwebs.

I relaxed while the lieutenant checked me over. My thoughts flowed to my squad, all those around me in the battle. "What happened to us? Fourth Squad?"

When he moved my right arm an inch, pain shot through my shoulder. It wasn't horrible, but enough to make me flinch.

He nodded, as if in approval. "Your Hispanic friend, she gave me some antibiotics you brought south with her. That sharply reduces any chance of infection."

"Lucia," I said. "What about her? How's she?"

"Well," Lieutenant Tuck said, hesitating. "Anyone intent on enforcing HIPAA privacy rules? No governing authority…"

I ignored his attempt at humor. "So?"

"She's checked on you like regular clockwork," he said with a smile. "That fact indicates that she doing well, Jack." He reached across and placed a hand on my uninjured shoulder. "She has shown deep concern for your welfare."

A sigh of relief escaped my lips. She was doing well, better than me. For some reason that turned my stomach, like I'd let her down. Looking up and away, I asked, "Tell me, Lieutenant. Are we safe from fallout?"

The change in topic threw him for a second.

"Radioactive fallout, currently is not a concern. My understanding is that even if the weather pattern changes, exposure to radiation every twenty-four hours would be equivalent to a high altitude flight from New York to Los Angeles and back."

The lieutenant stood up straight, his attention drawn to

someone approaching from behind me. "A corpsman will be around to check your bandages."

That seemed abrupt until he said, "Miss Lucia, your friend just inquired about you."

"He did, huh?"

Something was missing. Her voice lacked its usual confidence.

She'd lost some of her abrasive cockiness from before she'd teamed up with me at the park. Maybe she meant to keep a low vocal profile for the benefit of others in the nearby tents. Most of them were in far worse shape than me. One had passed away in his sleep, between when I'd woken up this morning, listening to the birds, and when the soldiers moved my cot outside the tent.

Despite the lieutenant's optimistic view on local radiation exposure—had he seen the impossible-to-miss mushroom clouds? It still concerned me. Injury and blood loss left me weak. Coupling that with pain, if the weather pattern shifted, I'd be in trouble. No way I could walk, drive or ride a bike, or a scooter. Any road bump while in a truck bed, even riding on a pile of blankets, the pain would be…a problem. My mind wandered back to all those in our column wounded moving south. I'd avoided them. Out of sight, out of mind. Most of them died along the way.

My present condition brought their suffering home to me. Even without travel, my chances were iffy. Lying on a cot in a tent packed with other wounded and dying men didn't remotely approach a 21st century hospital's ICU facilities.

Moving? Thinking on that I gritted my teeth. Better to suffer agonizing pain in the short term than die of cancer, or if the Mawks decided to counter attack.

I was slow to realize that Lucia was standing over me. She had her holstered .45 pistol and her sheathed Bowie knife hanging on her belt.

The lieutenant was gone. How long had she been standing there?

"You okay, Jack?"

The left side of her face, from high on her cheekbone down to her jaw, had three parallel cuts. A Mawk had raked her face, tearing deep with its talons. Her blood dripping on my face…I recalled that. Now, black-threaded stitches held each gash closed.

Lucia spotted me examining her cheek. She started to move her hand to cover it, but stopped. Instead, she turned away, hiding that side of her face.

"Smart move, getting someone a hundred times better than me to stitch you up."

"Looks like hell," she said.

"Not so much," I replied. "Bet it hurts like hell, though."

"Like a son of a bitch."

"Bet it hurts even more when you smile."

She still kept her left cheek turned away from me. "What's there to smile about, Jack?"

"I don't know, you tell me. What happened?"

"You hungry?" she asked, ignoring my question.

"Yeah, a little." Actually, a little was a lie. It felt like I hadn't eaten in a month.

"Be back in a minute."

She strode away, leaving me to stare at the tents and the sky. It was a cloudy day. Still a little cool, so probably morning. Men were talking and moving around nearby. No vehicle sounds.

I closed my eyes and listened, trying not to doze off.

"Hey," Lucia said. Instead of the foot of my cot, she stood on my left side this time.

She held a tin can and a spoon. This one did have a label, and that was handy. Better than the 'silver bullets' our squad spent time eating from. Roamer came up with the name for them. Not totally original, but funny enough. I'd miss him, like I'd miss a lot of people.

Lucia's lecturing voice brought my mind back from its wandering. "Alphabet soup. The lieutenant doctor—nurse guy—says you shouldn't eat too much at once yet, so we'll share."

That disappointed me. I was hungry. A pain spike interrupted my shrug.

"You're still not fully with it, are you, Jack?" She stirred the contents, and then put a spoonful in her mouth. She ran her tongue in and out once. "Concentrated, but I don't have a bowl."

"Give me a spoonful, then add some water from your canteen and stir."

She knelt down so that we were eye to eye, no effort keeping the injured side of her face turned away. "Hardly lukewarm as is."

"I don't care, do you?"

She gave me a spoonful. It was pasty and salty, and not bad.

While pouring a little water from her canteen into the can, she asked, "You still remember where you have tomato soup buried in our park?"

"What do you think?"

After stirring, she offered me another spoon of soup. This time she had to be more careful that it didn't spill. "We going back there, Jack?"

"That depends," I said.

"On what?"

"On what happened."

She paused. "Everybody's dead, Jack. Except for you and me, and Sergeant Yin and Josiah."

Josiah was one of the Ferals from the Cincinnati area. A quiet man, middle aged, short and thin. Who wasn't on the thin side these days? Well, I'd held my own after Luther and I got the park started. Lucia had filled out some after she'd gotten established in the park, too. But we were both thinner than before the attack, like everyone else. Some just more than others.

"Lieutenant Kuhn is alive. He drove our semi truck into the Mawks, Jack. Do you remember that?"

I nodded. "Yeah, I saw everyone…go down. Even you. I tried to—"

Lucia interrupted me. "I saw that. Dumbass move, Jack.

It's why one got on your back and bit ya." She stirred the soup in the can, and half smiled at me. "And why I'm still alive."

What could I say? We finished the soup in silence, alternating the few spoonful's left.

"Sergeant Eckstein, Private Washington, are they dead too?"

Lucia nodded once, tears beginning to well in her eyes.

I had to hear it, to make it real. But my needs weren't fair to Lucia.

"Don't cry," I said, fighting back tears myself. "Salt water'll burn that cheek of yours."

She reflexively turned that side of her face away from me.

"That doesn't matter, Lucia. This world, this war. We're all scarred."

"It don't matter." She meant it a different way than I did.

"I was wrong, Lucia. It does matter. The battle wounds, just like the scar under your chin. It's like patina on an antique. Means it's authentic, makes it more valuable, more attractive to someone with a cultured eye."

She scowled at me. Wiped away her tears. "Elmore and his horses, they're alive."

"That's great," I said, smiling.

She started to smile, then grimaced.

"You were right," I said, pointing at her cheek. "No smiling." Then I pointed to her ribs. "How about your side? Didn't a Mawk get you there?"

"Not bad. Didn't even need stitches." She set the soup can down and leaned close again. "So, are we going back? I got your guns and hand axe. Got them from the pile they gathered from where we fought. Nobody'd want that carnival gun anyway."

"We won here," I said. "That, or we wouldn't be alive and talking here in this camp. Do you know what happened with the thunder wells? Did we win more than just here?"

"Thunder wells? The nuclear bombs shooting out of

those mountains?" She pointed to her left, which didn't mean anything to me sitting with my limited view. "There's a colonel supposed to be holding a couple meetings tonight. Supposed to talk about that and what the United States is gonna do next."

I thought about that a second. I wanted to be there. "Lucia—"

"I know," she said, interrupting me and starting to smile. That caused her to flinch, and frown. "I'll talk to that nurse doctor, and if he says it's okay, I'll find someone that'll help me get you to it."

"Okay or not, I want to be there."

"Nobody'll stop you from walking on your own two feet, Jack." After a pause and wink, she said, "I'll get you there."

Thanks to Sergeant Yin's assistance, practically carrying me as I leaned on his shoulder, he got me seated on a metal folding chair, next to a long bench, off to the side in the large tent. It wasn't fancy. A white tent, like maybe a car dealership or someone having an outdoor wedding reception might have. Opposite the entrance and to my left stood a small podium. Probably where the colonel in charge of the underground base was supposed to speak. It was elevated on a platform built from cargo pallets. There were benches and chairs and stools aligned in rows, enough for maybe sixty people to sit. This was the third presentation, rotating through mixed crowds of troops, conscripts, cooperating civilians and a few scattered locals.

From the anxious looks, what was going to be said must've been important. Being the third group, gossip had to have spread some.

Lucia sat on the end of the bench to my right, keeping an eye on me while I slouched, waiting. My shoulder ached, despite the acetaminophen pills we still had. The ant-pincher sensation was gone, at least.

Sergeant Yin, who'd received more than his share of scratches and bruises, had come out better than me, Lucia or

Josiah. The latter had lost an eye, sprained an ankle, and had his shoulder knocked out of its socket. He was on the mend from the last two injuries. The first one, of course, was permanent. He wasn't around when Lucia had gone looking for Sergeant Yin.

According to Yin, Josiah was with Elmore, helping with the horse team.

On the way to the meeting we'd stopped at the memorial mound, marking the mass grave of those that had fallen in the battle, including Sergeant Eckstein and George, and everyone from our column. Everyone from Alabama and Georgia as well. Ours wasn't the only battle that took place in the area. Nine hundred thirty-seven in all. On the grand scale of deaths, that wasn't much. But on the scale of friends, and based on the number of humans left? It was enormous.

Sergeant Yin said they burned the alien bodies, and were scavenging what they could from the destroyed tanks and escape capsules. Information and equipment to study, and reverse engineer.

The tent was nearly full when everyone rose. Well, just about everyone. There was one man with an amputated leg and still in pretty bad shape, and me. I tried to stand but Lucia placed a disapproving hand on my good shoulder. I didn't have the strength to contest her insistence, and common sense.

The colonel was a short, mousy woman with mostly gray hair that had once been blond. She stepped on the platform, behind the podium, and signaled for everyone to be seated.

After arranging a few pages of notes, she introduced herself as Colonel Miller. Her voice and manner reminded me more of a college professor than a military officer prepared to give motivational speeches or spew military jargon. Still, her voice carried confident authority.

"I will get right down to business. The information I am about to impart, I encourage you to share. Word of mouth is one of the best tools we have, at the moment, to disseminate information to our fellow Americans. Those Americans that remain.

"It is estimated that, of the seven point five billion people populating Earth prior to the invasion, roughly fifteen percent remain alive. In the United States, of the three hundred twenty-five million, fewer than forty-six million are alive."

She paused, her unyielding green eyes scanning the crowd. There were a few murmurs of concern or surprise. To me, those numbers were optimistic. It wasn't like anybody could take a national census, let alone a world census. It made me wonder how much she was about to share would be truth and how much propaganda?

"It has been made clear to the failed invaders that we will not share our world. We will exterminate any and all of their kind we encounter. To do otherwise would be akin to inviting a wounded tiger into our house, and we all know how that arrangement is likely to end.

"We have taken some prisoners and will learn from them, but they will never be anything but tools for our own use, and our advancement of knowledge. They will not be allowed to breed. Once their usefulness has passed, they will be executed."

She leaned forward on the podium. "It is unnecessary to say that they came with the intention to exterminate us, and make Earth their home. Conquest appears to be in their nature, although there is information that an even more aggressive species is out there. An alien species that has defeated the Mawks, not only on their home world, but other worlds conquered by the Mawks. What we faced, as many of you may know, is from a Mawk colony world that scattered before their enemy arrived.

"The information we have on this other alien species is obviously biased, and it will take time to determine the truth of the matter."

She stood straight again, moving to the next page of notes. "The crawlers and dozers, lab-created creatures designed to hunt and destroy humans are soon to be a horrid memory, one we might share with our children, if we want to give them nightmares. They were designed not only to hunt us, and to a lesser extent our canine and equine companions, but also to have a compact lifespan, one that fortunately, didn't include reproduction. It is believed that they are now reaching the end of their lifespans, and all will be dead within the next thirty days."

She said it with confidence, but I wasn't so sure. Still, there had been fewer and fewer encounters, and I didn't think it could all be attributable to arrows made with split eye crystals and construction adhesive.

"Some of you here now," the colonel continued, "have been at this hidden base from the start of the invasion, the resistance, the war. Others, from Ohio and Georgia and Alabama, journeyed here to deliver the nuclear devices necessary to attack our adversaries. To strike them in orbit, where they mistakenly believed they were safe, beyond our reach."

She again leaned forward on the podium. "The Mawks, they are a technologically advanced and clever species. Patient and practical, willing to weaken us and throw us in disarray with EMPs and kinetic energy strikes and created tsunamis, and allow disease, and their predatory creatures…and our own unfortunate tendency to prey upon our own kind, to do the job.

"But their patience led to complacence and predictability, allowing us…" She paused, again scanning the crowd, making sure everyone was listening, which seemed pointless. Everyone was interested in the truth as to what happened, or at least the version of the truth being revealed. "Allowing us to prevail.

"And when I say *us*, I refer to all humanity."

She shrugged. "The term 'Thunder Wells' has been bantered around. It is accurate, both historically and descriptively." She pointed, circling her hand once above her head. "Not only here, across the USA, in the Appalachians and Rockies, the Cascades and Ozarks, but across Europe and the Middle East stretching across Asia, we dug the thunder wells. The enemy's complacency and predictability enabled us to covertly plan and target and, in the end, surprise them.

"They had thirty-eight ships orbiting our planet. The attack destroyed their carrier, a manufacturing and supply ship, their two colony vessels carrying the bulk of their colonists." The last word she said with a hint of sarcasm. "They lost destroyers and battle cruisers. In the end, they have fourteen ships left, four of those damaged."

She turned to her next page of notes without pausing. "For those who might be interested, our three slugs took out what is termed by the Mawks, as best as can be translated, their Science and Development vessel. It held many of their scientists and engineers, those that developed the influenza variant that proved ineffective. It also was where they genetically engineered and created the crawlers and dozers. Meaning they no longer have the ability to re-seed our planet with that particular, or any similar, scourge."

A cheer rose in the tent. I added my voice to it, but not any fist pumps and high fives.

Colonel Miller clasped her hands on the podium, covering her notes and waited. This wasn't her first time through the presentation, and she obviously expected the reaction. There honestly hadn't been much to cheer about in the past year.

Thirty seconds later things quieted down and everyone returned to their seats.

"Now for the somber news," Colonel Miller continued and held up a hand, signaling for people to remain seated. "Yes, it appears the Mawk invaders have left Earth's orbit, seeking another world to conquer, or possibly to join their scattered fellows. That may be good news or bad news for us. Even if it is bad, it is not an immediate concern.

"The possibility the Mawks might return, or a future encounter, or even confrontation, with the species that drove the Mawks to Earth, is out of our control. What is in our control is the enormous task of rebuilding here, on Earth.

"There were scattered emergency escape pod landings across the globe. The number and location of every one is not known. But whenever and wherever they are discovered, all nations have sworn to eliminate them."

Swearing to eliminate didn't fit with the notion that America had a few prisoners, and that we were pumping them for information and technical knowledge. Still, if nine out of ten discovered were killed, and none allowed to breed…

My attention returned to what the colonel was saying.

"It will take years, probably decades, to rebuild, and to be honest—my personal opinion—is that society will never return to what it was."

She held up a smart phone, its screen black and lifeless. No surprise.

"I don't expect this device to become functioning. Not in my lifetime. That is how much we have to do, ladies and gentlemen."

A grim prediction. Probably accurate, which gave me confidence in what the colonel was sharing.

After the murmurs died down, she continued. "The first thing the President intends to get up and working is communication, radio at first. Transportation, mainly railroads, and then the power grid will follow. Power generation and distribution? The majority will have to happen locally first. Electricity will enable some of the modern conveniences we once had, and set the foundation for manufacturing to begin. It will be like moving from the 1850s to the early 1900s, and then to the 1950s."

She kept talking for another ten minutes, about plans for restoring order, and dealing with renegade groups, like in Cincinnati, but I wasn't interested in that. Making it to and sitting through the meeting exhausted me, and a throbbing ache began in my shoulder.

My shoulder, injured, probably never reaching 100% recovery. Earth, would it ever recover 100%? Always, Earth's inhabitants, all of humanity, would be looking to the skies, metaphorically looking over their shoulder. I bet watching the skies and listening to them was a priority project not mentioned by Colonel Miller.

The colonel was right. It'd be years before the communication network was up. While I hadn't written off my family, and my friends, more than five out of six Americans were dead. A taboo of open discussion, one that had long ago infiltrated my thoughts. Long odds, their survival. The results of which could wait to be discovered. It wasn't something to give up on, but the way the world was, today wasn't the time for focusing time and energy on that discovery.

I tugged on Lucia's arm as the colonel descended the podium, everyone standing, except me and the other injured fellow.

Lucia turned and leaned down close to me. "What, Jack?"

"Our park, Lucia. We'll return. Rebuild there."

She smiled wide, stretching her stitches. The pain didn't matter, and that made me feel good, solidifying that it was the right choice.

Her hand slipped down into mine.

"Lucia, let's go home."

Epilogue

The trip back to our park proved much faster than the trip down to Tennessee.

Captain Kuhn invited us to join his northbound convoy traveling up I-75. In addition to our El Camino loaded down with our bikes, spare gear and food, Elmore Foltz drove the cabover semi, pulling an extended horse trailer filled with his team, and eight sheep to start a flock. It was much more ambitious than our small trailer holding five goats—two males and three females—to start our own goat herd. I wasn't sure if the term 'herd' was proper, but then again, I didn't know squat about goats. I didn't know much about 'rebuilding' the United States either.

The goats were our payment for supporting the column's delivery of the nuclear device, and serving as conscripts in the battle. Better than gold or silver which, while a recognized medium of trade, carried less value with what we faced in the upcoming years.

The column was on its way to Michigan to exterminate the Mawks from four escape capsules reported to have landed west of Flint. Tagging along until we reached Toledo offered us safety, especially through Cincinnati.

Lucia did most of the driving, with my shoulder still healing. Still, I did what I could, claiming that gear shifting was part of my physical therapy. That, and helping to scrounge fuel for our vehicle, Elmore's truck, the Army's nine civilian vehicles, which included old vans and pickup trucks. Lieutenant Kuhn's column also boasted six regular Army Humvees with roof-mounted machine guns, towing trailers of gear and equipment and two artillery pieces.

He also had bona fide combat vehicles. Three modern semi trucks, rebuilt to bypass their computer components, hauled a single Abrams tank, along with two Bradleys, on lowboy trailers. The combat vehicles would prove most valuable in dealing with the Mawk infestation, one of many in the United States.

The alien invasion fleet abandoned tens of thousands of their fellows. What remained of the fleet simply didn't have room for them.

The Army column had two tanker trucks of fuel. Nevertheless, our scrounging efforts were important in conserving what they had. Usable fuel, ounce for ounce, was more valuable than gold, at least until oil wells and refining facilities were back on line. Coal and wood would be the main energy source for train locomotives, and the process of converting from diesel was already under way. Then, power plants, especially coal-fired ones, could be brought back on line.

All of those, like the modern semi trucks, had to be reengineered to bypass their EMP-scrambled microchip computer components. The electric distribution system? It would take decades, reconfiguring components mile by countless mile.

The column stopped along the way, allowing me, Lucia, Captain Kuhn, Sergeant Yin, and Elmore to pay our respects to those of the 37th IBCT who died in the Mawk's ambush attack. Together we remembered the brief battle where Colonel Davis met his fate and where Private Barhorst died in a ditch, right next to me. They died in battle, like many others. Countless others, not only in our minor skirmish that'd never make the history books, if any were ever to be written, but in the countless battles fought in the United States, and across the globe.

Nevertheless, I placed a marker with as many of the names scratched into the wood that Lucia, Yin, Elmer and I could recall. Sadly, I'm sure we missed a few. That only reminded me of how the world had changed.

Humanity's 'Golden Age' was long gone. Survival, like our 1800s ancestors, was what the world faced. At least we had the 'know how' to build internal combustion engines, manufacture antibiotics, and more. And we had some leftovers from the Golden Age. They'd help get us through. Mainly firearms, vehicles, scattered medicines and canned food for emergencies, until they all too went bad or ran out.

Basic shelter, and a source of building and repair materials were on hand. Thousands upon thousands of abandoned homes, apartments, shops, factories, and more, until they fell into complete disrepair and decay.

Lucia and I made it back to our park. Little had changed. There was evidence of a few attempts to discover our hidden and buried treasures. Elmore and a female companion he picked up along the way home decided to settle in the Boy Scout park across the highway from our park. Elmore said it was better than returning to his isolated farm. I couldn't argue with that.

Also, along the way, Lucia proposed to me. How could I say, "No"?

Captain Kuhn performed the marriage ceremony. Sergeant Yin stood as best man and Elmore's companion, Loraine, served as Lucia's maid of honor.

The area around Toledo, from my count, had fewer than four hundred individuals, making the President's estimate of forty-six million Americans even more questionable. The lower population density, however, meant that, in addition to not having to worry about crawlers and dozers as before, we didn't have to be on guard from human predators 100% of the time. It freed us up to discover how annoying goats could be, and for harvesting the crops planted before joining Colonel Davis and the 37th IBCT's mission.

I should clarify, saying, what crops the deer, rabbits, insects, and other wildlife hadn't devoured in our absence.

Dr. Gurrie, the veterinarian, one of the area's few survivors, became an important member of our social circle. We received monthly visits on her rounds, which was a good thing because, before winter set in, Lucia was carrying our first child.

Lucia and I both agreed, if it was a boy, we'd name him Luther.

The End

ABOUT THE AUTHOR

Terry W. Ervin II is an English teacher who enjoys writing Fantasy and Science Fiction. He is the author of the Crax War Chronicles, the First Civilization's Legacy Series, and Genre Shotgun, a collection of his previously published short stories.

When Terry isn't writing or enjoying time with his wife and daughters, he can be found in his basement raising turtles. To contact Terry, or to learn more about his writing endeavors, visit his website at www.ervin-author.com or his blog, *Up Around the Corner.*